THE
DOUBLE
CROWN

MARIÉ HEESE

THE DOUBLE CROWN

SECRET WRITINGS OF THE FEMALE PHARAOH

HUMAN & ROUSSEAU
CAPE TOWN   PRETORIA

Copyright © 2009 by Marié Heese
First published in 2009 by Human & Rousseau,
a division of NB Publishers,
40 Heerengracht, Cape Town, 8001
Cover design by Michiel Botha
Cover photograph of pyramids by
Samantha Villagran, stock.xchng
Map and illustrations by Wiekie Theron
Designed and set in 11 on 15 pt
Adobe Garamond by Chérie Collins
Printed and bound by Paarl Print,
Oosterland Street, Paarl, South Africa

ISBN 978-0-7981-5036-1

1959 - 2009

This book was published in
Human & Rousseau's fiftieth anniversary year.

In memory of Andries Johannes Heese
1 February 1972 – 14 March 1999

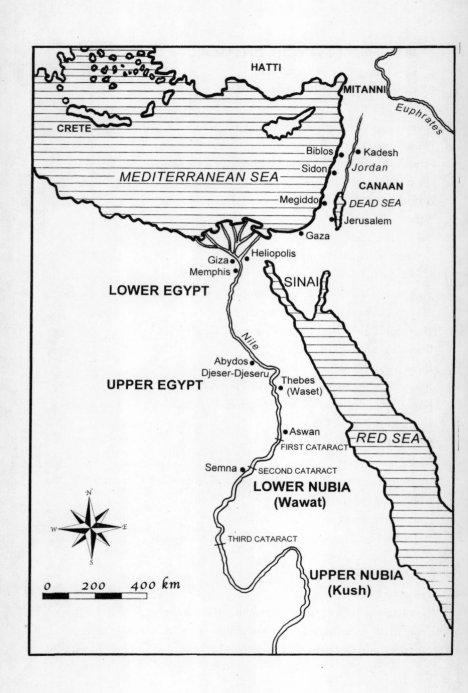

LIST OF CHARACTERS

Ahmeni, head of the Party of Legitimacy

Ahmose, a scribe

Ahmose, Queen, mother of Hatshepsut

Amenhotep, a steward

Amenhotep, son of Meryetre-Hatshepsut by Thutmose III and
    grandson to Hatshepsut

Amenmose, Prince, elder brother of Hatshepsut

Aqhat, a captain

Bek, a slave and a dwarf

Dhutmose, Vizier of the North

Hapu, the royal physician

Hapuseneb, Vizier of the South, Prophet and later Chief Priest of Amen,
    and Overseer of the Royal Tomb

Hatshepsut, Princess, Queen, King and Pharaoh

Ibana, an enforcer

Ineni, an architect

Itruri, tutor to the royal children of Thutmose I

Khani, from the Land of Kush (Southern Nubia), now a member of the
    Egyptian army

King of Punt

Mahu, a scribe

Meryetre-Hatshepsut, second daughter to Hatshepsut by Thutmose II

Minhotep, a physician

Neferubity, younger sister of Hatshepsut

Neferure, first daughter to Hatshepsut by Thutmose II

Nefthys and her twin boys

Nehsi, a general

Prince of Kadesh

Satioh, a Mitannian princess, Thutmose III's first principal wife

Senenmut, scribe, tutor to the royal children, later Chief Steward of
    Amen and Overseer of all Royal Works

Seni, a senior counsellor

Sitre, royal nurse (known as Inet)

Thitui, treasurer

Thutmose I, Pharaoh, Hatshepsut's father

Thutmose II, Pharaoh, son of Thutmose I and the Lady Mutnofert, and thus Hatshepsut's half-brother; also her husband

Thutmose III, Pharaoh, son of Thutmose II and a concubine, Isis; thus Hatshepsut's step-nephew and stepson

Wadjmose, Prince, elder brother of Hatshepsut

Yunit, a slave and a dwarf

I AM THE CHOSEN OF THE GODS. I have always known that. This knowledge has been the source of my strength and my power, and it is the reason why I know that those who now seek my death and desire to usurp my throne shall not succeed.

Yet I have decided that I must make a secret record with details about those whom I do not trust. I shall give the scrolls that I produce into the keeping of my scribe, the faithful Mahu. If I die a wrongful death, he must hand them to someone in power who will avenge me. Mahu will have to decide who the right person might be. I shall ensure that there will be sufficient evidence to see to it that the guilty, if such there are, suffer the just punishment of the gods and do not reap great benefits from treason.

Also I intend to write down the truth regarding my time as Pharaoh, ruler over the Two Lands. It is so that the main events of my reign are engraved upon the walls of the funerary temple at Djeser-Djeseru that my devoted Senenmut built for me, and upon the steles I have had erected. The living stone will bear witness to my deeds. But I fear that those who seek my death, should they succeed, might even attempt to destroy that proud record. Although I am certain that I can prevail, I shall nonetheless ensure that another record exists on the humble material created from papyrus, a record that Mahu could hide if needs be and that would survive. For those who would take my life would also steal my name, and so they would deprive my spirit of its home in the Afterlife. I will not let them take either my life or my immortality. I will not.

Besides, one can write on papyrus what one cannot write on stone. I am not an old woman – although I have seen forty risings of the Nile I am still vigorous – yet I feel the need to record my experiences, and to reflect on them. Sometimes it seems to me that time slides through one's grasp like the waters of the great river, and what one has done and what one knows cannot be writ in water.

I have lived a life of some significance, I do believe. I followed a destiny unusual for a woman. I achieved greatness and I paid for it. Loss and loneliness have been my portion; but I have always served the Black Land and its people to the utmost of my ability and they have loved me in return. As I feel hostile forces gathering around me, as I begin to sense age taking its inexorable toll, I wish that my life may not be forgotten, neither its greater deeds nor the smaller things that have given me joy.

I have sailed the Nile at sunset, floating on a sheet of living gold. I have tasted the roasted liver of fat geese. I have heard the haunting songs of the blind bard. I have felt a child's soft arms, a dying woman's bony grip, a lover's warm caress. I have inhaled the incense of the gods.

I feel that I must record these things. Here follow the secret writings of Ma'atkare Khnemet-Amen Hatshepsut, Female Horus of Fine Gold, King of Upper and Lower Egypt, and hereto I affix my seal.

I AM MAHU, SCRIBE TO PHARAOH HATSHEPSUT, may she live for ever. With these few words, added later and scribbled in haste, I wish to attest that these scrolls were given into my keeping by the Pharaoh and that they are written in her own script. But I have not given them into the hands of any of the men of power, for I do not know whom I should trust. The scrolls are stored in a safe and dry place where they must be kept secret until I have decided who should read them.

Of course Her Majesty sealed the scrolls she gave into my keeping with the imprint of her royal cartouche. But I did not have the strength of mind to keep them in my possession without reading what she had written. I needed to know what I was involved in, but also I am only human and I was most curious about unfolding events and about Her Majesty's intimate thoughts and feelings. So I confess it here: I broke the seals and I read the contents. Then I resealed the scrolls with my own scribe's seal. But never did I alter anything Her Majesty had set down. So if one day these scrolls are found, whoever reads them will be reading the very words of Her Majesty. This I solemnly swear by the Ka of Thoth.

I did however add some writings of my own to support and to amplify the writings of my Pharaoh so that the record may be complete and correct, for that is my task as a scribe. Those that follow after should know the truth about Her Majesty. Certainly there are many records of King Hatshepsut's reign, sculpted in statues, carved into the walls of temples, engraved on obelisks. Yet even that which is written on the living stone may be altered, as we have seen when a new Pharaoh takes over the temple of a predecessor and strikes out his cartouches, replacing them with his own. After all, it is written: *"Be thou a scribe, for a book is more durable than a stele or pyramid; it will preserve thy name better than any monument."*

These writings could lead to my immediate execution should they fall into the wrong hands. It is a dangerous commission that Her Majesty has honoured me with, but by the Ka of Thoth, I shall carry it out faithfully. I have ever been a loyal follower and humble servant of King Hatshepsut, may she live for ever. May the gods help me not to fail the Pharaoh.

THE FIRST SCROLL

It is a fact that I possess the blood royal, that I am the only one of four children borne by the Great Royal Wife Ahmose to the Pharaoh Thutmose the First, may they live for ever, who grew to adulthood. I am the last of the old royal line that runs through my mother, for my father the Pharaoh, may he live, came to the Double Throne as a great general and it was his marriage to her that made him royal since she was own sister to Pharaoh Amenhotep. Oh yes, I am the entirely legitimate occupant of the throne of the Two Lands. But to be legitimate is not enough for a woman to accede to the throne. She must also be the chosen one. The one the gods would have. And that am I.

For Hathor suckled me, Hapi cradled me, and Apophis spared me for my destiny. Since I was very young when these events occurred I do not myself recall them exactly, but they have been told to me so often that it seems as if I do remember. Perhaps I have some memory of the third and most significant event. The one who knew, who saw all three events as they happened, was the Great Royal Nurse Sitre, known as Inet – the ancient of days who had nursed my siblings and me and later took care of my daughters Neferure and Meryetre-Hatshepsut. She was my witness and unlike many who surround me, particularly now, had no reason whatsoever to lie.

Looking back, I realise that Inet's tales did much to direct my dreams of greatness. My earliest memories are of her voice telling me stories, always using the same words as the illiterate do and as children indeed demand. She would lisp a little because of her sparse teeth – she had only a few rotted stumps left, the rest ground down by years of chewing gritty bread. Some of her stories were those that all Egyptians know, such as *The Tale of the Shipwrecked Sailor*, or legends of great battles, or comic stories about animals.

But others concerned me personally and those were the ones that I liked best just as she loved to tell them. She used to nod her head, the plain black wig framing her wizened brown face with its little black eyes like olives in desiccated bread. The nods punctuated her tales as if she were listening to herself and agreeing that yes, that is quite correct, that is exactly how it happened.

Alas, my dear Inet is dead now and her voice is still. Ah, there have been so many deaths. I have seen to it that she is properly buried and well supplied with all the grave goods necessary for a good life in the Fields of the Blessed. Yet although sometimes it seems that her Ka breathes so close by that I feel it upon my cheek, she can no longer bear witness for me. But I can never forget the love she bore me, and her unwavering faith in my destiny.

So I shall set these tales down, just as she told them, for they have significance as regards the legitimacy of my rule over the Black Land. They prove that I am the chosen of the gods. During the time of rest after the midday meal I have some privacy. Usually I rest on a day-bed on the cool, spacious portico overlooking the flower gardens with their splashing fountains at the side of the harem palace in the royal city of Thebes. I shall use that time to write down these accounts. The slaves who bring fruit juices and keep me cool with ostrich feather fans are illiterate. They will not know what writings these are. My bodyguards keep a tactful distance while I rest, although they remain alert.

Tale number one was about Hathor, mother of Horus, foremost of the gods who have held me in their protective embrace all my life. I loved to hear it, for it made me feel that I had been singled out, that I was somehow special to the Goddess. It concerns the first year of my life, in the reign of my late father, may he live, Thutmose the First, year 4.

"Tell me again, about how Hathor suckled me," I would demand, during the sultry afternoons when everyone in the palace rested but I, being full of energy, did not want to sleep.

"You were a lusty babe," said Inet. She always said this proudly. "Came into the world kicking and squalling, tight little fists pumping as if ready to fight the world. Such a voice! Such a voice for a newborn! Demanding attention. Demanding food. Frightened the palace doves, you did, sounded like Bastet in full cry."

"I sounded like the cat goddess," I said boastfully.

"You know it, little one. A wet nurse was quickly found, the wife of a scribe whose child had died for it was born too soon. She had milk aplenty and she was honoured to be called to the palace."

"But the human milk was too thin," I chimed in.

"The human milk was too thin," agreed Inet, nodding. "You screamed with hunger, hour after hour. You could get no satisfaction from the woman's breast. And yet she had so much that it dribbled down, wetting her tunic. But what you needed was the milk of the God."

"Hathor," I said.

"You know it, little one. The chief physician attending the Great Queen, may she live for ever, advised us to procure cow's milk for you. It settles heavier in the stomach. It has more strength. I have seen it before," said Inet. "I have seen it in big, strong baby boys who are very hungry. But you were the first girl child I ever saw who thrived on it."

"I was suckled by Hathor," I said with satisfaction.

Of course; it had to be true. When I ordered my temple to be built at Djeser-Djeseru, I had a record placed on the walls showing the cow goddess suckling me.

"It was an omen," said Inet. "I do believe that you will be under her protection all your life. The Goddess is tender as a mother in caring for those she loves, fierce as a lioness in defending them from danger and evil. She will keep her hand over your head."

Indeed, I have often felt the arms of the Goddess bearing me up. There have been times in my life when I felt that all my strength was spent; then I pray to Hathor, and she infuses me with new vigour. She watches over me.

I reached out for more ink to begin recording the second of Inet's tales. At that moment a shadow at the far end of the portico seemed to suddenly solidify. There was no footfall to be heard yet I knew that it was Khani, come to report to me. He is known to the guards and they let him pass.

"Khani," I said. "Come. I see you."

He walked quietly across the cool tiles with his characteristic feline lope and stood before me, his three cubits of powerful muscle, dark as polished ebony, blocking out the sun before he bowed.

"Majesty," he said, in his deep voice, the voice of a bard. "You have eyes in the back of your head."

"I have need of them," I said. "And of more eyes scanning the kingdom on my behalf . . . Eyes that I can trust, such as yours, my faithful guardian."

"And you may require the support of Hathor also," he told me. "Inet used to claim that support for you."

"And Inet was right," I said. "I have indeed lived in the shelter of Hathor's vigilance. My sister and two brothers have gone to the gods. But I, beloved of Hathor, I thrived. To this day I am strong and I am never ill."

"Indeed, Majesty," agreed Khani. "You are strong."

There seemed to be reservations in his obsidian eyes.

"What is it?" I asked. "You have bad news?"

He would tell me, I knew, but in his own way. He would marshal his facts with care and tell me first only what he knew to be true. If there was gossip or speculation, he would report that also, but with a warning that it could not be substantiated. I rely greatly on his acute observations and intelligence.

I sent the slaves and the guards away. Everyone in my household knows that Khani is to be trusted. He has been loyal to me ever since he was brought to the Kingdom of the Two Lands as a prisoner of war. Soon after his accession as Pharaoh, my late husband Thutmose the Second, may he live, received news of an uprising in Nubia. Naturally he could not leave the court and the capital when his grasp of the sceptre was so recent. He dispatched an army under the command of his most trusted general, who quelled the rebellion, killed many men and captured the ringleaders.

They also captured Khani, a Nubian prince, son of the Kushite rebel chieftain, and brought him with the other captives to be paraded in the presence of the enthroned Pharaoh. The young prisoner was but one year older than I and I had at that time seen thirteen risings of the Nile. I can never forget that day when I stood beside my husband on a massive dais outside the administrative palace, facing the broad avenue lined with masses of people eager to see the victorious general, the great Ahmose pen-Nekhbet of el-Kab, ride into Thebes with the spoils of war. And the captives.

As the general's war chariot swept up to the dais, then those of the division commanders, followed by a mule train laden with Nubian gold gleaming in the sun, elephant tusks, ebony, and many bulging sacks filled with more booty, a huge roar went up from the watching crowd. The noise intensified when the soldiers climbed down to make deep obeisances while the charioteers held the horses in check. Some way behind came the infantry, led by the standard bearers, row after row of the flower of Egypt's men marching to the rhythm of drums and trumpets. I had a sudden thought that we needed more broad avenues in Thebes for great processions. Not only for military parades, but also for the festivals when the god Amen-Ra is brought from his shrine for the people to see. Then I forgot about the God as the captives came into view, greeted by yet louder roars and jeers.

Some of them had been badly injured and were loaded on mule-drawn carts, but several were able to walk and they shuffled along between their captors, urged forwards by prods from spears, their steps hobbled by the chains that bound them. Yet they walked as straight as they were able to, tall men, their dark naked torsos powdered with Theban dust; men who still held their bodies with the swagger of power, men with rings of gold in their ears and hatred in their hooded eyes.

So, I thought, these must be the rebel leaders from the wretched Kush. They should know better than to challenge the dominion of Khemet. Prompted by the soldiers with spears, they fell to their knees in front of the dais and kissed the ground. On the far right, I noticed a young boy, considerably shorter than the rest. He must be about my age, I thought with a shock. Walking into Thebes to meet his death, while I stood on a dais above him, a new life growing beneath my heart.

Indeed, it was at that very moment, when I caught the young prince's eyes – for prince he surely was, else why had he been brought before the King and not simply executed – it was then that I felt, for the first time, the delicate butterfly tickle of a new babe stirring in my slightly swollen abdomen. I put my hand on it. Perhaps, I thought, it is my son. Coming to life while that one comes to death.

My husband conducted the hearing with great dignity. The captives were prodded to their feet, to face the Pharaoh and hear their fate. They stood impassively. "Hear ye," he said, "thus Egypt punishes those that question our sovereignty. For we have been given dominion over our vassal states, of which Nubia is one. Therefore you are bound to honour the Pharaoh and obey his laws and pay his tribute. To rebel is treason, and punishment for treason is death." Screams and ululations went up from the crowd. "You, as leaders of the rebellion, are hereby sentenced to be killed and hung head downwards from the walls of Thebes." Another roar echoed along the dusty avenue as the sentence was pronounced.

I felt a sudden wave of nausea as I looked at the young prince. He must have expected that he too would be executed, but he showed no fear, standing straight as a young tree. Even then he already had a striking presence. When the sentence was pronounced, he did not flinch. He held his head high and his eyes met mine and did not slide away. One day, I thought, I shall have a son whose courage will match his.

Without planning to, I suddenly found myself speaking. "Husband," I said, "Pharaoh. I beg a word."

He turned to me courteously but with some surprise. The ranks of senior advisers and priests ranged below our thrones shifted and shuffled. It was not customary for the Great Royal Wife to speak at such occasions. Yet now that I had begun, I had to continue. "It is of course right that rebels should be punished, and in a manner to deter all who might dream of such actions," I said. "Pharaoh has dealt with them according to their deserts. But Ma'at demands not merely punishment for those who disturb its order. Ma'at is also justice." I was glad that my voice did not tremble and that it was bold but not shrill. I raised it so that I might be clearly heard. "And justice," I said, "includes mercy. There is one young man among the captives who surely had no hand in the planning of this rebellion, who fought, if he did fight, on the orders of his father, as would any young Egyptian in his place. I beg the great Pharaoh to show mercy towards him. Let him not be executed. Please, great Lord. Let him be spared."

For a long moment, my husband frowned as he deliberated. One or two of the priests were nodding. They seemed to agree with my comment about Ma'at. "Very well," said Thutmose. "We shall be merciful. The prince is spared." Now the fickle crowd cheered this pronouncement also.

So Pharaoh gave him life and decreed that he was to be educated and sent back eventually to a position of trust in his own country – with, of course, an outlook favourable to our kingdom. Khani was tutored with the children of the upper classes in Thebes, joined the military and progressed to the rank of Officer Commanding the Division of Sobek, currently quartered in Thebes. Commander Thutmose (my nephew-stepson Thutmose, he who would be King) would have sent Khani back to Nubia long ago, but I insisted that he remain here in Egypt. I tell Thutmose that we have need of him because he is an outstanding trainer of soldiers and he is always able to convert the children of conquered enemies into faithful warriors in the Pharaoh's army. But in truth I need him because his loyalty is to me. I have need of men whom I can trust absolutely.

When I look at Khani, I remember with great clarity the day when he stood before my husband the King together with the other captives from Nubia. Thinking of that day, it seems to me that we were both no more than children then, but at the time I felt mature. Especially I recall that when the youth inclined his head, it was to me that he bowed, not to the King. So he has always been my loyal supporter and, I think, my friend – perhaps, since Senenmut passed into the Afterlife, may he live, the only true friend that the Pharaoh has.

And now he stood before me, an adult and a soldier, one who spied for me.

"Bad news," Khani informed me. "It seems that the Mitanni are stirring up trouble on our borders with Canaan, aided by the Hittites."

"Surely not true," I said, angrily. "The Mitanni are supposed to act as a buffer between the Black Land and the Hittites. They should be dependable, considering the amount of gold we send them. How accurate is your information?"

Khani just looked at me with his inscrutable obsidian eyes. I sighed. I knew that his sources were always impeccable. If he told me something as a fact, he had checked it carefully.

Of course I have a counsellor who advises me on foreign affairs, one Seni, an elderly bureaucrat who served my late father, may he live, and now faithfully serves me. He is spare of figure and sparing of words, but his advice is always well thought through and precisely expressed, and I pay attention to it. Yet my royal father, Pharaoh Thutmose the First, taught me never to depend upon a single source of information or advice and always to discover what the common people are saying. So I have sources of information that are not known to all. Khani is one of them.

"The Great Commander Thutmose is planning and preparing for a campaign," he went on. "The intensity of training has increased. He has ordered many horses."

"I have given no such instructions," I said furiously.

As Pharaoh I am the absolute head of the armed forces and they may undertake no campaign that I have not decreed should take place. The upstart is angering me seriously. He is assuming powers that he does not have. Of course, it is true that he was crowned. I cannot deny that fact, but it should never have happened.

The young Thutmose, child of my husband Thutmose the Second and Isis, a mere concubine, had been given to the priests to learn the rites, to become himself a priest of Amen and to serve the God. He was no more than a little-regarded juvenile. But when my husband passed into the Afterlife, may he live for ever, the priests suddenly realised that they had an opportunity to control all Egypt. With a little boy they could use as a puppet on the throne, they would have power over the Two Lands such as the priesthood had never had before.

There have always been factions in Egypt, but a single faction had never yet gained overall control. One faction that traditionally opposes the priesthood is the military. Since the Pharaoh is also the

Ultimate Commander of the army and usually sides with them, they are extremely powerful. At this moment, the priests of Amen saw their chance to tilt the balance of power in their own favour, and they took it.

So, when one fine day in the temple of Amen-Ra it appeared for all the world as if the choice of the God fell on the child as he stood among the priests who had the care of him, there was a simple explanation for that event and it was not a supernatural one. That much should be obvious to anyone with half an understanding. It was not the child's doing, of course. He had seen only ten risings of the Nile when my husband died and he did not have the wit to plan and execute such a drama at that age. But the priests did.

During a ceremonial procession in the temple of Amen-Ra that day the gilded barque bearing the God, its carrying poles shouldered by eight strapping priests, paused in its stately circling of the enormous hall. It hesitated, reversed and bowed down in front of the surprised small figure of the child Thutmose, seeming to indicate that the God wanted him to ascend the Double Throne. But there was no truth in that pivotal moment. No mystery. No magic. It was a spectacle thought up and carefully executed by the priesthood. But the country believed the lie. So they crowned him.

Yet I have never acknowledged his supremacy. He is not the chosen of the gods. He does not have the blood royal. He was never inducted into the Mysteries of Osiris as I was, by my late father the Pharaoh, may he live, who intended me to rule. The coronation of the child was a hastily organised, superficial affair: He did not grasp the cobra, nor run around the white walls at Memphis, nor did he shoot off the symbolic arrows.

But they did crown him and it made me sick. I, who had been the Queen of the Two Lands, occupying the throne by my husband's side, I who had in all but name actually reigned more effectively than that sweet but ineffectual man, I who had the pure blood royal – I was relegated to an inferior position. I would be regent, they said. But everyone knew that the priests would call the tune.

I gritted my teeth and I bided my time. Two years after the misjudged coronation of the little upstart a vision came to me: a vision that proved my incontestable right to the Double Throne. I was shown how my heavenly father, the great god Amen, impregnated my mother, and told her that the child would be a daughter, Hatshepsut – and she would reign. I then took steps to have myself properly crowned; I have worn the Double Crown ever since. I sent the child back to the priests. I insisted that he should remain merely a very junior co-regent, with no independent powers. Later he went to the military and now, in his thirty-second year, he is the Great Commander of the Army and he is angering me.

Although I am a woman, I have been the Son of Horus, the Pharaoh Ma'atkare, Ruler of the Two Lands, for more than twenty years. In that time I have balanced the opposing forces in Egypt in a delicate game of power. I have controlled the priesthood, the nobles, the bureaucrats and the military. I have prevailed because I am able to read men, to charm them when need be, to inspire loyalty, to manipulate and in the final analysis to outwit them. They do not expect a woman to be cleverer than they, and therefore they are at a disadvantage. A woman, yet a king with might and majesty. It has been a potent combination and it has served me well in maintaining the balance of power. I have always enjoyed this game and I have played it adeptly. Yet I am tiring. There have been too many deaths and the wolf pup at Memphis keeps snapping at my heels.

I sighed again.

"Majesty," said Khani, who had stood silently while I considered his news. He was always able to be still, to be patient. Most men cannot. "You must keep your eyes open. Especially those at the back of your head. You must be vigilant."

"I always am," I said shortly. "Why this particular warning? What do you know?"

But clearly he had no specific information to give. "Just be vigilant," he repeated. "I am due back," he added. "I was given a document to deliver to the Grand Vizier. But I should not tarry. None saw me come here."

"A document? From Commander Thutmose?"

He nodded. This too was disturbing. Usually there was no love lost and little communication between those two. Something was decidedly going on.

"Thank you, Khani," I said. The shadows under the lush trees closed around his disappearing form as he strode away.

I was deeply concerned, too much so to return to my writings. Instead I sat down, knowing that at least one of my pet cats would jump onto my lap. Bastet came at once and settled down, purring. I stroked her creamy fur thoughtfully. She blinked her blue eyes at me. The other one, Sekhmet, has tawny fur and golden eyes like her namesake the lion goddess. She was probably off somewhere looking for mice. Like myself they are both daughters of the sun, but only Bastet has her nurturing qualities; the destructive powers of the sun are to be seen in Sekhmet. She is less companionable but she keeps the vermin down.

Even Bastet did not do much to soothe my troubled spirit. I wished that I had someone to talk to other than a state official. I wished Khani could have stayed. I wished that Inet could have been there with me, assuring me by her repetition of the known and familiar that the world is a safe and predictable place; keeping the threatening forces that I feel closing in on me at bay.

Here endeth the first scroll.

IT IS INDEED an important and a dangerous document that King Hatshepsut has entrusted to me. I am overcome that it should be given to me, a mere assistant scribe, and not to the Chief Royal Scribe. Yet I think I understand why this is the case. First, if it is true that there are those who seek Her Majesty's life (and I have reason to fear, alas, that this may be so), then they will keep a close watch on all those in her employ and especially those known to have her trust and thought to have ways of influencing her. The Chief Scribe may soon find that documents in his care are confiscated under some pretext or another. But nobody will expect me to have anything worth reading.

Second, I am Her Majesty's faithful servant and great admirer and she knows that she may depend on me. Indeed, she may be sure of my entire loyalty since already once I almost gave my life for the King. It happened some five years ago. Her Majesty had expressed a wish to sail to her great temple at Djeser-Djeseru, which was built for her by the late great Senenmut; it has a shrine to accommodate the god Amen on his annual procession from Karnak, but it also has a double chapel for King Hatshepsut and her royal father Thutmose the First where she wished to make offerings to her late father's Ka.

Pharaoh also wished to view some samples of white marble reported to have a beautiful tracery of green veins. It had been unloaded at Djeser-Djeseru, where the ramps for transporting materials were still in place. This unusual marble had apparently been located in the Eastern desert, and if the Pharaoh found it pleasing, orders would be given for extensive quarrying. I was instructed to accompany the group, for I have knowledge of such materials due to the fact that I spent a portion of my training as scribe in a number of quarries.

The journey was not to be a royal progress, just a trip on a simple barge, an opportunity to get away from the pressures of the court and the never-ending demands of governing the kingdom, so it was a fairly small group that set out that day and the atmosphere was informal. Her Majesty reclined on the deck beneath a striped awning, attended by two slave women waving basket-weave fans, for the day was searingly hot. Her ladies-in-waiting were seated around her on cushions, one of them playing a merry air on a long lute. Two bodyguards were on board, but their usual vigilance had relaxed in that seemingly safe situation. They were joking and throwing sticks. We sailed smoothly northwards with the flow of the great river. A light breeze carried the scent of damp earth. The water was the colour of lapis lazuli between the lush, palm-lined green banks. In the shallows small boys played with a bleating goat.

Suddenly the low prow of the barge dipped. A swimmer had approached the boat unseen under the water and had clambered aboard. Moving with the agile grace of a predatory lion, the man leapt past the astonished rowers and onto the deck where the Pharaoh was enthroned. In his hand he clutched a dagger. Only I registered immediately what was happening. I had no time to think, I just acted. I lunged forwards from my seat just below the deck and caught the man's wrist. He turned on me ferociously and I smelled garlic on his breath. When he struck at me I felt a burning sensation in my arm. We struggled mightily on the swaying boat. I had not the strength to overpower him, for he was powerful and wild with hatred, but I held him at bay. My intervention slowed him sufficiently for the Pharaoh's bodyguards to come to their senses and assist me.

He was tied up and taken ashore at the first opportunity. It turned out later that he was a farmer who had lost land which he believed to be his in a case before the Grand Vizier some days previously and he blamed the Pharaoh. For his attack on the King he forfeited his life.

As for me, I was bleeding from a gash in my arm, but I accounted the pain as nothing since I had been of service to Her Majesty. She herself attended to me once the attacker had been subdued, stopping up the wound with her own kerchief. Her hands were deft and gentle. I remember that she smelled of myrrh, even after a morning in the sun, and I remember the golden colour of her eyes, looking so closely into mine that I could only blink, and stutter.

"M-Majesty, it's n-nothing, you should not bother . . ."

"Of course I must," she said, in her low, clear voice. "You have been extremely brave. You might have lost your life for mine. I am indebted to you. There, I have tied the kerchief tightly, it should stop the bleeding for now."

I have it yet. She ordered the barge to be turned around and had me carried to the palace at Thebes where Hapu, the Chief Royal Physician, sewed the lips of the wound together and gave me a potion for the pain. But I was not aware of suffering; I could only relive those moments when Her Majesty had leaned close to me and tended me carefully with her own lovely hands. Since that time, five years ago, I have often been called to the palace. I live to serve the Pharaoh.

I wish that I had skill in portraiture, so that I might paint a picture of Her Majesty, one that would better show than the cold stone what Pharaoh Hatshepsut's appearance is. But I have skill only in words, and that the official kind. I do not have the eloquence of a bard, for I am a civil servant and accustomed to the writing of lists and dry reports. Yet I have a sharp eye and I miss little.

So I shall set down as accurately as I can what I have noted. The great King is fair of face and form. Her skin is light brown, with a bloom as of apricots; her hair is a wondrous red-gold, touched with henna and braided into many small braids so that it forms an imposing frame for her round and resolute face. I believe it is her own hair and not a wig as many ladies wear over a shaven skull.

Her eyes are most exceptional. They hold one's gaze and seem to read with a piercing regard what one would rather keep private. They are almond-shaped and the exact colour of a lion's golden gaze. I have on occasion accompanied my uncle on a hunt and I have seen a lion.

Her hands are small, with tapered fingers, well kept and decorated with henna. Also she has slender and elegant feet. She is quite tall for a woman and she walks with dignity and grace. Further I have noted that although Her Majesty is a god and a king she has the scent of a woman and the ability in passing by to stir a man's loins.

Her voice is arresting, low and clear. She seldom raises it, but when she does all those within hearing know that it is the voice of power, the voice of authority. She is able to quell a hall full of argumentative men with ease, and I have heard her stir up a multitude of the common people to adulation. Yes, the people of the Two Lands have loved the Pharaoh Hatshepsut and they have worked for her and bowed their heads to her these twenty years. It is not the people who would be rid of her.

Enough, enough. I must store these writings where they will not be discovered by prying eyes.

THE SECOND SCROLL

The faithful Mahu has taken the first scroll away and hidden it. Of course he now holds my life in his hands, and also the life of Khani. Yet I trust my little scribe who follows me around with the brown eyes of a loving dog. He would give all to protect me and he has a scar to prove it. A pity he has not the insight and the political intelligence – and the craftiness – that I once could call upon in one who began as a scribe and rose to greater things. If I still had Senenmut at my side, I would feel less threatened by the dangers that I sense around me now. But I am the Lord of the Two Lands and I, alone, have held sway for a score of years. I am divine; the gods range at my back. I will prevail.

Today I shall record Inet's second story that goes to prove my undoubted divinity.

"Hathor is not the only one of the gods who have favoured Your Majesty," she would begin. This is true. There has also always been Hapi, God of the life-giving Nile, Hapi the bountiful, the fruitful, the generous, who each year without fail causes the great river to flood its banks, drawing back to leave the rich black earth behind, bringing fertility to the Black Land; Hapi who has both beard and breasts, and is therefore both male and female as all my life I too have had to be. I have always thought it appropriate that I should have been in Hapi's especial care.

This is how Inet told the tale.

"You were just like a boy child," she said. "A rough little girl, always tumbling about with your brothers, running, jumping, climbing, throwing things, shouting . . ."

"I fought them, too," I said, lifting my chin. "And I beat them."

"You bit them," said Inet severely. "You did not behave like a princess of the royal house, not at all."

"Go on about Hapi," I said.

"One day the boys decided to go fishing," she continued. "They had small harpoons that one of the slaves had made for them. And a coracle woven of reeds, light enough for the two of them to handle."

"They weren't very old, were they?" I asked.

"Prince Wadjmose had seen eleven summers and Prince Amenmose nine," Inet confirmed.

"And I three," I said.

"Who is telling this tale?" Inet demanded. "If you know it all, why do you make me repeat it until I have to find some cooled wine to soothe my throat?"

"I like to hear it," I said. "Go on, tell me. I'll be quiet."

"You insisted on going along," she resumed. "Even with only three summers you knew what you wanted and you insisted on getting your way. Wilful, wilful." She shook her head with its stiff black wig. "Truth to tell, you threw yourself upon the ground and drummed your heels and screamed, and even I could not calm you down. So for the sake of peace they took you along."

"It was a beautiful day," I said dreamily. "The sun was shining and the river was blue as the sky, except around the edges where the reeds and papyrus plants made it look green."

"How would you know that?" asked Inet. "Surely you were too small to remember?"

"I think I do remember," I said. Actually, Inet had always described it thus, and I had heard the tale so many times that I no longer knew what I could really recall. Besides, the sun always shines in the Black Land.

"Yes, well, the day was fine. The boys were instructed to keep an eye on you and on no account to let you handle a harpoon. And naturally you were accompanied by a small retinue. It's not as though you went alone," said Inet, still suffering twinges of guilt as she reflected on what could have happened. "I should have gone too, but I had the headache that makes me blind on the one side."

"Itruri went," I said. "And two slaves."

"Itruri wasn't a great deal of use," sniffed Inet. She always was jealous of the elderly man who was the tutor of the royal children. "Sat on the bank under a sycamore tree and watched as disaster came close to wiping out the entire royal line, that's what he did. The river was just beginning to rise."

"As the goddess Isis wept for her dead love, Osiris," I said.

"You know it, little one. Osiris was dead and the summer solstice was approaching. But his death was only temporary."

"As is all death," I said.

"You know it, little one. But on this day Isis wept as she searched the world for the pieces of her beloved husband's body that had been cast to the four winds."

"By his wicked brother Seth," I added. I have always had a sneaking admiration for Seth. He was so clever and so ruthless in seeking his brother's throne.

Inet ignored me. "The waters were swelling," she continued. "The shoals on the banks where the boys fished were perhaps deeper than usual. There should have been two slaves in the coracle, but because they had you along, there was only room for one. The other one cast off and the boys paddled out briskly."

"And Amenmose speared a fish," I said.

"He did."

"And he was so excited that he fell over the side."

"He did. And Prince Wadjmose leaped in after him. Wadjmose could swim," said Inet, "but Amenmose was not yet a good swimmer, and finding the water deeper than he was used to, he panicked and held on to his brother in his fright and the two nearly went down together."

"So the slave jumped in too," I said, "leaving me in the coracle."

"He did. And the coracle bobbed out into the stream."

"And I could not swim. But Hapi cradled me," I said. "Hapi protected me. I did not fall in. I did not drown."

"Praise be to the gods," said Inet devoutly. "Reaching the middle of the river, where the current at that time ran strong, the little coracle sailed briskly downstream with you alone on board."

"I was not afraid," I said.

"No, you were not. Itruri said you waved at him and you were laughing, enjoying the ride."

"The wind was in my hair," I said. "It smelled of spice."

This time Inet did not question my memory. "Itruri was distraught," she said. "It had all happened so fast that he was at a loss. The slave had managed to get the two princes safely ashore, but there you went, all alone in a fragile boat of reeds, three summers only . . ." Inet shook her head as she contemplated the scene.

"But some peasants in a felucca saw my boat," I said. "And they saw that I was too small to be sailing alone. They didn't know I was a princess, though, did they, Inet?"

"They did not know. But they saw a small girl child alone on the wide water and they came to your rescue."

"And they carried me home to the harem palace, and my mother was terribly upset," I said, remembering how she had wept, and held me so tightly that I was almost unable to breathe. Only the previous year my little sister Neferubity had died, of something in her throat that stopped her breath, and my mother had wept, it seemed to me, for months. "Not this one too," she had cried, clutching me. "Please, please, do not take this one too!"

"I told her I was quite safe with Hapi, but she was not impressed," I said to Inet. "And my father the Pharaoh, may he live for ever, rewarded the men."

"He did. But he was angry with you, and you should never forget what he said to you then."

"He told me, 'Always remember that your life belongs to Khemet. Do not be careless with it.' But he did not understand that Hapi cradled me," I said. "Hapi did not let me drown."

"That is so," said Inet.

Truthfully, I have felt a bond with Hapi all my life. I am never happier than when I am sailing upon her bosom. (Although she is both male and female, I believe her female side predominates, for does she not nurture the Black Land like a loving mother?) In times of sorrow, I have fled to her banks and my tears have mingled with the sacred water. As a child, I often escaped from supervision to run down to the river and sit staring at the grand sweep of it, or to cool my hot feet in the soothing shallows. It was not difficult to slip away from the harem palace, where I lived with the rest of the palace children, in the silent, sultry afternoons when all the adults were asleep and the tutor who was supposed to keep an eye on his charges while they rested had also succumbed to the heat.

Here I was interrupted in my writing as my little dwarf Bek, one of my favourite slaves, came running out onto the portico, throwing himself into a series of rolling somersaults as he came. I could not help laughing and refrained from reproving him. He knows he should not rush unbidden into my presence, but he also knows he pleases me and he presumes on my lenience. In truth he is a grown man of some twenty-six summers, but he is no larger than a child of five, although he has broad shoulders and a large head atop his small body.

"A riddle! A riddle!" he cried, coming to a stop with his feet folded neatly onto his thighs. His fine brown eyes sparkled with mirth.

"What is it?" I asked.

"What is small, but potent? Single, yet multiplies? Finite, yet filled with potential?" He looked at me expectantly.

"A seed," I guessed.

He tilted his head. "A good guess, Majesty. It could be so. But I meant . . ."

He always wanted his audience to beg.

"Go on, tell me."

"Me! Me! Me!" he crowed, doing a backward somersault and sitting upright again.

"You multiply?"

"Me and Yunit," he announced, beaming with delight. "She is with child."

"Why, Bek, that is wonderful," I said, sincerely. Bek has been married to Yunit these seven years. She is also a dwarf, although slightly taller than he is. I had not thought they would have children.

"Two moons gone already," he told me proudly. "And sick to her stomach with it. She is only able to fancy pomegranates."

"Oh, so? And I suppose I must order my head gardener to supply my slave with pomegranates?"

"Majesty is kind. Majesty is as kind as she is beautiful. I mean he," and Bek shook his head. It confuses him that I am king although I am female.

"Think of me like Hapi," I said. "Hapi is both male and female. Strong and bountiful. Destructive and nurturing."

He nodded, his face clearing. The idea of the river god having a dual nature was familiar to him. "Majesty," he said, dropping his voice, getting up and sidling closer to me. He glanced at the guards who are never far from me, even during the time of afternoon rest.

"Speak softly," I said. Bek, small and odd though he is, has eyes and ears that I trust and they are always at my service.

"There is talk in the taverns," he murmured into my ear. Bek likes to frequent a number of taverns, where he is a great favourite because of his jokes. He earns occasional debens of copper or silver from the patrons, which he stashes away with a view to eventually gaining his freedom, when he hopes to acquire a smallholding where he and Yunit will plant vegetables for the market. He does not know I am aware of this, but Pharaoh must know whereof his servants dream. Dreams can be dangerous.

"Tell me."

"The Great Commander Thutmose prepares for a major campaign," he said, echoing what Khani had told me. "The soldiers are getting their gear ready. There is much admiration for the Commander. They are saying he is strong, he is aggressive, he is a lion whose roar will be heard as far as the Euphrates."

"Go on," I said, thinking: This is bad news. If there is already this kind of talk in the taverns, the plan must be well advanced, and other than Khani's message this report is the first I have heard of it. "What else are they saying?"

The discipline of the army is strict and Thutmose, he who would be King, is a stern commander who punishes loose talk. Yet in their cups men will let things drop, and Bek can make himself invisible; he crawls beneath tables and nobody notices him.

"They are saying the Great Commander is decisive. They are saying he will not hesitate to do whatever is necessary to defend the Black Land. They are saying he would not be attending to building operations and gardens while our enemies muster on our borders," he said. He avoided my eyes as he whispered, staring down at his sandals, from which his small toes protruded like a row of olives.

He knew what he was reporting was serious in the extreme. It was criticism of the Pharaoh; implied, oblique, but criticism nonetheless. It was treason.

I sent him away with a deben of silver for his trouble. He who would be King is moving in on me. It is time for me to gather my resources.

Here endeth the second scroll.

IT IS TRUE that there is much admiration for the Great Commander Thutmose. His soldiers and officers revere him, but the general populace admire him also. I have seen him myself, for although he is stationed in Memphis, where the army undergoes training, he comes to Thebes for the festivals. Indeed, he was here only three months ago, for the Celebration of Nehebkau, when all Khemet rejoices in the rebirth of Osiris. The festivities rivalled those of the New Year, with grand processions, marching bands, dancing, singing and roistering, and there was beer and food aplenty supplied to everyone from the Pharaoh's stores.

Commander Thutmose took part in various athletic games and competitions, winning almost every time – and there were no allowances made for his status. His physical strength and abilities are truly extraordinary. I was present for the archery competition on the last day, in which several officers of the army and some younger nobles pitted their skills against each other. In the final round, there were three targets instead of just the one, set up a few strides apart, and the test was to shoot at them from a military chariot moving past at speed.

It was a demonstration of the high level to which the soldiers have been trained, for quite a number were able to hit all three. But then the targets were moved further back and at last only Thutmose and one other, a standard bearer from the Division of Horus, were left. The standard bearer, one Metufer, was taller than Thutmose by almost a full head, slender and lithe, and it was a delight to watch him draw his bow to loose off one arrow after another with smooth and practised grace. A cheer went up from the watching crowd as his arrows struck home.

Then the chariot bearing Thutmose came thundering along the circuit. His charioteer was driving it at an even faster pace than Metufer's, whipping the sturdy brown horses into a tearing gallop, the white plumes streaming from their heads. In comparison with the taller man, Thutmose looked almost squat, but one could see the powerful muscles in his naked torso and upper arms rippling as he snatched his arrows from the quiver on his back with economical movements and sent them winging from the tremendous bow that, rumour has it, few other men can bend. The roar that greeted his third bull's eye could, I swear by the breath of Horus, have been heard in Memphis. Since Metufer's arrows had not all struck the exact centre of the targets, Thutmose was the winner.

The prize was a golden bracelet awarded by King Hatshepsut. The Pharaoh was enthroned on a wooden dais and as Thutmose strode up to it the crowd broke into a chant, rhythmically repeating: "Thutmose! Thutmose! Thutmose!" He turned and acknowledged the adulation of the crowd with a victorious salute, his oiled skin gleaming in the sun. The women around me were shrieking with excitement. He passed close by to where I stood, squashed between sweating female bodies, and I noted that he grinned at them, showing his white, somewhat protruding teeth. He has the intense physical presence of a predatory animal. It made me shiver.

Her Majesty had the expression of one who has bitten into a sweet date with a rotten tooth, but she congratulated him graciously enough. His obeisance was sketchy at best. Then he arose and slipped the bracelet over his arm, thick as a mooring rope. Again he turned to wave at the cheering crowd. The chant accompanied him to his chariot: "Thutmose! Thutmose! Thutmose!"

The women around me were going crazy, leaping to try and get a good look at the champion. All that jiggling bounty pressed up close against me was dizzying to the senses, especially as it was accompanied by a somewhat piscine scent growing more powerful by the minute in the hot and humid air. I fought my way clear, desperate for a cooled beer. As I trotted to the nearest tavern, one that I often frequent, I found to my embarrassment that I had to carry my linen bag of scribe's tools in front of my kilt in order to preserve my dignity.

There was a slave girl serving at the tables whom I have noted before, a well-fleshed wench with plump arms and dimples in her round cheeks. A Syrian, I think, brought here as a child after a punitive expedition in the time of Thutmose the Second, may he live. She was jiggling too, as she threaded her way through the crowded room balancing a loaded tray on an upraised hand, calling saucy answers to the raucous patrons. Her face creased into a huge smile when she recognised me.

"Well, well, the little scribe is here! And walking like a duck!"

I fell onto a chair. "I am not walking like a duck," I said indignantly. "I have hurt my heel. Now bring me a jug of beer and some bread."

"Of course, great lord," she said, and winked.

I sat fanning myself, contemplating Commander Thutmose. He is a dangerous man who has the admiration of the people as well as the respect and loyalty of the army. An outstanding leader of men, who has shown himself to be both crafty and courageous, winning battles through clever stratagems coupled with discipline and utter determination. Yes, yes, indeed a dangerous man.

Truly, the Pharaoh should watch her back.

THE THIRD SCROLL

I now continue with my task of setting out the proofs that I am the chosen of the gods. I loved hearing the tales of Hathor who had suckled me and Hapi who had cradled me. But the one I loved best was the story of Apophis, who had spared me from a certain early death. Apophis, the serpent god who lives in the nether regions of the world and is the enemy of men and gods, terrified Inet so greatly that she disliked even saying his name. As a child who was assured of safety, I greatly enjoyed the sense of danger that the tale gave me. "Tell me about Apophis," I would beg her.

"Speak not of him," said Inet, clutching at an amulet that always hung about her neck to stave off evil spirits.

"But he is on my side," I said. "Otherwise I would be dead. Unless, of course," and I glanced up at her sidelong through my lashes, "you have always lied to me about it."

"Sitre, Great Royal Nurse, does not lie," she said, her small black eyes narrowing to furious slits. She was own cousin to Hapuseneb and so of noble descent, although she had not been educated as he was. Sometimes she could be quite imperious.

"So tell me. It was two years after I sailed in the coracle, wasn't it?"

"One," said Inet, reluctantly. "You had four summers. In fact, it was the middle of the fourth summer of your life. The midday meal was over and everyone was resting in the heat of the day. It was extremely hot. Even your brothers were resting in their rooms."

"It was here, in this very palace, wasn't it?"

"In this very palace, right here, in hundred-gated Thebes. You and I were on this self-same portico with the stone pillars that looks out across the flower gardens."

"I could hear the fountains splashing and the doves murmuring in the palms. I remember that."

"I was resting on a wooden day-bed with cushions stuffed with wool," went on Inet, "and a slave had been keeping me cool with an ostrich-feather fan. You lay on the floor on a thin cotton rug because the tiles were cool, and soon you fell asleep."

"So did you," I said. Another reason why Inet hated to tell this tale.

"Just for a minute," she said, defensively. "It was so hot. And it was so quiet. Even the cicadas seemed to have gone to sleep."

"And the slave went away," I said.

"To fetch some cooled fruit juice, so he claimed. Since we would be thirsty when we awoke. And indeed, I did awaken. I am sure I had only just dropped off. But I sensed a presence," said Inet, warming to the drama of her story. "An evil presence. An imminent danger. I looked around, but I could see no human being. And then I looked down at where you were sleeping. And in the shadows, on the edge of the portico, close, oh so close to your little sleeping head, with your child's lock of hair falling across your face, cheeks rosy with the heat . . ." Inet clutched her amulet and made a sign to ward off the evil eye, her voice falling to a whisper . . . "there he was."

"Apophis," I said, shuddering deliciously.

Inet gulped and nodded. "Apophis," she confirmed. The serpent god. The narrow-hooded cobra, who attempts to ambush Ra when he sails through the nether regions of the world in his solar barque.

"Swaying from side to side," I added.

"Five cubits of dark evil, coiled up," said Inet dramatically. I think that the snake grew in length with each telling of the tale, but no matter. "I was petrified," said Inet. "I was truly turned to stone, like a statue hewn from granite with my feet planted in rock. I could not move. I could not utter."

"And I slept," I said.

"Praise be to the gods, you slept. The evil one swayed and his tongue flickered and he looked at me. I knew I looked at death. Nothing moved. And there was no sound. It was as if I had gone deaf as well as dumb."

"I did not move either."

"No, you did not move. Just breathed a little faster than usual because of the heat. And then Apophis lowered his head. And he slid forwards." Her voice dropped even further. "Right across your body. Clear across your chest. I swear it. But you did not move. And then he slipped over the edge of the portico and he disappeared into the shadows of the apple trees and he was gone."

"And the slave returned with the juice," I said.

"He did. And then I screamed and he dropped the pitcher, which shattered on the tiles, and I rushed forward and picked you up and hugged and kissed you and you were frightened by my anguish, so you cried, and . . ."

"It was general mayhem," I said. I liked that phrase.

"It was. But soon we all calmed down and the floor was mopped and we drank some juice."

"Apophis spared me for my destiny," I said with satisfaction.

This event finally confirmed Inet in her belief that I was the chosen of the gods. Suckled by Hathor, cradled by Hapi, and spared by Apophis: How could I not have a high destiny? It must, she devoutly believed, be so. Of course, when I was a little girl and my brothers the princes were still alive, it was not clear exactly what the gods had called me to do. Perhaps, suggested Inet, I might become the God's Wife of Amen, a position of great influence and power. She did not whisper the supreme title of Pharaoh in my ear. Yet within a few years of the visitation by Apophis, the Crown Prince was dead. Well I remember the day.

There was consternation in the palace. Just after midday, when as a rule the rooms were silent, with only the splash of water from the courtyards and the occasional soft footfall of a barefoot slave to be heard, there were suddenly voices exclaiming, people rushing about and weeping and wailing.

"What is it, Inet?" I demanded to know. "What has happened? Has war broken out?" I rather wished it had, for it seemed to my youthful imagination that it would be very exciting.

"No," said Inet grimly. "I think not." She vanished into the passage and reappeared soon after, shaking with shock.

"Inet! Inet, what has happened?" The palace women were now rending their clothes and tearing their hair. I had not seen this before and it was frightening.

"It is your brother Wadjmose," she said, in a tone of disbelief. "He has gone to . . . to join the . . . the Fields of the Blessed."

"Wadjmose is dead?" I was too young to understand that one did not use such terminology in Egypt.

"Hush. He will be with the gods," she told me, but somehow she did not look delighted by the news.

"But just yesterday he was playing with his pet lion cub," I said, stupidly. "He can't be . . . he can't have . . . gone anywhere."

"It was a flux," said Inet, wiping away tears with the back of her hand. "They say . . . they say his bowels turned to water, black water, and he . . . and he . . . he could not live. My child, you must come. The Queen your mother wishes to tell you herself."

I was ushered into the chamber where my mother sat: the Great Royal Wife, clad only in a thin linen shift, her head that normally bore an intricate wig topped with a crown now shaven and bald, her face hard yet wet, as if hewn from basalt and naked to the rain. I looked at her and I turned and fled. This could not be. I could not bear it. I ran from the palace as if Seth and all his devils howled at my heels and I headed straight for the river bank. Such confusion reigned that nobody stopped me, at least not until I had almost reached my goal. Then a hand shot out to grab my arm.

I blinked away my tears. It was Thutmose, my half-brother, borne to my father the Pharaoh by the Lady Mutnofert, a minor wife; he was walking up from the river with a fishing pole on his shoulder. I knew him from the palace school, where I had just begun to learn, painstakingly, to write a clean hieratic script, and he was among the seniors, since he was eight years older than me.

"Little sister," he said, "where do you rush to so heedlessly?"

"T-to the river," I stuttered, hiccuping. "Wadjmose has died of a flux, and everyone has gone mad and Mother . . . and Mother . . ." I could not find words to convey the horror of my regal, self-contained and always beautifully groomed mother stripped to the bone by grief.

"Wadjmose has . . . gone to the gods?" He was astounded. "You are sure of this?"

I gulped, and nodded. "It was a f-flux," I whispered, wiping my running nose on my bare arm.

He handed me a linen kerchief. "Indeed," he said. "And you are going to the river to . . . ?"

"To talk to Hapi," I told him. "I often do."

He nodded as if this made sense to him, put his arm around my shoulders and began to walk with me. "They will not seek me for some time," he said, "nor you, I think. Let us go and sit upon the bank."

So we went down to the river's edge, and we stared at the water surging by; it was at the time of the first rising and the Nile was green, promising a good inundation and rich harvests to come. I wept on my brother's shoulder and his hands were gentle as he stroked my hair. The humid air was scented with damp earth and rotting leaves. I could not tell him that it was not so much my brother's passing for which I wept, but for my broken mother with her naked suffering skull. My world was rent. Mothers did not weep. Divine royalty did not weep. I wanted somebody to tell me that the thing that had happened was not so.

He held me till I finally became calm.

"How do you talk to Hapi?" he enquired.

I peered at him from between my clotted eyelashes. Was he laughing at me?

"Is it necessary to speak aloud?" He appeared to be truly interested.

"No," I said. "You can just . . . you can just . . . think."

"Then let us think together."

We were quiet for a while.

"And does Hapi ever answer you?" he asked at length.

"Sometimes . . . sometimes it seems to me . . . that an answer comes," I said. "Sometimes she sings to me."

"And today?"

I tilted my head, listening. Today there was nothing but the wash of the water through the reeds and a croaking frog.

"Nothing," I said, forlornly.

"Your question, no doubt, was why?"

Of course he was right. I nodded.

"And you hear nothing."

I agreed wordlessly.

"Not quite nothing," he pointed out. "I hear the water. And the water is rising. What has that meant, little sister, for many thousands of years?"

"It has brought life," I said. "Hapi brings life." For every year the great river swells and floods its banks, so that the entire land looks like an enormous, turgid brown lake in which villages sit like islands and the trees seem half their size; this annual inundation deposits rich black earth all along the banks of the great river. Then when it recedes men can plant new crops, so that seeds may germinate under the sun, and harvests sprout and mature and be brought in.

I still did not understand why our brother had had to go to the gods, but the images conjured by the rushing water comforted me. Thutmose's understanding presence comforted me. In truth, before he was my husband and the Pharaoh, he was my friend. I put my hand in my brother's hand and struggled to my feet. "They will be looking for us," I said.

"Yes. We must return. But, little sister . . ."

"Yes?"

"You have a personal slave? One who can taste your food?"

"Yes."

"Eat nothing that has not been tasted," he warned me.

"But I . . . but I am only a child," I said.

"A child who bears the blood royal," he reminded me.

"And there is still Amenmose," I argued, "and . . . and you."

"But there are power-hungry men in Egypt who would love nothing better than to rule over the land. We do not know for sure – do we? – why Wadjmose died. Should the Pharaoh – the gods forbid it – pass into the Afterlife soon, all of his children might need to have a care." His dark eyes were very serious.

"I see," I said in a small voice. I had seen no more than seven risings of the Nile that day, yet it was the end of innocence for me.

I mourned my brother the Crown Prince. But I began to entertain a secret dream. I dared to dream of greatness.

It was the songs of the blind bard, coupled with Inet's tales, that gave form and direction to my dream.

He came to the harem palace when I had seen nine risings of the Nile. It was the first time that I was allowed to attend a formal banquet where the King my father presided, instead of being sent to the children's dining room with the rest of the palace children.

I wore a simple white linen shift and a little string of blue glass beads, but Inet had refused to let me line my eyes with black kohl and paint the lids with green malachite. There would be time enough for that later, she said. Yet she had tied a wax perfume cone on top of my head just like the other ladies had and I felt very grown-up. During the course of the evening it melted gradually, keeping me cool and scented with myrrh.

It was hot and noisy in the dining hall. I was given a gilded, richly decorated chair to sit on, just like the rest of the adults and their guests, a deputation from Syria who had brought tribute and gifts and all manner of things to barter.

The dinner went on and on. Female servants kept bringing more dishes piled high with delicacies, piping hot from the kitchen, where (I knew because I loved to go there) the chief cook sweated and shouted and swore and threw things at his minions. At the tables, though, all was decorous. I enjoyed the tender veal and the freshly baked wheat cakes, dripping with honey, and I had a slice of sweet melon afterwards. Naturally the adults ate far more – joints of roast beef studded with garlic, fat roasted ducks stuffed with herbs, rich goose livers pounded to a paste, steamed green beans, lentils and carrots, fig puree, cheese and dates. And of course, plenty of wine that had been cooled in earthenware jars. How could people eat and drink so much, I wondered.

I remember all these things so clearly because it was the first time, but also and mainly because of the blind bard. He was a member of a group of musicians, most of whom were girls; they played on double pipes and lutes and shook tambourines; the smallest rhythmically thumped a drum and several were expert at clicking the menat. But the bard, whose bald head shone in the lamplight like polished cedarwood and whose eyes gleamed milky white like pearls, played on a small portable harp and his music could have charmed the dead out of their tombs.

His first song was merry to begin with, ending, however, on a plaintive note. His fingers on the strings were gnarled, but the sound was like water over rocks, like the wind in the trees.

> *"Weave chains of blooms to give to your beloved,*
> *Rejoice, rejoice in the days of youth.*
> *Be happy, breathe in sweet scents.*
> *Keep your loved one ever near,*
> *Do not stop the music,*
> *Do not stop the dance,*
> *Bid farewell to all care!*
> *Pick delights like flowers in the fields.*
> *For soon, too soon the time will come*
> *When to that land of silence*
> *You and your love will both be gone."*

The bearded Syrians in their gaudy robes were becoming very merry and did not take kindly to the sad, haunting quality of the last lines. "Give us a song of great deeds," their leader shouted, banging on the table with his fist.

"Aye," chorused his fellows, who had already looked deep into the wine jar. "A song of great deeds!"

The blind bard inclined his head, swept his knotted fingers deftly across the singing strings, and said, in his deep voice: "I sing *The Song of the Godlike Ruler.*"

The rowdy Syrians cheered. Soon the power of his music had charmed them into stillness, and they listened even as I did.

> *"Hearken to the Song of the Godlike Ruler.*
> *His Majesty came forth as the Avenger.*
> *For the enemies of Ma'at were many*
> *And the Black Land suffered, aye it suffered much.*
> *His Majesty came forth as the Destroyer.*

> *He smote the adversaries of righteousness,*
> *He washed in their blood,*
> *He bathed in their gore.*
> *He cut off their heads like ducks."*

This was far more to the taste of the Syrians, who cheered and then settled down again.

> *"His Majesty drove back the fiends of Seth.*
> *He triumphed over all the foul fiends.*
> *Aye, he was victorious over his foes.*
> *He fixed his southern boundary-stone,*
> *He fixed his northern one like heaven,*
> *He governed unto the eastern deserts."*

Now the rest of the musicians joined in, in a swelling chorus.

> *"His Majesty came forth as Atum.*
> *He crushed iniquity.*
> *He repaired what he had found ruined.*
> *He restored the boundaries of the towns.*
> *He rebuilt the temples of the gods.*
> *His Majesty restored Ma'at,*
> *And all the people praised him."*

A trumpet sounded a clarion call above the singing strings and the flutes. Cymbals clashed.

> *"Aye, His Majesty was a godlike ruler.*
> *He came forth as Atum.*
> *He held the Black Land in his hands,*
> *He held it safe.*

He triumphed over evil.
He was a shining one clothed in power.
And all the people praised him."

There were more songs that night and much carousing – and drunkenness, I have no doubt. But Inet came to take me away before things became too rowdy and I did not protest. I lay in my bed, on my sheets of fine linen over a mattress stuffed with lambswool, and I kept hearing the thrilling words of the blind bard:

"Aye, His Majesty was a godlike ruler.
He came forth as Atum."

How wonderful, I thought, to be a godlike ruler. As indeed my father the great Pharaoh was. How wonderful to hold the Black Land in one's hands. To hold it safe, to triumph over evil. And to be loved by all, and praised:

"He was a shining one clothed in power.
And all the people praised him."

A shining one clothed in power. Oh yes, I thought. That was a destiny to desire. Not a tame existence in the harem. And although at that time my elder brother Amenmose was still alive, yet I felt in my bones that such a destiny would be mine.

Early the next morning I went out into the palace garden and encountered one of the Syrian deputation sitting on a bench in front of the fish pond, staring despondently into its depths. He must have been a young man, but to my eyes then he seemed quite old. He had a curly beard and curly locks and his brown eyes were bloodshot.

"Good morning," I said.

He groaned. "A good morning it is not," he responded. He spoke our tongue passably well and he had a pleasant voice, although it came thickly from his throat. "I looked too deeply into the wine jar and I am paying the price for it."

"Why then are you up so early?" I enquired. "When my brother Amenmose has drunk too much, I think he sleeps until the afternoon."

"I am not up early," he said, "I am still up late. I mean, I have not been to sleep as yet. We caroused all night and then we began to gamble and I lost." He rubbed his face blearily. "Somehow, someone seems to have stuffed a lambswool sock into my mouth," he complained. "One that was not recently well washed."

"Nor were you," I said.

He looked affronted. "You are remarkably pert, for a child," he said, regarding me with more attention. "Ah, the little princess." He leaned back lazily. "The little princess with the golden eyes. If I give you a bracelet, as golden as your eyes, will you send it to me by messenger when you are come of age?"

"Why should I do that?"

"Because I think we might have more to say to each other in a few years' time," he said. The expression in his eyes was one that later I would learn to recognise, but at that time it was new to me. It disturbed me somewhat and yet I liked it.

"When I come of age, I shall be Pharaoh," I said. I had not meant to speak my dream but it slipped out.

He laughed, then groaned and held his head. "Beware of what you desire, my dear," he said. "You might achieve it. Besides, you have a brother, do you not?"

I dropped my eyes. Of course I did not wish my brother harm. "I am younger than he," I muttered. "One does not know . . ."

"I shall send you the bracelet," he promised, with a grin.

He did so later that day. He knew who I was but I did not know him; when the slave brought the bracelet, of beautifully chased gold, in a little cedarwood box, he told me that it was a gift from the prince. He was the youngest scion of the royal house of the Mitanni in Syria. I had not thought that a prince could smell so. Yet I had liked him and I kept the bracelet. I have it still.

Here endeth the third scroll.

THE FOURTH SCROLL

When I was eleven, Inet's prediction came true: I was called to serve my father as the God's Wife of Amen. I was also Divine Adoratrice; this position can only be held by one who is unmarried and pure. I took enormous pride in my task. I had to be present during the daily temple rituals, so that I knew and understood them. I helped my father destroy by burning the names of Egypt's enemies, a ritual that gave me great satisfaction. I led groups of priests to the temple pool to be purified. I learned the dances that kept the God in a state of arousal. Young though I was, I was assisting my father the Pharaoh, as he explained, to guarantee the eternally recurring recreation of the world through the life-giving powers of the God. And a thrilling experience it was for a girl child who otherwise might have been restricted to the palace schoolroom, or learning to spin flax.

I also accompanied my father on some of his trips around the Black Land, for my mother, the Queen Ahmose, may she live, had much to do in the harem and was at times not well. I remember the first official journey that my royal father and I made together. Up to that day I had never travelled very far from the harem palace where I grew up, and I was very excited. We would be sailing to Heliopolis, to visit the priests at the temples there, and I would have a role in the rites.

We were to travel by boat, but although it was an official journey it was not a royal progress and the way would not be lined with cheering crowds. The boat would not be the exquisitely decorated solar barque on which the Pharaoh sailed during the major festivals. It was a large, comfortable vessel, though, with a high bow and stern, and a dais packed with soft cushions and shaded from the harsh sun by a colourful canopy. Slaves stood to attention with fans to keep us cool, and of course the royal guard would attend on us. Several smaller boats bearing bureaucrats and servants sailed with us, and the kitchen boat, from which delectable aromas wafted across the water, was never far behind.

This was the first time I met Senenmut. He was the scribe chosen to accompany us. At that time, when I was eleven years of age, he was a young man of eighteen. He was deferential, as was only right, but he did not seem overawed at the company in which he found himself, for he had a natural dignity and carried himself with assurance.

I liked his looks at once; he was taller than most men, with broad shoulders and a strong nose. His dark eyes under thick brows regarded the world with a slightly amused expression. I tried to observe him indirectly, with sidelong glances, and I noted that he had elegant hands with long fingers that were not stained with ink as a scribe's hands so often are. His hair was thick and dark and he wore it long; when the sun caught it, it had blue-black gleams. It looked as if it would be soft to the touch. I would like to run my hands through it, I thought.

He helped me onto the dais with a firm grip, and when I looked up to thank him, he actually winked at me. Well! A scribe with some audacity, I thought, feeling my cheeks grow warm. I lifted my chin and pretended to ignore him.

Once we had taken our seats in the shade, the King my father removed the crown of Lower Egypt that he had worn while being borne to the quay in his sedan chair, and which he would wear again when being met at Heliopolis. I saw that he had but little of his own hair left and the remaining tufts were grey. His dark eyes could still pierce one with a hawk-like glare, but the kohl he wore (as most adults do to help deflect the sharp rays of the sun) could not hide the surrounding folds and lines, and he looked – I must write this down, for I am bound to write the truth – like a leathery, tired ex-soldier with a stiff hip and a soft belly that overhung his studded belt. Clearly his teeth pained him, for he rubbed his jaw and sighed.

I was saddened by this view of my royal father. I knew that he had been a great general and a renowned warrior, about whose achievements on the battlefield many admiring tales were told. Always he had seemed to me to be a person of great stature and dignity, a person invested with authority and not a little mystery. But I took comfort from the reflection that his royal Ka would surely maintain its force even as his earthly body became diminished.

We would be sailing with the current, but against the wind, which almost always blows from the north. However, there was very little wind that morning, so the rowers would not have as hard a task as they would have done had the wind been strong. High on the bow a tall Nubian stood, keeping time for the rowers with a large brass gong; the rowers chanted a rhythmic song as they bent to their oars. As usual the river was busy. Other gongs from similar boats could be heard across the water. Shouts and orders echoed. Light boats woven of reeds slipped between the heavier barges carrying large cargoes of materials and food and the fine boats similar to ours that would be bearing persons of status.

We had set forth early but already the day was warm; the sky was a cloudless blue reflected in the water slipping by. My father was resting with his eyes shut; he seemed to have dropped off to sleep. For a moment I wondered whether he still breathed, but then a gentle snore reassured me. But I was far from sleep and I sat upright next to Senenmut the scribe, imitating his scribe's pose with the folded knees. Ah yes, time was when I could sit like that for a long time and then jump up and run.

I was fascinated by the bustling river traffic. Between the smaller boats some large ships were ponderously navigating the waterway towards the quay that we had left, bringing, I knew, cedarwood from Lebanon, gold from the mines in Sinai, ivory, ebony, strange animals and more gold from Nubia.

"Look, Princess," said Senenmut, "there go the Keftiu. They have sailed from very far away, where few Egyptians have ever sailed." He looked envious, as if he too would like to sail to distant lands.

I decided to allow him back into my favour. "Would you like to do that?"

"Above all things," he said, with a sigh.

"So why are you not a sailor?"

"My father thought a scribe would have better prospects."

"I think our sailors should be more venturesome," I said. "There may be rich lands that we know not of, with whom we could also trade our grain and wine, our linen and pottery. When I am Pharaoh . . ." I bit my lip. "If I were Pharaoh," I amended, peeping at him from under my lids. He kept his face straight, but his eyes were twinkling. I had the feeling that very little would ever escape him.

"Yes, Princess?" he prompted politely.

"I would order our sailors to explore," I said. "To go further than they are used to."

He nodded. "You too would like to go further than you are used to, I think," he said.

"Indeed I would," I said. "Indeed I would."

Just at that moment we were approaching a bay of striking beauty on the western bank, where stark, massive rock formations reared up behind a broad plain. A white building, not very big and partially fallen in, stood against the cliffs. Yet it had graceful lines, fronted by crumbling terraces linking with the plain.

"What place is that?" I asked sharply, jumping up from the dais and moving to the side of the boat. Senenmut rose to join me.

"The bay, Princess, is Djeser-Djeseru, a holy place where Hathor resides. The building is the temple of Mentuhotep the Second, may he live. He was a great Pharaoh, a unifier and a builder."

"I like the sound of that," I said. "A unifier and a builder. Good things to be."

"Yes," agreed Senenmut. "It is a mortuary temple, of course."

"Of course," I said. The temple of Amen-Ra at Karnak lay at our backs on the east bank and it was a living, working community. If I turned around I could see its impressive pylons and pillars. The west bank, I knew, was the abode of the dead; many mortuary temples stood there, with shrines where offerings were made to feed the Kas of Pharaohs who had gone to the gods. "It is a pity that the temple is in such a state."

"Mentuhotep and his successors saw to it that Egypt prospered," said Senenmut, "but Mentuhotep the Fourth was overthrown by his chief minister, Amenemhat. Maintaining the mortuary temples of the previous dynasty was not . . . ah . . . a priority."

"He must have been a fool to allow his throne to be usurped," I said scornfully. "Yet the temple could be restored. Or rather . . . something of greater . . . greater magnificence . . . could perhaps be built beside it."

"Djeser-Djeseru calls for a structure that dominates the plain," observed Senenmut, staring at the soaring, rugged cliffs that glittered in the early sunlight.

"I agree," I said, excitedly. "That would be wonderful. It would be the most wonderful temple that the world has ever seen."

He whistled faintly. "That would demand an extraordinary design, Princess."

"Yes, it would. But it could be done."

The bay was slipping past as our boat sailed on.

"It could be done," agreed Senenmut. He stared at the site as if measuring it with his eyes. "In fact it should be done. One day."

"One day," I echoed, trying to hold the image of those magnificent cliffs as the shore sped by.

From that moment he held a special place in my life. I think that there are few things that so bind two people as a shared dream; especially if it be somewhat outrageous and a difficult one to real-ise.

Together we leaned on the railing, looking back as the boat left the magnificent bay behind. I was standing downwind and suddenly noted the masculine scent of the scribe at my side. Involuntarily I leaned closer, inhaling him. Oh, I do like this man, I thought. I like him so much. I would wish . . . I would wish to . . . to dance for him as I do for the god Amen-Ra. When I looked at him sidelong, he was smiling down at me as if he knew my thoughts. I could feel my cheeks flushing hotly.

Just then there was a slight lurch. We had had to avoid a funeral boat carrying a gilded mummy case on its deck that had cut across our prow. Then the rowers recovered their rhythm and we approached a bend in the river. The temples of the living and the dead were left behind. We returned to perch upon the dais again. A slave girl began to play on a lute and sing and we sat listening companionably. Her voice was like clear water running over stones. It seemed to me that it was the very voice of Hapi, the river god who had sung to me so often, singing in my heart; singing a song of limitless possibilities. I closed my eyes, thinking: This must be what it is like in the Fields of the Blessed.

Suddenly the voice of the royal guard who rode the bow of the boat shouted a warning: "Beware, hippo!"

We had just rounded a bend in the river and were passing a small bay with a gently sloping sandy shoreline fringed with palm trees and lush green pasture. In the background white hills shimmered in the lucent sunlight. I realised with a shock that what I had taken to be a cluster of boulders in the shallow water near the shore was in truth a huddle of hippos cooling themselves. There appeared to be a number of calves, little boulders resting close to the huge bulk of their mothers.

At this moment the kitchen boat – considerably smaller, of course, than the royal barge – passed us on the shore side. Doubtless the chefs wanted to get to the place where we would stop for lunch before us so that the tables could be set out. Then a peculiar sound filled the air, a sort of honking wheeze; several of the cows in the shallow water opened their cavernous mouths as if they were yawning.

"Look out!" exclaimed Senenmut. "Here comes trouble."

I noticed that one of the hippos was moving towards the kitchen boat with a bobbing motion, almost a gallop, blowing explosively every time it sank below the water. The boat's rowers had now seen it too and were attempting to pull away into deeper water, but the charging monster attacked at such a speed that they could not evade it. The vast jaws opened and closed on the stern of the boat with a crunch. A high-pitched scream rent the air. The boat tilted as water streamed in through the gash, spilling rowers and other slaves into the river.

Again the huge jaws yawned and snapped together. I stared in horrified fascination as a sundered leg floated past us, colouring the water pink. Some servants still clinging to the foundering boat belaboured the hippo with oars. It roared and chomped once more. The royal barge had swung around to come to the rescue and two of the royal guards had flung their spears at the attacking animal, but to no avail as they simply bounced off its hide.

My father, who a moment before had been nodding against the cushions, had leapt to the side of the barge. Now he clambered to the bow and grabbed a spear from the hand of the lookout. Balancing on bent knees as the barge swayed, he waited for the next angry lunge. Suddenly he was once more a powerful warrior. Tautly poised, he almost seemed to shine. Into the open throat of the furious hippo he hurled the spear, straight and true as if aiming at a murderous enemy upon the battlefield. It struck home. The hippo coughed gouts of blood, emitting thunderous, gargling bellows of pain and anguish. It thrashed around in the reddening water. But it would fight no more. Pharaoh had triumphed. He had come forth as the destroyer and the danger was past.

The survivors were taken aboard our barge and we sailed onward. The physician who had of late begun to travel with the Pharaoh assisted the wounded. Someone would take care of the wreckage and salvage what they could. The other hippos would probably not attack anyone, Senenmut told me; it seemed that the kitchen boat had come between a mother and her calf, which had been sucked into the middle of the river by the current, running strongly since it was the season of Akhet.

I no longer remember everything that happened on the rest of that journey. There have been so many journeys since. Yet I recall every word that Senenmut and I exchanged. I remember how much I liked his voice, deep and resonant. I wanted to see more of him, but at that time our paths did not often cross.

In the year that followed, the royal house was again plunged into mourning by the passing of the Crown Prince. My brother Amenmose, who was an expert hunter and a superb soldier, broke his neck falling out of his fast-racing chariot during an ostrich hunt. He was killed instantly.

They brought him to the harem palace amid fearful weeping and wailing and laid him down on the bed in the room that had been his before he went to the Kap to be trained as a soldier. As soon as I heard the ululations of grief, I knew that something momentous had occurred. I ran to the room that seemed to be the centre of the storm. There he lay, with nothing more out of the ordinary to be seen than a graze running down the side of his cheek. Otherwise he looked just as if he slept: a young, handsome man, with a pronounced nose like that of our father the Pharaoh, and powerful arms and legs thanks to his military training. He might have been resting quietly on a long march.

The Royal Physician came and confirmed that the prince had indeed gone to the gods. My mother sat by his side holding his cold hand, but this time she did not weep, although I could see that shudders shook her frame. My father walked the floor and raged at everyone who had gone along on the expedition. He needed someone to blame. Nobody noticed me.

This time I did not run to talk to Hapi. Instead, I walked to one of the courtyards and sat down next to a fish pond. In the water golden carp circled.

A shadow fell across the water. I looked up. "Oh, it's you," I said, recognising Senenmut. Sad as I was, my heart lifted at the sight of him.

"I have heard about your brother, Princess," he said. "It is grievous news."

"Yes." We were both silent for a bit. "Sit down and talk to me."

He folded his legs into his scribe's pose. More silence.

I closed my eyes, picturing the moment of sudden flight that had ended my brother's life. "A terrible shock," I said. "A sad loss."

"Are you?" he asked. His dark eyes were questioning.

"Am I what?"

"Are you sad? Truly?"

"Why should I not be?" I asked indignantly. "I have lost my brother!"

"Then why do you not weep?"

I glared at him.

"It brings you closer to the throne," he reminded me. "If you would still be Pharaoh."

I had, truth to tell, been trying not to think this, yet thinking exactly this, and feeling at the same time enormously guilty to be thinking it. But I did not like this scribe looking so clearly into my shameful heart. "How dare you!" I said furiously. "You presume much!"

"You have the full blood royal," he observed. "It would be natural, to be thinking about the succession. You need not feel shame."

"I am not ashamed!" I scrambled to my feet.

He tilted his head back, looking at me with eyes like slits. "Then do not be so angry. It suggests guilt."

He had thrust me into confusion and I liked it not. But I did not know how to depart with dignity.

"They say . . ." He stopped, tantalisingly.

I took the bait and sat down again. "Well, what do they say?"

"They say that the axle may have been . . . tampered with. It seems that the chariot had lately come from a complete overhaul. It should have been sturdy."

A chill ran down my back like a small, cold snake. "Who would have done such a thing?"

"Someone in whose interest it would be for there not to be a strong Pharaoh when the current one passes, may he live for ever."

"Such as?"

"Such as the priests, perhaps? It would greatly increase their power and influence."

I nodded. This made sense. I trailed my hand in the cool water. The fish rose, snapping, as if expecting food. I glanced at the scribe. His eyes were calculating, as if he was not sure what to think of me. He could not – surely! – imagine that I had known, had in any way been involved . . .

"I did not wish my brother harm," I said. "Truly, I did not. He was years older than me and I did not see much of him before he went to the Kap, but I did not . . . I would never . . . I did not wish him harm. You must believe it."

He nodded and stood up. "I was called to the office of the palace housekeeper," he said, "but that was before all of this. Yet I should go and see . . ."

"Of course," I said, shortly. "Go." He should wait, I thought crossly, to be dismissed. I was a princess, after all. But to him I was a child.

I looked after the tall figure with the broad shoulders as he walked away. I was affronted that he had looked at me suspiciously. I wanted him to look at me differently. Like . . . like the priests looked at me when I danced as the God's Wife. Like that.

With my brother lying dead, I should not have been thinking of such matters. But I have sworn to write the truth, and the truth is that I did think of him so. I did.

Here endeth the fourth scroll.

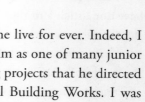

I KNEW THE late great Senenmut, may he live for ever. Indeed, I knew him well, for I often worked with him as one of many junior assistant scribes on the numerous building projects that he directed for Her Majesty as Overseer of the Royal Building Works. I was included in listing different types of building materials because I was a quarry scribe for a time and I know materials, especially marble. I was often present when Her Majesty came to inspect a site or to confer with Senenmut on a particular statue or decoration that she desired.

He was, I think, the only one of her officials who ever dared to oppose her in any matter of considerable importance, but he actually did that on more than one occasion when I was present. Mostly they were in complete accord as to what should be done, but sometimes she had an idea that he did not accept. He would not agree to build anything impracticable, nor would he allow her to make changes that would affect the integrity of the completed work. At times I feared that she would send him to the quarries for impertinence, but in the end he always had his way. And instead of falling from favour, he seemed only ever to rise – at least until shortly before he went to the gods. Something must have happened then, for he came less often to the palace and their behaviour was coldly formal and stiff. Her Majesty began to call on me more often at that time. And then he was gone.

I have my own opinion as to why he got away with so much. I noted how his face blazed with joy when he saw the royal barge approach a building site where he was working on the river bank. She would lean on the side, looking out for him. They would look at each other with such intensity that . . . well, he might as well have thrown out a grappling hook. I saw how her gaze followed him as he moved about giving orders and checking completed work. There was great admiration in her face, but a sadness also. A kind of yearning look. And then she would compose herself, and shake her head, and attend to the various complaints.

There have always been rumours, of course, that Senenmut was more to her than an official. Others had also noted what I have written of. Those who were jealous of his swift rise and the many titles Her Majesty conferred on him spread such gossip maliciously.

But I do not believe it. No, no, I do not. For one thing, they could never have been alone. There are always many officials and servants and slaves about. For another, he was a commoner. Not only did he not have royal blood, he did not even come from a noble family. How could he aspire to be the lover of one who was a Pharaoh and divine? He, who came from a family of market gardeners, as Hapuseneb used to sneer. No, it was not possible. Besides, his abilities were so outstanding that they were reason enough for his remarkable career. Quite enough.

Senenmut was a legend among the younger scribes, for he was a wonderful example of how a person whose background is quite ordinary may rise to great heights through diligence and royal favour. He grew up, I believe, in the small town of Iuny, and his parents were worthy but dull and far from rich. His schooling he had from an elderly priest who retired to Iuny to grow vegetables. He first came to the attention of the late Pharaoh Thutmose the First, may he live, through the Pharaoh's architect, the incomparable Ineni, who identified the young Senenmut as a most promising student of architecture. He worked under Ineni's tutelage for several years and the old man drove him hard.

Being a man of many parts, Senenmut was also an able administrator and furthermore good with children, so Pharaoh Thutmose the Second appointed him to be tutor to little Neferure who was born to Queen Hatshepsut when she was the Great Royal Wife, and also made him steward of the child's property. Senenmut dearly loved that little girl and she loved him. He would bring her along on a trip to a new building site, but only if he was sure she would be safe. I often saw her sitting on his lap, listening intently to some story that he was telling with much drama, or giggling uproariously because he was tickling her. They were always laughing together. He had a finely developed sense of the ridiculous and could mimic pompous officials and priests with wicked vividness.

I remember how one day he was doing a fine imitation of Hapuseneb for the amusement of the child and several junior scribes, myself included, during a time of rest under some trees at Karnak, where a section was being added to the hypostyle hall on the orders of the Pharaoh. The two men, the scribe and the priest, were similar in some ways, mainly in being very competent, but utterly dissimilar in others, and they never got on well. That day Senenmut had tied a huge bush of some kind to his head to represent Hapuseneb's imposing ceremonial wig, and was pretending to pray to the gods, while responding in asides to his wife Amenhotep. This lady, as everyone knows, rules the roost at home and the Grand Vizier and Chief Priest of Amen jumps at her commands.

"Blessings and thanksgiving to thee, O my Father, my Lord!" intoned Senenmut in the high-pitched, slightly nasal tones of Hapuseneb. *"Hear my prayer! The earth waits for thy precious seed!"* Then he ad-

ded, in an aside to imaginary words from his wife: "No, dear, I have not spoken to the builder. He is still completing the alterations at the palace. Amenhotep, my dove, I am busy. *The earth waits for thy precious seed! Come thou and inseminate it!* No, my dove, I do not want you to live in a hovel. Of course not. I assure you . . ."

By this time everybody was laughing. The imitation was brilliant.

Senenmut was getting well into the swing of things: *"All people sing thy blessings and praise thy name,"* he prayed, in the very voice of Hapuseneb. "We must be patient, my dove. The pyramids were not built in a day, you know." He did not notice that a group of priests had emerged from the pylon behind him and were fast approaching our resting place. Nor did he realise that the jeers and cheers around him had suddenly fallen silent. *"O give ear to our pleas!"* he wailed, clutching the bush to his head. *"Be thou generous, be thou . . ."*

At last a loud cough from one of the minor priests attracted his attention. Senenmut turned around, to be confronted by Hapuseneb in person. *". . . merciful!"* he said, tailing off. The bald, immaculate priest stood glaring at him with his arms crossed. Sheepishly Senenmut removed the bush and shook some leaves from his thick dark hair. He was as tall as the other, but rangy rather than elegant, and he was covered in dust from the building works. "Sorry," he said, carelessly. "We were just . . . fooling around."

Hapuseneb looked him up and down with a sneer. "And you are the appropriate person," he said, his high-pitched voice even higher with anger, "to play the fool."

"At least I do not have a wife who makes a fool of me," snapped Senenmut.

Hapuseneb blinked twice. "But then you are the Pharaoh's fool, not so? A flea-bitten base-born buffoon."

I thought the scribe would strike him for that. He did make a forward movement, but then he restrained himself, with a visible effort. "Better than being a two-faced onion-eyed footlicker."

At that they almost did come to blows, but two of the priests accompanying Hapuseneb laid restraining hands on his arms. "Vizier, come away," one of them muttered. "This is unseemly." With one last glare, the Vizier and Chief Priest turned on his heel and left the scene. Senenmut gave a yelp of laughter and the junior scribes giggled, but not too loudly, for it does not pay to anger such a powerful man.

Her Majesty, I observed, used to pit them against each other. She would often call upon them both to offer suggestions for solving a problem, and they tried to outdo each other with their advice. But in the end it was usually the Pharaoh who cut through to the core of the issue, and it was always she who decided what was to be done. There was never any doubt as to whose hand was at the helm of state.

I pray that her grip may never falter. That she may hold the Black Land safe.

THE FIFTH SCROLL

As I sat there at the fish pond trailing my fingers in the water and watching Senenmut walk away, a strange mix of feelings was roiling in my heart, like one of Hapu's pots in which he boiled up medications. There was sorrow for my brother, so young and strong, so suddenly bereft of breath; there was sadness for my parents who had to weep again for a lost child; there was a measure of fear, for if someone had killed the prince, might they not think also of me, who was the last of Pharaoh Thutmose's children with the pure blood royal? And there was beneath all these a shiver of excitement . . . and more than a touch of bitterness. Because I should be next in line for the Double Crown when my royal parents passed into the Afterlife; but since I was a girl, I knew I would be overlooked. I sighed. I should go to talk to Thutmose, my remaining half-brother, I thought. This disaster would change his life, and mine as well.

The corridors echoed with the grief of ritual mourning, but as I walked along them towards my half-brother's suite of rooms, I heard a different sound. A thin keening, full of such deep sorrow that the hair on my arms stood up. I pushed at the door whence it came. There I discovered Inet, huddled into a tight bundle on a low seat, hugging her knees, rocking and moaning.

I went to kneel beside her and took her in my arms. Why, she is quite little, I thought in surprise. I had looked up to her for so long, but now she seemed to have shrunk with age and grief. "Oh, Inet, please don't," I said helplessly. I was yet young enough to be greatly upset by adult weeping.

"My last prince gone," she sobbed into my shoulder. "Gone to the gods. It isn't right, it isn't right for young ones to go first. The gods have got the order wrong. All wrong. Quite wrong." She shook her head and moaned and rocked. I patted her heaving back.

I realised that she had loved my brother Amenmose every bit as much as my mother had. She had indeed seen more of him as a small child. She had brought him up. Of course she was bereft. "There, there," I said, as she had so often said to me. I searched for something to say to her. "He will be waiting for you in the Fields of the Blessed, and he will be young and strong, and he will always remain so," I offered at length. "He will never grow old and have a stiff hip and painful teeth and joints that ache. Think of that."

She calmed a little and sniffed.

"He will come to welcome you, Inet, when your time comes to go to the Fields of the Blessed," I told her. "To take you by the hand, and you will row in a little boat together and he will shoot ducks and the sun will always shine." I found it strange that I was now trying my best to comfort the one who had always comforted me.

"But I want him to be here," she said childishly. Then she gave a deep, tremulous sigh. "Well, well, it cannot be. We must put up with it. The older one gets, the more one must put up with." She looked at me closely with her little swollen eyes. "Praise be to the gods that you are strong," she said. She squeezed my hands. "Thank you, my child. I shall rest now."

I called for a slave to attend to her and then strode on to Thutmose's rooms. When I reached the tall bronze doors to my half-brother's suite of rooms, his guards knew me, of course, and stepped aside to let me through. Inside the heavy scent of incense mixed with medications hung in the air. I recognised the signs: Thutmose was ill again. I walked straight through to his bedroom, ordering fussing slaves out of the way. He lay on a day-bed piled with cushions, clad only in a light kilt. His skin shone with perspiration and he breathed shallowly. It was clear that he was having one of his attacks of fever, that also caused him to have much pain in his joints.

"Brother," I said.

He opened his eyes. "Ah. Hatshepsut." He put out his hand.

I stepped forwards and took it. It was clammy and trembled a little in mine. "You have heard?" I asked.

He sighed. "I have heard."

For a few moments we sat wordlessly. Then he said: "Now I will be Pharaoh. When the time comes. Your blood is better than mine but you are a child and a girl child to boot. The Double Crown will come to me. And I do not want it. It is a heavy burden to bear and I am so often tired. But know this: Bear it I will. I must do it for Khemet."

I nodded. I understood that Pharaoh was Egypt. "I will stand at your side," I promised. "I will help you bear it. I already help my royal father."

"I know," he said, smiling faintly at my stout words. "I know, and I will depend on you."

Shortly after the death of Amenmose, my mother the Queen Ahmose, who had been ailing for some time, fell seriously ill. I think that the shock was too much for her.

Some dire disease took hold of her and seemed to squeeze her chest so that she could not breathe. No medications, incantations or prayers to the gods could drag her back from the brink of the Afterlife where she hovered for weeks. They would not let me near her for fear that the devils that caused her to be ill would attack me too. Then one day she called for me.

I entered the room quietly and sat down on a little stool next to her bed. Incense hung upon the thick air in the chamber. I hoped that it would be strong enough to keep the lurking devils at bay. I waited. She did not speak at once, lying with her eyes closed. She had always had a strong face and an attractive one, but now it was drawn and looked like a mask carved from very ancient ivory. I sat quietly waiting while Her Majesty collected her thoughts.

At length she sighed. "Four children," she said, her voice a little creaky as though through disuse. "Four children have I carried under my heart and brought into this world with much travail. And now there is only the one."

This statement caused me to feel guilt – although I could not see why it should, for certainly I had had no fault in my three siblings' deaths.

"I am sorry, Mother," I said.

"First, I lost my little Neferubity. You remember your little sister, do you not?"

"Yes, Mother. But . . . time has passed, since she went to the gods."

"Time has passed. But I miss her yet. Let me tell you how it is, to lose a child." She stopped speaking and closed her eyes. She was silent for a long time. I thought she had fallen asleep, but then she continued. "First, it feels as if a large and heavy stone with sharp edges has been laid upon your heart. It pains you, here." She put a closed fist to her breast. "Much like a wound, that bleeds. Then, as time passes, the sharp edges of the stone are worn away. It becomes smoother, like a boulder that has rolled down the river and the tumbling water and the other stones have ground it round. Yet it is heavy still, and there is no way to put it down. You must bear it."

I was too young, that day, to grasp what my mother was telling me. Yet now I know she spoke the truth. Only not the whole truth. Because from time to time that stone recovers its cutting edge. Quite suddenly. A scent can do it, such as the incense that the midwives burned on the day of the child's birth. Or, for me, the glimpse of a slave girl who has the same slender and graceful look as my own lost child.

"Yet at the time there were left two princes of the blood," my mother went on. Tears were now sliding out of her closed eyes.

I patted her hand, feeling helpless. "Do not distress yourself," I said, but of course this had no effect.

"It seemed . . . that the succession was assured. Two sons . . . two princes . . . strong and handsome. And yet, now there is not one to follow the great Pharaoh when the time comes, may he live for ever. Not one."

"May he live," I echoed.

"You are young, my daughter," she said, opening her dark eyes and looking at me. "I hope you may not ever know what it is to lose a child, but I fear you may have to bear that sorrow as I do. Children are so . . ." Her voice seemed to grow faint like the wind sighing in the sycamore trees. "So fragile. Even a strong male child is but a reed and can be broken, just like that." She dabbed her eyes with a linen kerchief. With a trembling hand, she drank some fruit juice that a slave had brought. Then she raised her head and her voice came back. "But you are healthy, are you not, my child?"

"Yes, Mother," I said proudly. "I am healthy."

She nodded. "You will need all your strength," she told me. "You know that the Double Crown will eventually pass to your half-brother Thutmose, son of Mutnofert. He will be the second Pharaoh of that name."

"Yes, Mother."

"And you must wed Thutmose. Through you he will have a clear entitlement to the Double Throne. Your role must be that of Great Royal Wife."

"I know," I said with some bitterness.

"Mark me well," she said. "Whenever a Pharaoh passes into the Afterlife, the forces of chaos gather and threaten the destruction of the Two Lands. Your father, may he live, is not well. When he . . . when he passes . . ." A coughing fit overtook her and she gasped for breath. I handed her some more juice. She sipped, and continued. "The Royal House must avoid any suggestion of weakness or the jackals will rend the carcass of Khemet and chew on our bones."

I shivered. "Yes, Mother."

"So, though Thutmose your brother is himself frequently ill . . ."

"I have seen it."

". . . yet he is able and dedicated to Khemet and I believe he will do well enough with a strong wife by his side."

"Yes, Mother."

"Pharaoh must hold the Two Lands safe." She gestured with her hands, her finger joints enlarged with age and the skin spotted with brown, yet enacting a powerful grip as if clenching on the reins of a runaway chariot and hauling it back from the brink of an abyss. "Never again must it fall to foreign invaders who reject our customs, ruin our temples and desecrate our gods. Never, never again. You must be strong."

"Yes, Mother."

"You must be strong for Khemet," she said, her dark eyes intense. "Promise me."

"I will be strong."

"After I am gone, you will act for your father in the place of the Great Royal Wife," she said. "Watch, and learn. And, Hatshepsut . . ." She extended a bony hand and gripped my wrist.

"Mother?"

"Trust nobody absolutely," she whispered. "Be ever vigilant. Remember, Seth and his cohorts do not rest."

I clutched the amulet I wore around my neck and made a sign to avert evil. "I will remember." I assured her.

She sighed and closed her eyes.

"Mother?"

No answer came.

I wanted her to say something more. Something meant for me alone – me, her daughter, Hatshepsut, not the future Royal Wife, not the Keeper of Khemet. Something simple and loving. But the strength had gone from her. She never opened her eyes again.

From that time, when he lost the last prince of the full blood royal and his Great Royal Wife soon afterwards, it seemed to me that my father changed. On the one hand, he too, like Inet, shrank; his girth, which had grown as he aged, now fast became reduced. On the other hand, he appeared to have somehow become . . . I can only describe it as hard. Hard in his body, as if he were a living embodiment of one of the many stone sculptures of His Majesty; hard also in his heart, for he no longer took joy from life as he had when my mother lived. He never went hunting, never practised archery, ate and drank little at feasts, derived no pleasure from tumbling acrobats and dancing girls, no longer called upon the bard to sing . . .

At this point in the writing of my memories, I was interrupted by a great commotion. A babble of voices and weeping and wailing, punctuated by sharp commands and footsteps, broke the silence of my afternoon rest. The noise went past towards the servants' quarters and then Mahu the scribe appeared on the portico, looking agitated. He made a deep obeisance.

"What is it?" I asked. "I did not look for you yet."

"Pardon, Majesty," he said. "There was – there was some trouble at the alehouse."

"Was there fighting?" I asked. "Was one of my servants hurt?"

"I fear so, Majesty," he said, with an extremely unhappy expression. "But he will be seen to. Majesty should not . . ."

"Who is it?" I demanded to know. "Come on, out with it. I shall soon find out in any case."

Mahu does not have the strength of will to oppose me, nor the guile to lie. "It is Bek, Majesty," he said reluctantly.

"My dwarf? But how did he get into a fight? He does not drink to excess, and he is so small! Who would set upon a dwarf?" I was upset. Bek is a great favourite of mine and as I have written, he spies for me in the taverns.

"It was a . . . a group of ruffians," reported Mahu. I could see that he did not want to tell me, but also he knew that I would find out the truth no matter how he resisted.

"Syrians? Nubians?"

"No, Majesty. Egyptians born."

"Which tavern?"

"The Happy Hippo," said Mahu.

"The tavern-keeper shall pay for this, " I said grimly.

"Majesty," said Mahu wretchedly, "they were extremely drunk. It was not possible to control them. They just . . ."

"Did they know him for my dwarf?" I asked, growing angrier by the minute. "Was this something other than mere drunken sport?"

"N-n-no, Majesty, they knew him not, but I t-told them. I go there often and I heard him screaming as I g-got there and I told them, I told them, the Pharaoh will be mightily displeased at this. I told them," repeated Mahu. "The ringleader was a huge man, almost a giant, Majesty, and he had a huge sharp knife, with which he . . . but then I came upon them, and I told them, and he . . . desisted."

Mahu's eyes were miserable. I had the feeling that he was not telling me the entire truth. He stutters when he is upset. But then, it must have been a frightening sight. My little scribe has not much courage in the general run of things. Yet he bears a scar to prove that once he protected me at the risk of his own life. I do not forget that.

"They were drunk and seeking sport. Some people like to make fun of those who are . . . different. They . . . they called him a dog, and . . . and . . . I tried to help," he said, huskily, "but there were four of them, and I . . ." He looked away. He knows I love the little man. "They almost killed him," he whispered, "but just then I arrived, for I often go there, and I shouted at them that he was the Pharaoh's jester, and they would be punished, and at length they let him go. I had him carried here in a chair."

"Thank you, Mahu. I am grateful that you were there. Would you know them again?"

"Yes, Majesty, but they disappeared. I think they may have been sailors," said Mahu. "I do not think they will be found."

"I must go to him," I said, setting aside my writing implements.

"Majesty, no! I have told them to fetch Your Majesty's own physician. He will . . ."

"I will see him," I insisted. I was beginning to fear for Yunit, who is already several moons gone with the child she carries. "What did they do to him?"

Mahu looked distraught.

"Tell me!"

"They . . . they broke his legs," he told me.

"By Seth and all his devils . . ."

"And . . . and . . ."

"Out with it!"

"They s-sliced off both his ears." Tears stood in the scribe's eyes. He too was fond of Bek.

"By the foul breath of Seth!" I was so angry that I could hardly breathe. I stepped past Mahu, who was almost dancing in his distress and urgent desire to keep me from seeing Bek, but he knows better than to touch my person. I strode swiftly down the passage to the servants' quarters.

In the small room that Bek shares with Yunit, the dwarf had been laid down on a table, the better to be seen by the physician. His face had been battered into a purple ruin, and there was much blood, which several female slaves had been attempting to staunch with linen rags. Both of his legs stood out at odd angles. The room stank; he had clearly fouled himself in terror. Yunit stood by his side, her small face pinched with distress, holding tightly on to his hand. He was whimpering like a puppy too soon taken from its mother.

"Where is the physician?" I raged. "Has he not been called?"

At this moment one of the palace physicians sidled in. It was the one who looks after women's complaints, an oily-looking fellow whom I dislike.

"You!" I said, contemptuously. "Get you hence and call the Chief Physician immediately! And he should bring one used to battle wounds. It is an emergency! Tell them if they are not here straight away I'll have their ears as well – and yours, you scurvy toad!"

He backed out and scuttled away much faster than he had come in.

I walked up to the table and took Bek's other hand. It felt like a child's in size but he gripped mine like a man. He turned his swollen eyes on me.

"Do not speak," I said. "Ah, they are curs who did this! I shall have their hides!" And yet I knew that Mahu had spoken true. They would probably never be found.

Bek groaned. The tears rolled down Yunit's face.

"You should sit down, my dear," I told her. "It cannot be good . . ."

"I will stay with him," she said firmly, sniffing. "Until he is eased."

The Chief Physician, one Hapu, appeared quite promptly with a younger man I did not know so well in tow. "Pardon, pardon, Majesty," said Hapu, who is portly and was out of breath with hurrying (no doubt he values his somewhat batlike ears), "we did not know it was an urgent matter. This is Minhotep, who is knowledgeable about wounds."

The younger man, taller than Hapu by a head and built like a military man, made a deep obeisance. When he stood up, he looked me in the eyes. I liked his straight and fearless gaze.

"See to my slave," I ordered. "He must have the best of care, do you hear me?"

"Of course, Majesty. Please to clear the room," said Minhotep, in a decisive voice. He had slender fingers, I noticed, as he gently touched the skewed limbs. "Bring boiling water and plenty of linen bandages," he ordered the fussing slaves. "And some pieces of straight wood, we must have splints. Ask the palace carpenters."

The slaves trotted off to do his bidding.

"Can you give him something to ease the pain?" I asked anxiously.

"Yes, Majesty. I will mix a draught," said Hapu.

The slaves departed to do their bidding, but Yunit would not be moved.

"Let her stay with him," I told Minhotep, adding in an aside: "But see to her also, she has had a great shock, and as you see . . ."

"A calming draught for her as well," he promised. "Now, Majesty should leave it to us."

I returned to my writings, but I was greatly distressed. Yet I set down what had happened, although my hand shook and it will be hard to read. I find that to write down what has occurred helps me to think it through.

I suspect Mahu of lying to me, although I had not thought he was capable of it. I think those ruffians did know who Bek was, and this was a clear indication of disrespect for my majesty. It smacks of revolt. I like it not.

Mahu waited until the physicians came to report. He sat in his scribe's position, seemingly more relaxed, but he was trembling. At last they arrived to tell me that they had set the broken bones and cleaned the dwarf's bruised body and his wounds and put on poultices and bandages. He had been given poppy juice for the pain. He would recover, Minhotep said. Soldiers survived far worse than this. Yunit was asleep with a girl to watch over her.

"Will he walk again?" I asked Hapu.

"He will walk," said Hapu, "but somersaults will not come easy.

He will not be entirely deaf, but his hearing will be impaired. Mainly, now, we should watch for a fever."

"Attend him daily," I ordered Minhotep, who bowed in assent.

This does not bode well.

Here endeth the fifth scroll.

HER MAJESTY HAS a falcon's eyes. I did indeed lie to her. There were no ruffians in that tavern; no, it was a group of soldiers from the fifth division, the Division of Horus, who attacked the dwarf Bek. They came into the tavern where I was having lunch, but I was sitting outside in the courtyard with my back to the wall under the window and they did not see me. The sun was warm and my beer was pleasantly cool and the bread stuffed with coriander leaves and mint and olive oil was freshly baked.

At first I paid no attention to the rumble of conversation from inside the main room, but then I realised that they spoke of important matters and I pricked up my ears. They were discussing a scouting expedition to Canaan. Of course, they should not have spoken about such things in an ale-house, but they were not sober and they thought they were alone. There were no other customers, for it was early yet. I heard them refer to rumours about the loyalty of the Prince of Kadesh. The Great Commander does not trust him, I heard them say, and he wants to send a few crack troops disguised as Syrian merchants to discover the lie of the land.

Pharaoh would never agree to such an expedition, I knew, for if they were discovered it would be hard to maintain diplomatic relations. Her Majesty much prefers quiet diplomacy to military incursions. She would be sorely displeased. But Commander Thutmose clearly scented danger, and equally clearly, he was about to act without requesting permission from Her Majesty.

"You will look fetching with a curly beard," said the one with the deepest voice to another of their number. "And rings in your ears."

The reply was indistinct.

Suddenly there was an oath and a strangled yelp.

"So, you would spy, would you?" boomed the deep voice.

"No, no, Sire, I was fetching out my ball," protested a voice that I recognised. It was Bek, Her Majesty's dwarf. "I was juggling for the patrons, Sire, and my ball . . . See, here I have it, it rolled under . . ."

"You lie, you little devil," said another voice. It was sharp and commanding. I ventured to peer over the windowsill. The room was dim and my eyes accustomed to the bright sun could at first make out only vague shapes, but then I saw that one broad-shouldered soldier had Bek by the ear. "So, you would spy, would you," he said. "Take that, and that, and that . . ." His huge balled fist slammed into the dwarf's head and body. I flinched for poor Bek.

The tall one with the commanding voice had drawn his sword. Peering at him, I realised that I knew who he was: Metufer, the standard bearer who had almost beaten the Great Commander at archery. "You were listening. You are a spy."

"No, no, Sire, a humble juggler merely," jabbered Bek. "Ask anyone, they know me, Sire."

"I say you spied. And we know what to do with spies." His sword whistled as he slashed twice, lopping off the little man's ears. An inhuman screech tore through the quiet afternoon. Blood flowed over the dwarf's tunic.

He cowered, rolling himself into a ball. "No, no, no," he gibbered. "No, nooooo!"

I ducked down and huddled under the sill, terrified that someone might have seen me too. Oh, oh, oh, I muttered, may Hathor protect me, may Wadjet spit into their eyes so that they see me not.

The harsh voice came again. "We have fixed your ears," said

Metufer, "and next we'll take your tongue and feed it to the dogs."

At this, I tipped my beer and bread into the fish pond and scuttled around the mud-brick tavern to the front door, pretending that I had just arrived. "Hold!" I yelled.

Metufer lowered his sword and stared at me.

"Hold!" I shouted again. "It is the Pharaoh's jester! Do him no more harm!"

The standard bearer sneered. Seen close up he had a face for sneering, that one; it was disfigured by a scar that ran across both cheeks; his nose seemed permanently drawn up.

"I have removed his ears," he snarled, "and I shall remove his tongue also. Nor will you stop me."

Bek gave another blood-curdling screech.

"You will not escape punishment," I said. "I am Her Majesty's scribe, and I know who you are. You cannot kill all of these witnesses." My knees trembled, but I stood fast. By this time, the howls and screeches had drawn quite an audience, including the tavern-keeper and his anxious wife.

"The Great Commander will back me," said Metufer. "I am within my rights to punish spies."

"This is Pharaoh's jester," I said. "He has done no harm. He speaks true, he juggles for the patrons, I have seen him. L-let him go."

Bek was sitting on the ground now, his hands to his bloody head, rocking and moaning.

"Please, we want no trouble," begged the tavern-keeper. "I keep a good house, Sir, please, no trouble here."

"I say this is a spy," said Metufer. "Yet you may take him away. Only be sure that he does not speak of what he may have heard. If anything occurs to make us suspect that he has told, he will not only have no tongue, he will no longer breathe. And as I do now to his legs, I shall do to your hands, Scribe." Deliberately, he stepped on

Bek's little legs that were spread on the ground and yanked them upwards from the heels. Bones cracked.

Another howl rent the air, followed by a series of yelps. The bile rose in my throat.

"Remember," said Metufer.

Oh, I will remember. I will remember till I die. But I will not speak of it, nor will the dwarf. Only I will write it, so that the record may be accurate. I will note my shame. For if I had acted sooner, if I had run into the tavern when first they began to strike the dwarf, I might have saved his ears. But I was afraid, and I waited too long.

Yes, I shall remember. But I will not speak.

THE SIXTH SCROLL

After the mourning period had passed and my mother had been buried in her great tomb for some months, my father one day called me to his office at the administrative palace. When I arrived, he was standing at the window looking out at the water clock that he had had installed in the courtyard. I waited quietly, then made an obeisance when he turned to me. His face was thinner than ever and looked very drawn.

"Your brother Thutmose has been ill again," he said, abruptly.

"I know," I said. "Inet has been much concerned. But he is better now."

My father drummed his fingers against the window frame. "He is a fragile reed," he muttered. "He has no strength." Then he walked to his gilded chair with its legs ending in lion's paws and sat down heavily. "Prepare for a journey of some weeks," he told me. "We leave tomorrow. We go to Abydos."

After the stifling sadness of the past months, it lifted my spirits to be out on the noble river. As we sailed northward, the rowers speeding us on with powerful, rhythmic strokes, my father spoke to me as if I was a child no longer, but had an adult understanding. "It may be that Thutmose your brother grows in strength," he said. "But on the other hand, it might be that he goes to the gods too early. I myself must make that journey soon."

I protested: "But Majesty, you are not old . . ."

"I am being consumed from the inside," he said shortly, his hand on his shrunken abdomen. "I am hardly able to eat anything."

"But the physicians . . . the priests . . ."

"Have tried everything they know, but nothing has much effect. No, I must go to the Afterlife quite soon. And I am tormented by the fear that everything that I have built up, with much trouble and care, the unity I have achieved, the prosperity I have brought about, the boundaries I have extended and defined . . ." – a spasm of pain twisted his mouth, but he drew in a sharp breath and mastered it – "that everything will be lost, will be destroyed, if there is no strong Pharaoh to follow me. So, Hatshepsut, my daughter, I believe that it may fall to you to hold Khemet." His dark, somewhat sunken eyes held mine intently.

"I will do it, Father," I said, standing very straight, trembling at the significance of his words.

He leaned forward. "You desire power, do you not?"

"I . . . no, that is, I . . ."

"Let us have no lies, daughter. No pretence. Do you? Desire power?"

I gulped. "Yes, Father, yes, I do."

"You should remember that it is easy enough to be ruled. To be a ruler, that is far more difficult."

I nodded, not trusting my voice.

"What Pharaoh must desire, above all else, is the well-being of Khemet. Pharaoh's power, and the exercise thereof, must have one aim and one aim only: to maintain Ma'at. Ma'at is all."

"Yes, Father."

"A just ruler, one who follows Ma'at, will have the love of his people. And the love of the people is a precious thing, a resource in adversity."

I was not sure that I understood this, but I repeated: "A resource. Yes, Father."

"And you must learn to take counsel from able men. But do not let them rule you. Pharaoh rules; he will take counsel when he asks for it. Yet ask for it often, listen with care, and then decide."

"I hear, Father."

"And one thing more. Mark this, my child. To rule others is

a burdensome task. To rule oneself is the hardest thing of all."

This last was beyond me. But I nodded as if I had grasped his words.

He sighed and shook his head. I knew what he was not saying: that he feared greatly for the Black Land, being left to a fragile king and a girl child. But I was certain that I could be strong, that I would not disappoint my father, would not let the Black Land suffer or diminish. I would hold Khemet.

It was a fateful journey, for that was when my father inducted me into the Mysteries of Osiris. I shall not write in detail what transpired, for these are sacred and very secret matters, that may be made known only to one who will become a Pharaoh. That it was done, proves that not only my heavenly father but also my royal father on earth considered me – me, not the little Thutmose – to be the chosen of the gods. Suffice it to say that we went together to the tomb of Osiris that is at the ancient sacred city of Abydos, that I underwent such stringent tests that I thought more than once that I would not emerge alive, but that I was able to survive them all and satisfied the Pharaoh.

Thereafter I stood at my father's side and I learned much. He was a man well able to judge people and he saw straight through flattery and lies. I noted that he was always thoroughly prepared and better informed than any of his advisers, and that he never depended solely on one official's view. I also noted that he allowed no single official, noble, general or priest to gain too much influence.

If there was a matter of great importance to be debated, he would call the key men to attend on him privately one by one, ask for their opinions, and have a scribe note their words. Then they could not suddenly take a new tack in debate if it seemed politic. He would marshal their arguments and think about them, then identify the crucial issues. These also a scribe would note. He encouraged me to comment – not publicly, of course – when there were matters to be debated, and sometimes he noted what I said. This made me enormously proud.

When I had seen thirteen risings of the Nile, my half-brother and I broke the jar together. It was no grand ceremony, for marriages in the Black Land are civil contracts between the families of the persons concerned and this contract was within the royal house.

The night before we were to be joined together, Inet came to see me in my rooms, where I had lived as a princess all my life. I would henceforth move into the women's section of the harem palace. My husband had his own rooms, to which he called his concubines when he had decided whose turn it was. He had several such – in fact, had sired the half-royal princeling, Thutmose, upon one Isis five years previously – but he had taken no other wives before me. I had seen much less of Inet since I had become grown than when she took care of me as nurse, but she loved me dearly and still assumed that she could come to me without an invitation, as she did that night.

Her neat little figure, now half a head shorter than me, was still upright and her wig was stiff and black, but her face was wizened as a fig left to dry in the sun and she had lost more teeth.

"I brought you something," she said, smiling slyly. "You must sleep with it beneath your mattress, so that Egypt may have an heir."

"Are you not a little precipitate?" I asked. "I am not wed yet and already you would have me bear a child?"

"The sooner the better," said Inet, nodding to herself. "Else it will be the little Thutmose born to Isis, and he does not have the pure blood royal. That is not good. Here, take it." She thrust her gift at me. It was a small amulet, shaped like Taueret, the hippopotamus goddess of fertility. I took it and held her hand between mine. She stared into my eyes. "You are not ignorant of the marriage bed, are you, my child?"

"No, I am not," I said. "My mother spoke to me before she became ill. Besides, I have seen mating in the Royal Zoo."

"Not quite what one would hope for as regards the royal nuptial couch," remarked Inet dryly. "Yes, I was married once," she answered my unspoken question. "But my husband died young, of snakebite, and then my cousin Hapuseneb found me the position as Royal Nurse. It has been a good life." She patted my hand. "Be happy," she said, her black eyes filling with tears. "Be happy, little one."

In truth, I was quite expecting to be at least content. I had always liked my half-brother, and he had ever been kind to me. Also I had always known that I was promised to him and that it was for the good of Khemet that I should be his wife. Yet when the wedding feast was over and he escorted me into his rooms, I did feel nervous. What if it was painful? What if I hated what he did to me? What if I was no good as a wife? I was trembling a little when we entered his bedroom together.

It was a cool and airy room next to a courtyard in which a fountain splashed. The bed was hung with curtains of the finest white linen; tall alabaster vases held lotus blooms that scented the night air sweetly. The walls were painted with flowers and leaves, ducks and fish, in deep greens, blues and turquoises, that seemed to swim in the soft light of small oil lamps glowing on little tables. Woven rush matting piled with plump cushions covered the tiled floor.

Thutmose settled down on a heap against the wall and pulled me down beside him. "Come here," he said, positioning me on his lap so that his left arm cradled me against his shoulder. "Close your eyes and open your mouth."

I obeyed, thinking: Whatever he wants, you must do now. He is your husband. Whatever . . . I steeled myself. And found myself eating a pink fig. "Oh!" I said. "My favourite!" Together we finished a small bowl of them. When he leaned forwards to kiss me gently on the lips, he tasted of figs and honey. As he continued to move his mouth stickily against mine, he began to caress my knees. The rich scent of myrrh filled the room and there was a creamy smoothness on my skin. I sniffed, inhaling the delicious perfume.

"Relax," he murmured. "It is an unguent. Do you like it?"

"Mmmmmm." I was feeling slightly dizzy, having drunk more wine than I was used to. I settled into his arms. My robe fell open. I wasn't wearing anything else beneath it.

He continued to smooth the unguent rhythmically, hypnotically, over my knees and up over my thighs. I let my knees fall slightly apart. He stroked me like a cat. Up his hand moved, ever higher. Ah, he was getting close. Close to the secret place between my legs, the spot that could engender so much pleasure. I had discovered it myself some years ago, but I was not sure whether all girls had such a thing or whether it was only me. If they all did . . . surely he would know . . . he had been with concubines, they must have taught him . . . on and on his firm hand went, nearer but not quite there. Around and around and about and down. I think I moaned. I would scream, I thought, if he did not find the spot. Should I tell him, I wondered. Perhaps he did not . . . I moved my hips upon his lap. Should I guide his hand, just a little . . . Closer. Closer. Oh, yes. Oh, yes. He did know, after all. He knew exactly . . . oh, oh, oh, OH! OH! OH! AH! AHHHHHH!

As his firm touch found the perfect place, smoothed it with the unguent, stroked it hard, knuckled and kneaded it, I was overpowered with wave after wave of pleasure, such as I could not have imagined, ever. "Oh!" I gasped, at last. And opened my eyes, to find his dark eyes smiling into mine.

"Are you ready for me now, my wife?" he asked.

"Quite ready," I whispered, and moved under him.

So I was initiated into the marriage bed without pain, and as time went by with increasing skill and pleasure. He did not call me to the royal couch very often, though, and these occasions became fewer as time went by. As my interest in such matters grew more intense, his waned; already, I think, looking back, he was more ill than he would allow anyone to know. Perhaps it was not surprising, therefore, that there were moments when I longed for . . . I could not have said exactly what. But sometimes instead of a partner who was slightly shorter than me, slim and somewhat fragile, and whose hip bones cut into mine, I dreamed of a lover with a body taller and stronger and more vigorous. A lover in whom the force of life ran powerfully. But I did not allow myself to see his face.

Perhaps it is not appropriate that I should write about such things. But this is the true record of my reign and it must tell more than the official one. For I have been not only the divine Pharaoh who maintains Ma'at but also a woman and a mother, and I have known great love. I do not wish that my life should disappear like water seeping away into the sand. I have achieved much and suffered much and I regret only the things I did not do, the child who never lived, and those people I have loved who have gone before me. My heart does not despise any of my days. So. I write what I write.

The very next day I moved into the women's section of the harem palace and I made sure that I was immediately given precedence over all the women there.

"I shall move into the largest suite of rooms," I informed the Overseer of the Royal Harem, an able manager whose sharp eyes missed neither a speck of dust nor the disappearance of a pomegranate from the royal kitchens. "See to it."

My husband's mother, Mutnofert, did not like that at all. She was a slim woman with a pretty enough face, but she had small breasts and big ears, and a childish voice that grated me. Since my mother, the Queen Ahmose, had passed into the Afterlife, may she live for ever, Mutnofert herself had occupied those rooms.

"I do not see why I should move," she protested petulantly. "You are not the Great Royal Wife."

"And you," I pointed out, "are not the Mother of the King. Merely a minor wife."

"But I took over many functions when the Great Queen went to the gods," she argued. "I watch over the household of the royal children, and I am in charge of the weaving, and the Inspector of the Harem Administration reports to me."

"You may continue with all those worthy tasks," I said. "While I help my father the Pharaoh to reign over the Two Lands, to dispense justice, to ensure the proper order, and to maintain Ma'at. Together we guarantee the continuing existence of the world."

She moved.

When my father passed into the Afterlife, Egypt was bereft, for Thutmose the First had been a much loved and highly respected Pharaoh who truly had maintained Ma'at and governed the Black Land well. There would now be a period of seventy days' mourning while the Pharaoh's body underwent a series of rituals and processes to ensure that he would attain eternal life. Previously I had not given such matters much thought, but now I found my mind dwelling on it. Senenmut had described it all to me when my brother Amenmose died; he had much knowledge of it since he had served for some time as a scribe in the House of Death, where embalming was done.

"It stinks, that place," Senenmut had said, wrinkling his nose. "Those who work in the House of Death can be smelled from a distance. The sweetish smell of death seeps into one's clothes, it seems to cleave to the skin. I was glad when I could leave for a different post."

"I can understand that. I would have hated it," I said.

I knew how important it is to prepare the body properly for when the Ka returns – especially, of course, for a member of the

Royal House, since the link between the Pharaoh and the next world cannot be broken for fear of chaos descending. Yet I shuddered at the image of the Chief Surgeon approaching my royal father's noble head and pushing a long bronze hook up through a nostril. I knew he would rotate it till the brain turned to mush and could be drawn out. I knew that the brain is a useless organ and if left in place would surely putrefy. I knew all that – but I did not like to picture it.

I found the thought of the ordeal that my father's Ka would face even more horrifying than the imagined treatment of his body. I had been taught that Osiris, god of the dead, is the chief judge in the Hall of Judgment, where it is necessary for the Ka to make Protestations of Innocence. You must attest that you have not murdered, stolen, lied, cheated, acted unjustly to the weak, and so forth. Forty-two gods sit in a tribunal to hear these negative confessions. For a Pharaoh, the test is particularly stringent. Did he contravene Ma'at? Did he allow chaos to take over the Black Land? Did he favour the strong above the weak, did he insult the souls of the dead? Did he let the temples fall into ruin, did he counter the will of the gods? These questions would be put to my father.

What if his spirit did not prevail?

I asked this of Thutmose, my husband who would be crowned after the period of mourning was over.

"It would be a catastrophe," said Thutmose, frowning.

"What then?"

"Then will Osiris command that he suffer eternal damnation in the Netherworld," he said.

I shivered. I knew that it is a dread place, dismal and dark, peopled with monsters, lost spirits and defeated gods. "My father will surely satisfy the Great Tribunal," I said. "He governed the Black Land well and he always considered the will of the gods."

"I believe it to be so," agreed my husband.

"He will surely also pass the crucial test," I said hopefully. "I do not believe that there was evil in his heart, to make it weigh heavy against the feather of Ma'at on the scales of justice." The alternative was too dreadful to think upon: If the heart is heavy with evil, it outweighs the feather, and then it is thrown to the hound of hell, Ammit the Devourer, to be gobbled up. "And surely the prayers and magical incantations of the priests will help?"

"Everything possible will be done to ensure that the spirit of the Pharaoh will reach the Mountain of the Sunrise," Thutmose reminded me gently.

I knew that. Yet still I lived with fear. How could a human heart be so free of evil that it did not outweigh a feather? I could not be sure that my own heart did not conceal some evil thoughts and wishes, even if I did not have blood upon my hands. That it might not rise up and testify against me when my time came.

For seventy days the fate of Khemet hung in the balance. The departed Pharaoh had to be found worthy and then he would be exalted and live for ever. He would become conjoined with the sun god, Ra, be newly reborn as the sun and sail across the heavens in triumph. Then would the Black Land be blessed and the new Pharaoh could reign. Failing that, the world would end.

Here endeth the sixth scroll.

OH DEAR, OH dear. I should not be reading Her Majesty's most intimate secrets, it is not right. She would be horrified if she knew. But now I have seen what I have seen and I cannot pretend that I have not. I wonder whether an act such as my reading what is none of my business could weigh against my heart in the Afterlife? I fear it could. But I will keep my counsel. Nobody will ever hear her secrets from me, unless I must pass on her journals to be used in testimony on her behalf. And even then, I think I shall select. I can be discreet. I shall never speak of this.

I swear it by the Ka of Thoth.

THE SEVENTH SCROLL

After the seventy days of mourning had passed, the burial of the Pharaoh took place. Since Ra still rose in splendour every day, I was assured that my royal father had undergone transition, resurrection and exaltation, and had become one with the sun god. Therefore I did not find the funeral to be a terrifying experience. Rather it was a comfort to me to know that I would be a part of the majestic ceremony, which would take place at night. The procession would escort the mummy to the stark valley amid steep cliffs where Ineni had created a deep and secret tomb for the Pharaoh.

The mummy of the King with its beautiful mask of gold modelling the late king's face was placed upon a sledge drawn by a team of multi-coloured bulls. They would draw the sledge to the valley where the tomb had been prepared. Slaves lit the way with flaming torches. At the head of the procession, accompanied by a group of chantresses and lesser priests, walked the lector priest, draped in a leopard skin. He chanted incantations, burned incense and poured libations of sacred wine upon the ground. The sweet incense and the sourish smell of the wine mingled in the chill evening air. Marching feet grated on the gravel and the runners of the sledge scraped over the sand. Now and then one could hear a snort or grunt from the bulls.

My husband Thutmose and I walked directly behind the sledge. He gripped my hand tightly and I think we both took comfort from this. Behind us a second sledge followed, bearing the richly decorated canopic chest that held the jars with the Pharaoh's organs within a shrine. Behind the second sledge walked a large group of professional mourners, weeping and wailing and tearing their hair. Next, a large group of minor wives, concubines, children, and other members of the royal harem.

Then came porters staggering under a huge quantity of funerary goods. Pharaoh should not lack for anything once he achieved immortality. The slaves bore clothing, food, bunches of herbs, furniture, weaponry, heirloom vases, jewellery with the colours of flowers, carvings in wood, ivory and stone, statues clothed in silver and gold, jars of oil and wine, flasks of perfume, pots of unguents, papyrus scrolls containing the Book of the Dead, models of horses and beautifully decorated sledges, a model barque and a full-size gilded chariot.

Naturally, many ushabti would also be interred with the King, for these small figures of soldiers, officials, scribes, servants and slaves would be transfigured into a host of subjects who would serve the King in the Afterlife and ensure that his every need was met.

The funeral procession wound solemnly through the desolate valley to the Pharaoh's final dwelling place. A full moon shed an unearthly light over the stark hills, naked as bones, and cast deep shadows across the canyons through which the long line snaked. The incantations seemed to echo in the vast amphitheatre:

"The being for whom you do this will not perish for ever.
He will live on as a glorious god.
No evil will befall him."

Yet despite these words it seemed to me that Seth and his devils lurked in the dark ravines, that in the shadows Ammit the Devourer panted and slobbered, lusting for a meal, the choice morsel of a Pharaoh's heart, while monsters and genii eagerly awaited the advent of a lost soul that they could drive into the depths of the Netherworld where howl the unregenerate damned.

"The furious tempest drives him, it roars like Seth," intoned the priest.

As we marched through the valley in the shadow of death, I was comforted by the thought that the power of sacred spells shielded the spirit of my father the King; I could feel it just as I often sensed the arms of Hathor supporting me.

The voices of the chantresses rose sweetly:
"The reed-boats of the sky are prepared for me,
That I may cross to Ra at the horizon . . .
I will take my place there, for the moon is my brother . . ."
The priest promised:
"The guardians of heaven open the divine portals for him,
He reaches the celestial kingdom of Ra,
And is seated on the throne of Osiris.
His lifetime is eternal, its limit is everlastingness."
The cortège had now reached the dark mouth of the tomb. The mummy of the Pharaoh was reverently taken from the sledge, put into the smallest of the nest of coffins, and made to stand upright upon the ground. Several priests assisted in ritual purification and anointments. The lector priest recited a eulogy of the departed Pharaoh, emphasising his dedication to Ma'at and his devotion to the gods. Then it was time for my husband, the new Pharaoh, to carry out the task of Opening the Mouth. If this was not done, the dead Pharaoh would not be able to eat or speak – in effect he would die a second time. Meanwhile the slaves would carry the grave goods into the depths of the tomb, so that it would be furnished as a fit dwelling for the Pharaoh when at last he was installed there.

Thutmose, my husband, stepped forward. He wore a white linen tunic belted with a sash of bright colours under a pleated robe with wide sleeves. Bracelets of gold, a jewelled collar and a ceremonial crown glinted in the moonlight. He had the implements ready that are required for the ceremony, and proceeded to carry out his task with grace and gravity, touching the mouth, nose, eyes, ears and chest of the mummy, from which the mask had been removed for the ritual. I was proud of him.

First he touched the Pharaoh's mouth, intoning:
"I have come to embrace thee. I am thy son Horus.
I open for thee thy mouth."

Then his nose:

"I open for thee thy nostrils that thou mayest breathe.

I am thy son, I love thee."

Next, his eyes, now blue jewels:

"I open for thee thy two eyes. Also thy two ears.

The dead shall walk and shall speak,

And thy body shall be with the great company of the gods."

Finally, he touched the chest where the heart had been preserved beneath the layers of bandages:

"I quicken thy heart, so that thou mayest live.

Neither heaven nor earth can be taken away from thee,

For behold, thou wilt rise again without fail and for ever."

At last, it was time for the mummy to be borne into the tomb and laid to rest in the huge sarcophagus. As the priests carrying the inner coffin with the mummy disappeared into the dark entrance, the lamentations of the mourners increased in intensity. I, too, lamented as the custom was. I noticed that Thutmose had tears in his eyes. The tomb would be sealed, I knew, with spells and curses to deter tomb robbers. Then the entrance to the tomb would be hidden beneath stones and rubble.

As the slaves set to work carting large boulders and loose gravel, other servants and slaves set out the funeral feast on small tables covered with cloths. We had stools to rest our weary legs. By this time the greater part of the night had passed and the sky was lightening in the east. The moon had paled. I was hungry and I did full justice to the baked meats and tasty cakes and fruit, but Thutmose, who was pale and near to exhaustion, did no more than pick.

When at last the barque of Ra appeared, the sun's rays seemed to reflect from every facet of every rock and stone in that vast valley. The surrounding cliffs, that had been so stark and bleak, were magically transformed into a glittering palace of light. It seemed to me to be an excellent omen. Just so, I trusted, would the spirit of my father continue to triumph over the powers of darkness and come forth by day.

The ritual of the funeral greatly comforted me, especially the part played by my husband in honouring his father and freeing his spirit. I saw these actions as a link with former generations stretching back over the centuries, an essential element in the framework that keeps the Black Land stable and satisfies the gods. A framework that the Pharaoh holds in place, as I have striven to do throughout my reign.

Ah, yes, many years have passed since that night spent in the valley. One day a funeral procession will march along that self-same route bearing my body to join that of my late father, may he live for ever, in that self-same tomb, for I have given orders that an additional chamber with a great sarcophagus be prepared in it for me. One day a funeral oration will be spoken for me out there in the moonlight. What will be said of Hatshepsut? What will my greatest legacy be?

The people will weep, for they always weep when a Pharaoh goes to the gods. But will there be a single person standing before my tomb who will truly weep for me? Only the gods can tell. Well, that night must come as it comes for all. But not just yet. I still have work to do and responsibilities to meet.

After the funeral of my royal father a grand coronation ceremony took place and my half-brother and husband Thutmose became the second Pharaoh of that name. I stood proudly by his side during the joyous festival celebrating his ascent of the Double Throne. Now I was the Great Royal Wife, and I undeniably outranked the lady Mutnofert.

From the beginning I played an important role during my husband's reign. In many ways I had been prepared for this. The years I had spent as the God's Wife of Amen stood me in good stead, as did the experience I had had assisting my royal father. I think that my dear husband would have much preferred to live the life of a noble with nothing more taxing than some wine farms to oversee. But there was no other choice. Even though his strength was not great, Thutmose had to follow his destiny and mount the Double Throne.

So he needed me to stand by his side and he needed me to be strong as he grew constantly weaker, in body if not in spirit. Within a few months I stood in his place more and more often, conferring daily with the viziers and the treasurer, conducting morning audiences, dispensing justice, calling for conferences with the appropriate counsellors in the small audience chamber, and hosting visits from nomarchs and foreign deputations. Yes, almost from the time of my royal father's funeral, I was the one who guided Khemet. As, indeed, had been his wish.

It was at this time that my husband sent the punitive expedition to the Land of Kush and Khani was brought back a captive. As I have written, I spoke for him and he was spared. He attended the palace school with the children of nobles and lesser wives and concubines and he did well. I often sent for news of him, for I felt a bond, and reports were positive.

Also at this time, I had quickened with child. In the beginning I was often nauseous, and it seemed to me that every scent in the world had intensified and turned strange just to torment me. Especially the smell of frying fish that so often wafts through the streets of Thebes was a sore trial to me, and I banned certain unguents that I had delighted in before. But soon the worst of the nausea passed and, as my abdomen swelled and my small breasts grew full, I gloried in my condition. I felt filled with vigour and blessed by the gods; it was a time of flowering and bearing fruit. I felt very alive and aware of being a part of the great river of time that bears the generations through the ages. I was convinced that I bore the next Living Horus beneath my heart.

Oh, my child. My child. My child. She was born when I was fourteen. I was young and strong and I did not labour greatly.

Just after my light midday meal, my waters broke in a rush of warm liquid that left me standing, shocked and embarrassed at this sudden dereliction of my usually well-behaved body, with my feet in a puddle on the tiles. Then the contractions began, soon coming thick and fast, and the midwives – no less than three – propelled me firmly to the corner of the room where they had prepared a structure upon which I was to squat while giving birth. One of them stood before me holding my hands, while one rubbed my back, which felt as if an ill-tempered mule had let fly at it with its hind hooves. The third kept doing inspections and cheering me on.

Truly, whether one be a fishwife or a queen, there is no dignity at such a time. Anyone may peer and prod at one's most private parts and make pronouncements on the state of them. One's body becomes nothing more than a portal, stretched and wrenched open for the new being to pass through, and one is wrung without mercy, squeezed together and torn apart alternately with no quarter given.

Fortunately I had spent only a few hours squatting on the bricks when, after one huge despairing push, she slid into the midwives' hands, and soon she cried lustily, so that one could be sure she breathed. Never, even at my coronation, have I felt as powerful and as proud of myself as I did when I held my first-born in my arms. I knew that the god Khnum had fashioned her body and her Ka upon his potter's wheel. But I had carried her and I had brought her into the world through my loins and I was proud. Not for a moment did I think it a pity that she was not male. She was herself, and she was perfect.

When I had been washed and dressed in a fresh robe and installed on a day-bed with the new little princess in my arms, Inet came in. She looked at her doubtfully. "Better it had been a boy, seeing that the Pharaoh is not strong," she remarked.

"There will be time for boys," I said furiously. "She is beautiful. She is a gift from Khnum."

The milk rushed plentifully into my tender breasts and I insisted on feeding her myself for the first few weeks, although Inet disapproved. In the core of my body something clenched like a fist when the baby suckled and I sensed that it was good, that it was right.

But I could not keep on for long. I had to agree to a wet nurse taking over. Since I was already shouldering a portion of my husband's many tasks even then, only one year into his reign, inevitably my child was taken to the palace nursery to be brought up with the other palace children. Soon Inet had come to adore the child and cared for her devotedly.

I began to conduct interviews in the small audience chamber. One morning the young Nubian whose life I had begged from the Pharaoh arrived to see me.

He strode in confidently and made a deep obeisance. He had now been a pupil of the palace school for about six months and he had already, I thought, grown taller and filled out.

"Majesty," he said.

"Arise," I said. "I know who you are, but I do not know your name."

"Khani," he told me, rising and standing very straight, with something wrapped in linen in his hands. "I came to thank Your Majesty. I know that I owe the Great Queen my life. It is yours to command, and will always be."

I smiled a little at his earnestness, yet I was touched. "If you live to serve Egypt, I shall be well content," I said.

"I serve Your Majesty above all," he insisted. "I always will."

"I thank you," I said, although I could not think what he might do for me. He would surely become a soldier, I imagined. "Will you go to Memphis, to be trained?" I asked.

"After I have had more schooling," he assented. "Then, yes, I must go to Memphis. I would like to become a standard bearer."

"A noble ambition."

He stood, silent and slightly awkward for a few moments. Then he went down on one knee and held out the object in his hands. "I have brought a gift, for the new princess," he said. "I made it for her. I wish it could have been gold, but it is only wood."

I took the gift from his outstretched hands and folded the linen wrappings back. It was a small bowl, beautifully carved and polished, with handles in the shape of birds sitting on the rim. The wood was a dull golden colour with dark brown whorls in it. "Oh, it's lovely!" I exclaimed. "You have the hand of an artist. I am sure that she will use it one day, and she will love it."

He looked gratified.

After that he came every few months until he left for Memphis, always with something for Neferure: sometimes a basket of fruit, or flowers, or another small item carved from wood or marble. It was almost as if he sensed that she had played a role in his escape from death. We began to have longer conversations as he mastered our tongue, and I valued his comments. It was interesting to hear the views of someone looking at our land as an outsider. He had a keen and most perceptive understanding. I would miss him, I thought, when he went away.

Neferure bloomed. I insisted that she be given precedence as the first-born of the Great Royal Wife. This did not sit well with Isis, my husband's concubine, who had given him a son some six years previously when he was still the Crown Prince. That son, of course, was Thutmose, that one who would be King. But I was adamant and I got my way.

I saw Neferure often; Inet would bring her to play in my rooms, and when she was old enough she loved to be told stories. She was a good child and a loving one, a true child of the sun.

When Neferure was one, something happened to Inet that made

her left leg lazy and her left hand weak. She was in bed for some weeks, but recovered and learned to walk with a stick. It was clear that Neferure would need someone with more strength to look after her. It was then that my husband suggested that we should appoint Senenmut as her nurse and tutor. He had been my steward for some time, and he had acquitted himself well. He already loved the little princess; he explained to me that he was the eldest of a large brood of children and had been accustomed to helping his mother cope with the little ones. Neferure adored him from the start. So the appointment was made, and it suited everyone.

Here endeth the seventh scroll.

YESTERDAY WHEN PHARAOH gave the latest scroll into my keeping and I left the palace, I had that feeling of chill on the nape of my neck that accompanies the presence of inimical eyes. I felt that I was being watched and followed. The scroll was tucked under my tunic top into a little inner pocket I had my slave sew for me. I would not be so foolish as to carry it in plain sight. I did however carry a couple of ordinary scrolls together with the implements of my trade in a linen bag, and I had taken the trouble to write down a list of instructions to be delivered to the clerks of the Royal Granary, as if that had been the purpose of my visit to the King.

I would not go home, I thought. Let me first see if I can flush out the mangy dog sniffing at my heels. I forced myself to stroll as if I had no cares and betook myself to a tavern near the waterfront where I ordered beer. A slave brought water for me to cleanse my hands and then provided a small bowl of salty roasted lotus seeds designed to increase one's thirst. It was a popular watering-hole and there was much chatter and laughter.

Within minutes a stranger had slipped into the chair facing mine on the opposite side of the small table. At least, I took him for a stranger, and one with too little acquaintance with bathing at that. He had lost an eye and an ugly gash across his cheek on the same side drew his mouth up in a permanent grimace. His head was shaven, his tunic scruffy and stained. But when he spoke, I realised that I knew him. It was one Ahmose, who had been in the same class as I was at the temple school for scribes.

"Good day, my brother," he said. "I see it goes well with you, since you have the King's ear. Better with you than with me, I fear."

"Good day to you, Ahmose," I said, to show that I had recognised him. "Will you have a beer?"

He accepted with alacrity. I bade a slave bring some bread and dates also, and the manner in which Ahmose devoured the food when it came proved that I had been correct in my surmise that he was hungry.

"Have you been following me? How do you know I have the King's ear?"

He nodded, flushing slightly. "I caught sight of you outside the palace," he explained through a mouthful of bread. "I thought I would presume on our old acquaintance." Although he looked like a ruffian, he spoke like the educated man I knew him to be. His single eye, brown and somewhat bloodshot, looked at me pleadingly. "I seek work," he said. "You know that I am capable. But nobody wants to employ a scribe who looks like me."

"What happened to you?" I enquired, calling for more beer and bread.

His sorry tale was soon told. Like myself he had done some of his training as a scribe in a stone quarry. There a fight had broken out among the workers, a tough and violent lot as I well knew. He had attempted to calm the men and they had attacked him with their sharp implements. He had been close to death and could not work for months. Now he presented a fearsome face to the world.

"The problem is, the upper classes who have need of the services of a full-time scribe are disgusted by my looks," he explained.

"Ah," I said, "I see, I see."

"I get single commissions," he told me. "Mostly from the poor. But as you know, they very seldom use the services of a scribe and they pay little. I need permanent employment, Mahu. Is there not a job somewhere in a royal warehouse where it matters not how a man looks, but only that his work is accurate? You know that I am competent."

I nodded. "Yes, I know you are." I called for more beer while I thought. There was indeed a position for which Hapuseneb, Grand Vizier of the South, who also held numerous other posts in the service of the Pharaoh, including Chief Prophet of Amen and Overseer of the Royal Granaries, had asked me to help find an incumbent. It was a job as clerk in the Royal Granaries, but not one that would require the person to go out to the farms, rather an office job keeping track of stores and dispersals. Not highly paid nor of much consequence. But no doubt Ahmose would jump at it, and I knew he would acquit himself well.

It could prove useful, I thought, to have someone I knew, loyal to me and under an obligation to boot, working closely with the Vizier. Priest and Chief Prophet of the God though he is, I do not trust Hapuseneb, and a pair of eyes and ears keeping track of what he does and says may be just what we need. I could spare a few debens of silver to augment my old friend's income if he would report to me.

"I do believe I have something for you," I said. "We'll have to get you cleaned up and looking more presentable. What say you . . ."

By the time we staggered out, somewhat the worse for wear, we had a deal.

It is as well that I have been given a fright by Ahmose; I realise anew that I must needs be very careful, very careful indeed, with the secret documents given into my care. As soon as I have enough to fill a sealed jar, I shall travel to my cousin's farm near the mountains, where he keeps goats and grows olives. I can take two jars on a donkey, one with wine and the other filled with scrolls. There is a cave there with a fissure at the back; I shall place the jar inside and cover it with sand and loose stones. Yes, I think that will do. My cousin will be glad to receive wine from me from time to time. Yes, yes, much the best plan.

THE EIGHTH SCROLL

I have been heartsore ever since the attack upon Bek; it was a dreadful shock to me. I know he is an adult man and not a child, but he is so small, and yet has always been so sweet-natured and fun-loving, that I feel about him as I have only felt about one other and that was Neferure, may she live. I live with guilt because I sent him into danger; I should have known that one day he would be set upon for my sake. I am convinced that those who did this to him knew him for one of mine – perhaps he was in fact caught spying, which neither he nor Mahu will admit to me. But I know wherefore a man's ears are chopped off. It is not the random cruelty of drunken sailors that does this.

Of course the Pharaoh sends men into battle and they are killed or they are wounded. I know there is a cost to pay and I do not flinch from it, although I always try to avert war if I can. Yet if war must be waged, it must and men will die. Men will be mutilated. But not my little Bek. Not him.

It has been some weeks since I had time to write and he has recovered fairly well. The young physician, Minhotep, has been to see him often and has pulled him through. He has even had a pair of false ears made for Bek by the workers in the House of the Dead; they fashioned them from linen and resin and painted them to look like skin. They are attached to a wig, so when he puts it on he looks very normal and he hears well enough. But the spark of fun has gone from him and he sits in a low chair with his short legs in their splints sticking out in front of him and he never jokes or laughs.

Yunit, the gods be praised, has not lost the babe. She has been indefatigable in caring for Bek and I have seen that her ankles have become thick, but she will not allow anyone else to look after him.

Truth to tell, she presents a very odd little figure at present. With her swollen belly and short legs she puts me in mind of the goddess of fertility, Taueret, the pregnant hippopotamus. May that be a good portent for her. I hope that there may be no problems with the birth. She reminds me of myself.

The third year of my husband's reign began well for both of us. The recurrent illnesses that so sapped his strength seemed to be in abeyance; we hoped that he had overcome them completely. He was better able to shoulder his duties as Pharaoh and began the comprehensive restoration of temples that the Hyksos invaders had allowed to crumble into ruin. At this time also he called me often to the marriage bed, and soon I was pregnant again – this time, I was certain, with the son that he so much desired, a son with the full blood royal and an indisputable claim to the Double Throne.

And I was right. In truth I had a son. I carried him for seven moons and he stirred often under my heart. The day of his birth lives in my memory.

It was extremely hot, I remember that well. So hot that it was hard to breathe. It was the time when the waters of the Nile run red. Red as the blood that flowed from my loins after my little son was expelled from my body in a rush. I had been beset by sudden pains for only a short while when the birth took place – despite the bitter potions prescribed by the royal physicians and despite the incantations and prayers and burning of incense by the priests who beseeched the gods not to allow the babe to come forth, for it was too soon; two months too soon, and that was dangerous. The physicians were useless, the priests were powerless and the gods were deaf.

The babe was born and he was perfect. A perfect little man child, whole in every way. All of the miraculous miniature fingers and toes were there, all of the limbs, the tiny sac and the small member that should have matured to plant the seeds of Pharaohs yet to come, all there. The Chief Physician held him by the heels and everyone rejoiced.

But alas! The gods did not cause his heart to breathe. Khnum, who creates the animals by the breath of his mouth, who breathes forth the flowers of the field, who breathes air into the noses of men, did not infuse my son's perfect small body with the spirit of life. And I, divine though I am, I could not endow my son with the life force. I could not kindle the divine spark. I failed him.

The women took him away and cleaned him and wrapped him in linen swaddling clothes. They washed me too, and then they brought my small son and placed him in my arms. I held him but for a little while. The milk had started into my breasts, which tingled with it; thin as yet but plentiful. I took some on my palm and anointed the silent little face, the forehead, the tiny perfect nose, the exquisitely formed lips that could not suckle. The unbelievably smooth cheeks. The delicate rosy lids over the closed eyes. He did not seem to sleep; oh, no. The living cannot sleep so still.

They took him away and I was utterly bereft. I could not rise from my bed; I could not eat, I could not sleep. I just lay and let the tears roll down my cheeks. My husband was distraught at the loss of our son, but when he saw me despairing, he became even more concerned about me. "Hatshepsut, my love, you must eat," he urged me. "You are so thin. Please, eat! We cannot lose you too!"

But I could not. Finally he sent Inet to me. She had not been well since her leg and hand became lame, but she struggled into my room with her walking stick and sat down on a small stool next to my bed, saying nothing, simply taking my hand in her two hard little paws and stroking it gently.

"Oh, Inet," I sobbed. "It is so hard. So hard."

"I know," she said.

"He should have had a name," I said, voicing my deepest concern. Because he never breathed, he was not named. "How can he be taken to the gods if he had no name? How would they know to call him?"

"It is written, '*The god knows every name*'," said Inet. "Even those that we do not."

"Even the name of a baby who did not breathe?"

"Oh, yes. And because he never breathed, his heart would have been light and Ammit would not have gobbled it up," said Inet.

She always knew how to comfort me. My son would evade the clutches of the hound of hell, I thought. He would not have been sent to perdition in the ghastly Netherworld with those whose hearts are heavy with evil when weighed against the feather of Ma'at. He would have reached the celestial realm; the doors of the sky would have been thrown open to him; he would have joined the never-dying circumpolar stars.

My greatest comfort at that time was Neferure. Small though she was, already she was a person of considerable charm. She was an intelligent and biddable and indeed a most delightful child. Her nature was sunny and she never cried, except perhaps when she fell and bumped her head or when the teeth were coming into her mouth. She had the loveliest chuckle, a happy sound that everybody wanted to hear.

I was young and strong and I recovered as well as one ever does from such a loss. My husband was travelling often at this time, inspecting the sites of temples that he wanted to be restored, conferring with Ineni, who had been my father's architect and who was, despite advancing age, still the best man in the kingdom to consult and to oversee these projects. So I stood in the Pharaoh's place in Thebes and handled many matters, large and small. It helped me to be busy. One morning when I was carrying out my duties at the administrative palace, Khani arrived.

He was carrying a cage woven from reeds and covered with a piece of cloth, which he set down as he prostrated himself.

"Majesty!" he said. "I come to say farewell. Soon now I must leave for Memphis."

"Arise," I said. "I am glad to see you." He had grown very tall, and I was sure that he would make a good soldier. "Please be seated, I shall call for some juice, it is hot."

A chattering sound came from the cage.

"What on earth do you have there?" I asked.

"It is a gift for Your Majesty," he told me. "I heard that there was a little prince who did not live. I am sorry for it."

"Thank you," I said huskily.

He whisked the cloth off, leaned forwards and opened the door of the cage, taking out a tiny monkey. It chattered again, ran up his arm and nibbled at his ear.

"Oh!" I was enchanted. "Where did you find it?"

"A sailor had it, in a tavern," he told me. "He brought it from another country. I thought it might amuse Your Majesty. It is quite tame, it will not bite."

The little creature stared at me with its huge dark eyes. I reached out a hand. In a flash, it had jumped onto my arm and then onto my shoulder, where it sat with a hand gripping my hair. It felt like a tiny child.

At that moment, Hapuseneb was announced and he swept in, wearing his Vizier's uniform of a wrapped tunic of spotless white linen with braces over the shoulders, plus a gold chain with a medallion hanging from it. He made an obeisance to me, then stared haughtily at the young Nubian seated in my presence. His eyes grew wide as he noted the monkey.

"By the tears of Isis, what an extraordinary creature," he remarked, in his high-pitched, nasal voice.

The monkey screeched, took a flying leap onto Hapuseneb's shoulder, grabbed the chain and tried to tug off the medallion.

Hapuseneb let out an undignified yelp and attempted to wrest his chain from the little creature's grip, without success. "No! No! Naughty!" he remonstrated. "Let go, get off me, you little pest!" He gave it a swipe, connecting with its head. It gave a piercing shriek, jumped onto his bald head and produced a stream of yellow ordure across his face and down the front of his pristine garment. His howl of rage could be heard as far as Memphis, I do swear.

I was laughing as I had not laughed since I was a child.

Khani's teeth were white as he grinned. He got up to remove the monkey and managed to retrieve the medallion from its grasp. "There, there," he said, stroking and petting it.

"Oh, Hapuseneb," I said, wiping my eyes. "I am s-sorry, but you sh-should not have hit it." And I laughed some more.

He was outraged and stalked out of the room without being dismissed, calling for a slave to bring water and towels.

Khani and I sat giggling helplessly. "Oh, dear," I said, "he's going to be furious for days. Oh, my. It has done me so much good to have a laugh. Thank you, Khani."

"I live to serve Your Majesty," he smiled.

The little creature afforded me much joy for a few months, but then it suddenly took ill and died. It seemed to me that it was too closely connected to my still-born son, that therefore it too could not have a strong life force. I was sad to lose it, and it made me miss Khani. So I wrote to tell him, and after that several letters passed between us while he was training, being delivered by ships travelling up and down the Nile.

When I had recovered my strength, my husband lay with me often and tried hard to make a son. It was not long before his seed had once more taken root. But I could not be joyous, as I had both times before. It was not a happy pregnancy as both of the two previous ones had been. Each time before, I had felt blessed. The third time I felt sick.

Yes, I was sick to my stomach every day for all those moons that I carried my third child. I was tired and I could hardly eat. It was as if a strange growth had taken root in my body, which wanted to be rid of it. As for my spirit, it was sick too. I have vowed to tell the truth in these writings and I shall set down what I have never admitted – not even, perhaps, quite clearly to myself: I never wanted her. No, I did not. It was just over a year since my little son, he who has no name (may he yet live), was born and did not breathe. I was very much afraid that the new babe would be the same and I could not envisage enduring such suffering again. And besides, I did not want another babe. I wanted the one who had been born to me, the child that should have been my strong, my valiant son, mastering horses, leading men and drawing a bow that none but he could bend.

It was a hard time I had carrying her and a hard time bringing her forth. Two days I laboured, and I thought to die squatting on the bricks. The pains swept through my body without mercy, shaking me, tearing my bones asunder like a prisoner on a rack and squeezing me inside until I almost had no breath. The midwives had begun to despair when at last she came into the light. A small and insignificant girl child, screaming as if in protest at what was happening to her. And she went on screaming, it seemed to me, with barely a pause, for at least five moons. I bade Inet and the wet nurse take her from my sight.

Inet was angry with me. "You should never, never reject a baby," she scolded.

"Inet, I'm not rejecting her, I'm just sending her away for a while so that I can rest. I'm so tired, and all she does is scream. Let the wet nurse feed her somewhere else. Besides, what can a baby know? It knows nothing of what is going on."

Inet shook her stiff black wig. "She knows. Believe it. It is not Ma'at, to push a child away." She limped out of the room after the wet nurse with the screaming baby, exuding disapproval.

Oh, what nonsense, I thought, the hot tears sliding down my cheeks. And the last thing I needed was for Inet to be cold to me. I had already had to contend with my husband's disappointment when the new baby was not a son. He sighed deeply and shook his head, although he said nothing. I believe he knew that we had had all the opportunities the gods would grant and there would be no full-blood prince to follow him. For once, I thought, I would like someone to think of me. I want somebody to sit next to my bed and tell me I have been brave, I have suffered weary months of discomfort and many hours of pain and I have endured it all, I have done well. I want my mother Queen Ahmose, may she live, to sit here and hold my hands in her cool hands and comfort me. Instead I must be a disappointment to all and get scolded by Inet. It is not just.

By the time Neferure had seen five risings of the Nile and Meryetre two, my husband the Pharaoh, may he live, was tiring apace. He had always used to visit his minor wives, and called for a concubine or two from time to time, but those visits happened less and less often, and soon he came only to my rooms. He liked to sit with me in the cool of the evening, drinking a little wine and conversing. Then we would move to the bedroom, where candles burned, incense scented the air and fine fresh linen decked the bed. One night especially remains in my memory, for it was the very last time we lay together.

His body felt strange to me as we held each other and kissed gently. My arms were surprised at how thin, how fragile his slight form had become. He nuzzled me, murmuring with pleasure as he inhaled the perfume of the unguent that I had rubbed into my skin. He began to lick my neck, my shoulders and my breasts, and soon I was pulsing with desire; it had been too long since he had been with me. I wanted him to take me – I wanted him to master, yes, to ravish me, as Shu had ravished Tefnut, in the beginning of the world when the gods coupled and brought forth creation. I could feel his member expanding against my thigh. I moved under him, our bodies slippery and warm, and I moaned with yearning.

I arched to meet his thrust, but alas, however hard he tried, there was no spear. Nothing more than a slightly swollen but wilted lotus bud. He gave a sob, and buried his face in my neck. His thin shoulders shook. I could feel his hot tears trickling across my face.

"I cannot," he wept, "I cannot, my love, I am so tired. I am weary in my bones and however much I wish for it, I cannot do this."

I patted his heaving shoulders and murmured: "There, there," as one does to a weeping child. "No matter. Do not distress yourself."

Gently I rolled onto my side and eased him down next to me. The desire in my loins was like a burning thirst in the desert but I willed it away. At length the sobs subsided and he fell into a light sleep, waking with a start from time to time and much disturbed by dreams. All night I held the Living Horus in my arms and comforted him.

Within months he was so often ill that it was clear he would not reign much longer. He was always tired, coughed a great deal, and bore dark bruises on his body even though he had not been injured as far as I could see. His joints ached. At night he perspired heavily and I had to keep a couple of slaves at hand to sponge him down regularly. His teeth pained him greatly and his gums bled. Seeing him suffer was hard for me, for though I never loved him passionately yet I was much attached to him; one must feel so towards the husband who initiated one into the marriage bed with skill and patience. Also he was a gentle soul who did not deserve the punishment of the gods.

He was deeply concerned about the governance of the Two Lands. One day shortly before he went to the Afterlife, he called me to his side.

I sat on a stool and held his hand. It was hot and felt papery.

"It weighs heavily on my heart that we have no son to follow us," he said. "I want you to make me a promise."

"Yes, husband?"

"You must promise to betroth Neferure to my son by Isis. She must wed young Thutmose," he said.

"Surely that will not be necessary? I . . ."

"It must be," he said, struggling to breathe. "She has the pure blood royal. He is but . . . the child of a . . . concubine. He will need her . . . to hold the throne."

I can hold the throne, I thought, but I did not say it, for it would have upset him even more. Why, I thought in impotent fury, why is a half-blood prince to be preferred to a fully royal princess? But I will show the Black Land that a woman can hold the throne. I will demonstrate the power and ability of a female Pharaoh. Then my daughter can follow me.

"Promise me," he insisted with the implacability of a weak man.

So I promised. Yet I could never bear the thought of Thutmose, he who would be King, that one who has hot eyes, touching and defiling my lovely child. I promised but I had other plans.

Soon the time came when the Pharaoh could no longer eat and he grew weaker with every wavering breath. Only the concoction that Hapu made from dried willow bark eased his suffering to any degree; he did not even need poppy juice to help him sleep, for he was drifting into a shadowy world where he was seldom awake. None of the physicians' charms, spells or incantations, none of the sacrifices or prayers intoned by the priests, had any effect.

Even though I was there, I could not tell exactly when his Ka took flight. I sat by his side inhaling the cloying scent of his favourite floral incense. Feeling light-headed. At one moment it seemed to me that a darkness shadowed the room, and then he was no longer with us. He simply ceased to breathe, and Egypt mourned. The men stopped shaving and grew beards. The women let their hair down and lamented. The Black Land mourned its loss, as I did mine.

I was sad that he lost his strength so soon, for he had great dreams. But I had strength enough, I thought, to live as I had dreamed. I acted as regent, with every intention of acceding to the throne in my own right when the seventy days had passed. For was I not the chosen of the gods? The one with the true blood royal? Who had in effect already reigned for years?

But I made an error that I would never fall into again: I relaxed my guard; I was not alert; I did not ensure that I had eyes and ears everywhere keeping watch for me. During the seventy days of mourning the priests must have made their plans; so the move that they made that day in the temple, when the barque of Amen-Ra dipped to the child of the concubine, caught me unawares. I had not expected that they could dream of placing a juvenile upon the Double Throne. It is Pharaoh's duty to sustain vigour and vitality, lest Khemet lose its life force and prove unable to maintain Ma'at, which would allow the forces of chaos and evil to conquer the land. Always, always those forces lie in wait and have to be opposed, and only a strong Pharaoh is capable of doing that. Certainly not a child of ten.

I was absolutely furious, but I controlled myself and none could tell what my true feelings were. Although this coronation was utterly unacceptable, I could not act in a manner that seemed to contradict the God's will. I saw that it would take some time and careful planning, but I vowed that I would gain the throne at last. While the child was yet young I would be regent, but it would not be for long. It is not unknown in the history of Egypt for two Pharaohs to share the throne, one always being in the ascendancy. I would ensure that I myself was crowned, and I would become the major power. It was inevitable and it was necessary. Khemet needed me.

I realised at once that I would have to counter the power of the priests; this could be done by gaining the support of those who did not wish the priesthood to become all-powerful, namely the nobles, who formed the Party of Legitimacy, and the military. And also the bureaucrats. I believed that the nomarchs heading the provinces of Egypt would support me if I assured them that such support would be profitable. In this way I laid my plans and made my moves. Yes, I became regent. Only for a while.

Here endeth the eighth scroll.

MY FRIEND AHMOSE, the scribe who now works for the priests, has brought disquieting information and I am in much doubt as to whether I should pass it on to Her Majesty or not. It is this: Many documents are passing from the Great Commander Thutmose of the Army to the Vizier of the South, Hapuseneb, and back again. These documents are sealed and sent to and fro by courier, so Ahmose has not been able to read any of them. At first they were but few; however, lately the traffic has increased.

I see Ahmose regularly, but always in a tavern, so that none should suspect that these encounters are anything more than the meeting of two old friends. He looks considerably more presentable these days, almost sleek. Certainly better fed and neatly clothed. His scar has faded and now that his face is fuller it appears less crooked. Yesterday when I arrived at the Wishing Well he already had two large jars of beer waiting, and a bowl of olives, the juicy black kind that I like.

After some inconsequential chatter, he lowered his voice and leaned forwards confidentially. "I have not yet succeeded in taking a look at any of the communications between Hapuseneb and the Army Chief," he murmured, "yet sometimes one can tell quite a lot about a document from its context without having read it. Such as when it was written, for example, and who was present at the time."

I nodded.

"I have noticed," he told me, "that a certain tax collector comes often to see the Vizier at his private residence, which is very suspicious. Also, I can think of no good reason why a tax collector should come around so often at the present time. It is the season of sowing, there is no harvest to report on as yet."

"No, certainly not," I agreed. "This tax collector works in the southern region, does he?"

"Purports to," said Ahmose in a low tone, checking around us with his single good eye. There was only one group of customers, a rowdy bunch of sailors who were making so much noise that they drowned out anything my friend might say. Mine host had joined them for a beer and his small, bustling wife was wiping down the counter and setting out bowls of olives and fresh bread. It smelled delicious and I waved to her to bring some.

"You think he works elsewhere?" I asked when she had returned to the counter. I chewed some bread; it was indeed excellent.

Ahmose nodded. He whispered, "I think he must be a spy. In fact, most probably a master spy with several men reporting to him. For he brings bundles of documents. And then he visits the Chief Vizier for some time. And soon a courier arrives and sets off post-haste for the North."

"I see, I see. So you think – but surely it is a dangerous matter for several men to bring secret reports to one tax collector . . . These reports would be coming from a number of vassal states, I suppose you to mean . . ."

"Yes, that would make sense. They would contain information about the numbers and the state of readiness of our enemies' armies, no doubt. And anything the source could discover about the intentions of the commanders who lead them, and the movements and activities of the troops. Dangerous documents, indeed. But such persons are ingenious, and probably pose as merchants, hiding these reports in their merchandise. Also, carrier pigeons might be used."

"I see, I see. Well, this is useful, if unconfirmed. I shall inform Her Majesty."

"The best way to confirm my suspicions," whispered Ahmose, "would be to have the courier intercepted. The Pharaoh could arrange for that."

I nodded, rather unhappily. I would rather not pass the matter on, because such a man would probably have to be killed, and if he were innocent his life would weigh heavily upon my heart. Might it not then bear witness against me in the Afterlife? But then, I argued with myself, Pharaoh would have given the order, not me.

I know, I know it is my duty to report suspicions of treason to the King. I must do my duty, that is all. And I shall do it. Soon.

THE NINTH SCROLL

After my husband had passed into the Afterlife, Senenmut became of ever greater importance in my life. He was acting as steward of Neferure's property and my own, and he was tutor to Neferure. I ordered him to instruct her in religious matters and she was an apt pupil. Since the priests were at that time effectively running the country on behalf of the child Thutmose, I had more time then than I later had as Pharaoh to enjoy a homely life, so I occasionally used to join the children at lesson time. Neferure soaked up knowledge like dry earth the rain, and she asked questions that I would have been hard put to answer, but Senenmut did his best. I recall a day when he was discussing the origins of the world with her.

Meryetre, three years younger than her sister, was playing with dolls, putting them to bed in a box with linen cloths, crooning to them a little tuneless song.

"Before the world began," said Senenmut, "the creator god Atum floated alone in the primeval ocean Nun."

What a pleasant voice he has, I found myself thinking. Deep and rich. A good voice for telling tales. Neferure was listening intently, sitting cross-legged like a little scribe, tugging at her plaited child's lock of silky black hair. Graceful, slender and almond-eyed, she formed a sharp contrast to her pudgy-legged younger sister who, alas, had inherited the buck teeth of the Thutmose family.

"At last, Atum found a place for his foot, and came to rest on a solid mound," continued Senenmut. "He then . . . ah . . . aroused himself with his fist. Copulating with his hand, he spewed forth his seed in the shape of Shu and Tefnut, children of the divine loins. So the first divine couple came into being: Shu, god of life, air and light, and Tefnut, goddess of moisture."

Ah, I thought, even a god may arouse himself. Since my husband's failing health had kept him from my bed, and more so after his death, what other recourse could I have had, given that I was yet young and filled at times with strong desires? I sighed, but I kept my eyes on my hands, pretending to study my scarab ring.

"From this couple came forth Geb, the earth god, and Nut, the sky goddess," the tale went on. "Now Shu raised Nut over the reclining Geb and from the physical union of Geb and Nut were born the gods Osiris, Isis, Seth and Nefthys; from them, the creation of the world could follow."

"But where did the first god come from, Senenmut?" Neferure wanted to know. Surely she has him there, I thought, glancing up.

But he was equal to the challenge, being well versed in religious doctrine, since he had been a scribe for the priests in the House of Life. "He was begot by himself from all eternity," he told her. "He was and is the principle of all life. Father of fathers and Mother of mothers."

"Both man and woman, like Hapi," said Neferure. Understanding this, she could easily grasp the dual nature of my kingship when it came to pass.

"Yes. And so the source of the life force in all that lives."

"But we have many gods in Egypt, Senenmut," objected Neferure.

"One god may have many representations," explained Senenmut. "It is easier for the people to understand. And of course the people love their local deities. So we have many sacred beings, many different gods, household spirits, elements of nature, animals, scarabs . . . but all receive the breath of life from the one god."

Meryetre set up a frustrated howling because she was having trouble taking off a doll's dress. Neferure reached over to help her and the howling subsided into sobs.

"Yet some believe the sun god first came forth from an egg, on the mound of Heliopolis," I put in.

"Just another image of beginning," said Senenmut. "And later the priests at Memphis began to speak of Ptah, a supergod in whom other gods could be contained."

"But what is the life-force in all the gods?" asked Neferure, wrinkling her brow.

"It is the sun, my child. The most perfect image of the god is the sun. The sun's soul is Amen-Ra, whose name means Hidden Sun. He is the source of life and the other deities are parts of his body. And the Pharaoh is always the child of the sun."

Well, my younger daughter was not, that much was clear. She had been trying repeatedly to get two dolls to sit up straight and both of them kept falling over. She squatted on her heels, small fists clenched on her fat little knees, and had one of her fits of weeping. She always seemed to have a depth of sorrow that she needed her whole small stocky body to express. She howled, her face scrunched up and suffused with a dark anger, and the fat tears burst from her eyes to drip upon the tiles.

Neither Senenmut nor I was able to cope with Meryetre's attacks of overwhelming grief, but Neferure knew what to do. She fetched a bowl of pink figs and sat down right in front of her sister and proceeded to peel them, delicately, one by one, making appreciative noises. Meryetre opened one streaming eye. Neferure held up the fig, admired it, and ate it. Meryetre screamed some more. Neferure peeled another fig. Her sister peeped at her. Neferure held the fig up, enticingly. Meryetre sobbed, hiccupped, and opened her mouth. Neferure popped in the fig. "Shut up," she said, "and have some more."

The weeping fit was over. I leaned down and scooped the little one onto my lap. She was a damp and rather smelly bundle. I leaned my cheek on her hair. "There, there," I said. "I'll sing you a lullaby. Senenmut, please take Neferure to Inet for her bath."

He departed, holding my eldest by the hand. She was skipping along beside him. Meryetre stuck a thumb in her sticky mouth and snuggled into my arms. Oh, dear, I thought. I love you, my little one. Your mother loves you. You came forth from me and I must love you. But it is so much easier to love a child that is blithesome and full of grace. How strange it is that sometimes Khnum fashions a being so beautifully, while at other times one might almost swear he was not paying proper attention to his work. It is not just.

Looking back now, that period when my darling Neferure was receiving her first religious instruction and Meryetre still played with dolls seems a time of such peace and innocence that I could weep for it.

As I have written, I had to be regent, but I never intended that to last, for am I not the chosen of the gods? I will now set out the most important, the absolutely irrefutable proof of my right to be the Pharaoh, to bear a Horus name, to wear the Double Crown, to reign over Egypt and its vassal states, to smite evil, and to maintain the rule of Ma'at. It is quite simple. It is this: I am divine. I am sun-begotten. I am both the daughter and the son of Amen-Ra. And how do I know this? Not from Inet. No, her tales merely confirm what I know through a vision granted to me by the sun god himself.

It came to me two years after my husband Thutmose, the second Pharaoh of that name, had died and the child Thutmose was crowned – a misjudged coronation that should never have been allowed to take place.

The vision came to me – significantly, I have always believed – on the Day of the Dead, that joyous festival when all Thebes marches to the necropolis, bearing gifts of food, flowers and scrolls with messages for those who have gone before and now live happily in the Afterlife. The main part of the festival would begin at sunset, and important celebrations would take place in the hall of the Temple of Amen at Karnak in the northern section of Thebes. I had had very little sleep the night before, since I had spent many hours in meditation; also I had fasted all of the previous day. I had my part to play in the celebratory rites and I wanted to be in a fit state for the early-morning rituals that would be carried out with especial care on this feast day in the sanctuary of the God.

It was before sunrise, therefore, that I was carried to the temple in a sedan chair. Karnak is a whole religious complex and there are many temples dedicated to a host of lesser deities. But it is the temple of Amen-Ra to which I here refer. The air was crisp and a fresh breeze scented with the wood-smoke of the peasants' fires blew chill upon the skin. The footfalls of the slaves thudded on the pathway. All around me the city dreamed. Soon the beer shops would open and market stalls throw up their shutters, while slaves, servants, porters with bundles and housewives bearing baskets would people the streets. Now, though, a sleepy silence reigned as Thebes awaited the golden benediction of Ra.

Then we reached the entrance and the carriers set me down. Flanked by my guards, two tall Nubians with military training, and bearing a basket filled with meat, bread, fruit and beer, I walked resolutely through the first pylon of the primary temple. Even at this early hour there was already a scattering of the common folk in the outer courtyard; soon there would be a tremendous press of people and it would become difficult to move. The second courtyard, to which only those of noble descent would be admitted, was emptier. I passed through the third pylon and paused at the fourth to gaze up at the obelisks that had been erected at the behest of my royal father, Thutmose the First, may he live for ever. Now my guards had to remain behind, for they would not be allowed inside the sacred precincts further on.

As I neared the fifth pylon I could hear the chantresses singing, their hymn of praise accompanied by the crash and rattle of sistrum and tambourine. The scent of incense greeted me as I walked forwards. At this early hour the inner chamber was filled with dark shadows.

I stood quietly, breathing deeply, closing my eyes as I whispered a prayer to Amen asking for guidance, for courage and for insight. I confessed that I feared the child king did not have the capability to govern the Two Lands with a firm hand, while the priests who stood behind him lacked a proper grasp of the political issues that were likely to rend the country apart without a wise ruler to maintain balance and give direction. It was at that moment that the vision came to me.

As clearly as anything I have ever seen with my bodily eyes, I saw my mother, the Great Queen Ahmose, may she live for ever, reclining upon a couch in her boudoir. In my vision she was younger than she then was in fact by some twenty years. She wore but a transparent robe of the finest linen with a scarab pin on the left shoulder. I could see the door through which all who entered there must pass. As I watched, the door swung open and a golden glow suffused the air. It seemed as if the air itself was moving towards her couch, coalescing into a more solid shape the closer it drew. Still it gleamed with an unearthly light. On its head shimmered the disc of Amen-Ra. A shiver ran over my watching body as I realised that I was seeing the very God himself, approaching the waiting Queen, my mother.

She looked at this apparition with amazement and awe, but without fear. Surely, I thought, she was a woman of great courage to confront a being from the spirit world with such aplomb. But then I saw that the being had changed once more. It had taken on the form, the very substance, of my late father the Pharaoh, may he live for ever. He was an avatar of Amen, but yet it was his true familiar self, and it was in his own body that he approached his wife the Queen. She smiled at His Majesty. His penis was erect before her. She was filled with joy at the sight of his beauty.

I watched as he reached out to her, put aside the delicate robe, covered her with his strong body and placed his seed in her. He gave his heart to her. His love passed into her limbs. The palace was flooded with the God's fragrance. It did not seem lewd to me to be observing this. It was . . . it was like a sacrament, a ritual, a consecration, to which I was an awe-struck witness.

I knew that he had impregnated her then because he told her so, just before he rose from the couch and took his leave, once more losing his solid human form and dissolving before my watching eyes into a shimmer of golden light. *"You are now with child,"* said his voice, seeming to resound in the space where I stood transfixed. *"You will bear a princess, whom you will name Hatshepsut. And she will reign."* The words reverberated. I was convinced that they were clearly audible to the priests who now walked towards me. "Do you hear?" I demanded, breathless with the wonder of my vision. "And she will reign! And she will reign! Hatshepsut will reign! The God has told me so himself."

Having been vouchsafed this vision, I knew that I had to make my destiny manifest to all. I would have to make my move and make it decisively. At once it was clear to me what I should do. I would make offerings directly to the gods. This is traditionally the task and prerogative of the Pharaoh, which he delegates to his priests but which no other mortal may carry out. It is the Pharaoh's sacred duty to satisfy the gods with divine offerings and to bring funerary offerings to the transfigured dead. I was well acquainted with the prescribed steps of the morning ritual, since I had been the God's Wife of Amen for several years, attending on first my father and then my husband when they as the divine sons of the sun god acted as the link with the spirit world. Now I would carry out these steps in person.

I knew I had to win that confrontation on the Day of the Dead. The officiating priest on that fateful day was Hapuseneb, Chief

Priest of Amen and a power in the land. As he came towards me, his white linen tunic emerging from the gloom, I knew that he intended to bar my way. He was attended by four assistant priests, one the lector who would chant the prescribed magic words. The Chief Priest was taller than I by a head, with broad shoulders; the right shoulder bare, the left one draped in a leopard-skin mantle. His skin was a deep shade of copper and, as he had not yet donned his huge ceremonial wig, his bald pate gleamed in the torchlight. Indeed, his entire body was completely hairless, as priests must be to ensure complete cleanliness. His lashless eyes, green and protuberant, put me in mind of a chameleon, that small dragon that moves with such deliberation and changes colour to survive.

"I will break the seal," I announced, lifting my chin. The seal on the door of the inner shrine that holds the God may only be broken by the Pharaoh or his deputed priest. It is a most secret place, less accessible than that which is in heaven, more secret than the affairs of the Netherworld, more hidden than the inhabitants of the primeval ocean. I dropped my voice. "I am the son of Amen-Ra," I told him. "I have had a vision. The God himself begat me."

His smooth face expressed doubt. Had he had eyebrows, he would have raised them.

"I have the backing of the Party of Legitimacy," I told him. "The nobles do not approve that the child of a concubine should be King when one of the pure blood royal is at hand." This was entirely true. Also the nobles knew that they might expect grants of land and other favours from my hand if I were the supreme Pharaoh, but nothing would be forthcoming from a young child manipulated by the priests.

Hapuseneb was shrewd and he knew that the nobles, motivated both by greed and a resistance to the immense power of the priesthood, were formidable allies ranged at my back. He shifted slightly, but he did not stand aside.

"The military are also with me," I went on.

This surprised him. He had underestimated me. "The military?"

At that time, I had not yet the services of Khani, who was in training at Memphis, but I had others who were my eyes and ears, particularly in the South whence came so much gold. I learned the value of timely information early and I have always made sure that it is brought to me.

"There are signs of rebellion in the Land of Kush," I told him. "They scent a weakness in us. They do not believe that a small child and a queen who is merely a regent can hold the vassal states. That rebellion must be crushed decisively. General Pen-Nekhbet of el-Kab agrees. The Living Horus must smite our enemies."

Hapuseneb looked thoughtful. He said nothing, but much as he respected the aging general, I could guess that he found it difficult to view me as the Living Horus. I would have to do more to convince him.

"I have been inducted into the mysteries of Osiris," I reminded him.

He certainly had to know that my late father, may he live, had indeed done this when he was already weak with his final illness, at the time when I served as the God's Wife of Amen. These are secret matters of great significance and none but the Pharaoh and the Chief Priest may know of them.

"Yes, I do remember that," he murmured.

"My father the Pharaoh, may he live, expected me to reign," I insisted. "Otherwise he would not have inducted me."

Hapuseneb seemed to be wavering. He did not contradict me.

"I have the complete support of the nomarchs, of both the North and the South."

"Ah, yes. The nomarchs."

I could see that it was beginning to dawn on Hapuseneb that I had done my preparations with great care and thoroughness. He well knew that each of the nomarchs who ruled the forty-two nomes into which the land was demarcated had been called to my presence over the period since my husband the Pharaoh passed into the Afterlife. Having been offered sufficient inducements, they would support me with enthusiasm.

Hapuseneb shifted from foot to foot. Clearly he was feeling beleaguered.

"Also the Vizier of the North is on my side," I stated. This was a telling point; there was no love lost between the two viziers. I knew that Hapuseneb heartily disliked the Vizier Dhutmose, an essentially lazy sybarite who yet had enough ambition and greed to ensure that he ruled effectively. I stared intently into Hapuseneb's narrowed, doubtful eyes. "It could be that the Two Lands would benefit by returning to the former system," I suggested silkily. "One Vizier for the Two Lands. Possibly the duties of Vizier of the South as well as the Chief Priest of Amen will prove too much for you."

He flinched, having understood me perfectly. Of course he realised that the matter at hand was crucial. I had him pinned; by forcing this issue in front of the assistant priests at the entrance to the holy of holies, I was giving him no opportunity to prevaricate, to think of alternatives or to work out other moves.

I knew exactly what his considerations were: I had such powerful backing that I would probably gain the throne. If he continued to oppose me now I would henceforth be his implacable enemy, and he would lose power. If he threw in his lot with me, he would be allied closely to the Pharaoh. Better, perhaps, than being the shadowy manipulator of a young boy who had no powerful factions other than the priesthood backing him. Maybe he was also thinking that he would be able to manipulate me. I smiled.

"A vision?" he said. "The son of Amen-Ra?"

"The very seed of his loins," I affirmed. "The Living Horus."

He nodded reflectively. Then he stood aside. "Majesty will break the seal," he told the priests, who had been observing the encounter between us with their mouths hanging open. The lector priest began to chant the ritual words which must be faultlessly recited to be magical. The singing of the chantresses swelled around us. I handed over my basket, strode forwards and broke the clay seal to the innermost shrine which had been put in place by the Chief Priest the previous day.

It was cool, very dark, and smelled musty. While the outer reaches of the temple are open and sunlit, with brightly coloured paintings on the walls, the corridors grow narrower and darker as they lead inward to the shrine where the God lives. I walked forwards and stood before the golden statue of the God in its niche. It seemed to me that its painted eyes regarded me with approbation.

Gently and reverently I took the God from his niche and, using the items passed to me by the assistant priests, I fed the God, robed him, rouged his face and adorned him with royal emblems. Outside the inner sanctum the chantresses rejoiced, their pure voices accompanied by the rhythmic rattle of sistrums and tambourines. The powerful scent of the flaming torches and the heady aroma of incense filled the interior of the shrine, driving out the mustiness.

The rites completed, a feeling of dizziness threatened to overcome me. My recent actions had inducted me into the ranks of the divine, a chain of living gods reaching back into the ancient past, all of whom had served to link the invisible and the visible. Through my life henceforth and through my spiritual strength I would sustain Khemet. It was an awesome task.

I replaced the image, which the God would now certainly inhabit until the following day, in its niche. Then I kneeled down and struck my forehead against the dusty floor, smelling the dry sand. "Great Lord, my Father, make me worthy," I murmured. "Make we worthy and help me, my Father, to maintain Ma'at. Let me never weaken. Be thou at my side."

It seemed to me then that I heard the God speak. *"Verily thou art the seed of Amen-Ra,"* I heard the God say, *"which came forth from him."*

I once more sealed the shrine. I left the sanctuary walking backwards while sweeping away my footprints with a palm frond, lest the devils that seek to attack the God follow my tracks into the shrine. Not by my doing would evil overpower the sacred centre of divinity. Hapuseneb accompanied me as I emerged from the dark and narrow canal into the raucous brightness of the outer courtyards, now tightly packed with people who raised a rousing cheer when they saw us. We stood side by side acknowledging their acclaim.

Hapuseneb turned to look me in the eye. "I too applaud the Living Horus," he said. "May life, stability and dominion reward the Pharaoh Hatshepsut."

I inclined my head. Joy suffused my being.

"The people will need a sign, though," he added, softly. "I think it would be appropriate to consult the oracle."

"Indeed, we should do that," I agreed. And so King Hatshepsut was born that very morning, at the dawning of the Day of the Dead.

I achieved the throne, but it has not been easy to hold it. Mahu the scribe has brought some information that I find very disquieting. If it is true that Hapuseneb and Thutmose, that one that would be King, are corresponding almost daily, it is not good. I shall have to order that the so-called tax collector be taken prisoner and interrogated and his belongings searched. Yet it must seem that he was set upon by thugs, for if Hapuseneb were to realise that Pharaoh's hand is behind an attack on his man, there will be trouble – and then the conspirators, if such they are, will have been warned.

Well, I shall confer with the head of my band of secret enforcers. There never used to be a need for such men, but during these past few years I have discovered that I cannot do without them. They report only to me and I keep them faithful by a combination of threats and rewards. After I had had two of their number sent to the quarries lacking not only ears and noses but also their manhood, because I suspected them of reporting to Hapuseneb, the rest soon remembered where their loyalty lay.

The leader of the band is a fairly young man and he appears deceptively meek. He comes to me as a scribe, which he is, but that is not all he is. His name – but perhaps I should not write it, even in my secret scrolls, for there is always the danger that Mahu may be caught with these writings on his person and the head of the enforcers knows things . . . Let me call him Ibana. Ibana, then, is small and neat, with a shaven head and unexceptional brown eyes, barring that they are never still. He is extremely concerned about cleanliness and I must always ensure that a slave girl brings scented water to him when he arrives and again before he leaves so that he may wash his hands. Yes, I shall call for him and give him instructions to investigate the matter.

Here endeth the ninth scroll.

THE TENTH SCROLL

THE REIGN OF HATSHEPSUT YEAR 1

Within days of my confrontation with Hapuseneb I caught my nephew mounting a female slave. By this time he had twelve summers and he was becoming both insolent and rebellious I was determined to remove him from Thebes completely. With Hapuseneb's aid it would not be difficult, I thought.

The girl was older than the young Thutmose by about half his age again, and willing enough to judge by her complicit giggling. As for him, he did not even look abashed. She fled precipitately, pulling down her homespun shift, while he stood his ground, his stocky, muscular legs planted like small trees. He shook out his kilt and grinned.

"I am Pharaoh, Aunt," he told me. I am in truth his stepmother also, but he never addresses me as such. "Pharaoh should have his pick of women. And women should know their place."

This made me angry in the extreme, but I would not let him see that he had riled me. I was co-regent at the very least. How dared he speak to me in such dismissive tones! Nor could he be allowed to assume authority. He was a child, and a child could not sustain the essential connections to the gods, nor could a child maintain Ma'at. Especially not such a one as he.

"It is children who should know their place," I said, "and you are but a child, nephew."

He grinned again. Certainly his actions had not been childish when I came upon the scene.

He has hot eyes, that one who would be King. Hot eyes and voracious appetites. Runt though he is, there is fire in his loins, as I later found to my detriment – but more of that anon. First I must write of how I came to power. That episode goaded me into action.

I began to implement the necessary steps to establish myself as the primary Pharaoh, legitimate occupant of the Double Throne.

First the oracle would have to speak. That could be arranged. Then a glorious coronation would take place. It would be such a feast as the common people had not seen and would never forget. They would crown me with fanfares and feasting, with merriment and magnificence, with music from trumpets and flutes, cymbals and tambourines. I would become divine, and I would reign.

I decided then that the child Thutmose should be sent to the priests at Heliopolis. Of course, they would not keep him celibate, but if he tried to treat one of their wives the way he had the slave, they would doubtless find a way to discipline him. They could keep him busy learning the rites and rituals appropriate to the Aten. Oh yes, I thought, let him be removed to Heliopolis and learn to serve a lesser god.

Besides, I wanted him far away from Neferure, who was growing more beautiful with each rising of the Nile. I did not want him casting his lascivious eyes on my eldest daughter, my dearly beloved, my most precious ewe lamb. No, no, better to put a considerable distance between them, I thought. Especially after the episode with the slave. My darling deserved better than to be mated with this runt with the goatish disposition. I would not deny the betrothal that my husband had made me promise to announce, but I would keep them apart.

It soon became clear to me that I had made a good decision in forcing the issue with Hapuseneb. He now acted decisively on my behalf, taking a number of helpful steps. He supported me in lodging the child Thutmose with the priests. As he had promised, he consulted the oracle as regards my succession to the throne. The oracle's response was a clear endorsement of my claim. This is what it said, in ringing tones: *"Verily, she is the daughter and the son of Amen-Ra; she works for him and knows his divine will; her heavenly father will reward her with life, stability and dominion upon the Horus throne. She will live for ever."* I would be crowned.

My coronation was indeed a glorious occasion. All the elements that had characterised such ceremonies over the ages were present, elements that had not been included in the hasty and ill-conceived coronation of the child Thutmose. The festival began in Thebes. Early that morning my ladies awoke me and accompanied me to the bathing room, whose mud-brick walls were lined with smooth, pale limestone. There a slave shaved me from head to toe, for on this day of days I must be completely clean. A small, nut-brown girl, her eyes were huge at the thought of the special task she had to perform. To begin with her hands trembled a little, but she soon became absorbed in her work and gained confidence.

First she cut off my locks of hennaed hair, which were swept away, and then she closely shaved my skull with a copper-handled razor. When she was satisfied that I had a totally bald pate, she moved to my underarms, thence to my legs, and finally she depilated my private parts, ensuring that not a single hair remained anywhere. There was something sensual in the touch of her gentle, deft fingers, and I was momentarily reminded of my late husband Thutmose, may he live, who was a gentle and expert lover.

Then sacred water from the Nile was poured over me from bowls made of precious metals, and my entire body was scrubbed with natron salt and wiped down with a strigil. It stung on the recently shaved areas, but I made no complaint. I was given natron tablets to chew on to purify my breath. The salty taste made me feel slightly nauseous on an empty stomach. There would be much feasting later on, but initially it was necessary to fast. I was dried with soft towels.

Now the ladies of the bathing chamber rubbed myrrh oil sweetly scented with lotus into my glowing skin; then one brought a small pot made of gold containing concentrated lotus balsam and perfumed my wrists and inner arms with it.

My dear Inet limped in, bringing the kilt of pure white pleated linen and the fine white linen shirt in which I would arrive at the temple. This was a man's attire and she looked a little doubtful, but she knew better than to question me. Later more layers of clothing and jewellery would be added, but I would go to Amen-Ra simply clad. Even my feet were bare. She helped me to step into the kilt and fastened it. Next she dropped the shirt carefully over my shaven head, pulling it straight. Then she stood on tiptoe, drew my head down and kissed my forehead. Tears glimmered in her small dark eyes.

"Tomorrow you will be Pharaoh and none may touch your divine body," she murmured, "but today you are still my child and I love you. I always knew that it was your destiny to be great. I knew it, for are you not the chosen of the gods?" She pressed an ankh-shaped amulet on a chain into my hand. "This is for you, so that you may live for ever. May the gods be with you. May Hathor support you with her everlasting arms and keep you safe."

There were tears in my eyes too. "Thank you, Inet," I said.

At that moment I wished my mother could have been present, the Great Queen Ahmose, who had loved me too. I imagined her standing by my side. But I was motherless and I had to go to the temple alone.

A gold-inlaid sedan chair was brought to carry me to the temple of Amen-Ra at Karnak, where the ceremonies would begin. Excited crowds packed the streets and rousing cheers greeted me as I was carried swiftly along the brightly decorated thoroughfare. Everywhere there were flags and arches twined with flowers; my devoted Senenmut, who was in charge of preparations, had done his job well. I knew that, in addition to the festive look, he had ensured that there were guards on duty to keep an eye out for anyone who might mount an attack to prevent me from reaching my goal.

On reaching Karnak, I entered the sacred house of Amen-Ra. Figures of priests wearing animal masks denoting the pantheon of gods came to meet me. Recognising none but Hapuseneb, who was the tallest and wore the mask of Horus, I walked forwards resolutely.

It was necessary to undergo another ritual purification, thoroughly though I had been prepared. Guided by Horus and Atum, I entered the hall of purification. Here I removed the kilt and the shirt and stepped into a shallow crystal bowl of sacred water, while four priests representing the four cardinal points of the world poured water over me. I felt no shyness at that moment even though I was surrounded by men, for was I not there in my capacity as the son of Amen-Ra? Yet I noted that Horus was stirred by the sight of my naked form. I ignored that and shut my eyes. In my heart I spoke to Amen, Lord of the Thrones of the Two Lands. Give me sovereignty over the entire Black Land, over the North and South, Delta and Valley, I entreated the God. Give me dominion. And make me worthy.

I was dried and anointed with sacred oil. Once more I donned the kilt and the linen shirt, but now there was added a heavy collar, a flat, circular shape made of row upon row of gold links studded with lapis lazuli and carnelian. I was given sandals of leather interwoven with gold thread, with portraits of Hittite prisoners on the inner soles. Onward I walked, treading on our enemies, to the House of the King, where I would actually be crowned. The masked priests accompanied me. All around us the sweetly scented incense and the rattle of sistrums drove away devils. The ancient chant of the coronation ritual sounded in my ears, working its magic. I began to feel light-headed.

Now Hapuseneb, in his role as First Priest of Amen, presented a live cobra for me to grasp. I did not shrink for a single moment, but took the cold and scaly body firmly behind the narrow head. The black eyes stared into mine and it hissed. Yet I had no fear, for Apophis had once before spared me for my destiny. I looked at evil and I mastered it. The priest took the snake from me and killed it with dispatch. Now the royal uraeus was placed upon my forehead: a golden cobra with jewelled eyes. The symbol of Wadjet, the mother goddess. She would never leave me henceforth; she would strike terror into the souls of all who faced the King. She would spit venom into the eyes of my enemies.

At last I was truly Pharaoh and divine. The two crowns of Egypt were placed upon my head, one by one: the Red Crown of Lower Egypt, and the White Crown of Upper Egypt. The false beard of the Pharaohs was tied under my chin, held in place with loops around my ears. The bull's tail attached to a gold-studded leather belt was fastened around my waist. The sumptuous coronation robes were hung about my form. The royal crook and the flail were put into my hands. Now a blare of trumpets heralded the announcement of my five royal names: *Horus Powerful-of-Kas. Two Ladies Flourishing-of-Years. Female Horus of Fine Gold Divine-of-Diadems. King of Upper and Lower Egypt Ma'atkare. Daughter of Ra Khnemet-Amen Hatshepsut.*

Finally I proceeded to the innermost shrine, where I stood face to face with the God, Amen-Ra, an impressive golden figure with intensely blue eyes. It seemed to me that the God looked upon me with favour and spoke so: *"Thou hast been invested with the double crown, thou art blessed. Thou art my heir, thou art my seed. This is my daughter Khnemet-Amen Hatshepsut, living for ever. She shall reign."* I was filled with exaltation.

The Divine Light had placed me upon the earth of living mortals to judge human beings and satisfy the will of the gods. For the King must displace disorder, lies and injustice with the harmony of Ma'at – that is, the cosmic order that came into being with creation. The King must assure justice, protect the weak from the strong, make offerings to the Invisible and venerate the souls of the dead.

I prostrated myself and I prayed:

"Oh, my heavenly father and lord of lords,
Amen, Lord of the Double Throne,
I smell the air coming forth from thy nose!

Adored art thou in peace, O lord of the gods,
Thou art exalted by reason of thy wondrous things!
Make thou glorious my beatified being, make thou strong my soul!"
It seemed to me that I heard again the very voice of the God:
"Thou art blessed."

When I emerged from the dark recesses of the holy of holies, I walked in a great procession through the passages of the shadowy temple. I will be worthy, I vowed silently as I moved forwards. I will be worthy. I will reign wisely over this land that the God has given into my care. On we went, through the great pylons and out into the bright hot day. The heat and the noise of cheering crowds assaulted my senses. Now an even more ornate sedan chair, inlaid with gold and precious jewels, but without curtains so that I might be seen, awaited me. It would be carried high on the shoulders of six stalwart standard bearers of military divisions. They stood to attention as I emerged from the temple. I was delighted to see that Khani was one of them.

They were all solemn as they made deep obeisances, but when I told them to arise, Khani could not keep his wide white grin off his face. "I see you, Khani," I said. "You have received promotion. Pharaoh is pleased."

He beamed, prostrating himself again. Then he assisted me to climb into the chair and I was hoisted aloft.

"Pharaoh!" The people chanted. "Pharaoh! Pharaoh Hatshepsut!" The scent of crushed flowers rose in my nostrils as my sweating carriers pounded them underfoot.

I was carried aboard a golden barque which sailed to Memphis, between banks lined with screaming and cheering onlookers. In Memphis I ran around the Palace of White Walls to commemorate the unification of the Two Lands, a race I repeated at my Sed festival six years ago. The fact that I grew up with two elder brothers has stood me in good stead, that and the fact that I have ever been brimful of energy. From the centre of the palace plain I loosed off four arrows to the four cardinal points of the compass, using a sturdy and beautifully decorated bow. Archery has been one of my accomplishments since I was taught to shoot with the royal princelings in the palace school and I have kept it up.

Finally I opened the casket full of pigeons and released them into the sky. After circling for a minute or two, an equal number set off in each of the four directions, flying straight and true. This clearly showed that I was indeed the ruler of the entire world, of which Egypt is the centre and over which we exercise dominion by divine right. The roar and ringing cheers that greeted the flight of the freed birds sounds in my ears to this day.

Ah yes, there was some manipulation there. My devoted Senen-mut, may he live, had gone to a great deal of trouble some months before the ceremony to identify pigeon trainers who could train the requisite number of homing pigeons to fly home to four places in the appropriate directions, and they were well rewarded. One does not reign over Egypt by leaving things to chance. But it was merely done to communicate the truth that had been vouchsafed to me in the vision on the Day of the Dead. Once I knew without a doubt that I was of divine parentage, I moved forward; I did everything necessary to implement the will of the God, which was that I should reign. I was crowned with full ceremony; the God acknowledged me and I became divine. That is why those who desire my throne and seek my death, if such there be, shall not prevail.

Here endeth the tenth scroll.

I WAS THERE that day when Her Majesty was crowned with pomp and ceremony. In fact, it is one of my earliest memories, for I was only six years old, and my father carried me upon his shoulders so that I might see over the heads of the excited crowds. "Look well," my father said, "you may never again see the coronation festival of a great Pharaoh. That is King Ma'atkare Hatshepsut, may she live for ever."

A king who was a woman? Strange, I thought. Perhaps she has both beard and breasts, like Hapi. I strained my eyes, and indeed, she did have a beard firmly attached to her chin. Extraordinary! But whether she also had breasts I could not quite make out, since she wore a mantle and much jewellery. She certainly was the Pharaoh, though, since the Double Crown sat upon her head. I cheered lustily with the rest of the populace. Then I ate too many dates and was very sick.

I never could have imagined that one day I would serve that self-same Pharaoh in the manner that I do. Nor that I might almost lose my life in saving hers. If an oracle had predicted such a thing, I would have thought it a joke, even a few years ago. Yet now I am Her Majesty's devoted servant. And if the truth were known, I hold her in my power, for if I were to make known everything that she writes in her secret journal, she would without a doubt be in a dangerous position.

But of course I will never do that. No, no, I would not betray her. Her Majesty trusts me. I must be worthy. And I will.

THE ELEVENTH SCROLL

The first serious test of my leadership and resolve came very soon in the first year of my reign. It arrived in the form of a plea for help from the Commander of the forts at Semna that overlook the Nile below the Second Cataract and are a key element in our control over the Nubians. His message was urgent: Rebels had taken the furthest fort. The slaughter had been dreadful. The other forts feared a total uprising, and the Commander had brought the garrisons of Semna East and South into the protection of the main fort, Semna West. They were being besieged, and feared that they might be attacked and overrun.

At this time, the young Thutmose was with the priests at Heliopolis. Khani did not yet hold a high rank, and in any case, I could not expect him to lead an expedition against his own people. This was also true of Nehsi, an able general of Nubian origin. I had one seasoned officer to whom I could turn: the tough but aging old campaigner Ahmose pen-Nekhbet of el-Kab. He had served my husband and my father before him. I called him to a conference with Seni, my adviser on foreign affairs, and Hapuseneb, who as Vizier also serves as Minister of War.

I read out the message from the Fort Commander. All present were agreed that the Nubians were testing me, and that retribution should be swift and merciless. The question was, what would be required and how soon could we be ready?

"We have seen such uprisings before," said Hapuseneb in a bored tone. "They rebel with the inevitability of the inundation, but they are always driven back to the wretched Kush and flee like the water receding after the flood. They seldom muster more than three to four thousand, and they do not possess war chariots such as ours."

"Correct." Pen-Nekhbet eased his hip, which had been stiff ever since his last campaign, when he was seriously wounded. "But they do have archers, although they tend to be a disorganised rabble. One well-trained Egyptian division plus one squadron of chariots should more than suffice to teach them a sharp lesson."

I looked at Hapuseneb. "How soon can we muster a division who can depart at once? Which division is quartered here?" I knew that there is always one division in the capital, although the main body of the army resides in Memphis.

"The Division of Amen, Majesty," he told me. "It will take several days to muster, organise provisioning and arm them all."

I nodded. I knew I could depend on him to know exactly what was possible. That meant that five thousand foot soldiers and five hundred war chariots would soon be dispatched to the aid of the beleaguered soldiers at Semna. "How long will it take to reach the forts?"

"It is a ten days' march," responded Pen-Nekhbet.

"Will they be able to hold out so long?"

"They will not be overrun," stated Pen-Nekhbet confidently. "The fort at Semna West is a sturdy construction with bastions and towers to the landward side. On the river side steep cliffs fall down to the water. They should be able to hold it until we arrive."

Anger at the presumption of the rebels rose in me. Doubtless they thought that Egypt, ruled by a woman and a child, would be an easy target. That rather than fight, we would leave the soldiers holding our outposts at their mercy. That we would give up our southern dominion by default. They would discover that they were in error. I was the daughter of a great warrior Pharaoh, who had marked our northern and our southern boundaries with massive steles, one in Palestine and the other deep in Upper Nubia. Under my rule these boundaries would not shrink, not by one cubit. At the same time I was myself the divine son of Ra, and the care of this kingdom had been given into my hands. I would not fail my people. I would not.

I lifted my chin. "In no less than five days, I will expect to depart," I told Hapuseneb. "You will govern in my absence and ensure that all the daily rituals take place."

Hapuseneb was not a man who easily showed his emotions, but he looked totally astounded at my words. "Majesty!" he exclaimed. "You cannot intend to go yourself!"

"I am Supreme Commander of the army," I pointed out. "Who better to lead the troops?"

"But General Pen-Nekhbet . . ."

"Yes. I trust, General, that you will command one last campaign. Well, in truth it will be a punitive expedition, not all-out war. Let us not exaggerate. Can we depend on you?"

The old soldier straightened his shoulders. "Indeed you can. But Majesty, there is no need for you . . . Truly, it is not . . . it is not appropriate . . ."

"It is entirely appropriate for the Pharaoh to protect the realm," I stated. "Also our dominions must know that we will tolerate no rebellions. And the soldiers must be heartened and inspired by the sight of their Pharaoh at the head of the host."

Seni was frowning disapprovingly. "Majesty, with all due respect, what do you know of a forced march through the desert? Of sleeping hard and going thirsty? Of hardships that wring the body, before even taking the field against the enemy?"

"What do you know of childbirth?" I asked him. He blinked. "I have been wrung too," I said. "If the men can survive, I can survive."

"Many will die," said Hapuseneb, his high-pitched voice rising in agitation. "In combat. We cannot afford to lose our Pharaoh, so recently crowned, to a barbarian horde. Surely, Majesty, you do not intend to engage . . ."

"I shall lead the squadron of war chariots onto the field," I stated, "and take part in the initial onslaught by the archers. I am well trained in archery as you all know."

They did know, but they liked it not. Seni muttered something about a stationary target and an attacking warrior, but I ignored him. "Thereafter I shall take up a position towards the rear, from where I may still pick off some of the enemy. I am determined to do this, gentlemen. Pharaoh has spoken."

They were silent. Then Hapuseneb sighed. "Very well. I shall order a litter for Your Majesty . . ."

"I have absolutely no intention of going to war in a litter," I told him. "You will find me the Pharaoh's war chariot to ride in and an able charioteer."

"Yes, Majesty," conceded Hapuseneb. He made an obeisance. But his back was stiff.

The next verbal battle I had was with Senenmut. He wanted desperately to accompany the expedition. Several scribes would of course be required, to help keep track of supplies, draw up dispatches and so forth. But I insisted that he remain in Thebes.

"I need someone to be here whom I can trust implicitly," I said. "There will be no coups in my absence as long as that person acts as my eyes and ears."

"But Majesty! Hapuseneb . . ."

"It is precisely the priesthood that I do not altogether trust," I said. "Remember that they have the child."

He nodded reluctantly. "That is true. But if you do not go at all – Majesty, you should not be doing this. It is not fitting for a woman."

I stated angrily: "It is my duty as the Pharaoh."

"Pharaoh can delegate the conduct of warfare to the generals. It has been done before, it will again. Your late husband . . ."

"My late husband, may he live, was not strong. It is time to show the vassal states that Egypt has become stronger now, not weaker still. I must demonstrate my absolute resolve. Surely you understand this?" I wanted him to agree. He always did understand my heart.

"You could be killed, and I . . . and . . . and Egypt would be bereft."

I looked searchingly into his dark eyes. "And you? Is that what you said?"

"I spoke out of turn, Majesty. Please forgive your humble servant." Yet though his words were humble, his regard remained intense. He stood erect, stiffly correct, but I sensed turmoil behind the discipline.

How I yearned in that moment to reach out to him, to feel his arms enfold me, to be held, to be kissed, to say farewell as one would to a lover! I knew in my bones that that was also his desire. I felt my own limbs tremble. But I was Pharaoh and I could not give in. Steadily, I said: "I hereby appoint you Chief of All Works and Chief Steward of Amen, with all the rights and privileges that those positions entail."

That surprised him. "Majesty is good," he said. A faint smile curled his lips. "Hapuseneb will not be pleased."

"Hapuseneb cannot hold all the offices in the land," I snapped. "These appointments will give you sufficient authority to keep a check on him."

This appealed to Senenmut. A twinkle appeared in his eye and he relaxed somewhat. "Majesty is good," he repeated.

Within less than a week the Division of Amen was ready to depart. I too had been making my preparations. Hapuseneb had had the war chariot of the King brought out of storage where it had been placed when my late husband, may he live, became too ill and weak to ride in it; sadly, this was soon into his short reign.

The small, light body of the chariot, slung between huge spoked wheels, was elegantly worked in gold and gleamed in the brilliant sunshine. The two hardy little horses that drew it tossed their heads and whinnied. Suddenly the expedition became a reality to me, and I was filled with equal parts of excitement and trepidation. Could I do this?

Clearly my charioteer did not think so. When he reported for duty I ordered him to take me outside the city walls for training exercises. He was a short, broad-shouldered fellow named Nofru, with beetling black brows and a jagged scar across his cheek. His manner was taciturn and it was obvious that he disapproved of my intention to lead the expedition. Nor did he look forward to driving a woman into battle. He knew better than to say this, though. Instead he did his best to put me off by driving the horses hard and banking into racing turns designed to throw me off balance as I stood beside him drawing my bow. But not for nothing had I grown up with two brothers, both superb charioteers, archers and hunters; Amenmose, especially, had let me ride with him and I knew how to brace my legs and bend my knees.

I had some young recruits gallop around the training ground holding shields with circles drawn on them so that I could practise hitting a moving target while at the same time moving myself; it was a far cry from archery as a stationary sport, at which I was accustomed to shine. At first my shots went wild. But I practised relentlessly, keeping at it for hours every day. Leather gloves protected my hands, which had else been raw. My eye had always been good and at last I was able to shoot with consistent accuracy. When I swung myself out of the chariot after the last practice session, Nofru gave a grudging nod. This was sweet praise to me.

The morning came when the entire division mustered on a plain outside the city. I was dressed in a leather kilt, linen shirt covered in metal scales, and wore on my head the khepresh, the Pharaoh's blue leather fighting helmet that is also a crown. I strode onto the dais where General Pen-Nekhbet and Hapuseneb already stood. The golden standard of Amen reflected the sunlight as if conveying the blessing of the God. The serried ranks of infantry, five thousand men, stretched out in three directions before me, the bronze tips of their lances catching the sun. They were flanked by the chariots, each bearing two riders, the charioteer holding the restless horses in check. It seemed to me that there was a kind of vibration in the air that intensified as I took up my position front and centre.

"Soldiers of Khemet!" I said. I had had practice in speaking to crowds but never to such a multitude as this. I pitched my voice to carry; I was glad to note that it rang out clearly without being shrill. "You are our response to a challenge that must not go unpunished. Our southern boundary is threatened, and if we allow it to be breached with impunity, all of our enemies will take heart. This must not happen. Instead, the foul barbarians must be taught a lesson that will cause all others who might plan rebellion to give up before they even begin.

"I stand before you today not as a woman, but as your Pharaoh, who holds the safety of Khemet unutterably dear. I know that I, and the people of Khemet, can depend absolutely on your valour and your fighting skills. No attack on our sovereignty will be tolerated! Retribution must be swift and it must be merciless. Take no prisoners! Go forth to glory!"

Ringing cheers swept across the plain. I stepped down from the dais and mounted my chariot, ready to fall in behind the Shock Troops, those battle-hardened veterans who bore the initial brunt of any onslaught and who would lead the march as they would lead the first attack. Of course, mounted scouts had already departed. Pen-Nekhbet would also ride; time was when he would have marched with his men, but his stiff hip precluded that. Close to us would march the Braves of the King, an elite group who had also seen much of war. Then the thousands of infantry, the least experienced bringing up the rear, followed by mules bearing tents and extra supplies. Riding in the vanguard of this military caravan gave me a heady feeling of exhilaration.

As the day wore on, I soon realised that battle dress was not the appropriate wear for a march across the desert, and I changed my metal-covered tunic for a thin linen shirt and set the blue helmet aside for the cloth nemset crown.

This was a different world from the Black Land, lying fertile and lush along the river banks; it was the desert, the Red Land, governed by Seth. Harsh and hostile to men. Indeed, it began to seem as if almighty Ra himself had become our enemy, for the sun blazed upon us mercilessly, as though determined to bake our very bones and grind us into dust. Onward and onward our wheels rolled; my eyes stung and watered and I chewed on grit. But not a word of complaint escaped my lips. I had undertaken to do this thing and do it I would. In this manner my warrior father had ridden forth to battle many a time; in this manner my brothers would have gone out to face the enemy; so too my husband, may he live, had his strength been greater. Now it was left to me. And I would conquer.

Our route took us across the sandy plains between the mountains and the Nile. Looking back over my shoulder at the undulating line of grimly marching men, I was suddenly struck by how small we all appeared in contrast to the tremendous rock formations rearing above us. How many times, I wondered, had these towering cliffs witnessed bands of soldiers bent upon destruction? How many of them had watered the desert with their life's blood, never to return? How many of these sons of Khemet was I leading to their doom? But I did my utmost to push aside such thoughts.

When at last we made camp near the river I was almost too stiff to dismount from the chariot and stumble to my tent. My attendant brought buckets of water to bathe me and massaged my weary limbs with unguents, but although I was exhausted, sleep was slow to come. I lay upon my cot shivering under the woollen covers, for the night air had suddenly turned sharply chill, listening to the crunch of my guards' footsteps outside the tent and wondering whether the gods were with us. Surely they must be, I thought, for right was on our side and the priests had assured me that the departure date augured well. At length I slept.

So the march continued, day after day, one punishing royal cubit after another, and the sun leached the breath and strength from us all. At times it seemed to me that I had died and entered the Netherworld, the dread Duat, and having failed the tests of righteousness, had been condemned by the tribunal of the gods to traverse that fearsome world for evermore.

Yet at long last we neared our destination. The forts of East and West Semna were built to command the river, for they sat on cliffs where the Nile, narrowly constricted, passes through a region of hard rock. The North-South road also passes through West Semna, so that the Commander can control land traffic as well. It was late afternoon when we came up to a rocky ridge, some distance from where the main fort lies.

General Pen-Nekhbet came with the battalion commanders to confer with me. "The enemy are encamped on the other side of that ridge," the general said tersely. "Our scouts report that they guard the road on both sides of the main fort, allowing none to pass, either in or out. I would suggest, Majesty, that we dispatch the Shock Troops, a thousand veterans and two hundred chariots to circle around under cover of darkness; then, when the first light breaks, we fall upon them from the north and south at the same time."

"We shall trap them in a pincer and crack them like a nut," I said excitedly.

"Majesty," ventured Pen-Nekhbet, "will you not content yourself with a position high upon the ridge, from where . . ."

"I will ride with the other chariots at dawn," I told him curtly. "Pharaoh has spoken."

The night wind was as cold as the breath of Seth. The moon was almost full and cast an eerie bluish light over the scene. Around our tiny tents the limitless desert stretched. A distant rumbling could be heard; it was the voice of Hapi roaring through the rocky cleft. Occasionally a horse neighed. Otherwise silence reigned. The officers had departed and, except for the ever vigilant royal guards outside the tent, I was alone. I had told my attendant to go to sleep and she lay curled up on the mat beside my cot, breathing evenly.

If ever there was a time to commune with the gods, I thought, it is now. Standing there in the desert I turned my face to the night sky, which glittered with a myriad points of light. Even now Amen-Ra was traversing the Netherworld in his solar barque, evading and conquering evil spirits and the serpent Apophis, to emerge victorious and powerful enough to recreate the universe in the morning. I had dedicated this expedition to my heavenly father and I had to believe that we had his support. Yet at that moment he seemed to be very distant, perhaps too preoccupied to pay attention to his earthly daughter in her hour of need. This was not a time to pray to Hathor, goddess of love, nor to Hapi the bountiful. This was a time to entreat the support of Sekhmet, the lion goddess of war, daughter of the sun as I was myself, and destroyer of men. I knelt on the cold and sharply gritty sand. Be thou with me tomorrow, Sekhmet, I prayed. Uphold my courage and resolve, and strengthen my arm. Grant us victory.

I slept fitfully and awoke before the dawn. As the sky began to lighten, the Braves of the King were forming up. Orders were snapped out. One by one the chariots rolled into line, drivers muttering to the horses, wheels grating on the sand. Soon I had taken my place beside Nofru, clad in my battle dress, the Pharoah's blue leather helmet on my head. The horses wore their protective leather quilts. I had my bow, the quiver strapped to my back, and Nofru had an axe stuck into his belt. He and I each wore a dagger strapped to our left arm. I cast a glance over my shoulder and noted the rump of the infantry fanning out.

General Pen-Nekhbet's chariot drove up. "The other arm of the pincer is in place," he told me. "A rider has confirmed it. Enemy scouts have discovered our presence and they prepare for combat. We will move forwards slowly until we have them in sight. Then the chariots will lead the charge at the trumpet call. Majesty . . ."

"I am ready," I said. My knees were shaking, but despite this I felt strangely calm. Still Amen-Ra had not ascended into the sky, but a pale wash of light across the desert announced that this was imminent. The host of warriors began to move inexorably forwards, a tide of men rolling across the sand like the waters of the Nile. As we breasted the rocky ridge, we could see the enemy. They had ringed the base of the fort with their tents. Westward of their encampment lay a stony stretch of desert, and there they had lined up, bowmen in position, a phalanx of dark figures motionless and ominous in the half-light.

Now the shining rim of the God's solar barque showed above the horizon, flooding the plain with brightness. At that moment our trumpets sounded the attack. I took this as a good omen and my heart leaped in me. I heard Pen-Nekhbet's shouted orders to advance and then all the chariots picked up speed to sweep across the plain and loose off a first hail of arrows. Mine lurched as the left wheel struck an obstacle, but Nofru had soon righted us and held the horses on track. A cloud of dust behind the crouching Nubians told me that the Shock Troops were falling upon them from the rear. I heard myself screaming as we tore across the sand: "Khemet! Khemet!" I fixed my eyes on one of their men and shot my first arrow, but we were moving so swiftly amid the churning dust that I could not follow its path.

A howling as of the damned souls in the Duat broke from the barbarian hordes; it seemed to be a battle cry and it caused the hair on my neck to stand on end. Then our infantry were engulfed by a raging river of violence, as the desperate barbarians, set upon on all sides, fought with the utmost strength and savagery and the Egyptians battled to overcome them. Nofru deftly wheeled the chariot around. His control of the horses was superb. We melded into a fine team as he guided the chariot away from the thickest of the fray and circled the perimeter so that I was able to target the enemy and loose off accurate shots. Several of the enemy fell to my arrows.

On the fighting went amid the boiling dust, as cursing men battered and tore at each other; the wounded shrieked and moaned as hacked and broken bodies began to cover the ground and blood flowed like recklessly spilled wine. Chariots were smashed and frantic horses whinnied and screamed in terror and pain. Although Nofru kept me out of the heaviest fighting, I could see that arrows and lances were no longer of much use. Now it was grim hand-to-hand combat with axes and daggers; it was chop and thrust and cut and slash. No quarter asked or given. The stench of horse dung mingled with the metallic odour of blood in the thickening air. It was fast growing unbearably hot as the sun beat down upon the plain.

As the struggle surged to and fro, backing up in whirls and eddies, I had no idea who was gaining the upper hand. For all I knew I had led the troops to a dire defeat. Panting, Nofru drew the horses to a standstill; an arrow from the outskirts of the fray had grazed his forehead and blood was running into his eyes. He wiped them with the back of his wrist. For a breathless interval I seemed to be in a small pool of quiet on the outer edge of it all. Then something whistled past my ear and I saw that a short spear hurled out of the mêlée had pierced his neck. Hot blood spurted over my face as he choked and died, the reins falling slack from his suddenly limp hands. Fury gave me the strength to grab them, steady the horses, and tug his axe from his belt with my other hand. I saw a figure detach itself from the wheeling masses and run towards me, spear in hand.

In that moment I was no longer Hatshepsut. I became as one possessed. I was Sekhmet, daughter of the sun, goddess of war, furious and invincible. I licked Nofru's blood from my lips. I would avenge him. I would have more blood. I hurled the axe at the running man as my brothers had taught me to throw hunting sticks. It struck him in the chest and he dropped to the ground, blood spurting from the gaping wound. Now another attacker came speeding towards me in a low crouch. I snatched my dagger from its strap and threw it in the same manner. It struck the warrior in the eye and he too fell. I howled with glee.

Next moment two Braves of the King had leaped to my side. One vaulted into the chariot, pushing out the lifeless body of Nofru with scant ceremony. "Majesty, we are winning," he panted, "but now they will target you. We must remove you from the battle ground." Despite my protests, he grabbed Nofru's whip and lashed the weary horses into a trot and then a gallop. We swept around the plain and up to the fort, where we were welcomed and whence, it later appeared, the Commander had led an additional force to help rout the fleeing Nubians. Since the Pharaoh had given the order to take no prisoners, men were detailed to slit the throats of all the enemy wounded, leaving them to the jackals.

Yes, we won the day. We taught the rebels a lesson that remained in their memory long enough for the young Thutmose to lead the next reprisal, after he had joined the military in Memphis. I did not personally fight again.

Here endeth the eleventh scroll.

Ibana came this morning to report to me that his men had investigated the suspect tax collector and the documents carried by the courier to Thutmose at Memphis. Somehow I cannot like that man. It is hard to say why, for he is always punctiliously polite and he carries out his duties faithfully. Yet there is something about him that makes me feel cold, like walking into a dark room at midday.

As usual, the slave had to bring a bowl of water for him to wash his hands. I had to order the door to the small audience chamber to be firmly closed and the guards to stand some distance down the corridor. Only then would he speak.

"It has taken a while," he told me, "but we have some answers. Now, the tax collector . . ."

"Yes?"

"He is at least that which he purports to be. Of course he may be more than that . . . we know of such instances . . ." He smiled, dryly. "But he does officiate as a tax collector. The reason why he comes so often to the house of Hapuseneb bearing redundant lists . . ."

"Well?"

"He seeks the hand of the eldest daughter of the house in marriage. She is indeed a pretty girl."

"Oh." I know that Hapuseneb and his wife, Amenhotep, have a large brood. It is generally known that at home she reigns supreme, and that despite all his titles and authority in the country at large he jumps to it when she speaks. It always amuses me to imagine this.

"The two eldest are sons, and then there is Henut. The one that has caught the tax collector's fancy. Hapuseneb would let him have her hand, but the mother . . ."

"He will not cross his wife, I understand?"

Ibana smiled austerely. He too finds it amusing that the great man is ruled by his wife. "She will not have it. Her daughter is yet young, she says, and she has need of her at home. The tax-collector seeks to convince them otherwise, but so far without success."

"He will not prevail against Amenhotep," I said. "So. Is that all?"

"In his case, we were unable to uncover any other activities that appeared odd. So, the next step was to intercept the courier. We made it look as if some desert brigands had attacked him to steal his horse. It is a remarkably fine animal. What does Your Majesty wish us to do with it?"

"Won't he . . . when he recovers . . ."

"He will not recover," Ibana stated, his voice devoid of emotion. "When the documents he carried proved to be unexceptional, it was necessary to interrogate him . . . ah . . . thoroughly. To be sure that he carried no more . . . ah . . . interesting communications . . . in his head, so to speak. It does not appear that he did."

"I see."

Just then, Sekhmet stalked into the room. She stepped daintily over to Ibana and leapt onto his lap. He stroked her tenderly. Looking at those hands on her fur, I suddenly felt quite nauseous. I cleared my throat. "And the documents . . . ? What . . . ?"

"The Grand Vizier receives reports on the progress of newly promoted officers. He sends reviews of new training programmes, as Minister of War."

"Nothing more?"

"Nothing. Unless there is some code involved. We examined the documents with great care and we could discover no coded messages."

"Oh," I said.

"So. As always we shall continue to keep a constant watch," Ibana promised. He unfolded his legs. "Do I have Your Majesty's permission to depart?"

"Yes, yes."

"Ah . . . the horse?"

"Keep it," I said. "But be discreet."

"I am always discreet, Majesty. If I might just wash my hands again?"

"Of course." I opened the door and called for a slave.

This matter has disturbed me. I do understand that the security of the throne must be paramount for Khemet to survive. I also accept that security must be paid for in terms of risks taken and that such risks may sometimes cost lives. One cannot be Pharaoh without allowing for such things. Yet I am not happy with the attitude that Ibana exhibits. I know that he must be ruthless, but to show not the smallest degree of regret that an innocent man has been killed – that surely requires an adamantine heart. For my part I do regret it. I regret it greatly. I wish that I could wash my hands of it as lightly as Ibana does. Sometimes, it seems that to maintain Ma'at one must contravene Ma'at.

Yet, as far as Thutmose is concerned, I must be vigilant. Throughout my reign, this one problem has dogged me like a wolf on the trail of a goat: the co-regency of my nephew-stepson. While he was a child, I could keep him from exercising power. As I have written, I sent him to the Aten priests at Heliopolis when I was crowned. After the battle in Nubia I had peace for four years and I could move forward with my programme of rebuilding the temples of the gods all over Khemet that the Hyksos had allowed to fall into ruin. This employed many men and it was good for the land as a whole. At the same time I consolidated the gains achieved through conquest by my royal father, may he live, whilst maintaining good relations with our vassal states.

When Thutmose was sixteen, however, there was trouble at the temple school. Hapuseneb reported that he had seduced the wife of the Chief Priest of the Aten, no less, and when that worthy objected, he knocked the fellow out cold and threw him head first into the sacred lake, where he would have drowned had not some acolytes gone to his assistance. After this episode, the priests advised me to transfer him to the army training centre at Memphis. That should absorb a good deal of his restless energy, I thought, so I agreed.

The life of a soldier suits Thutmose perfectly. He has developed into a fearsome warrior, excelling as an archer shooting from a horse-drawn chariot. He draws a bow that men much taller than him cannot even bend. Soon he had become a standard bearer and then, in his nineteenth year, I was forced to appoint him Commander of the Army. It is a post traditionally held by the Crown Prince; and besides, one is obliged to admit, it would have been his on merit. The military revere him and he has strong generals; he leads men well and he inspires devotion in his followers. Now, in his thirty-second year, he grows ever more restless and ambitious and it is hard to hold him in check.

Last week Khani came again to report on military activities. He told me that, according to his informants in Memphis, the general preparations for a military undertaking of some magnitude were still progressing according to the orders of Commander Thutmose.

"Majesty," he said, "he behaves more like a reigning Pharaoh every day."

"I have thought that I should send him on some kind of expedition," I said. "One that would make good sense, that he could not within reason refuse. But not to Hatti." I chewed some dates and winced. A tooth at the back of my mouth has been plaguing me and the sticky, sweet date caused me pain.

"No, not to Hatti. If he undertakes a punitive raid to the land of the Hittites again, he will probably prevail," said Khani, observing me shrewdly. "And then he would return in triumph, bringing booty, treasure, prisoners, women and slaves."

"And he would be an even more popular hero than when he returned after putting down the latest uprising in Kush," I nodded. "That would not suit me. But tell me, Khani – how necessary is it that Egypt should act against the Hittites? Are they indeed mustering? Will Syria remain loyal to us? Will they hold steadfast as a buffer? Seni has said that he does not believe an attack on our borders is imminent. Should I believe him?"

Khani considered. "At first I thought the reports were exaggerated, Majesty," he responded. "But we have had more informers bringing tales that should give us cause for concern. While I agree with Seni that attack on our borders is unlikely at this time . . ."

"Most unlikely, I imagine," I said. "Syria and Canaan are still our allies, after all."

". . . yet the Hittites are growing arrogant. Perhaps it will soon be time for the lion of Egypt to roar."

I sighed. I detest warfare – throughout my reign, ever since I myself went on campaign, I have tried to limit violent hostilities. Yet as Pharaoh I must keep my country safe and at times that demands acts of war. Then they must be carried out. I prefer Thutmose to bear that responsibility, and yet I do not want him to achieve too much success. It is a dilemma in more than one way.

"I shall send him to Kush again," I said. "I imagine he will not be loath to go, to return to the scene of his earlier triumph."

"Kush is at present suitably cowed," said Khani. I looked at him sharply, suspecting irony, for of course Khani is Nubian-born and it could be that he would wish his country to cast off the grip of the Pharaoh. But I believe he has lived in Egypt long enough to understand that Egypt is the centre of the world and that it has been ordained that we should have dominion over the outlying lands. I think of him as an Egyptian, usually.

"All the same," I said. "I might order Thutmose to take a couple of companies to the South, to inspect the line of fortresses that control our border with Nubia. I shall claim to have information that they are planning an uprising. He cannot deny that it is imperative for us to maintain order in that area . . ."

"Hardly," said Khani dryly, "Given the amount of gold Egypt receives from Nubia."

Again I wondered at his tone, but his eyes were steady. I nodded. "I will convince Seni to support me in this."

"But what of our defences in the north-east?" he enquired.

"Perhaps we should send a division or two northwards to demonstrate our might and readiness. That might be sufficient to avoid war altogether. You could take overall command."

His shoulders squared. "I have not the rank," he objected.

"Promotion lies in the gift of the Pharaoh," I pointed out. "Yours is overdue."

"The Great Commander will not like that. Not at all."

"I care not what the Great Little Commander likes or does not like," I told him. "I am Pharaoh. You should leave your second-in-command in charge here, and go north with the divisions of Horus and Sekhmet. If you travel to Memphis on horseback, how long before you could depart?"

"With just two divisions, we can take the field within three weeks." As usual he looked imperturbable, but I had a sense of tension being tightly coiled in him.

"I will give commands," I promised.

As Khani left, swiftly and silently as usual, a sudden movement caught my eye. It was Bek, my little dwarf, whose legs have been out of splints for several weeks now. He came trotting onto the portico, and then he attempted to do one of his trademark somersaults. It was a dismal failure. He battled to sit upright after the roll; his wig and the false ears came off and ended up on his lap. Disconsolately he shook his bald and earless head.

"When is an ear not an ear?" he asked me.

"I give up," I said, holding back tears.

"When it's an earwig," he said, cackling mirthlessly. He clapped the contraption back on his head. "And when is a double crown not a double crown?" he asked, peering slyly through the false hair.

"Tell me?"

"When there are two heads to wear it."

Yes, I thought, Bek speaks the truth.

I gave the matter careful consideration, and I have taken two decisive steps. The continuation of covert military activities that were not sanctioned by me cannot be allowed to carry on unchecked. Equally, though, the army must be ready for any genuine contingencies and fully alert at all times. Therefore I have promoted Khani to the rank of general and I have ordered Thutmose to lead an expedition to the South to ensure that all is well on our border with the Land of Kush.

Khani was amazed at his promotion. Despite my earlier promise, he had not expected it. "But . . . but . . . Majesty," he protested. "The other generals – will they accept me? A foreigner, and a Nubian?"

"Are you not an Egyptian now, Khani?" I asked, looking at him searchingly.

His black eyes did not waver. "Indeed I am," he said. "When we were conquered . . . when I was brought here . . ."

"Yes?" I had often wondered what his feelings had been, but he was never one to speak easily of what was in his heart.

"We lost to superior warriors," he said. "They were . . . unstoppable. We were comprehensively outfought. Naturally I was devastated, but still, I had to admire them. I thought that I too would die that day, when I was brought before the King. I was prepared for it. But Majesty, you spoke for me. I understood that, although I did not understand the language then."

"At the time I did not realise that," I said. "How stupid of me."

"Still, I understood that you saved my life," said Khani. "So my life is yours to order as you will. Egypt is my home and you are my King. I am committed to your service."

"I know it, Khani," I said. "The generals must accept you. You have been excellently trained, you are very able and you lead men well. Besides, General Nehsi is a Nubian and he is widely respected. I foresee no problems."

"Thank you, Majesty. I am greatly honoured. I pledge eternal loyalty to you and to Khemet." He made a deep obeisance.

His promotion has been due for some time, on the grounds of service and ability, not mere closeness to My Majesty. He serves me well. So have a large number of able men. I have always preferred men to women, who so often seem to think only about small things.

My orders led to an acrimonious and exhausting scene in the Grand Audience Chamber, but I was steadfast. I had insisted that Thutmose come from Memphis to receive my instructions, so that he could not get away with claiming to be out of the city on a hunt or some such excuse.

He was enraged and strode the floor like a caged lion. "If there is a rebellion on the boil in the South – and I have not personally had warning of this . . ."

"I have better spies than you do, nephew," I said.

"Then some other general could be sent. Why on earth must I, the Great Commander, lead a mere couple of companies . . ."

"The Land of Kush must be suitably cowed," I said, using Khani's words to me. "They must be in no doubt that Egypt takes any kind of rebellion with the utmost seriousness, and that we are absolutely determined to quash anything of the sort. What better way to convey this message than to send the Great Commander himself?"

"Must act decisively," agreed Seni, in his clipped tones. "Essential to be firm. Very firm."

"But what about the North?" demanded Thutmose. "Have we not had warnings that matters there . . ."

"All the more reason for you to go to Kush," I said. "We have the bulk of the army in Memphis, with competent generals, should it be necessary to ward off attacks on our northern borders. But if we neglect to secure the South, we could be caught in an enormous pincer that could crush the Two Lands like a nut. That would be disastrous."

Seni and the senior military advisers present were nodding.

Thutmose glared at me furiously but impotently. He could not question the capabilities of his generals, after all. Nor could he claim to be involved in preparations for a major incursion of which his Pharaoh was unaware.

"Take two companies from the Division of Sobek, since they are stationed here," I told him. "Khani is their commander, but it would not be politic to send him to quell Kush, you must admit."

"Definitely not," agreed Seni.

Thutmose opened and closed his mouth but found no words and ground his buck teeth instead.

"It may eventually be necessary for a serious military campaign in the North," I acknowledged, "but not immediately, and there are other options to be tried before we send our entire army on the Horus road. Prudence, and patience, my good nephew, may save both the Two Lands and the flower of its men. Prudence and patience are qualities sometimes underestimated by the military, but of great value in proper governance."

Several of the men present chuckled audibly at this. Thutmose was not known for his patience. It would do him good to be obedient.

"Perhaps the army could conduct some military exercises in the Sinai while you are gone," I proposed. "That would keep them sharp and show the vassal states, especially Canaan and Syria, that Egypt does not sleep. But the southern forts must be supported. You are to leave within seven days. Pharaoh has spoken."

Thutmose could do nothing else but acquiesce, but he did not do so graciously.

"Military exercises!" he muttered to his cronies as I turned to leave. "By Seth and all his devils! Pah! That is what comes of having a female Pharaoh who knows nothing of warfare and precious little of government!"

Had he said this to my face I would have had to have him arrested. But that would not have suited me. It could lead to serious unrest, and besides there is no more suitable royal person to follow me on the Double Throne. But while I breathe he is no more than a junior co-regent and he must know his place. He shall not usurp my authority, nor shall he force a showdown with me. I pretended to be hard of hearing and I swept out. Yet I heard him clearly, and I shall not forget.

It is not true that I know nothing of warfare. I have had experience of it, and it has made me detest war and avoid it by all means at my command. I have never been completely free of the after-effects of that battle in Nubia. For soon after we had returned to Thebes, when life had resumed its usual routine and I was securely positioned on the throne, I began to have the dream – the dream that has since then recurred throughout my life. It changes in some details, but in essence it is the same.

The first time it came to me was about one month later, when I had recovered physically and had, I thought, relegated the terrible memories of that experience to the past, put them away as I had my battle dress, neatly folded up and stored in a chest under some cloaks with the lid firmly tied down and sealed.

In this dream I am there again, on that battlefield. It is extra-ordinarily real, without any of the strange distortions and improbable events that usually occur in dreams. I dream that I am on foot and alone, armed with only my dagger. Well, that detail is strange, for in truth I never left my chariot that day, but it would not have been impossible.

I feel again the burning sun upon my skin and the perspiration running down inside my tunic with its metal disks. I smell the dry hot dust and the horse manure and the peculiar odour of fresh blood. I hear the horses whinnying and the thundering of hooves and the wheels of the chariots crunching on the sand as they race by. I hear the barbarians howl their battle cry. And then all these sounds fade and I hear only a voice, urgent in my ears, and what it says, over and over, is: *Kill him for Khemet! Kill him for Khemet!*

The confused mêlée parts and a man runs towards me. It is the Nubian soldier, the one I struck down by hurling my dagger into his eye. Indeed, as he runs towards me his left eye streams blood, which drips onto his naked torso. But unlike that day he does not fall. In my dream this makes me angry, for have I not killed him already? But still he keeps coming. So I have to strike again, and he is now so close that I do not throw the dagger, I drive it straight into his other eye. It feels like jabbing a melon. More blood spurts out and he stumbles blindly until he finally drops at my feet.

Now everything happens very slowly. Around me the sights as well as the sounds of the battle fade away. I roll the Nubian onto his back with my foot. I see that he has ritual scars upon his cheeks and long earlobes stretched by the weight of golden hoops. I kneel down on the burning hot sand, which grates into my knees. But I do not care. Because I am overcome with an overwhelming, insatiable, terrible thirst: a thirst for blood. I put my hands on the dead man's shoulders and I lean forward and I suck and lap at his bleeding eyes. I am so thirsty, but the blood is not enough. I must have more blood.

I look at my hands and they have turned into a lion's paws. I cry out, but my voice has become a roar. I am Sekhmet. I sit back on my haunches in the desert and I roar my lust for blood. As I look around me, there are no more human beings in sight. Nothing but the boundless desert that stretches around me, growing ever vaster as

I watch, while I become smaller and smaller until I am nothing but a speck upon the limitless sand.

Then I wake up.

This dream has taught me what the worst thing is about waging war – the true reason why war distorts Ma'at. It is not, in the first place, the violence and the suffering. It is not the cutting down of men who should have seen many more harvests and watched their children grow. It is not the wailing of the mothers, the widows and the fatherless children left to struggle alone. Dreadful though these things are, they are not the worst. The worst is: War makes desirable that which is terrible. That is not Ma'at.

Here endeth the twelfth scroll.

THIS IS DREADFUL, dreadful. I was afraid that some such thing might happen and now it has. As a result of my report based on the observations of Ahmose, an innocent man has died. A man who did nothing against the crown, a man who was merely doing his job. And now . . . because of me . . . It makes me feel quite sick to think of it. But in truth, all those visits from a tax collector . . . well, it did appear strange. There could have been a plot. How was one to know?

I do understand why Her Majesty has to be vigilant where the Great Commander is concerned. His shadow seems always to be looming over her throne. I understand that Her Majesty feels that she is being threatened and of course she must act. Yet it does seem . . . it does seem radical. One wonders if it might not be advisable simply to allow Commander Thutmose a greater role in government, particularly as regards military matters. The fact remains that *he has been crowned.* How long can she hope to keep him under her thumb? And is that truly best for Khemet?

Oh, dear, oh dear, I am not suited to involvement in political matters. I am a scribe. I note things down. I make lists. I write letters and formal documents. I record events. I do not want blood on my hands. I cannot sleep at night. I wish I had never begun to get involved in such things!

THE THIRTEENTH SCROLL

THE REIGN OF HATSHEPSUT YEAR 20:
THE FOURTH MONTH OF PERET DAY 30

Yesterday I had a long discussion with Dhutmose, Vizier of the North. I require him to report to me in person regularly and we have private talks before he joins in the deliberations of the Great Council. We met in a small audience chamber, but I made certain that I had a throne chair to sit on and I kept him standing for a while before I graciously invited him to be seated on a low divan. He is no longer young and he is fat and a low seat is awkward for him, especially when he has to rise again. Also I had my back to the window, through which the morning sun streamed, shining brightly on his balding head with the greasy black ringlets artfully disposed to seem more than they are. He had to mop the perspiration from his brow. I learned a trick or two from my late father, may he live; men are often uncomfortable in my presence without quite knowing why.

The slaves brought cooled and watered wine, some dates and roasted lotus seeds, and I had them all tasted. Then I ordered the slaves out and told the guards to stand outside and allow no-one to disturb us.

"Well, Dhutmose," I said, after routine matters had been disposed of. "What else can you tell me of note?"

He took a date in his fat, beringed fingers and chewed it thoroughly. I noticed that he winced slightly and thought to myself that he too seems to have trouble with his teeth. "An excellent harvest may be expected," he said. This was good news, which I had already heard from my network of tax collectors who checked on agricultural production across the Black Land on behalf of the Pharaoh.

"Hapi has been bountiful," I agreed. During the past flood season the Nile did indeed rise to just the right extent.

Dhutmose proceeded to report further on a variety of administrative matters. There were no problems of note, and furthermore they were introducing a new device called a shaduf that would help the farmers irrigate more fields, he told me. It would increase yields.

"Pharaoh is pleased," I said. "Well, if that is all our business, we have time for a game of senet before our consultations with the Treasurer, have we not?"

"Yes, Majesty," said Dhutmose, whose understanding is as sharp as his body is fat and who likes to match his wits with mine. I clapped my hands and ordered the senet box to be brought and set up on a low table that has the shape of a slave woman crouching beneath a slab of inlaid and polished wood. We set up the pieces and threw the sticks to determine who would move first. He had the better of me.

For a while we concentrated in silence, taking turns to move. I usually won the race to clear all my pieces off the board, but he was a shrewd player himself. His small black eyes, deep in creases of fat, scanned the status of the pieces. Then he murmured: "The Great Commander has taken the road to the South, we are told. A punitive expedition against the Land of Kush?" He moved.

"A rebellion smouldering at the primary fort," I told him. I countered his move.

"Ah. The Commander is a man of great courage in battle, of course."

"Yes," I said shortly.

"His reputation is known to all." The sly black eyes peered at me and then slid away. "I have a nephew, a division commander in the army, who assures me that it is well deserved. One hears that he is fearless when driving his chariot. Too fearless, perhaps. Accidents happen so quickly."

I looked at him sharply. Dhutmose was boxing me onto a danger square. He removed a piece from the board without meeting my eyes.

"An affrighted horse, a loose wheel," he suggested, silkily. "A fall in the desert, a head injury . . ."

I shuddered, remembering the death of my brother Amenmose, all those years ago. "The Commander has taken spills," I said, "and survived them." I managed to move onto a safe space.

"Ah, yes. And he has killed more than a few lions too, one hears."

"Yes," I snapped. "He is an able hunter." I removed a piece also.

"Yet nobody is completely invincible," said Dhutmose, making a crafty move. "If, for example, an asp were to slither into his tent one night . . ."

"That would be fatal," I agreed. There is no known cure for the bite of an asp. I removed another piece. Looked carefully at the board, planning my next move. I have been tempted, I admit, to have Thutmose permanently removed. But given the support he enjoys, it would probably not be politic. Also I do not know who might then succeed to the throne of the Two Lands when at last I undertake the journey into the Afterlife. I have always felt so full of vigour that the matter did not concern me much, but this season of seed when the crops are maturing under the winter sun has been a tiring one and I must consider it.

"One understands that General Khani has the support of the army," observed Dhutmose. "A man of great ability, and devoted to Your Majesty."

"But still a Nubian," I said, blocking his next move. "There is a limit to the level to which he can progress. I do not think, for instance, that Khemet is ready for a black Pharaoh just yet."

"Perish the thought," said Dhutmose. "Your Majesty is yet vigorous. Your Majesty will doubtless reign yet for many risings of the Nile."

Long enough, I thought, for another division commander besides Khani to rise through the ranks. When there was none of the royal house left to follow a Pharaoh it has been known for the Commander of the Army to take the Double Throne. Dhutmose's nephew might be such a man. Or was he merely angling to have the Pharaoh deeply in his debt? I stared at the board.

For a while the game proceeded in silence. I could be rid of him, I thought; freed for ever of the wolf cub from Memphis. I need only nod. It would not even be necessary to speak the words. Dhutmose glanced up and his black stare reminded me, for a breathless moment, of the hooded cobra whose head I had grasped on the day of my coronation.

Then I made my final move. His eyes dropped to the game. I said, firmly: "I have every confidence that the Great Commander will return in good health. There is no reason to believe that it will be otherwise."

"Of course not," agreed Dhutmose smoothly. I had wiped the board. "Majesty has won," he conceded.

I had indeed.

"Majesty will live for ever," he said. The prize, in a game of senet, is eternal life.

"I will," I said. I felt assured that my heart was light. It would not weigh heavily against the feather of Ma'at upon the scales of justice in the Netherworld. The thought of that judgement has been much in my mind of late. I leaned back and clapped my hands to order more wine. Bastet jumped onto my lap and settled down, purring. I stroked her, feeling well content. She licked my hand affectionately.

Dhutmose has his uses, but he must be kept in check. He knows that I set men to watch him, but he is never sure exactly who they are, so that he cannot subvert them. As to his implied offer . . . a debt of such magnitude coupled with such secret knowledge would give him power over me that I can never allow.

I sat stroking Bastet after Dhutmose had taken his leave, remembering how I had considered every move to establish My Majesty.

Two methods have served me well: controlling and using powerful men; and propaganda statements made in living stone.

From the beginning of my reign, I have taken care always to counterbalance the power of one man with authority granted to other men so that no-one could ever overshadow the Pharaoh. I alone would wield supreme command. Dhutmose as Vizier of the North has been one counterbalance to my Vizier of the South over the years, but I soon realised that I also needed someone nearer to the throne, both physically and in spirit, to contend effectively with Hapuseneb.

I searched the ranks of my advisers and officials for one who had sufficient character, and I found the very man I needed in a person who until then had not had much authority: Senenmut. Able tutor of the little princess Neferure. Reliable steward of my own and my daughter's property. If he was indeed the man I judged him to be, he would stand up to Hapuseneb. Yes, I thought, Senenmut would be advanced. My Grand Vizier would be surprised. Not pleasantly.

To celebrate my coronation I ordered two statues of myself to be hewn from pink granite, far greater than life-size, showing My Majesty wearing the cloth nemset crown, to be installed at the entrance to the administrative palace on the bank of the Nile in Thebes. I instructed the artist to depart from the usual way of depicting a woman, standing with her feet together, but rather to sculpt me with one foot forward like a man. The male attitude should, I thought, prepare visiting diplomats and ambassadors for an encounter with a woman who is also a King.

In addition, I ordered enormous obelisks to be quarried at Aswan before I was crowned so that they might be ready to be floated down from Aswan on the flood soon after the ceremony. They would be placed at the eastern end of the temple of Amen-Ra at Karnak, where the coronation ceremonies take place, and I would dedicate them to the God who had begotten me. The great architect Ineni, who had overseen such undertakings for my royal father Thutmose the First, may he live, had recently died. So I gave Senenmut the task of ordering, transporting and installing the commemorative obelisks. After all, he had been taught by Ineni, had he not? I would see what he could do.

Hapuseneb had of course assumed that he would be given this task and he was much displeased; more so when, as I had expected, Senenmut carried out the task with remarkable efficiency.

Great was the rejoicing in Thebes when the obelisks were brought on river barges, conveyed to the temple on sledges and installed. I had ordered both obelisks to be clad in gold entirely, not merely the tips, and I had them inscribed with the words of Amen, describing me as his beloved daughter Ma'atkare, and confirming that the God, as my loving father, had ordained me King.

The two colossal obelisks sparkled and shimmered in the brilliant sunlight. I ordered a feast, providing bread and beer for all my people, and a bull was ritually slaughtered. Senenmut was in his element that day and partook in the festivities with great delight. He was then in the prime of his life, having seen twenty-six risings of the Nile: a tall man, well built and charged with energy. He had a natural authority and gift of command that men older and more senior than he might well have wished to possess. He was delighted to have carried out his task successfully, and I was pleased with him.

Music and dancing acclaimed the new Pharaoh in the streets and marketplaces. Joyous hymns resounded in the temples; it was clear that the gods were satisfied. Khemet was safe.

Soon after my coronation, I called Hapuseneb and Senenmut to the small audience chamber. Hapuseneb, assured of his position as Grand Vizier of the South and Chief Priest of Amen, arrived first, impeccable in his white tunic, his coppery skin entirely hairless as a priest's must be. Senenmut reported out of breath with dusty sandals, though his hands were clean. I kept them both standing.

"Hapuseneb," I said, "you worked with Ineni on my late father the Pharaoh's tomb, may they both live, not so?"

"Yes, Majesty." He moved a little aside from the perspiring Senenmut.

"So, you will know exactly where the entrance is located?" Although I had myself walked in my father's funeral procession, I would never be able to find the entrance in that vast, barren amphitheatre once it had been closed up and hidden beneath boulders and scattered rocks.

"Of course, Majesty. I have the co-ordinates here." He tapped his egg-shaped head.

"I want you to open it up, and extend it, with a deeper joint burial chamber, where I may lie with my royal father, in my own sarcophagus."

"But . . . is there not already a tomb . . ."

"Yes, but it is only suitable for a Great Royal Wife. You shall become the Overseer of the King's Tomb, and prepare one suitable for your Pharaoh. With appropriate inscriptions, naturally, and paintings relating to my reign. I know that already you are almost over-burdened, but I confidently entrust this additional great responsibility to you."

"Thank you, Majesty. I am extremely busy, but I can manage one more important task." He stared smugly at Senenmut.

"And as for you, Senenmut, you are to undertake the task of planning and designing my mortuary temple at Djeser-Djeseru. You shall be Overseer of the King's Temple. We shall discuss your ideas."

A delighted grin from Senenmut; a sharp intake of breath from Hapuseneb. Who was immediately jealous, for the mortuary temple would be in the public eye, while the tomb would remain hidden, and no-one would admire what Hapuseneb had wrought.

"I know I can depend on your absolute discretion," I said to Hapuseneb.

"No-one seeing, no-one hearing," murmured Senenmut.

"Of course, Majesty," said Hapuseneb through clenched teeth.

Hapuseneb looked down on Senenmut as an upstart provincial, coming from the small town of Iuny, being born of undistinguished parents, and having been educated by a priest. Hapuseneb, on the other hand, was a child of the palace, since his mother – who was a noblewoman – had waited on my mother the Queen, and he had been educated with the royal children, though before my time. However, it soon became clear that in terms of intellectual power and innate ability he and Senenmut were on an equal footing, and it sorely irked Hapuseneb. But it pleased me greatly and it strengthened my hand in dealing with them. And it amused me to see Hapuseneb seethe.

Of all the building works that I have caused to be done, my temple at Djeser-Djeseru is the one I love the best. It lifts my heart to think of it and I try to visit it often.

Senenmut knew that I had long admired the setting and he understood that it called for something exceptional. He took some time to consider possible designs and then he made a model of his concept, beautifully crafted out of light wood and placed against the mountainous cliffs of the bay where it would stand, sculpted out of some kind of clay and painted to look very realistic. I have it still; it is kept on a table in the palace and little Amenhotep begs to go and look at it when he comes to visit me. I remember so well the day Senenmut showed me the model in his office for the first time.

The model was covered with a linen cloth, so I did not see it at once. I was extremely curious to see what he had designed. He was quite nervous, I could tell, for he walked to and fro and talked too much.

"It will arise beside the partly ruined temple of Mentuhotep the Second," he explained, "but it will replace the building begun for the late Pharaoh Thutmose, may he live. The rear will be hewn out of the rocks, but the main construction in front will be built of limestone, so it will be almost white. The plan . . ."

"Senenmut," I said, "enough discussion. Show me! Why are you so nervous? It is not like you."

"Because, Majesty," he answered, "it is unlike any other temple ever built, except to some degree that of Mentuhotep. It is a design such as the Kingdom of the Two Lands has never seen before. And I have put my heart into it. I am afraid to show Your Majesty." Truly, he was most anxious.

"Show me!"

He took a deep breath and flung the covering aside.

For some moments I stood perfectly still, staring at it. I said not a word. The silence lengthened.

"Majesty," he said, miserably. "Pharaoh is displeased? Perhaps Pharaoh would have preferred a series of tall pylons, leading to a hypostyle hall, enormous pillars crowned with lotuses, and . . ."

"Be quiet," I said. I walked around the table. I saw, indeed, a unique design. It had elements of the old ruin, but it was much grander in scope and it fulfilled my wish that it would dominate the plain. There were three wide porticos fronting broad terraces on different levels, rising gradually from the plain up to where the God's sanctuary would be, deep inside the tall cliffs behind it, hewn out of the Theban rock. The terraces were linked by imposing open-air stairways, dividing the structure into northern and southern halves and leading up to the sanctuary. Its proportions were magically harmonious.

He waited, seeming to hold his breath.

"It is perfect," I said. "It is exquisite."

He sighed deeply with relief and kneeled to kiss the floor in front of my feet. I put out my hand and drew him up. Pharaoh does not lightly touch a subject, but this was a special occasion.

"Do not kneel," I said. "It is I that must kneel to the creator of such beauty."

He bent his head and raised my hand to his lips. His eyes were fixed on mine. He kissed my fingers. It was as if some of his life force passed into me. I had trouble breathing.

Then I took possession of my hand again, taking a backward step. "Explain," I said, "explain the way it will be laid out."

He picked up a wooden pointer tipped with ivory. "As Majesty ordered," he said, "the temple will be dedicated to Amen." I noted that the pointer was trembling.

"My heavenly father, yes." So was my voice.

"Therefore, the main sanctuary will be intended for the secret rites and rituals of Amen. But, since the site is a holy place inhabited by Hathor, there will be a chapel dedicated to the goddess."

"Excellent. On the walls we can show how the goddess suckled me. Here." I stepped forwards again. Our shoulders brushed. He let his arm rest against mine. It was warm. It was as if his life force hummed beneath his skin. We both pretended not to notice.

"There will be smaller shrines within, dedicated to the blessed memory of Pharaoh's ancestors, other gods, and the Pharaohs Thutmose the First and Second, may they live."

"May they live."

Desperately, his hand sought mine and our fingers entangled. My hand clung to his. My knees were shaking. I could hear his breathing, fast and uneven.

"There will be long colonnades," Senenmut continued, after a pause, "with plenty of wall space to record Your Majesty's deeds and the chief events of Your Majesty's reign."

My reign. Yes, I thought. I am the Pharaoh. I withdrew my hand and stepped away from him. "The records should begin with the record of my divine birth," I said, flatly. "And my coronation must be shown."

"Of course. I shall so instruct the artists." He sighed. "And here, Majesty, there will be a chapel dedicated to Anubis."

Anubis. On the walls of that chapel I would depict myself making offerings to the jackal-headed god, who supervises the weighing of one's heart in the Netherworld. That should stand me in good stead when the day of reckoning came. "Most appropriately."

"The columns, as Your Majesty sees, may be square or rounded, but uncrowned. No lotuses."

"Good. I like the pure lines."

At this his tense face relaxed into a smile. "The uppermost level will be a hypostyle hall with twenty-four square-cut pillars faced by painted statues of King Ma'atkare looking out across the Nile. Majesty's mortuary chapel will be located on the south side of the upper courtyard, here." He pointed. "It will be a vaulted chamber, with a doorway in the rear wall leading to the realm of the Afterlife."

"Excellent. Now, in front, as one approaches . . ."

"There will be an avenue," he said, "linking the temple with the old Valley Temple on the Nile. Lined with rows of sphinxes, each with the body of a lion and the head of the Pharaoh. The king of the beasts and the king of men united in one powerful creature. I have not yet made models of these, in case Your Majesty did not approve."

"Pharaoh does approve," I said. "I think it is an exceptionally striking concept."

"Then Pharaoh's servant is happy."

I walked around the model once again. "It will be perfect for the Feast of the Valley," I said. "When we bring the god Amen from Karnak to the Valley Temple in the second month of summer. I often think of the dark and secret shrine where the God lives and I suspect it must be lonely."

Senenmut agreed: "I too have thought it. With only the priests who ever come near, to carry out the daily rituals and bring the offerings. A lonely existence."

"But we will bring the God out of the gloom into the brilliant sun and transport him across the Nile to spend the night with Hathor at Djeser-Djeseru."

"One night of joyous feasting," he said, smiling in delight. "And the populace will take part, and they will be amazed at the glorious temple raised up for Pharaoh Hatshepsut. It will be a memorable feast, in a magnificent setting."

I nodded. "Pharaoh is greatly pleased," I told him. I stood gazing at the model, musing. "How long will it take, do you think?"

"Many years," he said. "It is a huge undertaking. But I will do the best I can to complete it as soon as possible."

"Well, if the completion is to be well into my reign, I think one more element might be added," I said.

He frowned. "Added?"

"Yes. Here, at the bottom of the first flight of steps."

"What should be added?"

"A pair of obelisks, similar to those ordered for my coronation. I greatly favour obelisks. They should be hewn from white marble. The highlights of my reign should be inscribed upon them. They should . . ."

"No," said Senenmut.

I stared at him. "No? No!"

"No, Majesty, I do not agree. Such strong added verticals would upset the balance of the design. Obelisks would look out of place."

"They would look majestic," I said.

"The cliffs are majestic," said Senenmut. "Against that backdrop, obelisks would appear puny."

"I am sure you are mistaken. I think the design requires obelisks."

"I will not add them," said Senenmut. He closed his lips in a thin line.

"You will do as I say or I will put Hapuseneb in charge of this project!"

"As Your Majesty wishes."

"You forget yourself. I made you. I can unmake you. I'll relegate you to the ranks of junior scribes! Then what will you do?"

"Go back to Iuny," said Senenmut. "I have property there. I can live peacefully raising vegetables. And, perhaps, children."

"I will confiscate your farm," I raged. "I will hang you head downwards from the walls of Thebes! I am Pharaoh!"

"Yes, Majesty," he said, tiredly. "If my life is worth no more than a pair of obelisks, so be it." He knelt at my feet.

I looked down at his thick dark hair. The tide of anger that had coursed through me receded. My heart reproached me. I wanted to reach out and draw him to his feet. In truth, I wanted to be taken into his arms and kissed again, not on my hand but on my lips. But I was Egypt and it could not be.

I stepped nearer to the model. "Are you sure they would look puny?"

"Certain, Majesty."

"Very well, then. You are the architect. Do as you please."

"Thank you, Majesty."

I swept out of his office. He should not see the tears that burned in my eyes. Tears of anger, of course. No, he should not see the Pharaoh weep.

Here endeth the thirteenth scroll.

THE FOURTEENTH SCROLL

Looking back over my life there was one event that changed everything. There was the time before and the time after, and they were entirely different. Before it happened, I was strong, I was resilient; I marched forward, there was nothing that I could not overcome. I felt fortunate. Afterwards I had to muster my strength. I felt vulnerable, like one who has had a terrible illness and has lost some deep-seated vitality that will never return. I was no longer sure that I was the chosen of the gods. If the record I am making here is to be complete, I must write of it, but it is hard to do. Yet I have vowed to tell the truth and write of it I must.

It was Senenmut who first noticed that there was something seriously wrong with Neferure. They were always close, since he had been her tutor before his duties became too onerous and his half-brother Senimen replaced him. However, by the time she fell ill she no longer had a tutor, for she was fourteen years old and a great help to me as Pharaoh. Inet, who had been her nurse, was sixty years old and half blind by then, or she would have warned me. I was deeply involved with building plans at the time and the signs of danger escaped me.

Perhaps Neferure herself had a presentiment. She came to my office in the administrative palace one day, as if she were one of my subjects rather than my daughter. "Mother, I wish to talk to you," she said. "Seriously."

"Yes, my child?" I was reading a scroll with lists of materials and checking the costs, which seemed exorbitant.

"I want you to listen."

"I always listen to you, dear."

"No, really listen. Hear me, Mother."

I looked up, frowning. "Is there a problem?"

"Mother," she said, twisting the edge of her robe nervously, "am I never to be married? Am I only to be the God's Wife of Amen all my life?"

I set the scroll aside and sighed. This was a most problematic issue and I had put off thinking about it for too long. "It is a great honour to be the God's Wife," I observed. "By taking part in the daily rituals, you support the Pharaoh in ensuring the survival and the well-being of Khemet."

"I know that, Mother. But since one must remain pure, it is a lonely life. Never to break the jar with any man, never to bear a child . . . A lonely prospect."

"Is there a . . . a particular man that you have met, to make you feel like this?"

"No, Mother. I do not meet many men, except for the priests, and they all revere me as the God's Wife. It just seems to me . . ."

"Yes?"

"My life is passing," she said, in a rush. "My life is passing, Mother. When you were my age you had already borne me. Yet I am barren and likely to remain so." There were tears in her eyes. "I would like a child," she said. "Of my own."

"My dear, we need to give this matter some thought."

"There is Thutmose," she suggested, "my half-brother. I understand . . . that I am promised to him."

"Who told you that?"

"There are . . . rumours." Put about by the man himself, I thought furiously. She was a child when I made that promise to my late husband, may he live, and I had never mentioned it. I did not think it would be wise.

"He already has a wife," I pointed out. I had, indeed, found him a wife when he was sixteen and went to Memphis to join the military. She was one Satioh, a lusty baggage who I reckoned would keep him further occupied and make him forget that he was betrothed to Neferure. I ordered a comfortable palace to be built for them near to the training grounds. Satioh, a plump, light-skinned Mitannian princess with a high colour, proved to be as fecund as the black silt of the Nile, but she brought forth girl children only, which pleased me. Lacking a son, I had plans for my Neferure, and younger girl children borne to Thutmose could not take precedence over her while a male child might.

"But multiple marriages are common in the royal house," said Neferure, mulishly. "I would be the Great Royal Wife." She knew this would anger me, and indeed it did.

"Absolutely not," I said. "That runt is not a suitable husband for the First Princess of Egypt. No, no. Let me think about this. Come and talk to me again in a week's time."

I did think about it. I could not contemplate giving her to Thutmose. I have never liked him, nor does he like me. We are like two dogs whose hair rises at the scent of the other. No, no. Besides, such a union would strengthen his claim to rule beside me, and I spend much of my energy avoiding that. Yet perhaps she should be mated, I thought; most girls are married younger than she was then.

Perhaps there was a fine young man among the noble families, I thought. But the matter should not be rushed. Like me, my daughter had the pure blood royal and therefore a better claim than Thutmose to the Double Throne. I greatly desired that she should one day be the primary Pharaoh, as I have been. It would no longer be thought so strange to have a female Pharaoh as it was when I first acceded to the throne. I have shown the way. Egypt has been stable and content under my rule. I have maintained Ma'at and kept chaos at bay by honouring the gods, and Egypt has prospered under my rule. Everyone would know that a female Pharaoh is capable of reigning well over the Black Land.

Nonetheless, if I die while Neferure is yet young, I thought, he will assume the throne in her stead. Perhaps it would be a good strategy to match her with a noble's son, who could stand by her side and help her maintain her right to rule. On the other hand, my thinking went, if she marries some other person, she could be relegated to Queen and Great Royal Wife while her husband assumes the title and the power of Pharaoh, and that is likely to cause civil war. Thutmose would never accept it. It was a vexing problem. If only that one who would be King would suffer a hunting accident such as my brother Amenmose did, or die on the battlefield, we would be well rid of him, I thought.

I decided that I would ask Senenmut. He and I conferred daily and I did not delay in putting the question to him. "Do you think it would be advisable for Neferure to be married?" I asked him. "I cannot decide whether it would be well judged or not."

He looked uncomfortable. "Perhaps when she is better, it could be considered," he said.

"Better? What do you mean, better? She has not been ill, except for a bad cough a while ago, but that is over now!"

"Majesty, she has not been well for quite some time," he told me. "You have not noticed it? I assumed . . ."

"Noticed what?"

"The princess Neferure tires quickly and her skin is very pale. Also I have noticed dark marks like bruises on her arms and legs. It has been worrying me, but I thought . . ."

"She has said nothing to me," I answered defensively. "She has not complained."

I called my daughter's chief lady-in-waiting, an elegant and rather vain person, to my office and questioned her. She confirmed that the princess had been listless and had taken to sleeping for hours in the afternoons, which she used not to do.

"But I think the princess does not sleep well at night," said her lady. "She perspires much and she is restless. And she does not eat well. I have tried to tempt her appetite with choice morsels, but . . ." She shrugged her narrow shoulders.

"Why has this not been reported to me?" I asked furiously.

Her kohl-rimmed eyes widened. "Pardon, Majesty, if I have failed in my duty. But the lady is not a child. She did not want . . . I did not think I should presume . . ."

"I am her mother, as well as the Pharaoh," I said, "and I must know when she is ill." I was filled with dread. My late husband Thutmose, may he live, had exhibited the same signs towards the end of his life.

"Humble apologies, Majesty," said the woman, making a deep obeisance. "I will in future report all that I observe."

But already, alas, it was too late. The issue of a possible marriage soon became irrelevant, for within weeks Neferure took to her bed. I could not believe that I had noticed nothing wrong before. She was growing thinner by the day, almost translucent, like an alabaster vase. We tried everything – Hapu, the Chief Physician, had a new suggestion for treatment almost every day, but none of them worked. I fed her pomegranates, spoon by spoon, to try to bring back a blush to her wan cheeks, with no success; we put cool wet linen compresses on her forehead, which soothed but did not cure; she drank watered wine with pulverised dried willow bark in it, which did relieve the fever she had developed, but not for long; she ate various insects mashed up with fat and honey, which only served to make her sick and lose the little food she had been able to consume.

We fought the devils who had gathered around her bed with incense, sistrums, amulets and charms; we beseeched the gods to intervene with incantations and sacrifices; each morning and evening I made her swallow spoonfuls of blood fresh from a slaughtered calf to transfer its life force into her pale body, but all it did was to make her retch. Hapu gave her syrup of figs "to keep the channels open" and at night he prescribed poppy juice in wine. This at least helped her to sleep.

I did not sleep and I ate only a little, just enough so that I did not faint. I poured my spirit into prayers to Imhotep and Bes, imploring them to intervene, begging for a miracle. If the Nile could return every year bringing the good earth, surely the gods could return the life force that was ebbing from my child, I reasoned. Why should she be taken from me? Which of the gods was demanding her presence in the Fields of the Blessed? Was it Anubis, sniffing after her with his jackal's nose? Was it Osiris, wishing for another beauteous sister? It is too soon, I moaned, it is too soon. She has hardly lived.

Senenmut was not allowed to visit her in the residential palace, but he came to my office every day to ask how she was. Even at such a time, the affairs of state could not be set aside, although I tried to get through the necessary business quickly so that I could get back to the room where she lay. One morning, about two weeks after she first took to her bed, he was with me when Hapu the Chief Physician arrived, his round face shiny with perspiration and his eyes wide with dread.

"Majesty," he said, abasing himself and kissing the ground abjectly several times. "Majesty, I fear . . ."

"No!" I cried out. I did not want to hear what he had to tell me. "No!"

"M-M-Majesty . . ." Nor could he say it. He stuttered and mumbled.

"What is it, man?" demanded Senenmut. "Is she worse? Out with it!"

"The, the, the P-Princess Neferure, Majesty . . ." – globules of sweat broke out on his shiny forehead – "has departed to the Afterlife."

"How dare you let her go when I was not there!" I screamed. "I should have been there! You useless little toad!" I dealt his face a resounding slap. Before I could repeat it, Senenmut had caught my arm.

"Hapu," he said, "get out of here and close the door. Tell the guards to let no-one in."

"Y-yes, Sir, yes, at once, Sir," and he scuttled out.

Grief coursed through me like the waters of a desert storm when Seth lets loose his devils and the heavens weep. Senenmut took me in his arms and held me and I clung to him. In that moment I had forgotten that I was the Pharaoh and may not be touched, and so had he. I could not have remained standing without his support.

"The gods knew," I wept, "the gods knew she was the first in my heart. They have taken her to punish me."

He patted my back and rocked me like a child. "I know," he murmured. "I know you loved her. I know it hurts. Cry. You must cry."

I remembered a day when she came to share a meal with me and we were served lentils, which she refused to eat.

"Don't want lentils," she frowned, "want tiger nut sweeties."

She loved tiger nuts, the date and nut balls flavoured with cinnamon and cardamom, and coated in honey and ground almonds, that my chief cook made especially for me.

"Finish your lentils," I said, "they are good for you."

"No," she said, firmly. She had but four summers at the time and I did not take kindly to being opposed by a four-year-old.

"You will sit on that chair until you have finished those lentils," I insisted.

She stuck out her lower lip and lowered her head. And there she sat, as time went by. She did not beg. She did not cry. She just sat there and she waited me out. At length I gave up and Inet took her away. I wished then, remembering that day, that I had given her the sweet things she wanted. What was so important about the wretched lentils, after all? It was just my pride, I admitted to myself; I did not enjoy being crossed. But nor did she.

After the first storm of weeping had passed, I collected myself.

"I must go to her," I told Senenmut. "Please sort out the remaining matters in this office as far as you can and tell everyone else to return another day."

"Yes, Majesty," he said.

I looked at him sharply. His face betrayed that he too was grief-stricken; of course he had loved her dearly, and I had not even thought about his pain. "I thank you, Senenmut," I said gently. Then I went to her room.

The ladies-in-waiting had rent their hair and their clothing and were weeping and wailing as the custom is. I too would join in the public show of grief, but first I needed some quiet time to say farewell. I sent them all out and told them to bring a cake of natron, some soft cloths and a bowl of pure water, and then to leave me alone. This they did.

I kneeled beside the low bed upon which my daughter lay. The sweetness of incense hung in the air. Someone had closed her eyes and she looked peaceful, but it did not comfort me. I was filled with anger at the gods who had stolen her away while I was absent. Yet I would do this one last thing: I would wash her in preparation for what was to come. I took up a cloth and the natron and I began to bathe her carefully. I washed her lovely face and her long slim neck and her shoulders; under her arms, then all along her arms, down to the hands, still bearing traces of henna where her ladies had decorated them before she became so ill. I washed her breasts, which were small and pale like those of a statue, yet still flushed with life and tipped with red like wine. I washed her abdomen that would never carry a babe, her private parts that had known no lover, her long legs that would no longer dance. At last I reached her feet, and they broke my heart. She had such slim and elegant feet. Such perfect toes. I washed them one by one. Very carefully.

Then I turned her over and I washed her back. I washed and

washed. Only I could not wash away the bruises left like stains upon her flesh.

When I had done I laid her down straight and looked at her. Yes, the god Khnum, when he created her body on his potter's wheel, had wrought exceedingly well.

Then I began again.

At length there was a knock at the door and Senenmut peered around it. "Majesty," he said.

"Go away."

"But Majesty . . ."

"Go away!" I shouted. "I am busy here, can you not see? I am . . ."

He came in despite my orders. "Majesty," he said, "it has been hours. You must let her go."

"I am bathing her," I explained.

"I know," he said. He bent down and removed the cloth from my grasp. "But the priests will purify her now. You have done enough." He took my hand and pulled me to my feet. My knees were stiff and painful and I stumbled. Again he supported me. "You must let her go," he repeated.

"They will cut her open. They will cut her open, and they will take out . . . take out . . ." For the second time that day I wept so hard that it hurt my throat.

"Majesty," he said, holding me, "her Ka must have a home. You know it is necessary. You know it must be done. You must let her go, now. The shining ones await her in the Fields of the Blessed. She will not be alone."

"Her heart will be found light, will it not?" I asked. "Ammit will not . . . will not . . ."

"Her heart will be so light that the scale will dip towards the feather of Ma'at," he assured me. "Ammit will go hungry. I am sure of that."

"But they will put her in a sarcophagus," I said, voicing another thought that had preyed on my mind. "She was afraid of that, you know it." With a vividness that wrenched at my heart, I remembered a long-ago day.

When Neferure was eleven and Meryetre eight, Bek had joined the palace staff. He was a gift from General Nehsi, who had bought him on an expedition to Canaan. The same age as Neferure, he had followed her around, trotting in her wake like a little dog, offering presents and making jokes to see her smile. He made her a doll out of a collection of wooden spools – an oddly-jointed doll, with a carved box into which it fit exactly.

The two little girls played with it in the sleepy afternoons, on the palace portico, while Inet watched and I dozed on a day-bed.

"It's an Osiris doll," said Neferure to her sister. "See, it has a sarcophagus."

"His brother Seth made it," said Meryetre, who had been tutored by Senenmut's half-brother Senimen. "And he and his friends tricked Osiris into getting into it. One friend climbed in, but it was too small. And another friend climbed in, but it was too big. And then Osiris climbed in, and it was *just right*." She put the doll into the box. "And Seth closed the lid, and he cast the sar-sarphapocus into the Nile!" At this, she hurled the box into the nearby fish pond, where it floated, half-submerged.

Neferure burst into tears. "No! No! He doesn't want to be inside it! It's scary! It's very, very scary!" Her voice wobbled woefully.

Inet rose from her seat on the portico and limped forward. She reached out with her walking-stick and hooked the box back within reach. She opened it and took out the doll. "But Isis saved him," she reminded Neferure. "His sister-wife saved him, remember?"

Neferure sniffed.

"There," said Inet. "We'll set him down in the sun and let his box dry out. Come on, we'll go and find you a tiger nut sweet."

Meryetre, ignored by all, remained behind. My eyes fell shut.

When Neferure and Inet returned, I awoke to consternation once again. Meryetre had continued the saga of Osiris by sawing the doll into bits with a sharp knife and burying them around the fish pond.

"My doll!" wept Neferure. "You've broken my doll!"

"Well, Seth sawed Osiris up and buried fourteen pieces along the Nile," said Meryetre. There were indeed fourteen little heaps of dirt around the pond. "That is what happened." She stuck her lower lip out.

Neferure sobbed.

"But Isis searched and searched," said Inet, desperately, "and she found all the bits and put them together with her magic. He even gave her a son, Horus, who triumphed over Seth. You know this, Neferure darling. That is why every Pharaoh is the Living Horus. I will dig up the bits and mend the doll, I promise, sweetheart." She glared at Meryetre.

"It will not be the same," said Neferure forlornly. "You keep the doll, now that you've ruined it," she said to her sister. "And keep the sarcophagus too, I don't like it."

"She was afraid of being closed up," I said now to Senenmut.

"But her Ka and her Ba and her Akh will roam free," he reminded me. "You know that the body in the chest is in imitation of Osiris, who was so imprisoned yet is arisen and reigns in the Afterlife. You know it must be done. You cannot prevent it, Majesty."

"No," I agreed desolately. "I cannot prevent it."

"Majesty, you must leave her now. You must come with me, and you must eat."

My head did not seem to be attached to my neck. "Yes," I said. I stepped away from him. Oh, how I hungered still to be held, to be comforted by his strong arms. But I stepped away from him and I straightened my back. I said: "I am still Egypt." And I left the room.

Meryetre was twelve years old when her sister died. She tried her best to comfort me. She would come to my rooms bearing little gifts: a posy of flowers, a bunch of grapes, a cake. Her manner was gentle and she spoke kindly to me, as if I had been the child and she the parent. She has a motherly side that is the best of her. But I would not be comforted.

One day she noticed that the posy she had brought the previous time had lain just where she left it and was withered and colourless. She looked at it and then she looked at me. "Mother," she said. "I am still here. Do you not even see me?"

I looked at the funny little face with the prominent teeth and pleading brown eyes. "Yes, dear," I said, suppressing a sigh. "I do see you."

Three times I had carried a babe, I thought. Three times I had suffered the sickness and the discomfort and the lack of sleep. Three times I had squatted upon the bricks. And one child only remained to show for it. Just like my mother, I thought. Had she too looked at me and felt bereft?

It was from that time, I think, that I began to feel – well, not old perhaps, by any means, but not young any more. Somehow a lustre had gone from the world that it has never regained. Yet life goes on; whether one will or no, life bears one along like a boat of reeds upon the river. One is not given a choice.

Here endeth the fourteenth scroll.

THE FIFTEENTH SCROLL

With Neferure gone to the Fields of the Blessed, Thutmose lost a chance to strengthen his claim to reign. Yet still he harboured aspirations that would have seen him supreme upon the Double Throne had he achieved his desires. It is somewhat ironic that he is my son-in-law now, considering what happened eleven risings of the Nile ago, when I had twenty-eight summers and he was a man of twenty.

The summer was particularly hot that year. I remember that I wore a diaphanous linen robe and a light crown for the private audience that Thutmose had requested. I received him in a small chamber at the residential palace in Thebes. Of course he lived mainly at Memphis – as he does still – where the army has its headquarters, but he came often to the capital. I heard his deep voice greeting the guards by name as he arrived. He makes a point of remembering the names of all his soldiers – one of the ways in which he enlists their loyalty. Also he demands nothing of them that he does not do himself; he is harsh but he is just; he is an able and courageous soldier and by repute a master strategist and tactician on the battle field. One must grant him all of that. His fault is that he does not know his place.

He strode boldly into the room. "Greetings, Majesty," he said. Short though he is, he makes his presence felt.

"Greetings, nephew," I said coolly. We measured each other for a space of time. At twenty, I noted, he was no longer a boy. His shoulders were broad and his bare chest hairy, as were the sturdy legs beneath his brief linen tunic. His shaven head shone with oil and his dark brown eyes stared intently from beneath thick brows. The bulging muscles on his upper arms attested to the strength that enabled him to draw his legendary bow with ease.

For the first time in our lives I saw a man when I looked at him. I do not know for sure how he saw me. Since the death of my darling Neferure the previous year, may she live for ever, I had not had a good appetite, so I do know that I was slim. My women kept my skin smooth and supple with unguents, and because of the heat my head under the crown was shaven, but in any case I had not yet seen any grey hairs. I looked, I felt assured, at least presentable.

"No slaves," he said, glancing at the two young girls who were waving large feathered fans. "Let them bring some cooled wine, and go."

I was immediately angered by his presumption in giving orders as if it were his palace, not mine, but I bit my tongue. I was determined not to let him see that he could annoy me. I believe it to be one of his tactics, to make me lose my self-control and so feel foolish.

"Go and fetch some wine and some things to eat, and then leave us," I ordered the slaves. "Nephew, will you not sit?" I gestured towards a low day-bed.

He looked at it and then at me with a small smile. "Rather a chair, Majesty, if I may?" he said, swinging one closer and sitting down without waiting for permission. We were now eye to eye, or almost, for I am taller than he. "Soft seats do not suit a soldier." His smile broadened mockingly. Of course he knew that seating men uncomfortably at a level below my eyes is an old trick of mine. He set a small wooden chest that he had brought with him down on the tiled floor at his feet. I wondered what it was, but I would not ask. While we waited for the slaves to bring refreshments we spoke of unimportant things. At last we were alone.

"Well, nephew?" I said, leaning back with a glass of cooled wine in my hand. "What matter do you wish to raise with me that must needs be so private? Do you have another grand scheme to march to the Euphrates?"

He looked nettled. "The time will come . . ." he began, but then he bit his lip. "No, Majesty, let us not bandy words on military matters. Those are issues that should be discussed with the military advisers and counsellors. No, I . . . well . . ."

I was not accustomed to seeing him look embarrassed, but he actually seemed ill at ease. "Perhaps the question on your mind has something to do with the mysterious box that you have brought with you," I suggested. "Does it perhaps contain a new game? I must confess that I tire a little of senet." I am extremely good at that traditional game, as well he knew.

"No, it is not a game," he said, rising suddenly and picking up the box. He placed it on a low table that stood at my side. "Please, Majesty, open it."

I inspected the little chest more closely. It was beautifully constructed from cedarwood, standing on four finely carved claws, with bands of polished copper across the domed lid and a clasp shaped like a lotus bud. "It is most elegant," I said. I undid the clasp and folded back the lid. Inside, soft cotton cloths hid some kind of round object.

"Go on," he said, "take it out."

I did so carefully. The wrappings fell open to display a superb vase fashioned from alabaster, with a wide, flaring lip. Carvings on its sides depicted small and delicate birds. "Oh!" I exclaimed. "It's beautiful!"

"A small thing, merely," he murmured.

I rose, taking it over to a table that stood beneath a window. "If I set it here," I said, "the light falls on it and makes it seem to glow. Oh, it is most exceptional. Where did you find it?"

He too had risen and stood regarding the lovely thing that almost seemed to shine with its own light. "Oh, I – well, I . . . didn't find it, exactly. Only the – well, the marble. It is of a particularly good quality. As one can see."

"You found the marble? You mean you made it? You made this yourself?"

"Yes," he admitted. "Yes, I did. I like to work with my hands."

I was astounded. I had heard that he had some skill with design, but I had not dreamed he could be capable of such artistry. "It is beautiful," I said, sincerely. "I thank you. It is a beautiful gift. The chest, too, that it came in, is very handsome. Did you make that as well?"

"Yes," he said. "It has a secret mechanism. Let me show you." He brought the chest over to the table where I stood, closed the lid and pressed twice on the lotus bud. "See? Now it is firmly closed. Nobody can lift the lid."

"But how can it be opened again?"

"Ah. You must know the secret. You must twist it once to the left, and twice to the right." He did so deftly, and the lid clicked open again. "More effective than ropes and seals," he said, smiling.

"It is most intriguing," I said, pressing on the bud to close it. "And now . . . twice to the left . . ."

"No, once to the left. Like this." He stretched out his hand and guided my fingers. "Then, twice to the right." Click, went the lid.

The King in me stiffened, rejecting the forbidden touch. The woman in me responded to the warmth of skin on skin. And he knew it. His hand took possession of mine, he folded both of his strong, warm hands around my hesitant fingers. He turned his head to look into my eyes, so close now that I could see tiny freckles on his olive skin. His dark eyes were too intense for me to face. His gaze seemed to unlock feelings that I had kept under rigid control for so long that I had forgotten their existence. I closed my eyes in an attempt to hide them again.

I felt him draw nearer yet, lean towards me, touch his lips to mine. The King was furious, but in that moment the woman reigned, and she wanted his kiss. So delicately, like a bird alighting on a bough for the space of a breath, then taking flight again, he touched his lips to mine. Ah, his lips were warm. A second kiss, firmer and longer now. The taste of salt. The scent of unguent laced with myrrh and beneath that the perspiration of a man. I inhaled his warmth, his strength, his powerful intensity.

"Hatshepsut," he said, his deep voice lingering over the syllables. His arms had slid around me, one hand in the small of my back, pressing me against him, his desire hard between us.

Yes, yes, the woman groaned, this is good, I want this, oh, yes, I do, it has been so long . . . I want this, I do, I do . . .

But the King was aghast at the sense of losing control. "Oh no," said the voice of the Pharaoh, breathlessly. "No! This may not be!"

"Do not deny it," murmured Thutmose. "Do not deny us. You want it too. You know you do." His kisses were becoming more urgent. He thrust a hand into the top of my thin robe, caressing my breast, gripping it, moving his hard thumb across the nipple, erect and sensitive, sending a thrill of delight coursing through the woman's loins like a stream of water through a dry wadi.

I want this, moaned the woman.

"This must stop," ordered the King.

Thutmose was ignoring the King's husky command.

I began to struggle. "Stop! Stop! Stop it!" Suddenly terrified, I felt like one who was drowning and could no longer breathe. I beat my hands against his shoulders fruitlessly. He picked me up and carried me over to the day-bed. He threw me down on the piled cushions, pulling at my robe. Wildly, I rolled aside as he cast himself down too. He caught my left arm, dragging me closer, pinning me down. In desperation I lunged across, grabbed a copper lamp that stood nearby, and brought it down on his head with a tremendous swing. It was a large and heavy one and it struck him on the forehead, making a nasty gash that streamed blood. He roared with pain, increasing his grip on my other arm until I thought he would snap it like a stick. Frantic now, I hit him again.

The lamp caught him on the temple and he dropped back onto the cushions with a grunt.

By the foul breath of Seth, I thought, I have killed him. I have killed the Great Commander of the Egyptian Army. I knelt beside him, panting and shivering with shock. Then he groaned. I sighed deeply. He was alive, after all. I rose to my feet and rearranged my robe, which was crushed but fortunately not torn, and replaced my crown, which had fallen from my head during the struggle. I looked around me. Quickly, I took a glass of wine and spilled some on the tiles. I dipped my fingers in the blood on his forehead and smeared some onto the corner of the table upon which I had placed the vase. Then I picked up the vase and dropped it, deliberately. It shattered into tiny pieces.

I went to the large double doors, opened them and called the guards.

"Majesty?" They hastened towards me.

"Come!" I called. Two stalwart men entered.

"What has happened?" enquired the more senior.

"The Commander has had a fall," I told them. "He slipped in the wine that the careless slaves spilled, and his head caught the corner of this table, knocking off this vase – here, you see the blood. I managed to get him onto the day-bed. Call the Royal Physician, at once."

"Yes, Majesty." They dashed away.

I stood, still shaking a little, looking at the Great Commander, whose face was pale and bloody and who lay sprawled inelegantly with one hand dangling in a puddle of wine. He groaned again, rolling his head from side to side. It suddenly struck me as being very funny: Here was this fabled warrior, whom nobody had been able to fell in battle, almost killed by a woman. With a lamp. I began to giggle. Then it turned to laughter, and the more I laughed, the harder it was to stop. Then it became mixed up with tears of fright.

In the middle of this fit of mine, Thutmose came to and Hapu arrived, accompanied by the guards. The poor man could not decide whom he should attend to first, the Pharaoh or the Commander. He tutted and stuttered and fussed. Finally he stood on tiptoe right in front of me and bellowed into my face: *"Majesty!"* I do not know whence he summoned the courage to do this, but it had the desired effect of startling me into silence.

"Majesty," he repeated, quietly now, "you have had a shock. I see that the Great Commander has been injured. You should sit down, and I will have a slave bring a calming draught. Now, what . . ."

I repeated my tale of the slip in a puddle of wine and the knock against the table. Thutmose glowered but did not contradict me. I was not sure just how much he clearly remembered, for I have heard that men who suffer a bad blow to the head can sometimes not recall what went immediately before. But he would not be keen to tell the true tale, if indeed he did remember all.

Hapu knelt down beside the day-bed and gently touched the bruises on Thutmose's face. He clucked at the cut above his eyebrow. "I shall have to sew this together," he said. "It is quite deep." His exploring fingers found the second bruise on the temple, the one that had caused Thutmose to pass out. His eyes narrowed. He glanced at me fleetingly, but made no further comment. No fool he, I thought. "If the Commander is able to walk, perhaps it would be better in my office," he suggested. "Then this room can be cleaned and ordered, and Her Majesty can rest."

"Of course I can walk," growled Thutmose, sitting up. "It is nothing." Yet he swayed a little when he stood.

"I am so sorry, nephew," I said. "I hope you may not suffer much pain."

He grunted and left the room without another word, his hand on Hapu's shoulder.

If he did not hate me before that episode, he has certainly hated me ever since. Oh, yes, he hates me, the little man. I know that. He maintains the pretence that he does not, but a pretence is what it is. I think it is not just that I rejected him – rejected and then bested him – that rankles; it is the fact that I laughed. And I believe he knows that I broke the beautiful vase on purpose, even though he was out cold when I did it. He has never forgiven me, for taking first his throne, and then his dignity. To this day he bears the scar.

As for myself, I was more shaken than I ever wanted to admit. It was as if some of my strength and resolve had bled away along with the wound I had inflicted on Thutmose. Hapu was concerned about me. The next afternoon he arrived at the time when I usually rest, bearing a large jug. I offered him a seat on a stool next to my day-bed, feeling too lethargic to arise.

He set the jug down on a little table in the shade. "My wife has made some of her special cordial for you, Majesty," he said. His round face was creased with a worried frown. "She boils it up with herbs. It has restorative qualities. You should drink as much as you are able to stomach, for it is slightly bitter."

This simple act of kindness was suddenly too much for me. The tears began coursing down my cheeks and I was powerless to stop them. They simply streamed, as if all the old aches of loss and longing had filled up a deep reservoir of tears inside my body, and of a sudden it had reached saturation point and now it was spilling over. I lay back on the cushions and I wept and wept. I wept for Inet, who was too old to comfort me. I wept for my gentle husband and for my little son who had not breathed. I wept for my lovely lost girl child, beloved of the gods. I wept for the wife I would never be, for the lover I might not take, for the lonely road that I must travel. I wept for my father who had been so strong when I was little, and I wept for my wise mother, whose counsel and devotion I sorely needed.

Hapu sat quietly beside me on his stool. He did not remonstrate with me or try to offer comfort. Instead, he simply reached across and took my hand and held it. He knew that it was not allowed to touch the Pharaoh without express permission, but as a physician it must have come naturally to him. I clung to him and sobbed and sobbed.

At length he began to make gentle shushing noises. "There, now," he said. "There, now." He offered me a kerchief of soft cotton. Then he arose, a little stiffly, and fetched some of the cordial in a beaker. "Try a sip or two of this," he said.

I hiccupped and drank. It was indeed slightly bitter, but tangy and refreshing also. I sighed deeply and drank some more. "Thank you," I murmured.

"Your Majesty has suffered a sad loss, and now a sudden shock . . . one cannot meet it robustly. Sometimes . . . sometimes it is necessary to speak about . . . about anything that may . . . that may particularly trouble one."

"Perhaps. But I feel better now. I thank you for your visit, and for your concern."

He departed, looking relieved.

I would not have told him what had happened between Thutmose and me, although I believed he had guessed. Yet his advice, I thought, was sound. So I told Senenmut the whole tale. He was furious. "And he handled you roughly? He attempted to force you? Why, the . . . the . . . He should be punished with extreme severity! How dare he!"

"No, no. Best just to leave it now. He'll never speak of it, I made him feel a fool. Besides, I don't know . . ."

"What, Majesty?"

At last my deepest fear surfaced. "I don't know how much . . . to what degree I may have . . . he may have thought . . . that I encouraged him."

There was a long silence. He hunched his shoulders and folded his arms across his chest, looking thunderous.

Tears began to roll down my cheeks. Angrily I brushed them away. "But I did not . . . It is just . . . just that he . . . he has such a . . . conceit of himself."

"He does indeed," said Senenmut grimly. "You say he actually wanted to marry you?"

"Yes. Not entirely impossible, I suppose, with only eight summers between us."

"Majesty did not consider . . ."

"Oh, no. Not for a moment. I like him not," I said, firmly, "I never have. And he would become the primary Pharaoh at once, he would take precedence, he would plunge Khemet into war – oh, no. No. I vowed to devote my life to the Black Land. It is my destiny."

"Never to take another husband? Not even . . . perhaps . . . a commoner? One who could not usurp the throne? There have been Pharaohs who married a commoner."

I sighed. "Yes. It has been known. But the commoners were wives. A male Pharaoh is secure enough upon the throne to make such a choice. But I have had to struggle to establish the fact of my divinity. Marrying a common man, I fear, would cast great doubt upon my divine nature, and it would reduce my authority. You must understand how that is."

"Yes, Majesty. Yes, I see." There was deep sadness in his face. "Indeed, I do understand."

Here endeth the fifteenth scroll.

MORE SECRET KNOWLEDGE that I would rather not have had. Well, I am being punished for my curiosity. I shall have to take a trip to my cousin's mountain farm immediately, for to possess a document relating how the Great Commander tried to force the Pharaoh . . . it had better be hidden away as quickly as possible. It reflects extremely badly on a man hero-worshipped by many. Besides, how he would hate the story of her method of self-defence and, worse, her laughter, to become public knowledge!

One wonders, though, whether he might not have justifiably thought . . . well, it does sound as if . . . oh, dear. It is so hard to know what women want. I would like to see more of that plump little Syrian partridge who works in the tavern where I meet Ahmose. Her name, I have discovered, is Saria. She has many admirers, though; just when I think I have received her most brilliant smile, she bestows an equally generous beam upon a corpulent merchant with hair in his ears and yellow teeth.

Of course, she is merely a slave and I could simply make an offer to buy her. She would probably be expensive, though, since she is undoubtedly an asset to the tavern keeper, and I do not have many debens of silver or gold put by. And even if I could afford her, I would not want her if she did not like me. I would not force a woman; that would make me no better than . . . the Great Commander? What am I thinking! No, no. This is mere foolishness. Time to blow out the lamp!

THE SIXTEENTH SCROLL

In the tenth year of my reign I lost my beloved Inet. Somehow I had considered her to be indestructible. For many years she was a daily presence in my life. When I no longer needed a nurse, she became a sort of honorary lady-in-waiting; then my children came and they needed her; despite the illness that had affected her manner of walking, she took care of them. Then the children grew older and she again remained as one of my ladies.

When I was young she was always there, never going away on trips and leaving me behind as my royal parents so often did. With her oft-repeated tales of the gods and how they had favoured me, she made me feel safe and she encouraged me to think of myself as someone special, someone with an exceptional destiny. She never thought that I did not belong on the Double Throne; on the contrary, when I acceded to the throne, it was to her merely the fulfilment of predictions that she had been making since I was a child.

Yet she never quite seemed to have grasped that I was indeed the Pharaoh. Especially as she grew older and somewhat forgetful, I remained her dear child, to be scolded if she saw fit, to be cosseted if I was even a little unwell, to be told to eat, made to rest, comforted when sad, and above all loved. To be held. She knew, in principle, that the Pharaoh's person was sacred and not to be touched, but she forgot. If she felt it was needed, she would hug me or gently take my hand and stroke it. I never reprimanded her for that.

Of course, at times she irritated me. While it was soothing to be treated like a child when one was ill or very tired, at other times it was inappropriate and made me cross. Also, as her memory for recent matters grew worse, her recollections from the past seemed increasingly important to her, and she would retell her tales over and over, in exactly the same words, until I felt ready to scream. Trying to prevent her from doing this was hopeless. One could say, yes, Inet, I know, you have told me, you told me just a minute ago, but that did not stop her. The words would come relentlessly: "Hathor suckled you, Hapi cradled you, and Apophis spared you for your destiny. Did you know that?"

Yes, Inet, I do know. You told me . . . Don't tell me again. I cannot stand it.

She seemed to grow smaller as she grew older. Not merely thinner, although she did lose girth, but so stooped that she was at last not much taller than a child. She began to go blind, and for the last years of her life she was very frail. Then the time came when she took ill, with a pain in her abdomen that no prayers or charms or medications were able to cure.

"Inet," I said, "the time has come when you should lie down. I shall give orders for a wooden bed to be put into your room. You'll be more comfortable and it will be easier for the servants to assist you that way."

"A mat has always been good enough for me," she objected.

"But you struggle to get up." I was firm with her, and the slaves installed a cedarwood bed in her little room near mine, padded with folded linen and furnished with cool fine linen sheets and a cushioned headrest.

She went on protesting, but finally she could no longer fight the devils that were causing her to waste away and she let herself be put to bed. Hapu told me that the best he could do for her was to give her the juice of the poppy to dull the pain, which grew steadily worse, and to help her sleep. For some weeks she lay there like a good child, never complaining, slipping in and out of consciousness. I looked in often. Sometimes I sat next to the bed and held her hand. I was not sure that she even knew that I was there.

Then, one day while I was sitting beside her, her small black eyes grew suddenly bright in her wrinkled little face. Her bony grip on my hand tightened. "Majesty!" she said. "You are here! You are too good!"

"How are you, Inet?" I asked gently. "Is the pain very bad?"

"Oh, no. No. I am just . . . very tired. I think I just need to rest a little longer."

I thought: As always, she still thinks she ought to be up and busy.

"Rest as long as you like," I told her, stroking her hand.

Her eyes fell shut again. Then, after some time had passed, they opened again. "Majesty," she said. "My darling Hatshepsut. Now you are the Pharaoh Ma'atkare. You see, I knew."

"Yes, Inet."

"Hathor suckled you, Hapi cradled you, and Apophis spared you for your destiny. Did you know that?"

"Yes, Inet."

She lay breathing very shallowly, blinking. Her hands seemed to move of their own volition, plucking at the sheets. Then she opened her eyes wide, said: "Oh!" in a surprised tone of voice, and breathed her last.

Dear Inet. I miss her greatly. I had her properly buried, with plenty of grave goods to sustain her in the Afterlife, and I always see to it that she receives mortuary offerings on the Day of the Dead, wishing the sweet breath of the north wind to her loving spirit.

Sad though I was, I was somewhat cheered by the progress on the building of my mortuary temple at Djeser-Djeseru. Work was proceeding apace, but it did not always go smoothly. Aside from the usual problems that beset all building operations, Hapuseneb and Senenmut were often at odds. Hapuseneb was bitterly jealous of Senenmut. It irked him greatly that when I promoted him to First Prophet of Amen, Senenmut was made Steward of the Estates of Amen at Karnak. He also hated the appointment of Senenmut as Overseer of all Royal Works. But most of all he hated the fact that he, Hapuseneb, was merely responsible for my tomb, which was not in the public eye (exactly the opposite, of course), while the task entrusted to Senenmut was so spectacular.

One day they arrived at my small audience chamber towards the end of an early session, having made an appointment to see me together.

Both men made particularly deep obeisances to me, but avoided each other's eyes.

"Well," I said, "what is the problem? Vizier, speak."

"Majesty," said Hapuseneb, "it concerns the dispersal of revenues. I have always controlled taxes and also the revenue from the various possessions held by the priesthood of Amen across the land, and I have ever had a care for good husbandry."

"Yes, yes." I knew that the priests of Amen controlled around a third of the cultivated land and employed easily twenty per cent of the population. I knew they owned not only temples, but all manner of other income-generating properties, which included mines and quarries, sea-going ships and indeed entire villages.

"Majesty, naturally the priesthood has contributed towards the financing of the great project at Djeser-Djeseru. But now, Majesty, my . . . ah . . . colleague, the honourable Senenmut . . ."

I knew it cost him some effort to be so polite. I suppressed a smile. "Yes?"

". . . having, as Steward of Amen, access to the stores at Karnak, has diverted inappropriate amounts to the building project. Hugely inappropriate amounts. If this goes on unchecked, Majesty, we shall be beggared. Beggared, I say!" His nasal voice rose ever higher with aggravation.

"Well, Steward? What say you?"

"With all due respect," said Senenmut, "my honourable colleague exaggerates. I have been using considerable amounts of the temple surpluses, certainly, but there is plenty left. The problem is that the project is at a stage where it requires substantial contributions. Your Majesty knows that we employ many farmers during the quiet season . . ."

"I know, yes. I am happy that we increase employment."

"But as Your Majesty is well aware, the inundation is at hand, and we will lose many labourers. So we must push to complete the current phase as fast as possible. And that means materials, and materials mean transport, and all of it means more labour . . ."

"The pyramids were not built in a day," interjected Hapuseneb. "I see no need for this urgency."

"Why must the project be delayed because of miserliness? Miserliness and greed," said Senenmut, growing angry himself.

"Do you accuse me of greed, Sir? And I say, you are profligate! Better control – "

"I do control everything! Every single building block, every single tool is accounted for! I am a scribe, among other – "

"A scribbler from the provinces," Hapuseneb sneered, "advanced above his – "

"At least I am not a parsimonious snob!" retorted Senenmut.

"Gentlemen, gentlemen," I intervened. They had for the moment forgotten where they were and both looked guilty. "Let us have cool heads. Now then, it is true that the inundation is upon us. It seems quite reasonable to me that an attempt be made to complete the current phase as fast as possible. I cannot believe that the temple resources could be so drastically depleted. No, my judgment is that the building should continue apace. That is the end of it. Pharaoh has spoken."

They made obeisances and left.

I knew Hapuseneb would be seething, but it would be good for him. He should have known better than to complain to me about such a matter. I think he could not resist a bleat of protest at the curtailment of his powers by the appointment of Senenmut to the

Stewardship. But as I have written, it was an essential element of my grasp upon ultimate authority that the Vizier's powers be limited. It is a method that has served me well.

When the building operations were well advanced, Senenmut escorted me on a boat trip to view the site from the river. I was pleased at the reported progress, and I could not wait to see for myself.

It was the beginning of Akhet and the river, which had just begun to rise in the south, was calm and hinting of a change to green. We sailed north, the slight current aiding the rowers as they pulled against a light breeze. As ever, I sensed that Hapi held me, and I felt at home. The shouts of children playing in the shallows rang across the water.

As we neared the bay of Djeser-Djeseru, the sail was furled to allow the boat to swing around and come to rest, wallowing slightly, where we could view the building operations. As Senenmut had promised me, the temple was truly grand in scope and it did indeed dominate the plain. Two broad terraces fronted by wide porticos led down from the core of the temple, the God's sanctuary, which had been hewn out of the Theban rock deep inside the tall cliffs behind it. A third terrace was being added. Imposing open-air stairways linked the terraces, dividing the structure into northern and southern halves and leading up to the sanctuary. Already it was clear that the proportions would, as he had promised, be magically harmonious.

I sighed with satisfaction. "Oh, but it is beautiful. When I have not seen it for a while I forget, and then I am again surprised. Surprised and delighted."

"I am glad Your Majesty is pleased."

We sat companionably side by side on the cushioned deck platform and gazed at the superb structure that was coming into being because we had willed it. My eyes followed the movements of the builders and labourers, tiny, insignificant black figures against the white background. "It is hard to believe," I observed, "that men, who are such puny things seen at this distance, are able to create such a vast structure."

"That will stand long after they are turned to dust and have been forgotten," said Senenmut. "But Your Majesty will be remembered, and rituals in the temple will ensure that Your Majesty lives for ever."

"It will be a good thing," I said, "to be remembered for something of such amazing beauty. But you, Senenmut – you are the one who has above all others made this a reality. You, too, should be remembered down the years. You have my permission to have representations of yourself engraved upon the walls."

"Majesty!" he exclaimed. "You are too good!"

"In inconspicuous places, of course," I added.

"Naturally. I shall see to that." His eyes were shining, and he turned with a forward movement as if to take me in his arms. But he bethought himself, and his hands dropped to his lap. He looked away and sighed. "I thank Your Majesty," he said, in a suddenly flat voice. "It is an extraordinary reward. For a commoner."

It was indeed an extraordinary reward, for anyone. But then, he had always given extraordinary service. In fact, I had given him considerable recognition before then, by allowing him to order a large number of statues of himself, to place in the forecourts of the many temples dedicated to Amen. There are some of him holding Neferure as a small child that I cannot look at, for they make me weep. But this award was exceptional and he knew it.

He was silent for a while. Then he told me: "When the last terrace is in place, we will create the avenue linking the temple with the old Valley Temple on the Nile. Already the sculptors are hard at work carving the sphinxes, each with the body of a lion and the head of the Pharaoh, that will line the approach."

"Yes, I have sat for the head to be modelled. It will be very striking."

"Truly regal," said Senenmut with a touch of bitterness. "But now we must give thought to the gardens, Majesty. They too should be unique."

"You are right," I said, musingly. "You are quite right. I must think about it."

Very soon the answer came to me. And I say "came to me" advisedly, for I received the answer to the question as to how the temple gardens might be made exceptional in the form of a vision granted by the God himself, while I was carrying out the daily ritual at the temple of Amen-Ra at Karnak. As I stood alone before the shrine it seemed to me that I heard a voice addressing me.

"Hear me, my beloved daughter, King Ma'atkare Hatshepsut, hear my divine will. The route to the fabled Land of Punt must once more be found. The ways to the groves of myrrh should be discovered. For the Land of Punt is a wondrous portion of the God's land; I have created it for myself in order to lighten my heart. You must send an expedition to Punt, so that you may bring back incense trees, to establish for me a Punt in the garden of the house that you have built for me.

"I will lead your soldiers by land and by sea, to unknown shores where they will find incense as much as they desire. They will load their ships with marvellous plants in abundance and with all the good things of that distant land."

I made a deep obeisance to the shrine and kissed the floor. "I hear, Divine One," I breathed. "I hear and will obey."

When first I broached this plan, my counsellors expressed many doubts. All kinds of objections were raised and problems foreseen. Yes, tales were told of voyages to the exotic Land of Punt in the time of our ancestors, but some people doubted that these tales were true, and even if they were, such voyages had happened many generations ago. In the time of the hated Hyksos trading expeditions had been limited. It was now no longer certain exactly where this fabled country was situated, nor how precisely it might be reached. I dismissed all objections with scorn.

"There are records," I insisted, facing a phalanx of nay-saying advisers. "My late father, may he live for ever, used to speak of it. No, there can be no doubt that the land exists and that it can be reached from Khemet. What our ancestors did, we too can do." The proposed voyage to Punt would be the crowning achievement of my adventurous foreign policy. It would be a highlight of my reign. I would not be gainsaid.

"But, Majesty, the cost . . ." Treasurer Thitui was as usual concerned about this.

"Will be negligible compared with the riches we could bring back. Doubtless the natives will be content with relatively cheap baubles in exchange. And we will have much use for the ships that we shall build."

"Who is to lead the expedition?"

For a moment, I wished that young Thutmose had been there, instead of being away on a lion-hunting expedition. It was just the kind of adventure that would appeal to him. It would rid me of his bothersome presence for some years, I estimated. Indeed it was the kind of undertaking that might even result in his never returning to the Black Land. But he was far away, and besides, at that time he had held the position of Great Commander of the Army for only two years. In truth, he led the army excellently well and it would be hard to replace him.

"General Nehsi," I said. Nehsi has ever been one of my sturdiest supporters, a man of open mind and adventurous character. I was sure that he would see it as a challenge. Furthermore I considered it possible that the inhabitants of that distant land might understand the language of Nubia rather than ours. "He will exact tribute from the natives to admit their allegiance to their distant King Ma'atkare. What say you, General?"

"I say we essay forth," he answered. "I will search the records for details that might aid us. If we cannot find the fabled land – well, then we must return empty-handed. But let us try."

"You will not fail," I stated positively. "The God has spoken."

The planning was set in train and an order was placed for five large ocean-going ships. They were built, equipped and provisioned in the space of four months. As usual, my devoted Senenmut played a prominent part in ensuring that this was swiftly and efficiently done.

In fact, one evening when he arrived at the palace to share some wine with me on the cool portico, he begged me to send him.

"Let me lead the expedition to Punt," said Senenmut, his eyes shining. "I can do it. Nehsi can command the troops, but I would be the leader."

"It is not necessary," I told him. "Nehsi can command all perfectly well. Why should you wish to leave Thebes?"

"It is the challenge of a lifetime," he said excitedly as he strode to and fro. "To seek a land that may not even exist! To make a journey no man living has ever made before!" He gestured widely across the rose garden. "Majesty, I beg of you . . ."

"I cannot spare you," I objected. "The temple must be completed in the interim."

"But, Majesty – it is far advanced, another overseer could complete it. To travel to parts unknown . . . I have dreamed of it, I have desired it above all else! It has been the dream of my life – Majesty, you have heard me say it!"

"Yes, I have," I admitted reluctantly. "But without you, the men would grow lazy. Problems would loom large and none would see a way to solve them."

"I could leave detailed instructions, complete plans, there are men who could oversee the final stages as well as I. Amenhotep, for example, he is a younger scribe who . . ."

"It would not do. Without your authority, matters will undoubtedly stall. Hapuseneb would tie up the funds. You know he would. And then he would find a way to place the blame on you."

Senenmut folded his arms across his chest and glared at me.

"It will not be done without you, and you know it," I said.

"I am building your dream," he said, in a low, shaking voice. "I am causing your dream to take shape, to become real, to stand against the Theban rock until the water clocks run dry, to show to the ages that Hatshepsut was King and she did live. I eat and drink and sleep with building dust and grit so that your dream may happen. But mine! But mine! You cannot . . . you will not . . ."

"I cannot spare you from the building," I told him. "But even if arrangements could be made, I could not let you go, not so far away, not for years, not on a journey that might never bring you home! Do you not see?" I was trembling.

He took two strides towards me and stopped. He stared intently into my eyes.

I held his gaze. In those wordless moments, much was communicated, and much understood.

At length he said, with a sigh: "I am Your Majesty's faithful servant to command. As ever."

"I depend on you, Senenmut," I said.

The day the ships set forth was one of great festivity. They were seen off with marching bands playing loud music, hordes of well-wishers throwing flowers, and ringing cheers. Offerings were made to the divinities of the air to ensure a fair wind and a safe passage. The plan was for them to sail north down the Nile and then to pass through an ancient canal leading from the eastern delta that connected the

Nile with the Eastern Sea. I had ordered the canal to be cleared out by work teams sent ahead as soon as the plans had been made final. Once through the canal, the ships would hug the coast, sailing in a southerly direction, searching for the land that I for one was certain they would reach. Now all we could do was wait.

Here endeth the sixteenth scroll.

I WAS A YOUNG scribe then, working with Senenmut on the building of the great temple. Some of the men thought it was a strange design that would not look as imposing as the kind usually favoured by the Pharaohs. But I thought we were working on a masterpiece, and indeed, when the completed temple stood in its fragrant garden against those dramatic cliffs, it was evident that it is superb. Men have thought that nothing could ever compare with the pyramids, but my opinion is that Her Majesty's temple is as exceptional, if in a different way.

Of course, the temple serves a dual purpose, which the pyramids do not. Those structures are self-sufficient, monumental royal tombs, each a burial place for one Pharaoh, surrounded by sumptuous pyramid complexes all intended to provide for the Pharaoh's ease and comfort in the Afterlife. King Hatshepsut, together with Senenmut, devised an innovative approach: She attached her own mortuary chapel to a temple of the gods.

She will not be buried in the temple, however. Her tomb – the one she plans to share with her late father, the Pharaoh Thutmose the First, may he live – is located in the mountain behind the temple, to be reached by way of the valley where the entrance to the tomb lies hidden. Her mortuary chapel is not in the central axis of the temple, as one might have expected; King Hatshepsut seldom does what one might expect. Her chapel was placed behind the south colonnade of the upper court. It contains a hall where offerings will be made to sustain the Ka of the deceased King. The central axis of the temple leads to a shrine for Amen, Her Majesty's heavenly father, and his shrine was dug into the depths of the Theban rock.

There are further sanctuaries and shrines to various gods, such as Anubis and Hathor; there is a dark and secret shrine for the worship of Osiris, and an open solar complex for the worship of the sun god Ra. It has a small open courtyard and a monumental altar, positioned so that ceremonies may be conducted facing the rising sun. Then of course there are chapels for the royal family. Her Majesty honoured her royal father, may he live. So the temple serves multiple purposes and in many ways it is different from anything anyone has ever seen.

However, the strangest element, the one that is truly extraordinary, is the inclusion of images of Senenmut. There are more than sixty – I know, I have counted them – small images of Senenmut, some kneeling, others standing with outstretched arms, concealed within the temple. They are cleverly placed where they would be hidden by open doors of shrines or niches for statues, and they are accompanied by short inscriptions stating that he is engaged in worshipping both the god Amen and King Hatshepsut.

Of course there are images of the royal family throughout the temple, in the form of statues and painted reliefs. There is a beautiful relief, for example, of Her Majesty's daughter Neferure depicted with Her Majesty's little sister Neferubity, who also died young. They are shown wearing diadems, jewellery and girdles and nothing else. But to allow images of a person who was not royal, nor even nobly born – a mere commoner – in a sacred space: how could that be? It was completely and utterly unheard-of. There was much gossip among the workmen about this. Some of them even made the scurrilous suggestion that the royal children were not so royal at all . . . springing not from the seed of Pharaoh Thutmose, but from that of an upstart scribe.

But I do not believe it. As I have written, there were so few chances for those two to be alone together. And I believe Her Majesty to be faithful in nature; she would not have cheated on her husband in such a way. Above all, she values the blood royal, and she reveres the Double Throne. No, no, it could not be.

I have my own thoughts about the images of Senenmut. Her Majesty loved the scribe as she loved no-one else in all her life. I have always thought so, and now that I am reading her private journal (I confess to feeling some shame about this, yet I cannot resist it), I see that I am right. I think Her Majesty knew that in this life they could never be together; but perhaps, if she could ensure eternal life for both of them, and ensure that his Ka would be closely associated with hers, then maybe they could be together in the Afterlife. I may be quite wrong – it could just be that she wished to reward what was truly extraordinary devotion and service. But I think I am correct. Yes, yes, I do believe so.

THE SEVENTEENTH SCROLL

We are blessed with a good harvest this year. I have been able, at the new moon, to cut the first sheaf of wheat with the ceremonial scythe, and everyone is labouring mightily to assist the farmers in bringing in the harvest. The tax collectors are busy and our stores will be replenished, so I can be at ease about that.

However, I am not happy about Bek, my little dwarf, who was attacked while spying for me. Since then, he has been very quiet and downcast. His legs have healed, a tribute to the skill of the young physician Minhotep, who set them well. He is able to walk almost without a limp. But after a few poor attempts at entertaining me, he appears to have given up. He does not seem to want to do anything; he just sits and stares at his toes. Never makes a joke nor even tries to juggle. Only Yunit can sometimes make him smile, and then it is but a poor imitation of his broad grin that used to light up my days when he came bouncing in to ask me riddles.

Yunit grows ever larger with child. This Bek is proud of, as one can clearly see when she sits close to him and he gently strokes her swollen belly.

Yesterday he came to show me a cradle he had fashioned from olive wood, on a matching cart with a handle and small wheels.

"See, Majesty, the cradle is a low one, and it has rockers. So that Yunit can easily reach in, and also rock the babe while sitting down," he explained. "And it fits onto the cart, so that she can pull it around."

"It's beautiful," I said. "Beautiful and practical. How clever of you. Are you hoping for a son, Bek?"

"Either, Majesty," said Bek. "But it would be good if Khnum could fashion a child with proper legs."

Perhaps, when the child comes, it will cheer him – indeed, cheer them both. He lies heavy on my heart.

It further troubles me that I do not hear from Khani. It seems that he was wounded in a skirmish, but surely by this time he is sufficiently recovered to write to me. I miss his regular visits and his dependable reports. Of course, I do have men in my employ whose job it is to keep me informed of everything that may happen across the land: officials, tax collectors, scribes . . . and Ibana. Yet I do not trust him. He does not serve my interests, only his own; should he sense weakness in me, he will find a new master very soon. No, I have always placed more trust in those whose loyalty to me is personal. Such a one as Khani. I would trust him with my life. But why do I hear nothing from him? Even if he has been ill, he should be well enough now to send me a letter. It disturbs me. As I have written, we always keep in touch. He could send me letters and reports by courier, so why does he not do this?

I have kept letters that he wrote to me while he was in training in Memphis. Reading them now, I am still impressed by his youthful enthusiasm and his devotion to Khemet. Unrolling one of those papyrus scrolls, I am transported back these eighteen years.

LETTER FROM KHANI TO HER MAJESTY: THE REIGN OF HATSHEPSUT YEAR 2

Greetings and salutations to the Pharaoh Ma'atkare Khnemet-Amen Hatshepsut, living for ever, from her devoted subject and friend Khani, Standard Bearer in the Division of Sobek at Memphis. Majesty, I hope this finds you well as it leaves me. I write to inform Your Majesty that I have been selected to be trained in the Kap. I am extremely proud of this, since I am very aware that only those destined to become officers and commanders are allowed into this secret fraternity. If, as I believe, Your Majesty's good word had something to do with my acceptance, I wish to express my grateful thanks. I shall endeavour to fulfil your expectations of me. I live to serve Your Majesty and the Two Lands. May Your Majesty live for ever.

Indeed, it was true that I had spoken for him, but he would never have been accepted if he had not had the necessary qualities. He received the special training that the Kap has to offer, and he went on to become the Officer in Charge of Recruits in the standing army, where he did outstanding work. Although he was stationed in Memphis, he came to Thebes several times a year for the great festivals, wherein the military play an important part, and then he would always come to see me.

For the past four years he has been the Officer Commanding the Division of Sobek, currently stationed in Thebes. Naturally there must always be a full division in Thebes to defend the capital in case of incursions from the south. The various divisions of the army, the main rump of which is stationed at Memphis, are rotated to take terms of duty in Thebes. So, for these four years we have been close and it worries me that he does not write.

Well, it is bootless to keep brooding about this. Let me return to my story.

As the months went by, there were periods when I forgot about the expedition on its way to Punt. Then again I would remember and I would try to imagine the five ships with their sails bellied out in the wind, bravely voyaging into the unknown for my sake. I wondered whether they would be able to locate that fabled land. Would they reach it safely? Would the trading go off well, and would they succeed in returning home with their precious cargo? I worried about them and I thought how awful it would be if they were lost at sea, never to return, and never to be properly buried in the earth of Khemet so that they might attain the Afterlife. Indeed, those men ventured much for my sake, for they risked not only their lives on earth but even their claims to eternity. Yet the god Amen had spoken. I could not believe that they would be lost.

It would have been a great comfort to receive letters, but of course, given that they were at sea, that was impossible. However, General Nehsi understood my deep interest in the journey and realised that, if they were successful, a full record would be invaluable to anyone coming after them, and of course equally for those who would inscribe the events of my reign on my mortuary temple walls. So he kept a detailed journal that afterwards came into my possession. I shall add his scrolls to mine so that the story of that remarkable undertaking may be kept safe. As we have seen in the past, even the living stone where their actions were to be recorded may be altered. Let his writings attest to what they did.

FROM THE JOURNAL OF GENERAL NEHSI, BEGUN IN THE REIGN OF HATSHEPSUT YEAR 11

The trip along the Nile to the delta passed speedily and without any problems. The sailors were doing what they knew well how to do. The weather was hot, but it was cool on the water and everyone on board the five ships was in a festive mood. We lounged on deck drinking beer and watching the densely green river banks slip by. In places hippos loomed like round rocks and ducks quacked amongst the reeds. The sailors often caught fish and the cooks served them with a delicious sauce; we could obtain fresh vegetables and fruit from small boats that plied the river. It felt like a holiday.

The blessings of the gods be upon the Pharaoh, we all said when we reached the ancient canal leading from the delta to the Eastern Sea and found it in good order and easily navigable. King Ma'atkare's foresight in sending work teams to prepare the thoroughfare made it smooth going for us, otherwise there had perforce been a considerable delay. So the second leg of the journey was also trouble-free and pleasant.

But now we have reached the open sea and turned southwards along the coast, and the journey has ceased being easy. Every day brings its own challenges. I fear that the sailors are no longer at home upon these rough and unpredictable waters; there are not many who have had any experience other than on the river, although some tell me they have sailed to ports such as Sidon and Byblos. Most of the soldiers are seasick, retching and wretched, and curse the evil day they left the stable land.

The captain, a swarthy Phoenician named Aqhat, fortunately does have experience of seafaring. He is a taciturn man who grunts his orders but otherwise hardly speaks. Also he seems to sleep very little, and only for short periods, trusting no man better than himself to keep us safe. He holds course close to the coast, but not close enough to see land at all times, else should we crash upon rocky promontories. Days go by that we can see nothing other than the limitless, rolling ocean stretching to the horizon on all sides, with the other four ships of our fleet tossing about somewhere within sight, looking frighteningly frail. We have been fortunate in the weather, having had a brisk following wind most of the time.

Hardly had I noted that the weather had been reasonably fair, when, of course, it changed. As I sat on the deck one night, it seemed to me that the stars low upon the horizon were dimming. The night was warm and still, and there was a slight wind; the ship was not making good headway, but was ploughing and wallowing in the dark water, which had an oily look. Something ominous was approaching from the southeast; there seemed to be a blackness there that was sending advance guards: a heavy swell, a closeness in the air, an oppressiveness that made it hard to breathe.

Suddenly Captain Aqhat was at my side. "Stormy weather coming, Sir," he said. Almost at once a rush of wind arrived, bringing with it pelting rain. Sharp orders had the sailors jumping to their tasks, taking in the sails, bringing the ship heeling around. The air had grown cold very quickly. The motion of the ship was uneasy. I understood that we could not sail freely before the wind, for the direction was wrong; it would result in our running aground on the rocky coast. I could no longer sit, but I would not go below; it was too close down there, and besides, more of the soldiers would be seasick, for sure, causing a most disgusting smell. It was exhilarating to be out on deck in the dark night, riding the huge swells that now ran beneath our hull.

The weather turned thick and wild; the wind became a gale and lashed the towering waves into gleaming white foam. Taller and taller they grew, looming hugely as if they would smash down upon us and send us to the depths of the ocean in little pieces of wreckage. But the gallant ship mounted each swell, sometimes almost standing on end, and crashed down to the further side, wallowing until the next mountain of water bore down. It seemed as if Seth and all his screaming devils had descended upon us and were tossing us about for their sport. At our departure from Thebes our ship had looked large and sturdy compared to other boats on the Nile, but now it seemed to be but a tiny, fragile barque. When the sea grew calm again, it seemed to me miraculous that we had survived.

How presumptuous we were, I thought that terrifying night, to venture upon the fathomless deeps with such frail vessels and with so little knowledge of the vagaries of the gods who reigned over that vast world of water. By and large the gods of Khemet were far more predictable. Hapi could usually be counted upon to deliver the inundation year after year. One knew what to expect. The flood would bring the rich black earth and recede and planting would be done; the crops would germinate and ripen under the winter sun and when the time was right, the harvest would be brought in. It was comfortable and familiar. Out on the boundless ocean all was strange, and savage storms might at any moment descend to punish human audacity.

And yet, survival in such circumstances brings greater satisfaction than one derives from comfortable routines at home. To go beyond the known, the familiar, the safe and predictable; to venture, to dare, to challenge unknown gods – ah, therein lies a delight that the homebound *and the faint-hearted will never experience. I shall be forever grateful to Her Majesty that she afforded me the chance to learn this truth.*

Once we had lived through that first wild storm upon the open ocean I lost my fear. I had seen that our captain was a very capable seafarer and I became confident that we would reach our goal. And so, after a long and often wearying journey lasting many months, at last we did. One hot and humid day, we neared a widely curving bay edged with a broad sweep of white sand where the waves broke in curving lines of glittering foam. Further back a thick tangle of green foliage sheltered a village with curiously conical huts set high above the ground. Thin trickles of smoke ascended into the cloudless sky.

"Sir, I believe we have reached Ta-Neter," said the captain. According to the few reports that I had been able to find before we departed, left by the ancients who had made this voyage before us, it seemed that we had indeed. Ta-Neter: the fabled Land of Punt.

Captain Aqhat suggested that at first only the lead ship, ours, should sail close enough to be sighted and that we should anchor well offshore, sending but a few small boats towards the beach. That way we could establish contact without their assuming that we were attacking them. I thought his plan well judged, and so we carried it out. I went ashore unarmed, carrying my staff of office, but escorted by eight armed soldiers. We were not a sufficiently large group to intimidate their king, who stood ready to greet us, accompanied by one wife, a daughter and two sons. He welcomed us in a friendly manner.

The king was a slender man with a reddish skin, wearing a loincloth and rows of anklets on his left leg. His long, thin beard straggled to his chest. He did not look so very different from ourselves, but the queen of that wondrous land was truly remarkable to behold. Never had I seen a woman of such ample girth. So heavy was she that she found it difficult to walk about and was carried everywhere upon a small ass, which seemed hardly capable of carrying such a load, yet bore her valiantly.

She wore what seemed to be a short, split kilt, a shirt without sleeves and a necklace made of a thong with large, colourful baubles strung on it. She had fine eyes that flashed with laughter, and a wide smile showing strong white teeth.

The king was clearly very proud of her. We concluded that ample girth was considered beautiful, a strange idea for Egyptians, for our women are admired when they are slim and able to move with grace. However, one must expect that foreign lands will have foreign concepts and foreign customs.

We had brought some samples of the items we wished to use to barter with and upon landing we spread them out on the sand and stood back, showing that we had come in peace. They chattered among themselves in their strange tongue. It would have been difficult to communicate, but by great good fortune it appeared that there were some among them who had a knowledge of the tongue used in my country of Nubia. Besides myself several of our soldiers are able to speak it, so we managed better than I had anticipated. Soon their king had found an interpreter and had indicated his willingness to trade.

Thereafter, the other four ships hove into view and anchored offshore in deeper water. The soldiers who now arrived in larger numbers were made welcome also. The village where the Puntites live I judged most attractive. Their houses, with the oddly conical shapes we had noticed from the sea, are constructed from plaited palm fronds and set high off the ground on poles, so that they require a ladder to gain access to their homes. These structures are well suited to their climate, which is hot and sultry. The lush trees surrounding the houses provide cool shade. Chattering monkeys play in their branches, where we also noted many nesting birds. We saw ebony and incense trees as well as palms, and realised at once that we would be able to bring back the trees that Her Majesty desired to create an incense garden for the God at Djeser-Djeseru.

The Puntites were delighted with the items we had brought: brightly coloured beads and bracelets, and some useful tools. Cordial relations were quickly established, and I gave orders that a tent be prepared in which we could receive the chiefs of this land, so that we might present them with bread, beer, wine, meat and fruits – all the good things of the land of Egypt, as was ordered by the Pharaoh, to whom all life, strength and health are wished. So a tent was raised in the harbour of Punt, on the shore of the sea, and there was a small outpost of the Black Land on a strange and distant coast.

Captain Aqhat explained to me that it was necessary to await the reversal of the prevailing winds to carry us back to Egypt. So we spent several weeks travelling westwards overland, assisted by Puntite guides, to the interior of that wondrous land, to collect ebony and incense and to gather other treasures such as elephant tusks and panther skins, as well as a number of live animals, some more extraordinary than those told about in any ancient tale. From a number of villages on our route we collected tribute to their distant Pharaoh in the shape of sacks filled with precious metals. Several sturdy donkeys were required to transport the goods back to the shore. We would indeed have a rich haul to present to Her Majesty and to the god Amen.

At long last, Captain Aqhat deemed the time for our departure to have come. We had been received with much graciousness, but I found that my longing for home was intense: for the warm lips of my wife, for the cooled wine and the dry air of the Black Land. I wondered whether my children would even know me. I had ventured far and I had experienced much, but now I yearned for comfortable familiarity. I was ready to go home.

While the fleet was away, life in Thebes went on as usual. A year went by. Thutmose for once was living a quiet life. The spies I paid to keep an eye on him reported that he spent a great deal of time at his palace in Memphis. By that time he had expanded his harem. This is the prerogative of the Pharaoh, not common among Egyptian men, and it has always irked me that he assumes it as his right. But then he was crowned, after all, and besides, anything that keeps him busy is a benefit to me. Satioh, the Mitannian princess he wed at sixteen, remained his Chief Wife and favourite, the mother of several little girls, all of them black-haired and plump like their mother.

Yes, it did indeed seem as if the young whelp had settled down.

"Commander Thutmose devotes many hours a day to studying plants," Ibana told me one day.

"Plants? He likes to garden?"

"He plans the gardens, but he does not dig or weed. For that he has slaves and workmen," replied Ibana. "No, he studies plants, it seems, in order to understand their nature. And their properties. Medicinal uses, for example."

"Indeed?"

"Yes. I am told he brews an infusion that takes away the headache very promptly."

I should ask for the recipe, I thought.

"Also, he has redesigned the interior of the palace at Memphis altogether. It is much grander and yet at the same time more comfortable than it has ever been."

"A man of many parts," I commented.

"And he composes verses, which he reads to the Princess Satioh as they sit in the rose garden. He has imported many exquisite new roses from Syria."

"Verses," I repeated, rather faintly. Could this be the chief warrior of Khemet, the scourge of lions, the destroyer of a hundred elephants?

I was astounded. Furthermore he appeared to have reconsidered his attitude to me. He seemed to have decided that it would be fruitless to oppose me on almost every count as he had been doing until then. Instead, when called to Thebes to join in discussions in the audience chamber he only spoke on issues that he had clearly thought about carefully and made comments and suggestions that were so sensible that I often found myself in agreement with him.

"He is attempting to impress you," said Senenmut when I related all of this to him. "He is trying to behave like a Pharaoh instead of like a petulant child."

"What do you think he hopes to gain?" I asked.

"More of a role in governing the country," suggested Senenmut. "A greater measure of co-regency."

"I will not share the Double Throne," I flared up. "There can be only one true Pharaoh."

Indeed, the situation was becoming extremely difficult. While there have been co-regencies before, this happened when an aging Pharaoh called upon his heir to stand by his side and learn the principles of good governance and the daily rituals, to be inducted into the mysteries of Osiris and so forth. Then when the elder died, the younger could take over the reins smoothly. But never to my knowledge had there been two co-equal Pharaohs; the concept did not make sense. I was not nearing my end and I would not, could not surrender the throne.

"I cannot allow him to edge me out," I stated angrily.

"No, but you might allow him to play a more prominent role on some formal occasions, such as in processions and at feasts, without diminishing your authority," suggested Senenmut reasonably. "It might keep him more content."

I sighed. "I suppose I should. Also, the Party of Legitimacy has been pressuring me to allow him to marry Meryetre. You know that he was betrothed to Neferure, may she live, but . . ." The nobles, no doubt encouraged by Thutmose, wanted to ensure that there would not be two separate contenders for the crown of the Two Lands when I passed into the Afterlife. They do not forget that my stepson is merely the child of a concubine.

"It is probably inevitable," said Senenmut, "and although I understand that you are loath to do it, I think you should. She has the pure blood royal and were she to marry any other man, he could lay claim to the throne when Your Majesty passes into the Afterlife. Then there could be civil war, for Thutmose would not accept it."

"Their argument exactly," I said. "Very well. Let them break the jar together. Perhaps then Meryetre will be more content."

But she was not. I think it is not in her nature to be happy.

"I should be the Chief Wife," said Meryetre angrily, the night before they broke the jar. "I have the full blood royal of the Pharaohs. Satioh is only a foreign princess."

And if you did not have royal blood, I doubt you would even have been a minor wife of his, I thought to myself, but I refrained from saying so. Perhaps she may fall pregnant quickly, I thought; rumour has it that Thutmose knows very well how to pleasure a woman. If she has a son, perhaps it will make her feel better. I contemplated the idea of becoming a grandmother and I was not sure that I would care for it. A grandmother is by definition an old lady, went my thinking, and I did not yet feel old in the least. Well, perhaps that would not happen too soon.

In the end Meryetre settled into life in the harem well enough. There are often tiffs among the women, of course, and sometimes outright battles, about precedence, about servants, about children squabbling – once, by the tears of Isis, about access to a new loom! I was often regaled with complaints when she came to visit – as I still am. But then, as now, I did not have much patience with her. My attention was concentrated on the return of the fleet. But from the time they left, two years were to pass before there was any news of them.

Here endeth the seventeenth scroll.

THE EIGHTEENTH SCROLL

We were still waiting for the fleet to return when Meryetre informed me of her pregnancy. The child had been conceived on a most favourable night, she informed me smugly, and she was sure that she would bear a son. Beyond my expectation, I felt a leap of happiness within my heart when she told me the news. Perhaps, I thought, she would indeed bear the son that had been denied to me. And so it might yet come to pass that another great Pharaoh would be given to Egypt from my loins. So Meryetre waited for her child and I waited for my ships.

There were times when I was convinced that the entire fleet had been lost at sea, that they would never return to the Black Land, all those strong, brave men who had dared to undertake that extraordinary journey for my sake and for the greater glory of the god Amen. I found it hard to look the wife of General Nehsi in the eye, for it might be that I had caused her to become a widow. But Senenmut never lost his faith.

"Majesty, have patience," he counselled me. "The mysterious country of Punt is far away and they will have had to wait for favourable winds. They will come home. Perhaps in the first months of Akhet, when the flood swells the river."

Month after month went by and there was no sign of the five great ships. My eyes grew tired of scanning the horizon to no avail. I gave gold to the priests to ensure regular prayers and incantations, begging the gods to protect the ships and bring them safely back. Yet when at last the first news came, I was caught unawares. I was conducting an interview with diplomats from Canaan in my Grand Audience Chamber when a herald arrived post-haste from the North, covered in dust, and demanded immediate audience as he brought momentous news.

I was afraid that he would announce an insurrection on our borders, but I would not show the visitors any hesitancy. "Let him in," I ordered, remaining outwardly calm.

A slight youth strode up to the throne and prostrated himself.

"Arise," I said. "What news have you?"

"Majesty, the ships have been sighted," he told me. "The fleet has traversed the canal and sails upon the river!"

"By the breath of Horus, that is wonderful news!" I exclaimed. "Our ships have returned from Punt," I informed the assembled men. A murmur of amazement and admiration from the swarthy Canaanites greeted this announcement. "But tell me – are they all there? All safe? We did not lose any ships?"

"Not a single one, Majesty," he assured me. "All five are there. Low in the water, as if they bring much cargo. And the people who have seen them pass tell of many monkeys that scamper about and clamber on the rigging."

"We must arrange a suitable welcome," I said. "You will be rewarded for your pains."

His tired face broke into a smile and he kissed the ground again.

Of course they did not arrive that very day, as I would have wished; it still took several weeks for them to ride the rising flood towards Thebes. There was time enough for Senenmut to arrange a welcoming party of appropriate size and grandeur. As the days wore on I became ever more impatient and awaited the progress reports from the cities lining the river with great anticipation. At last the morning came when they would sail into harbour.

I had decreed a public holiday and the crowds were out in full force, eating, drinking and making merry. Bands played on the quay. Brightly coloured flags flew in the brisk breeze and looped chains of flowers swayed along the way that the procession would take to the palace. I had a special throne erected for myself upon a platform on the wharf, so that I might see over the crowds. I was dressed as if for a festival, in a gilded kilt and a pleated robe with a gold sash, with jewels at my throat and on my wrists, and the double crown of Egypt proudly on my head. A temporary awning protected me from the brilliant sun, and I was flanked by my guards, a pair of tall Nubians.

The water was running fast and green, but the wind blew from the north, and when the first ship rounded the bend in the river it was making good time with a full-bellied sail and the aid of the rowers. A ringing cheer went up and trumpets sounded a clarion call of welcome. The beat of the rowers' gong echoed the thump of my excited heart.

The plan was that I would wait until all five ships had been safely moored and then I would welcome a deputation of the five captains and their first mates, led by General Nehsi. Thereafter we would proceed to the palace for a banquet while the unloading went on and the cargo was brought ashore and transported to the palace.

When Nehsi strode onto the quay I almost did not recognise him. He had grown lean and his hair and beard were bushy. But I knew him by his brilliant smile. Directly behind him walked a person who had to be from Punt: a sinewy fellow who had a magnificent beast on a leash and a whip in his other hand. Behind them came the captains and their mates with the rolling gait so typical of sailors. Then followed some soldiers, each bearing a gift: items made of gold, silver, lapis lazuli and malachite, amphorae containing incense and myrrh, ebony, a vast pair of ivory tusks, a small chattering monkey on a chain and two trees planted in baskets slung from a rod. They all knelt and presented the gifts. The beast snarled. His handler dragged him back onto his haunches.

"Majesty," said Nehsi, "I have the honour to present the fruits of our expedition to the Land of Punt. These are, of course, but samples. We have brought a rich cargo, and many strange animals."

"Welcome home, Nehsi," I said. "You have done well. Pharaoh is pleased – nay, Pharaoh is delighted. The god Amen will be delighted also."

"Then is Pharaoh's servant glad," said Nehsi, who can at times be suave, for a bluff soldier. "Majesty, we have also brought some visitors from Punt. They insisted on coming along to see for themselves the great land of Egypt from which they are all ruled, and to see with their own eyes the greatness of Your Majesty."

"Bid them welcome," I said. I now saw the small group of rather bedraggled-looking strangers, garbed in beads and loincloths, who had disembarked from the lead ship and followed, hesitantly, behind the soldiers bearing gifts. "But will they understand? What language do they speak?"

"Some of them understand the tongue of Nubia," explained Nehsi, "they interpret to the king."

"Very well, then. Tell them that they shall be our honoured guests, but when they wish to return to their own land, we shall help them."

"Thank you, Majesty."

The beast snarled again.

"Nehsi, what animal is that?"

"It is a panther, a special gift to the Pharaoh from the Chiefs of Punt."

"It is beautiful," I said. The handler brought it forwards, until I could smell its feral scent in the hot air. Its sleek black sides rippled in the sunlight. Golden eyes stared into mine. It had a look of scorn, I fancied. *You will never own me,* it seemed to say. *I am your master, as you will discover if ever I am unleashed.* I shivered. "We should move on to the palace," I said. "Please invite all these people to the banquet. See to the animals also."

"Yes, Majesty."

The cargo that the fleet had brought was unloaded and indeed, there were many wondrous goods. In addition to the precious stuffs, there were extraordinary animals, and a large herd of cattle that lowed piteously as they tramped the streets of Thebes. But the best of all were the incense and myrrh trees. Now we would be able to make our own sweet-smelling unguents, using the best ingredients in the world. And I could at last have the garden around my mortuary temple completed as I had promised the God.

Being the dutiful daughter of Amen, I dedicated the best of the goods to my heavenly father. The God was brought forth from his shrine to the palace in his golden barque to receive the offerings. Senenmut and Nehsi stood by my side as I proudly laid the items at the feet of the God. I had the scene recorded on the walls of my mortuary temple at Djeser-Djeseru, where it may yet be read: *The King himself, King of Upper and Lower Egypt, Ma'atkare, takes the valuable things of the divine land of Punt, offering the gifts of the southern countries, the tributes from the wretched Kush, the treasures of gold and precious stones to Amen-Ra, the Lord of the Double Throne. The King Ma'atkare lives for ever, she is full of joy, she rules over Khemet like Ra eternally.*

I was happy that I had been able to carry out the instructions of the God, but more than that, I felt that the amazing success of the expedition had vindicated my reign. Surely, I thought, it was now abundantly clear that I, the female Pharaoh, was not some unnatural being; that I had not angered the gods and that I truly had maintained Ma'at.

Shortly after the fleet had returned from Punt, Meryetre went into labour. It was long and hard. I was extremely worried, remembering my little son who had not breathed. I gave plenty of gold to the priests to ensure that they would say prayers and make offerings, and I myself prayed and offered sacrifices, especially to the hippopotamus god Taueret, the protective deity of expectant mothers and women in childbirth. I could not pay attention to my daily tasks and left everything to Hapuseneb. For one long night and an even longer day, I was not the Pharaoh; I was a mother and a grandmother-in-waiting and I was distraught. Inet had died some years before, so we missed her loving support.

Hapu of course was by Meryetre's side, also the one who sees to women's matters in the palace; there were priests to chant the incantations and shake the sistrums and there were the women who were versed in childbirth. I was useless and powerless in that situation and I liked it not. I could do little else but pray, and wait.

Meryetre surprised me. My self-centred daughter, who was continually dissatisfied with life and ready to whine, did not utter a single complaint. When the pains came thick and fast, racking her stocky frame, she emitted low, guttural groans; in between she gasped for breath and panted shallowly; she swung her head from side to side, staring at me like a cow I once saw labouring when I was a child and had gone into the fields with my brothers, dumb with pain and effort; but she did not complain. Although I had had a fairly hard time birthing her, it was nothing compared to this, and my other birthings had been relatively easy. She struggled on with a kind of animal endurance and courage that I could not, I think, have matched. I looked in often, and hardly slept myself.

Towards the beginning of the second night, Hapu came to me, his round face slick with perspiration. It was the second month of Akhet and the weather was hot. "Majesty," he said, drops falling to the floor as he made an obeisance, "if the child does not emerge soon we shall have to remove it. Do we have permission to do this? It is a dangerous procedure, especially for the mother, but it may be the only way."

"Do you mean to . . . to cut her . . ." I had heard of such operations, but I had never actually known any woman who had been so treated.

"Yes, Majesty. We will cut across the abdomen and remove the babe. We will then sew up the wound as we do for soldiers on the battlefield. But there will be much blood. And afterwards there may be fever. I do not know . . . I cannot tell . . ." He was sorely distressed.

"Whether she will live. I know."

"Or the babe," he added, miserably. "The risks are great."

"Well, if you must . . . if there is no other way . . . then it will have to be done."

He nodded. "We will wait just a little while longer," he said, straightening his shoulders. "The women are making her walk, in between squatting on the bricks. Perhaps the child can still come naturally. It should be a lusty babe. A big one, to have given this much trouble."

"If it breathes," I said. I went into the birthing chamber with him. If it were to be done, I would stand by. Two more physicians had arrived, and the priests who were chanting prayers and incantations in the background intensified their volume.

"The princess should lie down now," Hapu instructed the women. They glared at him, but assisted Meryetre to a wooden bed. She staggered, breathing out on moans, and almost fell as we eased her down. I leaned over her hugely swollen belly and took both her hands. She gripped them so hard that I grunted. I inhaled her sour sweat that overpowered the incense in the room. I felt the spasms rack her in a vicious, inexorable rhythm as the babe surged towards the light.

Finally, just before the physicians were about to make the incision, Meryetre gave a great cry and the child came forth. The women caught it, tied the cord and cut it free. It gave a loud squall. Yes, like me, it came into the world kicking and squalling, tight little fists pumping as if ready to fight the world. It did indeed sound like Bastet in full cry, as Inet used to say of me. And it was a boy. She had produced a Pharaoh for the Black Land.

"Praise be to Taueret and to all the gods," I said fervently. I took the child into my arms. He was wet and slithery and his head was covered with something white and sticky. His eyes were scrunched shut and he yelled deafeningly. But I would not let the women take him away. "See to his mother," I told them. "I will hold him for a while. Let him grow calm. Then you may go and bathe him. Give me a linen wrap."

They did not like it, but they could not gainsay me. I wrapped the angry little being and went to sit on a large chair padded with cushions in the corner of the room. While the women were busy with Meryetre, I held the child, crooning softly.

I sang to him:

> *"Be quiet, little one. Be at rest.*
> *You have come to the Black Land.*
> *You have a mother who loves you,*
> *You have a father who will love you,*
> *You have a grandmother whose most precious thing you are.*
> *Be quiet, little one. Be at rest."*

Soon he did become calm. I gave him a finger and he gripped it firmly. Oh yes, I thought. Indeed a lusty babe. Khnum had fashioned his tiny body most beautifully on his potter's wheel. May his Ka have been fashioned equally well. I held him up against my breast and patted his back. He snuffled in my neck and went to sleep.

As soon as she had been washed and settled on her bed, Meryetre demanded to see her child. I took him in and laid him on her chest. Her face was swollen with effort, but she smiled proudly when she looked at me across the small form. "I have a strong boy child," she said, and sighed with satisfaction.

"Yes. You have done well, my child. You have been brave."

She smiled a tired smile.

"You should sleep now."

The women bustled over and removed the babe. Hapu brought

her a draught of medication. "This will ease you, Ma'am," he said. "You will have many aches and pains for the next few days." She took it obediently. Already her eyes were closed. She was clearly exhausted.

I invited the physician to sit down with me in an antechamber and share some bread and watered wine. He looked close to exhaustion himself and his hands shook as he helped himself.

"Hapu, you have done well," I said.

He nodded. "I was much afeard," he confessed, munching. "We were like to have lost them both."

"But you triumphed."

He sighed. "So often we do not. There is much, much more to know about sickness and healing than we can even imagine, I think. Why is it that sometimes we can wrest the Ka from the clutches of the devils who would carry it off, and at other times our best efforts do not prevail?"

"We cannot know," I said.

"I believe that healing has more to do with the power of the Ka itself than with anything that a physician does," he told me. "If it is determined not to leave the body, often it does stay, even though the body is extremely sick. I think that if we knew more about the Ka, we would be better healers."

"Yet you are gifted at healing, Hapu. I too dreamed of being a healer, in my way. I have tried to bind the wounds of Khemet inflicted by the Hyksos. I have tried to make the Black Land whole again."

"Majesty has indeed restored the temples across the land," said Hapu, giving a little belch.

"Why did you become a physician? Was it your father's profession?" I have always liked to converse with someone who is good at what he does.

"Yes, but it was also my own desire," said Hapu, sipping some watered wine. "I can smell devils, Majesty. I mean the kind that make one ill. It is useful for a physician."

It would be useful for a Pharaoh too, I thought. "What do devils smell like?"

"Not all the same," said Hapu. "Some smell sourish, some bitter. Yet others smell sweet. One can choose the right charms and medications, depending on the smell."

"Sweet? You mean, like myrrh?"

"No. A kind of rotten sweet." He shuddered but it did not stop him from taking a big bite of bread stuffed with mint. "A person into whose body a sweet-smelling devil has crawled will go to the gods without a doubt."

"Can you smell gods as well?" I asked.

"No. Only devils. Perhaps it is better to understand devils. I have thought it might be dangerous to understand the gods." He looked at me with bleary eyes. "Majesty should rest now."

"Thank you, Hapu. I will lie down as soon as I have made offerings of thanksgiving to the gods. You shall have some debens of gold for this night's work."

"Majesty is kind." He made an obeisance, swaying with weariness.

By this time it was early morning and time for the dawn rituals. I decided that I would go myself to the temple of Amen instead of leaving it to the priests and I would give thanks for the boy child who had been safely delivered this night. When the carriers set me down and I alighted from my sedan chair in front of the huge pylon entrance, I stood still for a moment, savouring the crisp air with its scent of wood smoke. I looked up at the pale blue expanse of sky arching over the city. And there it was, as I had known it must be: a falcon, circling lazily far overhead.

Yes. It was an omen. I had held another Living Horus in my arms. He would reign upon earth and he would wear the white crown and the red crown on the throne of Geb and smite the enemies of Egypt. He would be the strong Bull, Appearing in Truth, the son of Ra. It would come to pass.

Here endeth the eighteenth scroll.

I HAVE HAD a tale from Ahmose that is causing me sleepless nights. This time it concerns General Khani, who is a great favourite with Her Majesty and I know has her complete trust. That makes it even more difficult to know what best to do. I am greatly disturbed, for the last time I passed on information from Ahmose an innocent man died.

In truth, I do not even think this report can be designated as information. It is only a rumour and it is based wholly on hearsay, having passed from someone else to Ahmose to me. So quite possibly it has been distorted, or it may worthless to begin with. Yet it is such a dreadful rumour that were it true . . . well, I do not like to think of it.

This is what Ahmose had to tell me. He slid into his seat opposite me at the tavern obviously bursting with news. As soon as we had our beer in hand, he leaned forwards and whispered conspiratorially: "I have a juicy rumour for you today, brother!"

"What is it?" I asked, warily.

"You know that the Division of Sobek is quartered here in Thebes as we speak?"

"Yes, I know. General Khani's division. I used to see him at the palace sometimes, before he departed to the North with two other divisions."

"Some of the soldiers in the barracks here in Thebes are talking sedition," whispered Ahmose.

"Sedition? What are they saying?" I felt positively ill. "Have you actually heard them, yourself?"

"Well, no, but I gamble with a group of men which includes one who knows the soldiers. He tells me that they are saying that promotion has gone to General Khani's head. That he now feels he should be the Great Commander of the Army instead of Commander Thutmose. That he is laying plans to eliminate the Commander by arranging for him to die in the next battle by a mercenary's hand."

"But Khani has always been a most exemplary soldier. Why should he now . . ."

"But that is not all they say," whispered Ahmose, his scarred face contorted with glee. The man is an inveterate gossip and I am sorry that I ever became involved with him. I do not want to hear these things. "They say that this will be merely a preliminary to General Khani's ultimate ambition, which is to eliminate King Ma'atkare Hatshepsut also . . ."

I drew in a sharp, hissing breath.

"Hush, brother, do not exclaim . . . to become the first Nubian on the Double Throne, and to consolidate the empire of Egypt with his country, after which he will march to the Euphrates and subjugate all of Egypt's vassal lands that are currently restive in the north-east. And he will reign over the greatest empire ever seen."

There. I have written it. And reading it over, I fear, I greatly fear it sounds as if it might well be true. By the Ka of Thoth, it would be a magnificent revenge for all the times the Egyptian soldiers have quelled rebellions by the wretched Nubians, for the massacre in which all of General Khani's relatives were killed, and in particular for the execution of his father as a rebel when they were brought to the Black Land in chains. Nor would it be the first time that a general in the army becomes the Pharaoh. There are precedents. Also, for the Great Commander and the Pharaoh to be one and the same would consolidate enormous power in one person. I can see that it would seem highly desirable to a man of ambition, and General Khani is, I believe, an ambitious man.

Yet for all its plausibility it remains a rumour and nothing else. I cannot in good conscience pass it on. Or not before I have at least heard it from more than one source. This could cause far, far greater trouble than the previous rumour. This could be perfectly disastrous. Maybe I should just . . . just warn Her Majesty to have a care, without stating anything specific. Or perhaps it would be best to remain silent altogether while the Great Commander Thutmose is away in the South and General Khani in the North. When they return . . . then we shall see. Yes, we shall see.

THE NINETEENTH SCROLL

The wonderful plants that the expedition from Punt had brought were exactly what were needed to complete the gardens at Djeser-Djeseru in a manner pleasing to Amen-Ra. Among many other treasures, Nehsi had brought back baskets of incense and myrrh, but to my mind the most precious things were thirty incense trees, half of them frankincense and half myrrh, which would provide us with the precious resins required to manufacture excellent incense ourselves.

When the new plants arrived from Punt, the gardens surrounding my mortuary temple were already superb. As each terrace was completed, from the topmost one down, gardens had been laid out and planted on either side. Trees that had been planted when building began – sycamore, acacia, tamarisk and willow – had grown to a good height. Ornamental ponds stocked with fish and waterfowl had been made, around which bulrushes and lotus lilies flourished. The green oasis so created soon attracted a myriad of colourful birds, butterflies, and plenty of frogs. The new incense trees were planted in the gardens with great care, providing the finishing touch to a glorious creation. The whole was enclosed in a thick limestone wall with an ornamental gate.

In the thirteenth year of my reign the temple at Djeser-Djeseru was at last complete. Directly after the expedition from Punt had landed, I had given orders that the history of this great undertaking be carved in relief upon the temple walls. The artists who did the work were two young men who had actually been members of the expedition, and they depicted the events and the people involved with amazing liveliness. The large numbers of colossal sculptures of My Majesty had been completed and were in place.

Now that the gardens were flourishing, all was ready for the God to be brought across the river to spend one night with Hathor, goddess of love, beauty and joy, at Djeser-Djeseru. Usually, of course, Amen dwelt in isolation in the dark and lonely shrine at the heart of his temple at Karnak. But for the Feast of the Valley a group of priests would carry him out of his deep seclusion into the brilliant sunlight on his golden barque, then transport him across the river on his barge to the new temple, where religious rites would be performed. Excited crowds of people dressed in their best, together with dancers, jugglers and acrobats, would accompany the procession as far as they were allowed.

Once he reached the cool, dark heart of his own shrine, cut deep into the living rock behind the temple, only the Pharaoh and designated priests might gain access to perform the secret, sacred rites by the light of guttering torches and to set out the offerings to the God: meat and bread, wine and beer.

The people would depart to spend the night in the private tomb-chapels of their relations and ancestors. The night would be whiled away merrily with feasting and drinking by the light of hundreds of torches, as Thebans celebrated their reunion with the transfigured dead. At the dawning of the new day a religious ritual would wind up the festivities, and then the God would be conveyed back to the east bank and his gloomy, reclusive home at the heart of the Karnak temple.

Late one afternoon, some weeks before the Feast of the Valley, Senenmut and I sat at ease in one of my reception rooms, as we so often did. He had a large jug of beer; he never really enjoyed wine very much. I thought that he looked tired, as well he might, for the last few months had been a strain.

"Well," I said, "my dear, devoted friend, it is done at last. Did you ever think, that first time that we saw the bay of Djeser-Djeseru together, and conceived of creating an extraordinary building there, that it would come to pass?"

"I always knew we could do it," he said. "I knew that we had the determination – you, Majesty, and I. We dreamed it and we built the dream."

"You built it," I said. "Without your dedication, there would have been nothing."

"Without your vision and unfailing support, there had been nothing either."

"Well, there it stands. The most beautiful building in all the world."

"Majesty is gracious," he said, his tired face lighting up with pleasure.

"It requires a very special celebration," I said, musingly. An idea had come to me. Some might say, an outrageous idea. Yet having thought it, it filled me with delight.

"Soon the Feast of the Valley will take place, and the God will come to the temple," he reminded me.

"I know it. The God will have his night. One night of freedom and love. Just that once, the God may follow his heart in its time of fire and night. If the God may be allowed such freedom . . ."

He was staring at me.

"Why not the Pharaoh?" I whispered. "Why should we not celebrate the completion of Djeser-Djeseru together?"

"Majesty? I do not understand."

I jumped up and began to stride up and down, speaking excitedly but in a low voice. The guards were on duty as usual, but out of earshot, and I had sent my ladies and the slaves away. It was almost impossible for us to achieve true privacy for any length of time. Always there were slaves and servants hovering around and guards at hand, if not directly in sight, with household officials going about their duties. Several ladies-in-waiting constantly attended on me. But I had thought of a plan.

"Two nights from now, the moon will be full," I said, urgently.

"As Pharaoh, I could journey to my mortuary temple then and carry out some rites to consecrate it. Then from there I could continue the journey to visit my palace at Heliopolis, where I have not been for some time."

"Yes, Majesty?" He too was on his feet, concentrating on my muttered words.

"I will arrange that we be transported to the temple, you and I, for a . . . for a private ceremony at sunset. A royal barge from Thebes can take us there, but they shall have orders to depart. Then . . . yes, yes, I see how it may be arranged! Another royal barge from Heliopolis can come to take us further."

"Ah," he said. "We shall have an hour or so, between barges."

"Not so," I told him softly. The plan had fallen into place in my mind. "If we inform my servants at Heliopolis that the ceremony is to take place at sunrise on the following day, not sunset, they will not come till morning. Don't you see? The early part of the night will belong to the God. But the rest of the night will belong to us."

He drew a deep, wavering breath. "Majesty proposes to spend the night alone on the west bank? The abode of the spirits?"

"Not alone, Senenmut. You will be there with me. And why should I fear the spirits of the transfigured dead? There are more people in the Afterlife who loved me, and whom I loved, than are left in the world of the living."

He reached out a hand and gripped my arm. This was forbidden, but given what I had just proposed, I could hardly object. "You will risk this? To be . . ."

"To be with you," I murmured. Tears pricked in my eyes. "Just this once, let me not be the King. Let me not be the God, and alone. Just once."

My lady of the bedchamber arrived to assist me to my rest. Her plucked eyebrows rose at the sight of a commoner touching the Pharaoh.

Senenmut promptly let go of my arm and stepped back, making a deep obeisance. "Pharaoh has spoken," he said.

I gave the orders. Naturally, there were remonstrations. Surely I should be accompanied by priests, to assist in the rites? No, I said. This was for me to do as Pharaoh, for it was my mortuary temple. The priests would have their turn during the Feast of the Valley, soon. But one barge could undertake the whole trip, why need one come from Heliopolis? Because the Vizier of the North wished to see the completed temple, and he had offered to come and fetch me, I said. But surely I would require my ladies-in-waiting? Others would be arriving almost immediately from Heliopolis to attend on me, I said. I could survive a brief span of time without them. But how could I spend even a short time unprotected by my guards? This was not advisable. Nonsense, I said. It would be for a short time only, I would have Senenmut at my side, and in any case, most people were terrified of the west bank at night. I doubted any attacker would have the courage to land there.

With sweet reason, I overcame all objections to the plan. I had set my will on this and I would not be gainsaid. It would happen, and Senenmut would make all the arrangements, including the orders to the contingent from Heliopolis, so that they would know exactly what to do. With some reluctance everyone capitulated.

Two days later, we set sail from Thebes just as the sun was about to drop below the horizon. It had been a brilliant day, and hot, but it was as always somewhat cooler on the river. The stately barge was rowed out among the river craft that plied the waterway. As we moved steadily onward to the rhythmic thumping of the rowers' gong, the sun began to colour the water all around us. The surface of the water, a little choppy due to a light breeze, took on the appearance of a sheet of living gold stretching to the north and the south and bearing us up. The thick vegetation on the verges looked darkly soft and shadowy. On we sailed upon this magical river as if in some rich fantasy.

They set us down upon the west bank and then the royal barge took off again towards Thebes. Senenmut hefted two baskets that he had packed according to my instructions and we began to walk along the broad sweep of the avenue. On either side of us crouched the rows of sphinxes, each one with my face. But I was looking ahead, to the temple set against the towering crags. The sun had now dropped below the horizon and the cliffs in front of us, stark and glittering by day, were softened by the fading rose-tinted light. For a few moments they appeared to have been hewn from amethyst. Against that dramatic background the graceful limestone temple gleamed pearly white. All around us the fragrant gardens bloomed.

Then, as we continued walking uphill, the shadowed crags turned to grey. We reached the lowest portico before the light had faded altogether. Senenmut set the baskets down, extracted a torch and a tinder-box, lit the torch and handed it to me.

"First, I must honour the God," I said. "Walk with me up to the shrine."

He picked up the baskets and followed me. We ascended the sweeping staircases together. However, when we reached the God's dwelling deep in the heart of the rock behind the third terrace, I moved forwards alone. I unsealed the ornamental doors. I held out my hand for the basket of offerings. Then I walked on into the chill and musty darkness, alone.

Inside the shrine there was an altar for the God. I put the torch in a socket against the wall. I knelt and kissed the ground. Then I took incense from the basket, lit it and placed it on either side of the altar. I placed the dish with bread and meat and the vessels containing wine and beer upon the altar. I intoned the incantations that I knew so well, the magic words that knitted together the real and the spirit worlds, the visible and the invisible. Then I spoke a special prayer, dedicating the temple and especially the garden to the God. I concentrated hard, causing the Ka of the offering to feed the Ka of the God.

At last I felt sure that my heavenly father must be satisfied. Now Senenmut and I could share what was left. I gathered the offerings into the basket, took the torch and left the shrine, where incense mingled with the dank smell of the dark, rock-walled enclosure. I resealed the doors.

Emerging into the fresh night air, now decidedly cooler than when I went in, I felt my spirits lift. Frogs clamoured in the ponds and an owl hooted. In the distance I heard a clear, pure, singing sound: surely, I thought, the voice of the goddess Hathor, Mistress of Music, lyrical and true. I followed the wordless song. Down it led me, down the great ramp and the staircase, calling, calling.

Then I came to the northern colonnade of the middle terrace overlooking the lower courtyard, with its lovely garden. On the rear wall relief sculptures depicted ritual hunting and fishing in the sacred ponds. With his back to the wall sat Senenmut, in his old pose as a scribe, playing a flute. Numerous candles burned around him. In front of him cushions on a soft rug covered sycamore branches to make a couch. The wavering light kept the surrounding shadows at bay and illuminated the rich golden colour of the images carved into the ivory limestone walls. They seemed almost to leap into life. He did not notice me at once, but gazed out into the darkness as if he could see all manner of things that I could not.

I set the basket down and blew out the torch. I removed the crown from my head and set that down carefully also. Beneath it my hair, which I had allowed to grow, had been pinned up; I removed the pins and shook it loose. It had been washed in perfumed water, but not braided. I untied the broad gold sash made of embroidered silk from my waist, holding it in my hand, and let the thin linen robe fall free. Then, slowly, obedient to the music, I began to dance. I have ever been a good dancer, having been taught from my eleventh year when I acted for my father, may he live, as the God's Wife of Amen. I had practised anew when I taught my darling Neferure, may she live. It is the task of the God's Wife to maintain the God in a state of arousal. I had not forgotten those skills.

The wide, pleated sleeves of my robe fell open like wings as I spread out my arms and danced forward into the circle of light. There was a momentary catch in the music when Senenmut saw me; then it continued, with renewed rhythmic energy. And I continued to dance: twirling, whirling, backing and advancing; stretching, leaping, balancing for the space of a breath on the toes of one foot, then spinning away again; like a willow in the wind, I swayed and bent; like a bird I flew, alighted, and escaped; like a flame I reached upward and like a shadow I melted away. The golden sash in my hand flashed and rippled like a captive flame.

My robe fell from my shoulders, down to my ankles, then I snatched it up and covered myself again. I let it fly out, brought it back; swung it high and finally discarded it. Now I wore only my pleated kilt and a necklace of blue faience. The golden sash hid my breasts from view; then it was whipped aside; then brought into play again. I whirled and twirled, and then I lost the kilt. Now I had only the sinuously waving sash to hide behind; it was a ribbon of light, it was a delicate screen, it was a veil. But I did not wish to hide. No, I gloried in my nakedness. I dropped the sash.

The music stopped as Senenmut rose to his feet and took me in his arms. He too had discarded his kilt. His body was hard and warm and he smelled of lotus oil. He lifted me off my feet. Together we sank onto the couch, and when he entered me all the years of longing, of loneliness, of discipline and denial burst from me in a long howl of agony and delight. We cleaved unto each other like thirst-stricken travellers who have been lost and at long last find a deep fresh well.

When we finally came to rest, sated, breathless, and tangled in each other's arms, as if to touch as much as possible, the moon had risen and a pale wash of silver light spilled in bands across the pillared portico. It was a place of magic, a gold and silver bower, a playground fit for the gods. And oh, how we played! In that night, I was everything to him: I was his mother, and suckled him; I was his lover, and delighted him; I was his slave, and knelt to him; I was his child, and he cradled me in his arms and crooned to me.

At last we were spent and weary. He lay back upon the cushions, holding me close as I lay beside him, my cheek pillowed on his shoulder, one arm and one leg thrown across his body. I felt his breathing slow. His free hand stroked my arm, gently, gently. Then he turned my wrist so that the tips of his fingers rested just below the base of my thumb, holding it like that for a while. His warm breath tickled my ear.

"What are you doing?" I enquired sleepily.

"Listening to the voice of your heart," he told me. "I can sense it through my fingers. It speaks to me."

"What do you mean?"

"Here, feel my wrist," he said. "With your fingertips, like this. Don't press hard, just touch it."

I did as he told me. Then I could indeed feel it: a rhythmic throbbing. "Is it truly the voice of your heart?" I asked, wondering.

"It is. It falls silent when one's life force is spent. It stops when the heart stops," he told me. "And it speaks of love, for close to the beloved it rushes with joy. Yours is rushing, my beloved."

"So is yours," I murmured against his skin.

He drew the rug over us so that we were warmly cocooned in the moonlight, listening to the frogs. Enfolded in his arms, I felt entirely safe, as if no danger could ever come near me. Briefly, we slept.

The barge from Heliopolis would arrive just after dawn, since they were expecting the consecration rites to have been carried out at sunrise. I awoke as the last stars were fading on the horizon. Senenmut slept on, sprawled on the couch he had made for us, his face pillowed on one hand. Now the portico was but a stretch of cold, grey stone. The air was crisp, but I walked down to one of the ornamental ponds to splash myself, washing away the scents and the stickiness of passion with the icy water. My nipples puckered with the cold and with remembered pleasure. But there could be no more of that. I rubbed down with a towel and dressed carefully in my robe, tying the sash tightly. I slipped on my golden sandals and fastened the clasp of the flat jewelled collar that emphasised my royal status.

I picked up my crown, the red crown of Lower Egypt that I would wear on arrival at Heliopolis, and stood turning it in my hands. I looked up: A moment before, there had been only a hulking dark mass; now the towering crags and the elegant temple were taking form as a pale light washed the sky. It was as if they were being created from nothing as I watched. Just so does the world emerge from chaos each morning thanks to the rituals that the Pharaoh observes to link the Invisible and the visible. Just so does the Pharaoh maintain the existence of Khemet.

For a single night, I had laid all that aside. I had been another person, a different woman with a different life. I had not been the King nor the God, and Senenmut had not been my servant. In that moment, standing there in the chill before the dawn, I wished that I had chosen to walk a different road. I wished that we might have lived together simply, a man and a woman, that I might have gone to his arms each night and suckled his babes at my breast.

But I was Egypt. I had desired this high destiny; I had desired to become the Pharaoh, and divine. Yet I had not known that a god could be so lonely.

I tied up my hair and fitted the crown to my head. I walked back and awoke my love. "We must be ready," I said. "Everything must be packed away, and we must be standing on the quay to welcome the deputation from Heliopolis."

He rose to his feet in a lithe movement and reached for me, but I evaded his arms.

"No," I said. "No, my darling Senenmut, it is over. I am the King."

"So easily? After such a night, no more than this? *It is over?*" he mimicked me incredulously.

"It is not easy," I said. "The gods know that it has always been hard and it will be much harder now. But I am Pharaoh. I must reign alone. I do not have a choice."

"How can the all-powerful Pharaoh have no choice?" Now he was furious. "The one who has but to speak and everyone obeys? Ruler over the Black Land and all its dominions? Divine offspring of Ra? No choice? No choice!"

"No, none." I too was angry now. "I could never take a secret lover. It would not remain a secret very long. You know that I very seldom have privacy. And if such a thing about me became known, I would be laughed at. I would have become an ordinary, weak woman, seduced and mastered by a man. I could not rule."

"But . . . but could we not . . . would it not be possible . . . I . . . I cannot believe . . ."

"We could never break the jar together. I have told you that before. I thought you understood."

"I understand nothing!" In his agitation he began to stride to and fro. "If that is true, then why this night? Why plan so carefully for this, why raise my hopes, why treat me like . . . like a prince, and then . . . then simply cast me aside like a worn-out robe? Why?" There were tears in his eyes as he stopped pacing and faced me.

"I wanted . . . I wanted to have one perfect memory," I said, blinking away tears myself. "For just one night, I wanted to be free . . . to be simply a woman, spending time with her lover. Even the God has a night of freedom. Just one night."

"Even the God. Yes, of course, we must never forget that Pharaoh is divine," he sneered. "And a god cannot be mated with a mere human being, especially not a common man born in a little house built of mud bricks. No, we cannot have that!"

"Well, it could not happen. Then I would be the wife of a commoner while Thutmose, who is half royal, would be married to a wife of the full blood royal. You see what a weapon that would be in their hands?"

He sighed deeply, looking around him at the superb monument he had built for me, testimony of love and devotion beyond compare. Then his gaze returned to mine, suddenly sharpened. "And if there should be . . . issue . . . from this night?"

"There will be no issue," I said. "I have made sure of that. No, this was one precious night, and I thank you for it, but there will never be another."

He stood there staring at me, bafflement and fury in his eyes that had been so loving but moments before. "I cannot believe this," he said. I saw that he was shaking. He folded his arms as if to hold himself still. "I cannot believe that you could do this."

"You should believe it," I told him.

There was a long silence. Then: "Pharaoh has spoken," said Senenmut with deep bitterness. I could not blame him.

"I know that you will take our secret into the Afterlife," I said. "I depend on your discretion."

He nodded curtly. He bent down and collected the pile of branches that had been our couch and hurled them away. He packed up the baskets and stalked down to the shore, ignoring me completely, in absolute silence. The dawn found us standing on the quay, shivering in the chill wind that blew from the bleak water.

Here endeth the nineteenth scroll.

I THINK THEY were observed. It is merely a suspicion that I have, yet it could be true. The reason for this suspicion is to be found upon the temple wall – the outer northern wall – low down, almost hidden behind some bushes. It is a scurrilous little drawing, crudely executed with some sharp instrument. Not done by an artist, far from it – merely a few lines scratched by some common person with dirty thoughts. Yet it has sufficient detail for one to recognise the female Pharaoh, who is depicted on her knees, being mounted like a dog by a man who could be Senenmut.

My guess would be that it was done by one of the undergardeners. But is it a drawing of something actually observed, or is it merely the scribble of someone with a grievance, an expression of hatred intended to reduce the great King to a common slut? It is true that most people are terrified of the west bank at night, for they fear the spirits whose abode it is. But perhaps a worker missed the last boat home, and crept up to the temple to shelter from the chill; a worker who saw, perhaps, some lights, who heard a flute, drew nearer, peered . . .

I do not like to imagine this. No, no, it must have been mere spite. Besides, there were never any rumours about that night. About the relationship of Her Majesty and Senenmut, yes, of course there were rumours. But there was never anything as specific as the events related in this scroll. I would have heard.

I will never, never, speak of this. I should not have read this scroll at all. I regret having set eyes on these words, but it is too late. Yet now at last I understand the coldness that came between them in the end. It was obvious to all who had seen how they were together before. Oh, yes, I understand.

THE TWENTIETH SCROLL

THE REIGN OF HATSHEPSUT YEAR 20:
THE THIRD MONTH OF SHOMU DAY 15

Yesterday Mahu came to me with a tale of rumour-mongering in the taverns that has left me shaken. As usual he was reluctant to speak, but I could see that he had been brooding on this and he knew that I ought to be told. He hates to be the bearer of bad news, so he stuttered and stumbled through his report, avoiding my eyes. But tell me he did.

"Come on, Mahu, out with it," I said, irritably. "You asked for an audience. You must have something to say."

"It is merely a rumour, Majesty," he said. "Truly, there is no proof – no proof whatsoever – only what is said, in the taverns, and then only when men are drunk, and careless."

"What do they say?" No doubt more mutterings about the un-natural nature of a female Pharaoh, I thought. Every so often somebody starts that hare.

"It concerns Khani," said Mahu, rocking forwards and backwards as if he would much like to flee. He spoke so softly that I was not sure what I had heard.

"Who? What did you say?"

For once he looked straight into my eyes. "General Khani," he repeated. "It concerns him."

"Continue." Now he had my attention.

"They are saying . . . s-saying that the promotion to general has gone to his head."

Well, there would always be those who would say that. I was not surprised. "Continue."

"They are saying that his ambitions now . . . know no bounds. That he seeks . . . that he seeks . . ."

"To become the Great Commander?" I enquired.

"Yes. B-but more."

"More?"

"That he seeks the throne," whispered Mahu. "That he would be rid of both General Thutmose, Majesty, and yourself. That he has borne a deep grudge, all these years, for the humiliation that his c-country suffered, and his family, at Egyptian hands. That he seeks r-revenge. That he envisions a . . . a N-Nubian on the throne and Egypt a vassal state of Nubia, instead of the other way around."

I stared at him, aghast. This is a possibility that has never occurred to me. Yet perhaps it should have. Now that it has been spoken, it sounds dreadfully plausible. By Seth and all his devils! A Nubian on the Double Throne! It shall never be!

I was much perturbed by Mahu's report. Yet once I had grown calmer and considered the matter, I reminded myself of how easy it is to start a rumour and how often such rumours have no vestige of truth in them. There have been rumours about me that were entirely devoid of truth. It is a sly and underhand weapon, but it can be very effective. This tale about Khani has already succeeded in causing me to doubt him, to lose my absolute trust in his loyalty. This is terrible, considering our long and close relationship.

I have cast my thoughts back over the years and I can find no single instance of any action on Khani's part that would support these rumours. I remember the day I spoke for him, and how he bowed to me, not to my husband the Pharaoh. From that day there has been a bond between us. I remember the little monkey he brought to divert me when my son was still-born, and how it messed on Hapuseneb's tunic. I remember Khani's wide smile when he helped to carry me through the cheering crowds on the day that I was crowned. I remember how he came to me when the division of which he had been made Commander was quartered in Thebes, four years ago.

He had asked for an audience in my small audience chamber and when he arrived, he indicated that we should speak completely privately. I sent the guards away and closed the door.

"Yes, Khani?" He has an extremely imposing presence, I thought. The years of military training had filled out his frame and he stood tall and powerful.

"Majesty." He made a deep obeisance.

"Please rise. Pharaoh is pleased that your division is quartered here. Now we shall see more of you," I said.

"I have a suggestion to make, Majesty," he said in his deep voice.

"Tell me."

"While we are quartered here, I could make regular reports to Your Majesty, about . . . anything that might be of particular interest. In my position I hear many things. Naturally, I also know what the military are planning, especially . . ."

"Especially the Great Commander Thutmose?"

"Exactly. It might be helpful to Your Majesty to know what he intends before he imparts that information himself."

"If at all?"

"If at all. I know he has reason to feel . . . hard done by. Such men are dangerous."

I nodded thoughtfully. It would indeed be of great assistance to me in maintaining my supremacy.

"And, Majesty, I think it would be best if these regular reports were made discreetly. Let me not come too often to the audience chamber. Let me come quietly, while most people are resting, in the afternoons, to the residential palace. I can travel in a closed sedan chair, carried by men I trust."

"Very well," I agreed. "I appreciate your devotion, Khani. Thank you."

"I live to serve Your Majesty," he said.

In truth, he always has. And yet, perhaps Mahu's message is a timely warning to me not to trust anybody implicitly. Not one single person. Khani's words about Thutmose might well apply to himself: Was he not hard done by, as a child? Is *he* not perhaps dangerous? Khani himself told me to watch my back. Well, I shall do so. I shall watch my back and bide my time. Ibana must be told to observe Khani very closely. Yet of course – I must doubt even Ibana, just as I must doubt everyone else. How have things come to this?

I think poor little Bek saw me looking troubled, so he thought of a new way to divert me. He has found a lute and somebody has taught him how to strum it. He does not do so expertly, but he manages a few chords and accompanies himself as he sings. He has a remarkably fine voice, sweet and clear, and he sings with a kind of melancholy feeling that almost moves one to tears. Doubtless this is far from his intention, but that is what it does to me.

After Mahu had left, Bek sidled into my room, strumming. When I smiled at him, he sat down on the floor, stiffly, cradled the lute and sang. I think the song must have been his own invention, for I do not recall that I ever heard the bard sing those words. The tune was simple, but sweet, and memorable to the ear.

> *I sing of a seed that is sown*
> *In the earth, soft and deep,*
> *A seed that must wait for the sun*
> *To awaken it from sleep.*
>
> *I sing of a plant that unfurls*
> *Little leaves, brave and new,*
> *Of a stem that grows up to the light*
> *And of roots thirsty for dew.*
>
> *I sing of a tree, broad and strong,*
> *Bearing fruit, bringing shade,*

Where the birds may make nests safe and sure
In the midst of a cool glade.

Now he strummed more loudly, with deeper chords.

I sing of a storm that will break,
That will roar, that will rend
Branch from branch till the strong tree is cleft
Into halves that ne'er will mend.

Softer, now:

I sing of a tree fallen down,
Gone to earth, gone to earth,
And a drift of a handful of dust
Blown away by the God's breath.

"Why, Bek, that's beautiful," I said. "You shall become a bard!"

He smiled, looking almost like his old self. But his song has made me sad. It has brought memories.

Looking back, I think that the celebration of Djeser-Djeseru marked the high point of my life and of my reign as Pharaoh. Somehow, from that time onward, it was as if the gods began to withdraw their support from me, gradually but inexorably. Indeed, I had already forfeited the support of the one person on whom I had most depended.

Ever since the night at Djeser-Djeseru, Senenmut's attitude towards me had changed. He was no longer my beloved, telling me mutely of his love with every glance; he was no longer even my friend who sat with me companionably in the cool evenings sharing some wine. He became punctiliously correct, carrying out all his tasks with as much competence as ever, but he withdrew his heart from me.

It was my own fault, I knew. I had treated him badly. He had good reason to be angry. And yet . . . and yet, I could not regret that night. Nor, I would swear to it, did he. But he was angry and he punished me. I remember that he came, not long after that extraordinary night, to ask for leave of absence, standing stiffly to attention in my small audience chamber.

"Majesty," said Senenmut, "I beg that Pharaoh will excuse me from my duties for some weeks. The work on the great temple is complete, after all, and there are no major projects in hand."

"What would you do?" I asked.

"Return to Iuny," said Senenmut. He had been back to the small town where he had grown up a number of times over the years, but never for very long. "My mother has passed into the Afterlife and I wish to arrange an appropriate burial."

"Why, I am sorry for it," I said, sincerely. I had quite forgotten that Senenmut still had an aged mother living. "Of course, you should go."

"A suitable tomb has been prepared close to my own," he told me. "Work on it was begun some time ago. And since I am now a man of substance thanks to Your Majesty's generosity . . ."

His words were grateful, but his tone was sardonic. I merely inclined my head.

". . . it is possible for me to undertake, also, the reburial of my father, and even of some other members of my family who died earlier when I had limited means, and who were therefore given poor interments. I intend to have them all reburied together with appropriate grave goods. May they live."

"A noble aim," I said. "Certainly, we will spare you. When do you leave?"

"Tomorrow," he said.

"And shall we see you, perhaps, at the palace this evening?" I hated the sound of supplication in my voice. But I had missed him so, for he had stopped coming of his own accord and I would not order his attendance.

"If Your Majesty insists." His tone was flat.

"Pharaoh does not insist," I said, regally. "Naturally you will be busy. Go, go."

He kissed the ground. And he went.

In the year that followed, year 14 of my reign, two events took place that shook me seriously. I must write first of the one that caused me the greatest personal grief.

By that time I had lost many people who were dear to me. To some extent it was a comfort to think of them as happy spirits in the Fields of the Blessed, or in the case of my late father and husband (may they live) who had been Pharaohs, riding triumphantly with Ra in his solar barque. And yet sometimes I fear that the dwelling place of the inhabitants of the West may be deep and dark, with no light to brighten it, no north wind to refresh the heart. I hope I may be wrong. But it cannot be denied, as it has been written, that "*None has returned from there, to tell us how they fare*".

Be that as it may, that year I was to lose yet another beloved person to that unknown world. And it happened so suddenly, without a glimmer of warning. I do not know which is worse: to know that a loved one is ill, to snatch at hope, to search desperately for cures that do not work, only to watch that person suffer, dwindle, and at last depart; or alternatively to find that someone has been cruelly taken away with no chance even to say farewell. Both experiences are terrible. But in any case it matters little even if I could solve that conundrum – which I cannot – for one does not have a choice.

I had just completed a morning session in the Grand Audience Chamber, receiving tribute and holding discussions with visiting diplomats, when Hapuseneb urgently requested an audience. I was tired and tried to put him off, but he insisted on seeing me alone immediately.

"What is it, Hapuseneb?" I enquired crossly. "Can it not wait?"

"No, Majesty, I fear not," he said. His face was impassive. "I have grave news."

"Well, out with it," I sighed. I was expecting some political crisis to have blown up.

"We have received news that the Chief Steward of Amen was discovered dead in his house this morning," he told me.

"The Chief Steward . . ." I stared at him stupidly. "The Chief . . . you mean Senenmut? Is that what you mean?"

"Yes, Majesty."

"But that . . . that cannot be. There must be some mistake. Just yesterday he was with me. We . . . we spoke of additions to the gardens at Djeser-Djeseru. No, Hapuseneb, there has been a mistake."

"No, Majesty, I fear not," he said, inexorably. "Senenmut has departed to the Afterlife."

"How do you know? For sure?"

"It was discovered early this morning," he told me, "but we thought it would not be wise to disturb Your Majesty in the audience chamber. Naturally, I went to apprise myself of the accuracy of the information. The Chief Steward lay in the forecourt of his villa and he was not breathing. He was quite cold. I judged that he had not breathed for some time. To be sure, nevertheless, I called for the Royal Physician, and he concurred."

"You knew it and you did not tell me!"

"Majesty, there was no purpose. I made the necessary arrangements. He has been taken to the House of the Dead and I gave instructions for a full . . ."

"You did what? You had no right! No right to have him taken away! No right at all!" I was screaming now.

"But, Majesty, he has . . . he had no kin living with him . . . I could not leave . . ."

"You had no right," I sobbed. "I should have had the time . . . I would have wished . . . would have wished to say farewell. But you, you couldn't wait to get rid of him, you vulture, you have always hated him, and now you are alive and he is dead and you just . . . you . . ." I was weeping now, huge, shaking sobs, the tears running down my face and dripping onto my robe.

"Majesty, do not upset yourself so," he said, alarmed. "I shall call for Hapu. Please, Majesty, sit down." He stretched out a hand towards me.

"Do not dare touch me!" I shouted. "I am the Pharaoh! Touch me and I'll have you put to death! I should . . . I should . . ."

He made a deep obeisance, kissing the floor before my feet, and then retreated, muttering about Hapu. I sat down and buried my face in my hands.

I felt utterly bereft. And the worst of it was that he had gone to the gods with anger towards me in his heart. I knew I had given him cause. But with or without reason, he should not have parted from me so. Cold looks, and then nothing. Nothing. Gone. How could I bear it? The tears had dried up and instead I felt as if I had been dealt a huge, gaping wound. I wrapped my arms around myself. If I did not hold myself very tightly, I felt sure that my heart would fall out through the rent and lie bleeding upon the ground.

Soon Hapu arrived bearing some medications which he urged me to drink. "Majesty, you have had a shock. Please . . ."

"Oh, go away and leave me alone! You cannot do anything anyway! Nobody can do anything!"

"Just a sip," he coaxed me. "Just a sip. Please . . ."

I swallowed some of the bitter draught he held out to me. It made me catch my breath. I breathed deeply. "Did you see . . . did you see him, Hapu?" I asked. "There has been no mistake?"

"No, Majesty. No mistake."

"But how . . . what . . . how could it have happened? He was perfectly well last night. He had no complaints."

"His heart just stopped," said Hapu. "The signs were clear. He was no longer a young man, Your Majesty."

"Nor was he old," I said resentfully. "Only forty. That is not old."

"A fair age," said Hapu. "Not many live that long. And he worked hard all his life."

This was true. He had never been a sedentary scribe and nothing else. When they were working on the two great obelisks for my coronation, he had thought nothing of taking up a hammer himself; he told me this, proud to have made a contribution to the actual work. I saw his hands, scarred and callused in my service. Always he had had such energy, such strength. I could not believe that it had simply stopped, that that powerful life force had simply ceased to be.

"I would have wished," I said, my voice shaking, "I would have wished to say farewell. Before they . . . before . . ."

"I am sorry, Majesty," he said, looking woebegone, "we did not think. We acted for the best. The Vizier has given orders for a full mummification treatment to commence at once."

I nodded. The draught had taken effect and I was beginning to feel numb and distant, as if I were not truly present. "Yes," I said. "That should be done. Hapu . . ."

"Majesty?"

"Are you sure there were no signs of . . . of anything . . . no knife wound, for example? No . . . bruises . . . no injury to the head? Did you examine . . ."

"Majesty," said Hapu, whose judgement I had come to trust, "I looked with care. There were no signs of violence, none at all."

"Could he have been poisoned?"

"There were no signs of that either," he said. "Some kinds would leave a smell, or might have caused vomiting, or some foam around the lips, or a change in the colour of the skin . . . There was none of that."

"*Would* there necessarily have been one of those signs?" I wanted someone to blame for this terrible thing. I wanted someone to be guilty, someone to punish as harshly as possible.

"No," said Hapu. "There are some that do not leave a trace. Majesty, please, do not torture yourself with such thoughts. I looked and I found nothing. His heart gave in, it was tired. These things happen. You must resign yourself. It is a sad loss, indeed it is Khemet's loss, for he was a great man. But it was the time for him to journey to the Fields of the Blessed. The time to rest."

But first he would have to face Ammit, I thought. He would have to traverse the dreadful Netherworld and be judged by the gods. His heart would have to be weighed against the feather of Ma'at. Oh, Osiris, I thought, treat him with mercy. Surely his heart is light. I would do all that might be done to help him on his way. Every ritual, every prayer, every magic spell, every incantation, amulet, scarab or charm that could assist his safe passage would be ordered on his behalf. His body would receive the very best treatment that could be had from the House of the Dead. And I would have him buried with due ceremony in his grand new tomb with the stars on the ceiling, in the great sarcophagus that I had given him.

I made all these plans. But they did not comfort me. All gone, I thought, sadly, they have all gone, all those who had once loved and supported me. To survive is to be lonely. Nobody warns one of that.

Although my mother, the Queen Ahmose, had passed into the Afterlife many years before Inet, it was only after Inet went to the Fields of the Blessed that I felt like an orphan. And it was when Senenmut went into the Afterlife that I truly felt like a widow. It is strange that I felt like that, although we did not break the jar together, while when my husband Thutmose passed away – even though I had loved him, a gentle love, almost as if I had been his mother rather than his wife – I did not feel bereft. But now I did. My most able official, my most trusted adviser, my confidant, my lover of one magical night, my implementer of dreams, my best – indeed, my only – friend: all these were lost to me in one black night. I mourned him as if I had been his wife. I mourn him still.

But I had no peace that year, no time to recover from that dreadful shock, no time to gather my strength, no time to find my balance again. The second event that shook me concerned a rebellion in Canaan, centred in the town of Gaza, which posed a serious threat to our dominion in Asia. It was clear that the Canaanites required a sharp lesson and I gave the order to Thutmose to march there and re-establish our authority. He leapt at the chance to demonstrate the fighting ability of the soldiers that he had been training so assiduously. Taking two crack divisions, he departed with dispatch.

The expedition proved that the military had indeed reached a high pitch of professionalism under his guidance. In former years, this had not been the case. There had not always been a well-trained army on standby. Those predatory vagabonds the Hyksos were able to conquer Egypt because our arms and our soldiers were inferior, much though it pains me to acknowledge that. But we learned from them and we threw them out of Khemet, and ever since then we have maintained a powerful military. The expedition moved with the swiftness and deadliness of a striking cobra. Within only a number of weeks the rebellion had been crushed and the army returned victorious.

Thutmose rode into Thebes in his gilded chariot, standing with his thick legs braced as his driver guided the spirited horses, waving to the cheering crowds who threw flowers in front of his wheels. The army that marched in his wake brought prisoners to be pressed into slavery, and heaps of treasure piled onto groaning carts. This he had great pleasure in dumping in front of my throne in the Grand Audience Chamber while the assembled counsellors and nobles clapped and stamped their approval. He had a young prince in chains dragged in and set his sandalled foot upon the youth's bent neck.

"So," he stated in a ringing voice, "does Pharaoh punish those who rebel against the dominion of Egypt!"

More enthusiastic applause.

He makes it sound as if he were the Pharaoh, I thought. I waited for the noise to die down. "I thank the Great Commander, who has so ably executed Pharaoh's will," I said. "We shall reward him suitably. We shall bestow the Gold of Honour upon him at the next Window of Appearances."

That, I thought, was rather clever of me. It was a sought-after and rich award, that chunky gold necklace, and he could hardly refuse to accept it. But the ceremony would serve to emphasise my position as supreme: I would be enthroned in my great Window at the main palace in Thebes, surrounded by reliefs depicting myself as a crouching sphinx plus many emblems of kingship, while he would be below, clearly the humble recipient of the Pharaoh's gift.

Yet he had scored a signal victory, and not only in the field of war. The people were ecstatic. To them he was a hero, there was no denying that. All the way down from the North the crowds by the roadside had shouted their adulation. Naturally the military were united in their pride. Even some of my elderly counsellors, who had been inclined to see him as a juvenile, now treated him with respect. Tales of his remarkable achievements and bravery on the battlefield, that were of course soon embellished, did the rounds. It was said that he had personally killed thousands of the enemy, never missing a shot with his great bow from the back of his racing chariot. I doubted he had had that many arrows, but I knew better than to say so. He was the hero of the day; and for the first time in my reign I truly feared for my crown.

The night after Thutmose returned from his expedition I dreamed again of war. Once more I strode alone on that battlefield, on foot, armed with my dagger. Once more the scorching sun burned down upon me. I heard the barbarians howl. With frightful clarity, I saw the men rending each other and heard their piteous shrieks and groans. I smelled again the blood that had become mixed with the hot sand. And once more the sounds faded as the voice, that strangely familiar voice that I can never quite place, hissed to me: *Kill him for Khemet! Kill him for Khemet!*

As always, in my dream I knew that the Nubian soldier would come running towards me. And I knew that I would have to obey the voice. I would have to kill him again.

And so he came running, his eye bleeding as before. I knew that he would kill me if I did not stop his murderous rush. I raised the dagger and plunged it deep. He fell dead at my feet, his gore bathing my dusty sandals. I dreamed that I put my foot upon his neck. "So," I cried in a ringing voice, "does Pharaoh punish those who rebel against the dominion of Pharaoh!"

Once more I knelt upon the burning sand and experienced that overwhelming thirst for blood; once more I lapped his eyes. Oh, horrible, horrible! I struggled awake in such disgust that I found myself retching, and my attendant ran to fetch Hapu. I lay in a pool of perspiration, almost unable to breathe. Hapu gave me a calming draught, but I did not feel better until I had bade my ladies wash me, pouring cool water over my head, and perfumed myself with myrrh.

I hate that dream. I hate myself when I have that dream. I wish I could expunge it from my memory. But I cannot.

Here endeth the twentieth scroll.

THE TWENTY-FIRST SCROLL

Well, it is the new year, but it has not had an auspicious beginning. Yesterday afternoon, Hapuseneb came to the residential palace bearing bad news for me. He seemed anxious that I should hear it as soon as possible. I was annoyed, for I felt it could have waited for the morrow. But he was bursting to tell me.

Among the many duties of his office there is the task of monitoring the annual rising of the Nile. It is now that time of year when the green water should begin to appear in the south. However, it seems that this is not happening.

"Majesty," said Hapuseneb, "the water level is low. There is reason for concern." His lashless eyes were hooded, but I thought I detected a gleam of satisfaction. I have long suspected that Hapuseneb no longer supports me, and a poor inundation would undermine my powers as seriously as almost nothing else could do. He knows this very well.

"Are you sure?" I was immediately alarmed. I know that the dog-star Sothis is once more visible in the pre-dawn sky, so the flood should take place soon.

"It is too early to be sure," he answered, typically cautious, "but the indications are not good. I have had a report from Elephantine. The Nilometer there does not show the extent of increase that one would expect."

This was indeed cause for concern. "What about the vegetable harvest?" I asked.

"I fear the second harvest will not be very satisfactory," he told me. "At its lowest point the river was extremely low, so irrigation was difficult."

"We need to know the extent of food supplies in stock at depots across the country, as well as in the White House," I said. "You should send to all the nomarchs and ask for tallies."

"This has already been undertaken, Majesty." He looked smug.

Of course, he needed such reports before the flood was in full spate, since agricultural activities must be suspended for three months during this time. Then farmers are employed on public works and live from the table of the ruler. Naturally we would have sufficient stores for this period, but if the inundation were really too low and planting could not take place, we would need far greater stores to take care of the people for much longer.

By the breath of Horus, I pray that he may be mistaken. Never has there been a danger of a failed inundation during my reign. Last year's flood was normal and the harvest was very good. How can the waters not rise? Oh, Hapi, can you have forsaken me? This is Hatshepsut, whom you cradled and kept safe when she was a child. You have ever been on my side.

I shall make offerings. This cannot be.

Just as the Grand Vizier was leaving, a slave came running and made a deep obeisance. "Majesty," she said, "Yunit has asked me . . . Yunit says . . ." She looked very upset and stuttered without making sense. She was new to the palace and it was the first time I had set eyes on her. She seemed overwhelmed by my presence.

"Yes, girl, what is it? Out with it."

"Yunit is in labour, Majesty, and has been for some time. She . . ."

"Has the physician seen to her yet?"

"No, Majesty."

Hapuseneb looked at her severely. "Surely you are not bothering the Pharaoh with the problems of female slaves," he said. "Go to the palace housekeeper. Really, you should know your place."

"I shall come to her," I said, glaring at him. "Yunit is one of my favourites. I am concerned for her."

"A dwarf, is she not?" She had served refreshments when he was with me more than once in the past. I do not think he would have remembered any other slave, but the diminutive Yunit, who is also very pretty, had clearly made an impression.

"Yes. And I think she carries a very large baby. It will be difficult."

"Majesty is gracious," he said loftily, clearly meaning that I was ridiculous. I ignored this, saying farewell and then walking swiftly along the corridors to the slave quarters at the back of the palace compound. I knew that Yunit would have been seen to by midwives. Also there was a physician whose responsibility it was to see to the health of the palace slaves; after all, a sick slave cannot put in a day's work. But he was not a man who had had much experience of deliveries and the midwives would not have called for him to assist with a difficult birth. They could usually do whatever was needed.

As soon as I entered the room it was clear to me that the situation was bad. The room smelled rank; Yunit lay on a pallet drenched with sweat and her hair, normally thick and wavy, was nothing more than dank strings. Her eyes seemed to have sunk into her head. She lay staring at the ceiling, making tired little whimpering sounds, much as an animal might do that had been caught in a trap for many hours.

Two midwives, one considerably older than the other, fell to their knees and kissed the floor when they saw me. They too looked exhausted.

"Majesty!" exclaimed the older of the two. "You are too gracious!"

I walked to the bed and took Yunit's hand. She did not even turn her head to look at me. "Yunit," I said, softly. "It is I, Pharaoh. I have come to help you."

Dazed eyes turned to me and two fat tears rolled over her cheeks.

"It hurts," she whispered. "Can you make it stop? Please make it stop!"

"How long has she been in labour?" I asked.

"A night, a day and another night, and today also," the older midwife told me. "We have tried everything we know, but nothing will avail. She is too tired now to squat upon the bricks. She fell over and we let her lie down. It is not good, but . . ."

I turned to the girl slave who had fetched me. "Go and call Hapu," I ordered her. "Run. Tell him it is urgent."

"H-H-Hapu?"

"The Chief Royal Physician. You do know what he looks like?"

"Y-y-yes, Majesty."

"Well, then. Hurry."

I sat down on a stool next to the pallet and stroked Yunit's hand. "We will do the best we can, my dear."

"Bek," she sobbed, "can I see Bek?"

He had of course been banished by the midwives. "Soon," I promised. "We'll call him soon."

Hapu came promptly and conferred with the midwives. Then he said, "Majesty, I must examine the patient. But it has been so long . . . I think we will have to try the option that we almost tried when the little prince was born."

I understood. "Very well," I said, "you must decide. I shall await the outcome in my rooms. You will let me know?"

"At once, Majesty."

The sun was setting when at last Hapu was admitted to my presence. His round face was tired and solemn and his tunic was stained with blood. He made an obeisance.

"Tell me quickly," I said. "Could you . . . did you . . ."

"We cut the babe out of her body," he said, and sighed. His hands, I noticed, were trembling. "It was a perfectly formed little boy child, not a dwarf. Normal, and big. She was never going to be able to give birth in the usual way. Had I been called sooner, perhaps . . . But I fear, Majesty, that the babe was dead. It must have died hours ago."

My eyes pricked. I was reminded, naturally, of my own boy child who never breathed. It always seems to me to be such an enormous waste when a child does not breathe. For what did Khnum painstakingly fashion the little body, if he would not also breathe the life force into the newly-born? It does not make sense to me. Truly, at times the gods are strange

"And Yunit?"

"We sewed up the wound. Minhotep assisted me. But she was very weak. I do not know whether she will last the night. I am sorry, Majesty."

"You did your best, Hapu, I know that. It must be a hard thing to do."

"Yes, Majesty, it is," he said, looking surprised.

"Thank you. Thank you for your efforts."

Within an hour I was informed that Yunit had passed into the Afterlife. Bek had been with her, said the older midwife, who came to inform me, and when he realised that she was no longer breathing, he let out such a howl that the slaves thought Seth had descended upon the palace and there was consternation. But the slaves' physician had given him a draught of poppy juice, she said, and he was now asleep.

I told her that I would see him in the morning.

Now more than ever, I realise what a blessing it was that the little Amenhotep was born naturally and that he survived. And Meryetre, of course. Poor little Yunit. The burden borne so long, and all for naught. I think she was already very weary when her time came. I am tired myself, and I feel deeply sad. So sad that it is almost as if my bones ache. Somehow these events seem like bad omens.

Ah well, perhaps it will divert me to continue my journal.

By the fifteenth year of my reign, the Great Commander Thutmose was giving me considerable trouble. I did not like the airs that he had been putting on since his military triumph earlier that year. No longer did he live quietly and mind his tongue; my spies in Memphis reported that he was being openly critical of certain decisions I had made. I thought that it was time to blunt the claws of the wolf cub again, as I had had to do before.

Now the words of my royal father so long ago on that first journey together came into my mind: "*The love of the people is a precious thing, a resource in adversity.*" At last I understood his meaning. For I knew I had a formidable ally that I could call upon to support me: none less than the people of Egypt. Oh yes, the people of Khemet loved and revered me. They had known peace and plenty, indeed they had flourished under my rule. They did not desire a warmonger upon the Double Throne. I would call upon them to help me make it quite clear who the Pharaoh was and while I breathed would always be. Public acclamation of an overwhelming nature – that was what I needed and was determined to achieve.

So I decided that it was time for me to hold my Sed festival. My jubilee, my Myriad of Years. This is a tradition stretching back in time over more than a thousand years. It has been usual for the Pharaoh to celebrate the Heb-Sed after thirty years of rule, but my late father the Pharaoh, may he live, held his Sed festival after fifteen years had passed, not long before his death. If he could decide that this was right, then so could I.

I knew that this plan of mine entailed serious risks, for the Sed festival is a stringent test of the Pharaoh's spiritual and physical powers and the consequences of failure would be severe. I could not afford to stumble in the slightest degree. If I did, it would be said that I was no longer fit to reign. In the past the Sed festival had been a way to rid the throne of an occupant who had grown too ill or too weak to carry on. It could lead to my downfall. Should it be true that the gods did not want a woman upon the Double Throne, this would be the moment for them to demonstrate their ire, to repudiate and to destroy me.

Equally, if it were clearly successful, it would strengthen my position, proving positively that I belonged upon the throne. I well knew what the Sed festival entails, since I had assisted my father (may he live) at his Heb-Sed, in the role of the Great Royal Wife. It is the time when the Ka of the gods must mingle once more with the Ka of the Pharaoh. The time when the Pharaoh, providing he passes all the tests, becomes more than ever divine, marking a new cycle in the life of the King. And the influence of a successful Sed celebration, I knew, carries over into the Afterlife. It ensures that the Pharaoh's reign is perpetuated for all eternity. Indeed, I thought, that was worth striving for. High stakes. All to lose and all to gain.

Yes, I would go ahead. I would risk all. But I would plan everything meticulously and I would prepare with great thoroughness. I would begin at once.

My father had marked the occasion by having his architect, the great Ineni, erect a superb pair of obelisks before the entrance to the temple of Amen-Ra at Karnak. As I have written, my coronation had been marked by the erection of my own obelisks under the guidance of Senenmut, and they stood at the eastern end of the temple, their gold cladding glittering in the sun, proud witnesses to my ascension to the throne. Now, I decided, I would emulate my royal father once more. I would commission another pair of obelisks to mark my jubilee, and I would place them at the very spot where the God had dipped to the child Thutmose. That should send a powerful message to all concerned, I thought.

It was in fact my royal father who appeared to me in a dream and told me to do this. In my dream he instructed me to remove the wooden roof of his hypostyle hall in the temple at Karnak and to erect my obelisks in the space thus created. Who was I to gainsay the will of the transfigured dead? I gave the orders. These obelisks, I said, should be taller than any that had ever been erected by any Pharaoh before me; their points should reach the sky.

Since my devoted Senenmut had died the previous year, I entrusted the task of overseeing the creation, transport and erection of these items to my steward Amenhotep. He is a very different kind of person to the one who was my right hand, yet very efficient in his own way. He does not have Senenmut's endearing enthusiasm, but he plans everything down to the finest detail and nothing escapes his severely critical eye. I also charged him with the organisation of the country-wide festival itself, which would stretch over five days. I gave him a free hand in planning a feast that the people of Khemet would thoroughly enjoy, an occasion to remember. Of course it would demand deep coffers, but the nobles and others of high status would vie with each other in helping to bear the costs.

Furthermore, I gave orders that a fine new solar barque should be built for the God to be transported across the river at the time of the Nile festival during my jubilee year. For my part, I thought, I shall show in this manner that I honour my heavenly father, Amen-Ra, while on the tips of my obelisks I shall have engravings made to show myself as a youth kneeling and receiving the emblems of kingship from him.

According to tradition my jubilee would be proclaimed from Memphis on the first day of spring, the season of rejuvenation. This date was selected to emphasise the purpose of the celebration, which was to revivify the Pharaoh and reaffirm his fitness to rule. It was a public ritual of rebirth and rededication. But the festival would only take place several months later, in the first month of Peret, while the water is yet high, to allow time for work to be done on the new barque and on my obelisks. Then when they had been completed they could be floated down the river.

While work was progressing on these projects, I considered how I might best prepare myself. It occurred to me that the Royal Physician had served my late father, may he live, at the time of his jubilee. He might be able to provide good counsel, I thought. Since the occasion when I had knocked out the Great Commander with a lamp, and even more since my devoted Senenmut had died, I had come more and more to depend on the funny little man. He has a fussy manner, but he truly is good at healing people; above all, he has insight into how people think and feel, and somehow by that time I had come to trust him. I called him to my small audience chamber.

The rotund little man was sweating, for the day was hot. He looked at me anxiously. "What is the problem, Majesty? You are not ill?"

"I am never ill," I said. "No. I shall shortly announce my Sed festival, to be held later this year. I require some . . . advice."

"Ah," he said, nodding. "Yes. I was able to be of assistance to His Majesty King Thutmose the First, may he live for ever, at the time of his jubilee. But Majesty . . . it is a terrible risk. Are you sure . . ."

"I must silence my critics," I told him, walking the floor in agitation. "I must face down the Great Commander. I believe that he is mustering supporters behind my back. Since he quelled the rebellion last year he has the status of a hero, and there is always the resistance to a female Pharaoh that tends to surface at such a time. I must . . . I must do something spectacular."

"A successful Sed festival would indeed be a great spectacle," he nodded, "and it would impress the populace, since most people see only one such in their lifetime."

"But there is more than that," I said. "Yes, I am doing it for all the reasons we have spoken of, but . . . I . . . I need to do it for myself." Since the loss of my one true friend I never spoke intimately with anyone. I never showed weakness nor admitted doubts. But suddenly the kind regard of the little man undid me. "I am so tired, Hapu," I confessed. "Tired and heartsore and like to lose the way.

I need . . ." I bit hard on my lip as the tears threatened to slip over my cheeks.

"Majesty feels the need to be renewed," said Hapu.

"Yes," I said. "That is precisely what I need."

He nodded understandingly. "And that the Sed festival may achieve. Very well. How can I assist Your Majesty?"

"Tell me how best I can prepare myself. But, Hapu . . ."

"Majesty?"

"Nobody must know that I have consulted you on this. You understand?"

"Of course," he said. "I am Your Majesty's personal physician. I am a loyal servant." He looked somewhat injured.

"I know," I said.

"Well. As to the spiritual testing of the living Pharaoh I can say nothing. The Sed demands that he must have the strength of spirit to absorb and to channel the fierce energy that emanates from the gods. If not, the Pharaoh could be destroyed."

I shivered. I had faith in my own strength, but what if the energy emanating from the gods was too much for me to bear?

"But," Hapu went on, "Your Majesty has always shown courage. Courage and strength. Sufficient, I believe, even for this tough test." He did not say this is a sycophantic tone; his round eyes were earnest and fixed on me admiringly.

"Thank you, Hapu," I said, a little surprised. It has always been a strength of mine to engender admiration and trust in the men who serve me. Yet I had not thought that Hapu was one of my admirers.

"Well then, while the spiritual demands are great, the physical are equally so, and as for that I do have some suggestions that might help Your Majesty prepare. Ah . . . where . . . ?"

"The ceremonies will take place at Memphis," I told him. "At the Palace of White Walls where my coronation was celebrated. I have ordered the great palace courtyard to be refurbished and prepared for the occasion."

"Most suitable," said Hapu. "Majesty will need to begin at once, to build up the reserves of the body."

I nodded. The physical demands of a Heb-Sed are indeed daunting to contemplate. I recalled that my late father had had to call on every bit of his then waning strength to survive. The ceremonies go on for five days and the Pharaoh is fully involved throughout. There is no time to rest. For the first three days there are ritual processions accompanied by litanies, and offerings are made to the gods represented in the shrines lining the great courtyard. Then, on the fourth day, the Pharaoh must accept the testament of the gods that makes him the rightful heir to the throne of the Two Lands. It is a document encased in leather . . . but it is a supernatural object. If the Pharaoh has not properly absorbed the Ka of the gods, he will not have the strength to grasp it. This would be the crucial moment that would either confirm or destroy my reign. It was terrifying to imagine.

"Assuming that Majesty is able to grasp the testament of the gods, Majesty will of course have to run the prescribed ritual courses. This requires great physical powers," said Hapu, eyeing me somewhat dubiously.

I recalled that the ritual run must be carried out for Lower Egypt and again for Upper Egypt, to affirm the unity of the Two Lands, thus eight times in all, towards the four points of the compass. I pictured my late father pounding around the white walls, calling on the stamina that had been his as a great general, perspiration pouring from his face and dripping onto his naked chest. He had had to bear several ritual articles in his hands as he ran – such as the testament of the gods and the symbolic oar with which the Pharaoh steers the ship of state. In the enervating desert heat, this was not a task for the faint-hearted – nor for the physically weak. I could not afford to stumble, hesitate, or fail to complete the course.

"I know that it will be extremely demanding," I said. "But I must do it. Hapu, you must help me to prepare myself, yet none must know what I am doing."

"Very well," he agreed. "First, to build up Your Majesty's bodily strength . . ."

"Yes?"

"It would be . . . helpful . . . if Your Majesty were a little . . ."

"What?"

"Slighter. To run more easily," he said. "Good runners are slight."

"Oh." I could see that it had cost him some courage to come out with this. It was true that I was no longer as slim as I had been formerly. Since I had lost my devoted Senenmut the previous year I had turned to sweet things for comfort and I had gained considerably in girth, there was no denying that fact. I considered. It could help me to become clearly slimmer, especially if it were not made obvious until the festival, when it might appear that I had been magically rejuvenated by the rituals. I could wear loose robes while I was reducing myself. "Yes, Hapu, I think you are right."

"Majesty should just eat fewer sweetmeats," he suggested, "and smaller portions of all food. That should have the desired effect." He looked relieved that I had not been angry with him for his comment. "Then, Majesty should practise going without the midday rest."

"Often I do not rest," I said testily. "I work on documents. But all right. What do you think . . ."

"Majesty should practise running," said Hapu.

"By the tears of Isis, how do you think I must do that? The Pharaoh cannot be seen racing around the streets of Thebes! Be sensible!"

"No, Majesty, not in the streets. It is quite possible to run and yet remain in the same place," said Hapu. "Just lifting the feet, but not moving forwards."

"Oh, I see," I said thoughtfully. Well, I supposed I could do that in the afternoons on my portico. I always told the guards to remain some distance away and they need not see me. "Very well. I shall be sure to run regularly."

"The strength of the body must be built up," said Hapu. "I will come to the palace, if Your Majesty agrees, and demonstrate how the soldiers of Egypt train to build strength. With heavy weights."

"My father . . . did he train?"

"He trained. But, Majesty, the training is very hard going. A soldier of Egypt must be tough."

"So am I," I said, glaring at him. "So must Pharaoh be."

He shuffled. "Majesty recalls that it will be necessary to shoot four arrows into the four directions of the compass at the end of the ceremonies?"

"Yes, of course I do. Fortunately I have always been good at archery."

"Good. Then, it will be important for Your Majesty to sleep well every night during the celebrations. I shall provide a nightly drink with the juice of the poppy."

"That would be good," I said, nodding. I could imagine that one might lie awake at such a time and he was right, it would be exhausting.

"One more matter," he said, somewhat nervously.

"Yes?"

"If it should happen," he said, carefully, "if . . . if . . ."

"Yes? What?"

"If it should be the time for Your Majesty's monthly flux . . ."

"Oh, dear. That would be a disaster." I had not thought of it.

"Yes, it would be difficult. But I have a potion that will make it tardy. Not keep it away altogether, of course. But it does delay the flux by a few days."

"You are a wonderful man," I said, smiling at him appreciatively. He had given me courage.

His round face flushed with pleasure. "Majesty is gracious," he said, making a deep obeisance.

"Thank you, Hapu."

Now I felt ready to begin preparations. I was absolutely determined that I would survive the tests. And on the fifth and final day the double coronation would be repeated, just like the first time. I would stride forth regenerated. I would become new and strong and the Two Lands would once again be the fruitful fields of the Divine.

Here endeth the twenty-first scroll.

THE TWENTY-SECOND SCROLL

THE REIGN OF HATSHEPSUT YEAR 15

Everyone concerned laboured mightily to complete the pair of obelisks I had commissioned in time for my jubilee festival. As the date for the festival approached, I feared that the work might not be done in time, but all other work at the quarry had been suspended and the two mighty spears were indeed completed with only days to spare. On the day when the enormous barge arrived with its extraordinary cargo, there was almost as much excitement as the day the expedition returned from Punt. Noisy crowds lined the river banks and cheered loudly when the boats sailed into view. Musicians played martial music accompanied by drums and sistrums.

I myself was on the quay enthroned on a temporary wooden platform to receive the obelisks. I was much afraid that there would be some mishap, for the barge was very cumbersome, but fortunately my people are accomplished boatmen and the precious load was safely brought ashore.

Next, the obelisks had to be transported overland to the temple. Most of the inscriptions had already been done at the quarry, describing my relationship to my earthly and my heavenly father and emphasising my right to rule. But the gold cladding on the tips would be carried out at the temple itself. This time Thitui would not allow me to clad the entire shafts with gold. He said it would be needlessly extravagant and it might lead to criticism of My Majesty, so I heeded him.

I gave instructions that the inscriptions would also record these words: *My majesty ordered this work to be done for my heavenly father Amen. I did this for him with the love a king has for a god. It was my desire to make it for him, gilded with electrum . . . I undertake what my mouth speaks; I do not go back on my word. I gave the finest electrum for*

it, which I measured like sacks of grain. My majesty ordered this quantity,
more than the Two Lands had ever seen.

Well, admittedly, there was a slight exaggeration, since the first
two obelisks actually bore more gold than these two. But then these
were bigger. None larger had ever been erected. They would be the
tallest in the world.

The obelisks were transported on rollers to the temple, where
the space for them had been prepared. When the cladding had been
completed, the obelisks could finally be installed, their bases planted
fast in the earth of Khemet and their fingers pointing to heaven.
Again I was present to observe the work being carried out. The steward Amenhotep seemed to bob up everywhere.

"How will you get the obelisks into place?" I asked him.

He wiped his perspiring face. "Well, Majesty, as you see, the
roof has been removed from this section. We have prepared square
foundations in the floor. The foundations are notched and the bases
have been chiselled to fit."

I nodded, interestedly. I have always been fascinated by building
projects. "But it will be a challenge to raise them up and slot them
into place," I said.

"Indeed. That is what the mounds of sand are for. The pylons
will be dragged up the one side, base first, then tipped over and slid
into the pits," he explained.

"Ingenious." I watched as the first of the behemoths was man-
handled up the slope of a mound, guided by a network of ropes on
which many men hauled. As they worked, they chanted rhythmically.
The base teetered as the centre of balance shifted. Then it canted over.

"Hold the tip steady!" shouted Amenhotep, his voice shrill with
anxiety. The leaders of two teams on opposing sides yelled orders.
Then the colossal spear slid down the far side of the mound, grinding
on the sand, and slammed into place with a thud that echoed through
the hall. A ringing cheer went up.

The next one went faster. Unfortunately too fast. The men were overeager to complete the task. As the long shaft rocked on the top of the mound, the teams holding the ropes to the tips lost the rhythm and the obelisk began to swing from side to side, gaining in momentum as it swung.

"By the scales of Sobek, hold on, hold on!" yelled Amenhotep desperately.

But they could not hold it. It rolled over the side of the mound and the gold-plated tip crashed thunderously to the ground, pinning two unfortunate men to the stone floor. One, in fact, was only a boy, and as the falling shaft struck him it made his eyes burst from his head. An inhuman scream pierced the chorus of gasps and groans. Blood spurted, bright scarlet in the sun. It smelled like a sacrifice.

"Majesty!" My guards, who had been staring with as much fascination as I, leaped to my side. The chief guard gestured for my sedan chair to be brought. I was swiftly carried away from the scene.

Eventually the second obelisk was also successfully raised, and the feasting went on and a bull was killed. Yet some of my delight was gone. Afterwards it seemed to me that I could discern a dark stain on the tip of one obelisk. Imagination, of course. Gold does not stain.

The first day of my Myriad of Years dawned sunny and clear. I had travelled to Memphis before the festival was due to begin. I chose Memphis for two main reasons. First, the Palace of White Walls had been the site where I ran the ritual way when I was crowned, and I considered it suitable that I should repeat the ritual there. Second, Memphis is where the army has its headquarters, and the Commander had – indeed, still has – many supporters there. I needed to impress upon them, especially, my right and my fitness to reign.

There was an expectant buzz throughout the city, as jugglers and acrobats entertained the crowds, who were out in huge numbers, dressed in their best; marching bands celebrated with trumpets and drums, flutes and sistrums; hawkers cried their wares, legless beggars solicited alms, and pickpockets and prostitutes plied their trade. Over it all wafted the smells of freshly baked bread and frying fish. I had given orders for abundant food and beer to be distributed.

The palace had of course been renovated and equipped with the necessary vast courtyard, open to the sky, lined with shrines for the gods, with a platform at the one end holding two thrones and seating for the select audience at the other. The walls had been newly whitewashed and reflected the morning sun brilliantly. Brightly striped pennants on poles atop the walls snapped in the light breeze.

For my first appearance, I was regally dressed in a kilt and an intricately pleated robe, both of fine white linen decorated with gilt, golden sandals, a round, flat jewelled collar and the Double Crown. Dressed like that, I stood at the top of a flight of stairs leading down to the courtyard, flanked by two tall standard bearers. A roar went up when the crowd caught sight of me. This was, however, their last glimpse of the old King Khnemet-Amen Ma'atkare Hatshepsut. I now proceeded once more to the robing chamber, removed my rich garments and the crown and stood with my shaven head bowed for a purification ritual carried out by the officiating priests with their jackal masks. They poured sacred liquid over me from a vessel fashioned from pure crystal. It was cold, and I gasped a little from the shock as it ran over my warm skin. The scent of myrrh rose into the air. Next, I put on a simple, close-fitting linen tunic.

Two of the masked priests led me back to the courtyard. The roar that now greeted me was louder than before. As I slowly descended the broad stone steps, the roar intensified. Stripped of my crown and robe, with only the thin tunic clinging to my body, I was sure that all could clearly observe my slim, taut new form, the first indication that the old King that I had been was dead and a newly regenerated King was present, ready and willing to be tested as stringently as would be required.

From the base of the staircase a short figure now walked to meet me. Since I had no Royal Wife, the role that such a one would have played was to be carried out by my royal daughter, Meryetre. A regal figure she was not; since the birth of my grandson Amenhotep two years previously, she had not managed to lose the considerable girth she had put on. No matter: the contrast between us could do me no harm. However, she held herself proudly, two white plumes nodding in her hair. Her kohl-rimmed eyes were anxiously fixed on mine. I gave her a slight nod as she turned to face the crowd, then led me down the steps. It would be her task to protect me with ritual incantations throughout the ceremonies and to feed me with the celestial milk.

Thutmose had been given some minor ritual actions to carry out during the course of the festival, but nothing very spectacular. I was aware of his constant fixed regard as the days went by; no doubt he was waiting for me to flag, to stumble, to fail. I would disappoint him.

The lector priest who would read the prescribed text from the sacred papyrus over the next few days intoned the first words. The orchestra composed of harps, lutes and double pipes began to play a lyrical melody, pure, singing tones, punctuated by the deep boom of the huge drum. For three days we would proceed around the vast courtyard, paying homage to the deity in each shrine. It was very demanding, both physically and spiritually, for it was necessary for me to concentrate all the time, since it was my intervention that gave supernatural life to each deity. I was weaving links between the spiritual world and the one on earth, affirming the life force of the created world, so ensuring the continued existence of Khemet.

Yet I did not find it tiring; rather, the experience was affirming my own life force. I was becoming more and more exalted, moving into a state of being where everything seemed to become more intense, more infused with significance. Only the baleful stare of Commander Thutmose was fading into the background; otherwise, colours seemed sharp and bright, sounds crystal clear; the eyes of the gods, fashioned from precious stones, regarding me from their niches, appeared to me to shine with energy that poured into my being and bore me up.

I fear my poor Meryetre had no such uplifting experience; obviously her legs were growing tired with each day's slow march and her energy flagged. She had not had the benefit of months of preparation, as I had had; preparation that was standing me in good stead. Yet she continued to hold her head high and played her part with gritty determination. I was proud of her.

From time to time I would take my place on one of the two thrones, constantly alternating. This symbolised the reconciliation of the two highly diverse portions of the Black Land, emphasising that every element of the rituals had a dual phase, so that the land as a whole could be united in the person of the King.

On the fourth day of the festival I exchanged the long tunic for a pleated kilt, complete with a bull's tail, traditional symbol of the Pharaohs from time immemorial. Now the crucial test would be carried out, to be sure that I had absorbed the Ka of the gods and had been regenerated as the newly divine King. The leather case containing the testament of the gods would be placed in my hand. The question was: Could I grasp it without fainting? As Hapuseneb, wearing his jackal mask, put the sacred object into my hand, I closed my fist around it firmly. It seemed to me that a stream of energy coursed from it through my entire being. I held it aloft, and the cheers that rang around me could surely have been heard clear across the city.

Enormous relief almost did make me faint, but I breathed deeply and held on. Surely, I thought with elation, surely the gods were satisfied, for if they had not been, they could have destroyed me in that moment. I must yet be the chosen of the gods.

Next I received more ritual objects, and, descending from the platform where the test had taken place, I kicked off my sandals and proceeded to run the ritual courses prescribed by tradition: four times as the King of Upper Egypt, and four times as the King of Lower Egypt. Through my actions, I united the Two Lands, revived the life force of the Pharaohs who had gone before me, assured the continued existence of creation, confirmed the presence of the gods, and finally stood before my people as the rejuvenated King. I accepted my bow from Hapuseneb, and, standing tall, I loosed off four arrows to the four points of the compass. A mighty cheer accompanied each arrow as it went winging forth. After all this I was somewhat winded, but not desperately so; I noted that Meryetre observed me with amazement. She had not expected her mother to have such strength.

Nor, clearly, had Thutmose. I caught his furious gaze as I acknowledged the applause of the crowd. Well, let him be angry, I thought triumphantly. After this, I have the upper hand. And the best is yet to come.

The fifth and final day of the festival was the day that would see me crowned again. For this occasion, the two thrones had been replaced with a single one: larger, higher and more richly ornamented than either of the other two. Again the day began in the robing room, where I was dressed in the full regalia of a Pharaoh. Preceded by standard bearers and accompanied by priests wearing jackal masks, I walked the length of the courtyard to ascend the platform and thence the throne. As at my first coronation, I was crowned first with the white crown and then with the red. Together they formed the Double Crown, symbolising my kingship of the Two Lands. The two sceptres, the crook and the flail, were placed in my hands.

Now there remained only the last ceremonial act: The Great Ones of Egypt were to come forward one by one and wash my feet, so indicating their acceptance of my authority and their submission to my reign. The first would be Hapuseneb, in his capacity as Grand Vizier of the South, now without his jackal mask; next Dhutmose, Vizier of the North; then Seni, as my senior counsellor; Ahmeni, the noble who heads the Party of Legitimacy; and then Thutmose, as the Great Commander of the Egyptian Army.

An ornamental bowl holding sacred water was brought, together with a cake of natron and an embroidered cloth. I removed my golden sandals and stretched out my feet so that the men, kneeling on the steps below the throne, could carry out their ritual task. In Hapuseneb's eyes I thought I saw respect and admiration. He strode forward quickly and worked fast. The cool water was soothing, for my feet were hot and tired by this time. Dhutmose, sycophant that he is, practically kissed my toes. Seni nodded austerely as he meticulously wiped my feet. Ahmeni acted with solemn dignity.

Then it was Thutmose's turn. Across the bent back of Ahmeni, our eyes met. His were smouldering. He knew, of course, exactly what I had achieved with this festival. He had wished me to fail and I had not. Now he had to carry out this act, which to him would be degrading – I knew it. Yet there was no escape. For a few breaths he did not move. Then he marched across the platform, knelt stiffly, avoiding my gaze, and gave each foot a cursory wipe. A slave darted forwards to dry my feet and help me replace my sandals. I stood, to the ringing acclamation of the crowd.

Then I indicated that they should be silent. I had composed a prayer for the occasion that I would now speak. My voice was clear and steady as I said the words:

I have done this with affection for my Father Amen,
I have executed his plan for this first jubilee;
I was guided by his excellent Spirit,

and I omitted nothing of that which he demanded.
My Majesty honours the Divine Lord.
I did it under his guidance; it was he who directed me.
My heart took counsel from my Father; his heart spoke to my heart.
I turned not my back upon the All-Lord. I did his will and I honour
him.

I looked at the officials standing in the front row of the select audience. Among them I noted military commanders, and right in the middle – there was Khani, at that time Commander of Recruits. His eyes held mine as they had all those years previously, when my husband had been the Pharaoh and I had spoken for him. Once more he bowed his head to me as he had done then.

I was borne out of the palace in a litter and carried along the avenues to be greeted by the jubilant populace. The old King, myself, tired and troubled, was dead; I went forth as the new King, younger and more vital, rededicated to his people. Reborn and strong. Able to maintain the unity of the Two Lands and the sanctity of Ma'at, able to preserve the miracle of creation, to satisfy the will of the gods. Fit to wear the Double Crown. The Living Horus.

Ah me, I wish that I could feel like that now. But I fear that I have lost that slim young form; I could not now run around the white walls, with or without the oar of state. I am weary and my heart is heavy in my breast. I have just come from an interview with Dhutmose, Vizier of the North, who was here to deliver his usual report. This time the news was not good. It is the first month of Akhet and the farmers of the North have heard that the waters show no sign of rising. They too fear that the inundation will be late and less than usual. May the gods forbid that it does not come at all.

Here endeth the twenty-second scroll.

WELL I RECALL Her Majesty's Myriad of Years. I was then twenty-one, employed in a quarry, but I made sure that I was in Memphis to witness the great festival, and an impressive one it was. Of course, I was not one of the select audience in the palace where the ceremonies took place, but I did see Her Majesty run around the white walls before going back inside to complete the ceremonies. She amazed everyone, for she was fleet of foot and did not seem to tire. She ran clad only in a simple tunic, and anyone could see that the Pharaoh looked young and slim.

The common people were astounded. I stood, cheers ringing in my ears, the scent of flowers crushed underfoot in my nose, near a stout peasant woman who was lost in admiration for the Pharaoh. "The great King has surely been renewed," she said in awe. "She gained in girth after her Steward died, and she seemed very tired and downcast, and now look! She seems slight, and young, and strong! Truly, the gods do favour her!"

As for myself, what struck me most was not the demonstration of renewed vigour. No, as I stood among the crowd and watched the procession move past, with Her Majesty carried high on a kind of jewelled and gilded throne, the Double Crown upon her head and the crook and flail held in her hands, what I thought was that after all, the great King was but a slight female figure, and that she looked very much alone.

THE TWENTY-THIRD SCROLL

This new year, which began badly, has grown worse. First I had a visit from my daughter Meryetre that disturbed me greatly. As I have written, I was forced to give her hand to Commander Thutmose. For him, I believe it was a political marriage and not one he entered into with his heart. However, she was with child very soon. It must have been a most auspicious night when he bedded her to plant that seed, for my darling grandson Amenhotep is a child of great virility, cleverness and charm. He is also a very loving little boy, much attached to his wet nurse, who sees far more of him than his own mother. The year of his birth was indeed a very good year for me, when my great expedition to Punt returned and the gods were pleased. The child has now seen eight risings of the Nile and grows more delightful every day.

Meryetre comes from Memphis to visit and brings him to see me, not as often as I would wish, but they do come. When she arrived for her most recent visit she was in a state of great excitement. In fact, she could hardly wait for me to find the little model war chariot, a present from Khani, that Amenhotep loves to play with when he visits me. I saw to it that he had a tiger nut sweet and some grape juice, which he likes, and ordered some watered wine and dates for us.

"And how is it with you, my daughter?" I enquired with a sigh. Usually this question would bring forth numerous complaints, but not that day.

"It goes well, Mother," she said, her dark eyes shining with some pleasure that she was hugging to herself with glee.

"Oh? Am I to be a grandmother a second time?" I asked. This seemed unlikely, since she had miscarried twice after the birth of her son. The second time I had gone to her, since I had to travel to Memphis at the time in connection with a building project, and I had been surprised at the urgency with which she had clung to me and at the depth of her sorrow. It was not the same, I would have thought, not as heartrending as losing a fully-formed babe, yet she had been distraught. There was not much that I could do, but I listened as she bewailed her loss, and I made her bowls of warm goat's milk with honey as I had done when she was little and it seemed to comfort her.

"What? Oh, no! No, I am not with child. No, no. It is Thutmose, my husband, who has made me very happy."

"Really?" Had he bought her jewels, I wondered. She has rather flashy taste and a collar of gold studded with jasper and carnelian can make her eyes light up.

"I am to be his Chief Wife," she announced proudly. "He has set aside that Satioh who brings forth girl children only and who has become a slattern and a nag."

At this I frowned. Satioh is a Mitannian princess and the Mitanni would not take kindly to an insult offered to one of their royal house. Could that have been his intention, I wondered. I suspect him of trying to create an excuse to take the field against the Mitanni.

Well, well, I thought. This is a shrewd move on the part of the runt. On the one hand it might enrage the Mitanni sufficiently to cause them to attack, which would force my hand in declaring war. On the other hand it strengthens his claim to the Double Throne. And since he has five daughters from the first wife, while his other sons by minor wives and concubines are all younger than Amenhotep and do not have the full blood royal, Meryetre will doubtless in time become the Mother of the King. So, it is certainly politic to make her the Chief Wife. No fool he, one must admit. And a move I could hardly oppose. No fool, indeed.

"Mother, you frown," said Meryetre in an injured tone. Her voice had taken on the whining note I knew so well, that grated me as it had done all her life. "You are not pleased for me," she complained. "You should be glad that he has given greater honour to me, who am Egyptian-born. She is no longer the sun of his eyes. He loves me better now." She sniffed and a tear rolled down her cheek. "She has grown fat, and slatternly," she added, wiping it away.

Yes, perhaps she has, my poor child, I thought, but while she may have lost her looks you never had any. In fact, you have always looked a great deal like your husband Thutmose, which may be the reason why he finds you acceptable. Both stocky little figures, both brown of eye with strong, slightly hooked noses and both with the buck teeth so common in the royal family, although mercifully they passed me by. For that matter, both bald, although of course Meryetre wears extraordinary, intricately plaited wigs. How two sisters could look as different as she and Neferure, my darling first-born, may she live, I do not understand. For Neferure, as I have written, was beautiful and made men catch their breath as she walked by. Perhaps it is not surprising Meryetre is always discontented, I thought.

I put my hand on hers and patted it. "I am happy if your husband honours you, my child," I said. "It is the thought of possible political effects of a slight to the Mitanni that makes me frown. Be happy."

She sniffed again and was partly mollified. But I lay awake most of that night, as I now have for several more. I feel as if I cannot draw enough breath. Also I am afraid to sleep, for I do not want a recurrence of my dream of war. I am being encircled, I am being pressed on all sides. They will force me into armed conflict and I do not want it. Yet that is not all; I must write truthfully. There is another matter that steals the sleep from my eyes.

Only a day later an event occurred that I still find virtually impossible to believe. For two people to be so close over so many years, and for the one to . . . His heart was tied to mine, and mine to his.

Indissolubly. He knew that. How could he, how could he then . . . No, let me write it as it happened.

I had finished my morning session in the Grand Audience Chamber and had moved on to a smaller room that Hapuseneb as Vizier of the South uses as an office. I had matters to discuss with him. Praise be to the gods that it was private; if this episode had happened in front of large numbers of people, I do not know how I could have maintained any dignity. He was not there, but I was glad to sit for a few moments collecting myself. These days a full session tires me. I had sent my lady-in-waiting to fetch some cool juice, but she had not yet returned.

Hapuseneb does himself proud, I thought, looking around me at the elegant furniture, woven floor covering and superb collection of vases, many of which were surely imported. They were carefully set out on tables and chests. I noticed fine pottery vessels and others fashioned from rock crystal, alabaster and glass. A man who does well with the support of the Pharaoh.

Suddenly an altercation met my ears; someone was trying to obtain entry and the guards at the door were not allowing it.

I heard the guards' low rumble and then a high-pitched woman's voice arguing urgently.

"The morning audiences are over," I heard one guard say, through the half-open door. "You must come back tomorrow."

"The Pharaoh will wish to see me," the female voice insisted. "Just enquire, that's all."

"We are not going to disturb Her Majesty, woman, I tell you, come back tomorrow!"

"Tell the Pharaoh it concerns the late Senenmut," said the voice, clearly intending that I should overhear these words. "Just tell her, you'll see . . ."

I went to the door. "Let her come in," I told the guards. "Keep all others out. Come, then."

The woman walked in, smiling triumphantly at the guards. Then she made a deep obeisance. "Thank you for seeing me, Majesty," she said.

"Rise," I said. "Your name?"

"Nefthys, Majesty." She stood. I saw a woman somewhat smaller and also younger than I am. She was quite elegantly dressed in fine, pleated linen with a coloured sash and wore a necklace of silver set with amethysts. Many small plaits framed her oval face. A person of some status and means, I thought.

"You mentioned . . . Senenmut? He who was the Overseer of the King's Temple, the architect of Djeser-Djeseru? That Senenmut?"

"The same, Majesty."

"Well, what of him? You were related?" I wondered whether there could be a matter of property that she had come to me about. Yet Senenmut has been in the Afterlife these six years; surely all such issues will have been sorted out, I thought.

She nodded. "It's about my sons, Majesty," she stated confidently. "A pair of twins. They are now of an age to be properly trained as scribes, both having seen seven summers, and I wished to beg admittance to the palace school for them."

Well, she had considerable presumption. I wondered who could have sired them that she should believe them to have such a claim on royal patronage. She herself had no connection with the palace, I was sure of that. I would have known of her, for she could be neither a servant nor a slave.

"Why should I allow them in?" I asked.

"Because he would have wished it, Majesty."

"Who would?"

Her almond-shaped, amber eyes widened. "Senenmut, Majesty."

"Indeed. So, you must be his sister. Yet I did not know he had one of that name. I know of Ahhotep and Nofret-Hor, but . . ."

"No, not his sister, Majesty. His wife."

I stared at her blankly. "He had no wife," I said.

"Majesty, he did. He had me. He was the father of my sons."

I was angry. This was clearly an imposter, a woman with a scheme to promote her children by this wretched lie. "Not true," I snapped. "He had no sons."

She was unrolling a scroll that she had taken from a basket on her arm. Silver bracelets jangled. "I have the contract, Majesty, between his family and mine. Signed and attested, and sealed as you see."

I barely glanced at it. "A forgery, no doubt," I said. "Senenmut never lived anywhere but in Thebes, where his home was. To be near . . . to be near the court. He had no time for a wife and family. His . . . his work took all his time."

"He had a second home," she told me, "in Iuny, where he was born and grew up."

"He was never there for long," I insisted, "and when he went there, he went to visit his parents, and old friends."

"Many women have husbands who go away for long periods of time," she argued. "Sailors. Soldiers. Tax collectors. I could bring witnesses from Iuny," she added, "who will attest that when he was there he lived with me."

"Bribed," I sneered, "doubtless there are enough townsfolk who would swear their mother was a whore if promised a goodly supply of food for a year or so. No, no, my good woman, it will not do, it will not do at all."

I was shaking, but still in command of myself.

"Majesty," she whispered, "I know where the entrance to his second tomb is located. I know that at first he wished to be buried in what is now his funerary chapel, and his great quartzite sarcophagus was delivered there. But he feared tomb robbers, as do all rich persons, and he commissioned a secret second tomb, hidden beneath the precincts of Djeser-Djeseru. He had the permission of Your Majesty. I know that the ceiling of that secret tomb is decorated with a calendar showing the lunar months and depicting heavenly bodies."

"Someone betrayed him," I retorted. "Some workman, some artisan told you these secret things. It was not Senenmut. Why," I demanded furiously, "why have you come here to tell me these lies?"

"It was his wish," she said inexorably. "It was his wish that his sons should be palace children. He made me promise to come to Your Majesty when they were of the right age. He said . . . he said, 'If the Pharaoh does not believe you, say: Remember the celebration of Djeser-Djeseru.' Her Majesty will know that message must come from me."

Now I knew that she spoke the truth. My heart howled in my breast like a jackal, but I would not let her hear it. Twins! Twin sons born to this woman, and my son never breathed! Oh Senenmut, how you have punished me! I turned my back and pretended to be studying a vase. "When were your sons born?" I asked. I had to force my voice to speak.

"One year after the great temple was completed," she told me. "Before that, I used the juice of the silphion plant, for he did not want children at first."

"When did you break the jar?"

"Twelve years ago, Majesty."

When I was twenty-eight years old, I thought. The year that Thutmose, that one who would be King, tried to seduce me. When I laughed and told Senenmut of his impertinence. When I affirmed that I would never take a husband. That year. And the children begot upon her soon after the "celebration of Djeser-Djeseru". By the foul breath of Seth, I believed her now. The hot tears began to roll down my cheeks. Oh, how I was betrayed! How he had cheated me! I thought I held his heart, that it was mine alone!

"He said, Majesty, that you would allow the boys into the palace school, once you knew that they were his."

Yes, he was right. I could not refuse. I could not risk this woman going about and telling everybody that the Pharaoh would not accept the sons of the late great Senenmut into the palace school because of jealousy. I could not risk her telling what she might know of . . . the celebration of Djeser-Djeseru. I did not know what he had told her, and I could not, I would not ask. And he, who knew me so well, would have known that.

Oh, I was angry. I shook with it. It was a double, no, a triple betrayal. First, he had not been faithful to me, as I had been to him. I had been celibate, I had spent lonely nights aching with desire, I took no substitute lover! In my thoughts, we were in the same case, and I took heart from knowing – imagining – that he too was lonely, longing for what could not be. I believed that we were two of a kind, both sacrificing love because we served Khemet. Often when I could not sleep and longed for him, I believed that he too was awake and that the voice of his heart spoke my name to him.

Worse, he did not tell me. If he had, I would have been heart-sore, but surely I would have understood. Very well then, if you must, I would have said – a man has needs, and this woman will not be important in your life. But he left me ignorant, he went away to Iuny, not to a concubine, but to his wife, to loving arms, to *twin sons* – by the tears of Isis – and I did not know! How she must have laughed at me! How they must have laughed together! Not only they, but all who knew. Many must indeed have known. And many must have mocked the poor deluded Pharaoh! It does not bear thinking of!

But worst of all: He had told her of the celebration of Djeser-Djeseru! That is the worst betrayal that he could ever have conceived. He knew how absolute was the trust I placed in him. It was our secret, ours alone. He promised to take it to the Afterlife. Instead, he spoke about it to this woman. How could he . . . how could he have . . . How much detail had he shared with her, I wondered, cringing. Did he truly need to boast about his mastery of the Pharaoh? Was this how he achieved revenge for my refusal to take him as a royal consort? By shaming me from beyond the tomb?

He should have hung head down from the walls of Thebes. He should have been thrown to the dogs. He should have been fed to the crocodiles. He should have been burned alive. Still standing with my back to the woman, I wiped my cheeks with the shawl I wore over my shoulders. Gathered my strength. Collected my dignity. "Very well," I said. I turned around. "You may speak to the Chief Tutor. Tell him the Pharaoh wishes the boys to be enrolled."

She made a deep obeisance.

"Smell the ground," I ordered.

She kissed the floor in front of my feet.

"Rise, and go," I said. "But I do not wish ever to set eyes on you again. Is that clear?"

She rose. Her eyes were cast down, but they flicked up once, looked me up and down and then away again, and in that moment I caught the hint of triumph in her glance. "Yes, Majesty. Thank you, Majesty," she said.

I waited until she had left the room, and had had time to depart. Then I picked up the vases one by one and threw them at the wall. Pottery, glass, alabaster scattered in shards across the room. When Hapuseneb arrived, he stood aghast at the destruction, but he knew better than to remonstrate. I picked up the rock crystal vessel, which had bounced off the wall.

"There is one left," I said, putting it down on a table. "I shall speak to you tomorrow." I swept out.

Anger coursed through me like Seth bent on destruction, and like Seth I wanted to destroy. I called for a gang of strong workmen and I told them to go to the funerary chapel of the late Senenmut and to break the sarcophagus remaining there with its images and inscriptions into as many pieces as there were stars in the night sky. I told them to remove the names and images of Senenmut and of the Pharaoh from the walls wherever they appeared. I told them to remove all the statues of him, large or small, shatter them and cast them into a quarry.

As for his secret tomb, where he actually lies – of course that is a more difficult matter to dispose of. Ordinary people are loath to disturb an eternal house, especially of someone known to all, although tomb robbers are desperate enough to risk the possible effects of curses or the retribution of the gods that the dead one invoked with prayers, spells and amulets. Yet I found a greedy priest from the House of the Dead and offered him all of the grave goods if he would open the tomb, get a gang of slaves from the quarries to haul out that sarcophagus, destroy it completely, take out the coffins, remove the mummy and feed it to the crocodiles. A pity, I thought in my impotent rage, that it was not the living body of the faithless one. But I will be revenged. I will wipe out his name and banish him to the Netherworld, there to be devoured by monsters. He shall not live.

Here endeth the twenty-third scroll.

THE TWENTY-FOURTH SCROLL

I have now, I believe, written about the most important events of my life and of my reign. Yet I shall continue with my secret writings, recording what happens from day to day. It helps me to think matters through.

It is a strange thing, but when one begins to write, it is as if the reed pen has its own intentions that one's heart did not necessarily plan. More than once I have surprised myself by what I write; I have been more candid in some of these scrolls than I should have been. My pen knows what it wants. It wants to tell my story. But I can be obstinate, if I truly want to be, and I now note, here, very firmly, that I do not wish to write any more about the faithless one, whose tomb I have denuded and whose mummy I have had destroyed. No more of that. *I will write no more of that.*

I am still Pharaoh, and I still occupy the Double Throne. I must concentrate on serious things, matters of state. Thutmose has returned from the South, to a hero's welcome. They cheered him all along the river as he marched with his men; this even though they had fought no battles, other than a few skirmishes with desert tribes. Had quashed no insurrection, for there had been none. Still, the common folk revere him, and in the streets of Thebes they threw flowers beneath his feet.

I must reassert my status and authority. I have been considering my choices, and I have had an excellent idea. Six years ago, my Sed festival served me well. It impressed the populace and reaffirmed my kingship. What I had done once before, I thought, I could do again. I sent for Hapuseneb.

"Soon it will be time for the Festival of Opet," I said.

"Yes. But, Majesty, the water remains low. I believe it would be wise to keep the festival within modest limits this year. It must be held, of course, but . . ."

I said, "Precisely because the festival is linked to the rising of the Nile, it is necessary to praise the gods whole-heartedly."

Hapuseneb looked very uneasy. "If the inundation fails, we shall have to feed our people for many months. We must husband our resources. To be spendthrift now . . ."

"The inundation will not fail," I said, with more assurance than I felt. "Perhaps it may be somewhat less generous than usual, but that has happened before. We shall survive, particularly with the aid of the shaduf and the way in which it improves irrigation. It is early Akhet yet."

"The signs are ominous," he said, stubbornly.

"Well, all the more reason to propitiate the gods. We need a grand Opet festival with prayers and ample offerings to ensure a good inundation." I did not see how he could argue against this, since the Opet festival prescribes – among other ceremonies – communing between the Pharaoh and Amen-Min, who inseminates the earth and brings forth fruitful harvests.

He sighed. "What had Your Majesty in mind?"

"A truly magnificent event," I said, "continuing for a full eight days with, of course, music and pageantry and sporting events – races, archery competitions, wrestling matches, that sort of thing. And plenty of bread and beer to be distributed."

"As long as that? Majesty, I must protest! Most strenuously! In the circumstances . . . even two days . . ."

"Well, then . . . perhaps four. We must honour both Hapi and Amen-Min appropriately. We must demonstrate our total faith in the gods' blessings."

"Yes, Majesty," he agreed reluctantly. "But three days, truly, should suffice. We must husband our resources."

"Very well, then, three. But I shall order another obelisk," I told him. "Not a pair, there will not be time. But definitely one. And this one is to be the tallest, the most amazing spire the world has ever seen, reaching to the heavens. One solid piece of granite like my other two pairs. Not a single join. I shall dedicate it to the god Amen-Ra at Karnak."

"But, Majesty, surely they will not be able to complete it so quickly?"

"If only one is to be made, I believe it can be done. It is early Akhet now, and the festival will take place at the end of the second month, for the moon will only be in the right phase by then. I have made up my mind. Amenhotep must put a huge team to work upon it, to get it ready so that its erection may be the culmination of the festival."

He had by this time understood that I was determined. "Pharaoh has spoken," he said. But his lips were thin.

Of course, he knew and I knew the deeper meaning of the Opet festival. Besides ensuring a good inundation, it also emphasises the bond between the gods – particularly Amen-Ra – and the Pharaoh. It constitutes a renewal of the King's right and power to rule. The coronation rites are repeated. Once again the might of Amen is bequeathed through ritual to his son, the Living Horus. Hapuseneb could not deny me the right to carry out these ceremonies, so essential to the link between the visible and the Invisible and therefore also essential to the very survival of the Black Land.

Having set matters in train for the Opet festival, I slept better than I have for some time. But the lady-in-waiting who awakened me this morning brought ill news. She was clearly nervous as she prepared my clothing and set out the jewelled collar and studded bracelet I had elected to wear for the early session in the Grand Audience Chamber. A deputation from Nubia was due and I intended to look very regal. Once or twice she began to speak but swallowed her words and went on hastily with her duties, eyes averted.

"Oh, come out with it, woman," I said testily. "I can see that you are big with news. Doubtless it is bad, or you would not look so fearful."

"Majesty," she said, and fell to her knees in front of the low chair I sat in while a second lady arranged my elaborate wig. It has been so hot that I ordered my head shaved. The wig would later be replaced by the crown that was kept in the Vizier's office.

"Well? What is it?"

Indeed I was expecting bad news, for at present it seems there is no other kind. Yet I was not prepared for her announcement, nor for the force with which it struck at my heart.

"Majesty, it . . . it concerns the dwarf," she told me.

"Well, what of him?" Guiltily I thought that I had neglected Bek of late. When he was well he used to come daily to amuse me, but since he was attacked in the tavern I do not see him often. Yet I try not to let too many days pass without at least ordering some fruit or tiger nut sweets, which he loves like a child, to be taken to him.

"Majesty, he is dying."

"What!" I stared at her stupidly. She blinked and dipped her head.

"Hapu does not think that he will see tomorrow," she said. "He told me to inform Your Majesty."

"But why . . . he has not been ill, has he? Why was I not told before?"

"Not ill, Majesty." She pleated a fold in her tunic.

"What then? Surely he was not set upon again!"

"No, Majesty." At last she looked up. "He has drunk poison," she whispered.

"Poison! By Seth and all his devils! Who was responsible for this? He shall not breathe!"

"No, Majesty. He . . . he took it himself. He told the physician when the other slaves found him lying on the floor. He says that he does not wish to live."

Anger and grief coursed through me. Also guilt. This should not have happened. I should not have allowed it to happen. Bek was like a child to me and I should have cared for him better.

"I shall go to see him," I said, removing the heavy wig and dumping it on the bed.

My dresser was upset. "But Majesty! The viceroy from Kush awaits!" she remonstrated.

"Let him wait. Send word to the Vizier." I strode barefoot along the corridors to the slave quarters. I knew where Bek's room was, the one where Yunit had breathed her last. My lady had to trot to keep up with me.

In the small room with its plain brick walls Bek lay on a simple sleeping mat, flat on his back with his toes turned up. The sour smell of vomit hung in the air, but he was clean and so was the floor. Hapu sat on a low stool beside him holding his hand.

"Majesty," said Hapu, struggling to rise. The years have attacked his knees and he is no longer nimble.

"Sit," I ordered. "Tell me at once. Is there yet hope?"

Hapu collapsed back onto the stool with a deep sigh. I knew that he was fond of Bek himself and he looked miserable. "No, Majesty," he said. "I have tried emetics. They made him regurgitate, but I fear it was too late. He must have drunk the potion hours before he was found."

"Is there nothing . . . can you do nothing at all to help?" Tears were pricking my eyes. The small figure more than ever resembled a child as he lay there quietly, barely breathing, his eyes closed.

"No, Majesty. He has taken the kind of poison that paralyses the body. Some kind of snake venom, I suspect. Soon he will no longer be able to breathe. I can do nothing." Hapu shook his head and rubbed Bek's limp hand.

"But where did he get such a thing? Who supplied it? The guilty person must be punished! He must be found, he must . . ."

Hapu went on shaking his head. "Bek will have bribed some slave to fetch it. There are those who trade in such things, but they are very careful — nobody ever knows their names. Certainly, whoever brought it crept here in the dark and now is nameless also. Let it be, Majesty."

I knelt on the floor next to the mat and took Bek's other hand in mine. It felt cold.

"Bek," I said urgently.

His eyelids fluttered.

"Bek? Speak to me!" Somehow I could not bear to lose him without a word.

Slowly his eyes opened and his gaze fixed on mine. "Majesty," he whispered. His breath was as light as a spring breeze in a sycamore tree. I leaned closer, gripping his cold fingers.

"Majesty, I am . . . sorry."

"Dear Bek," I said.

"I can no longer . . . do . . . what I do well," he breathed. "And all those I loved and . . . who loved me . . . have gone . . . into the Afterlife. I long . . . to join them. Forgive me, Majesty."

Bereft of words, I patted his hand. He pressed my fingers weakly. I continued to kneel next to him while he breathed in short, shallow gasps. In a few moments he ceased breathing altogether. I rose awkwardly and stood looking at the small, utterly quiet figure with its spindly legs — still, I noted, crooked from the grievous injuries he had suffered for my sake.

The thought of this was too much for me and I began to weep. Hapu stood up also. He shook his head despondently.

"I am sorry, Majesty," he said. "Sorry that I could not help him. Could not prevent or cure. I failed him."

"You did your best, Hapu," I said through my tears. "If anyone failed him it was I. I should have taken better note of him."

"Well," said Hapu, "I hope that he will reach the Fields of the Blessed, and that when he does, he will be able to run again."

"And turn somersaults," I said, attempting to regain my composure. I yet had work to do.

Hapu smiled sadly. "May he live for ever."

"I shall give orders for offerings to the gods," I said. Perhaps they would be merciful, I thought, seeing that the supplications would be for Bek and not for me.

Shortly after Bek had gone to the Afterlife, Ibana came to report. He brought two persons with him, a soldier and a slave. The heavy door to the office where I held the interview was shut, and they all spoke in low voices. The slave was a short, thickset woman with black hair. She held something wrapped in linen in her hands. The soldier was a strapping young Egyptian, clean-shaven and bald.

"Show Her Majesty what you have found," Ibana instructed the woman. "Put it on the table over there."

The woman moved forwards hesitantly. Then she unrolled the linen and two small items fell out. She seemed not to want to touch them. She bit her lip and looked up at me.

I peered at the small figurines that now lay on the table top. Then I gasped. The one was a waxen likeness of myself – indeed, quite an artistic one. It even wore a miniature double crown and a false beard and a robe. Three sharp spikes were buried in it, one in the abdomen, one in the chest and one in the head. The second was a model of Thutmose, correct down to his special bow. It was pierced by two spikes in the side. Suddenly I felt as if I could not breathe.

"Where did you find these?" I demanded.

"In a . . . in a chest," the slave whispered.

"Whose chest?"

"Belonging to General Khani," she whispered.

I felt cold with shock. "I don't believe it! You lie, woman!"

Tears stood in her eyes. "Majesty, it is the truth, I swear it. If I lie, may my heart give witness against me in the Afterlife! I swear it by the risen Osiris!"

I stared hard at her. These were serious oaths. She was trembling, but her dark eyes held mine. Her manner spoke of truthfulness. I have learned to smell out liars with considerable success, but she did not seem to me to be lying.

"This woman cleans General Khani's quarters," said Ibana. "And sees to his clothing."

"That is true, Majesty," said the soldier, clearing his throat. "I serve as the General's factotum in Thebes. When on campaign he travels light, but here he likes to have a choice of cloaks. I told this slave to prepare for the General's return – he is due back from the North. She was airing the woven mantles that had been stored away, and she discovered these . . . objects . . . wrapped in a towel in the bottom of a chest. She brought them straight to me."

"You are suggesting that they were there for . . . some time?"

"Yes, Majesty."

For as long as Khani was away, I supposed. And that is just as long as I have been feeling not myself. If someone has been putting evil spells on me, that would explain it. But Khani! My friend, my most reliable informer! I could not credit it.

I looked at Ibana. "How did you come to know of this?"

"The factotum is one of my spies," he told me. "He keeps me up to date with the General's doings."

"Majesty, I serve the Great Commander, and I serve the Pharaoh. If any plan their downfall, it is my duty to report on them." Zeal shone in the young man's eyes.

I looked down at the terrible little objects. "Wrap them again," I told the slave. "And leave them with me." I turned to Ibana. "I will consider this carefully," I said.

"Majesty should act, and soon," he said. "I await instructions."

I would have to take these figurines to a priest, so that he could remove the spikes and devise some spells to counteract the evil magic. But what could clear the devilish suspicion from my heart?

This cannot be true, I told myself. Surely it must be a fiendish plot. Yes, I was inclined to believe that the two witnesses were speaking the truth, for their manner had been convincing, and they did not seem to be the kind of people who might be practised liars. Yet the figurines could easily have been planted for them to find by someone who wanted to drive a wedge between my last good friend and me. Someone who wanted me to be filled with suspicion, to fear for my life and to feel entirely isolated. Very possible.

And yet, as Mahu told me, there have been those dreadful rumours about Khani. Does Khani in truth desire the Double Throne? Has he harboured thoughts of revenge for all these years? Am I his enemy and not his friend? Would he rejoice to see me bleed? Does he seek my death?

Is there no loyalty, no faithfulness anywhere? This, added to the perfidy of Senenmut – but no. I have vowed: *I will write no more of that.*

This afternoon as I was resting on my portico with Bastet on my lap, Khani appeared as he always used to, silently, out of the shadows. I looked up and there he stood. He made a deep obeisance and said, "Majesty!"

"Khani!" I exclaimed. For a moment I was delighted to see him, and had I not been Pharaoh I think I would have jumped up and thrown my arms around him. But then I recalled Ibana's report and I resisted that impulse and just looked at him. He stood stiffly and the silence lengthened. I stroked the cat.

"Majesty is displeased with me?" he asked.

"You did not write," I said, accusingly. "I did receive reports, but none from your own hand."

"For some time I was too ill to write," he told me. "I was wounded early on, in a skirmish with a desert tribe. It was only a slight wound, but it festered badly and I was delirious. The physician Minhotep pulled me through with herbal concoctions."

"You do look very thin," I said, observing him carefully. His ebony face had a greyish tinge.

"But when I grew better, I did write," he said. "I wrote often."

"Often? I had no letters from you, all this time. None at all."

"Intercepted, no doubt," he said. "I have enemies in Thebes. As do you, Majesty."

"It is possible." Time was when I would have believed him implicitly. Now, though, I look at him and I see a pretender to the Double Throne, bent on revenge for old wrongs and greedy for power.

"Majesty," said Khani, "I bring a warning. There can be no doubt now that Khemet will have to go to war. Our dominions in the north-east are growing restless, and the Prince of Kadesh is the leader of the rebels. They are gathering around him in considerable numbers, ready to do battle. Not only the Hittites, but the Mitanni and the Canaanites also. Tough and determined soldiers, Majesty."

"And how do you know this? You did not travel north as far as Kadesh, surely?"

"No. But we have scouts, who went that far and observed what was going on. Also, we captured some Bedouin who turned out to be spies for the Hittites. They were . . . persuaded . . . to tell us what they knew. Large armies are mustering. Already their advance guard attacks and plunders our outposts. We shall have to act, and act decisively."

"What do you think should be done?"

"For a start it will be necessary to take Megiddo, to teach the rebels a lesson. Furthermore, we are reliably informed that they have laid up a substantial wheat harvest. It could be confiscated and brought to Egypt."

"And why, in that case, have you come home? Turned tail, did you?"

"I obeyed the instructions of my Pharaoh," he said, stiffly. "I came to tell Your Majesty in person what the situation is, since I had no responses to my letters. I came to urge the dispatch of an entire army, not merely one or two divisions."

"Should I send the Great Commander?" I asked, watching him carefully.

He did not hesitate. "Yes, Majesty. As soon as possible. I will gladly serve under him."

And you would have every opportunity of dispatching him to the Afterlife, I thought, and making it seem the fortune of war. You could then take the command, subdue the rebels (whose strength and determination you have no doubt exaggerated), return as a conquering hero bearing treasure and food, and usurp the throne. Probably also allowing an insurgency from the south, from your own country, the wretched Kush.

I could not believe that I was having such thoughts about my old friend and faithful supporter. Yet it was as if the devils of Seth had crept into my heart, making me fearful and suspicious. What should I do? What should I believe? What should I decide?

"I shall put it to my advisers," I said.

He made an obeisance and left silently as ever.

I was much disturbed. Bastet sensed my restlessness and jumped off my lap, whereupon Sekhmet chased her off the portico into the garden. I watched them streaking across the flower beds with a troubled heart. I do not want to do this. I think most of my advisors will think we should go to war. But I shall insist on a delay, while we first send more scouts to ascertain whether Khani speaks the truth or whether he exaggerates.

I have nobody left whom I can trust.

Here endeth the twenty-fourth scroll.

I AM HURT, sorely hurt, that Her Majesty does not think of me as someone she can trust, someone she can depend upon. It is not that she does not trust me, in truth. The fact is that she does not think of me at all. She forgets me altogether. She forgets that I breathe. And yet I saved her life once; and even now I hold it in my hands.

They are dangerous documents, these scrolls that I carry away with me. The one I brought out today, for example . . . It gives me power to have these words of the Pharaoh in my possession. Of course she does not know that I read what she writes. She believes that the royal seal keeps her words private. She never suspects that I have insight into her thoughts; that I am, in some way, an intimate confidant of the King.

It has occurred to me that I could betray her. Yes, I must admit that I have thought of this. More than once. I have considered showing the scrolls to the Grand Vizier and I have thought he would reward me. Richly. I might be given many debens of gold for making these writings known to him and to the Great Commander. I might achieve high office by such means. I might become a great name in the land, with many titles, with much property and many slaves.

Now it has occurred to me that General Khani might give much to read this latest scroll. For that matter, I could go and fetch all of the scrolls that I have so carefully hidden, and take them to him. He would know her heart, then, he would know all her weaknesses, her suspicions, her doubts. If indeed he is as ambitious as she thinks he may be, if he does indeed desire the Double Throne, what might I not gain by giving him these insights? What rewards might not be mine?

But no. But no. I have the Pharaoh's trust. Once I saved her life. By the Ka of Thoth, I will keep faith with her. Even though she does not think of me. Were I to betray my King, it would be an act against Ma'at. I will not do it.

THE TWENTY-FIFTH SCROLL

Today my steward Amenhotep came to me bearing bad news. He is not given to being emotional, but I could see at once that he was upset. He reported to my office at the palace, as he does regularly — indeed, daily when he is in Thebes. But of late he has been spending all his time at the quarry where work on my giant obelisk has been going on for weeks. His skin was blistered by the sun and his bony frame had lost what little flesh it had carried. A lean and sinewy man, he is as tough as a mooring rope, but he staggered a little when he made obeisance.

"My dear Amenhotep," I said, "you look ill. Please be seated and I will call for beer. I am sure you are thirsty."

He shook his head dumbly and shuffled. "Majesty is gracious," he said, his voice almost a croak. Then he stared at his feet. His toenails were cracked and ingrained with dirt. I could see that he had been working with the team of labourers and stonemasons himself.

"Well, talk to me," I prompted him. "What have you to report?"

"Majesty . . ." His voice failed.

"What is it? Has there been an accident?" Sometimes bad accidents occur at the quarries and men are injured. I hoped this was not the case, for I did not want deaths associated with my obelisk.

"No, Majesty." He cleared his throat. Then he looked me in the eye, and it came out in a rush: "The obelisk has cracked, Majesty. We have had to abandon it." He clenched his lips, which were trembling.

I saw that he was very much afraid. No doubt he expected some awful punishment to descend upon him. Or perhaps he merely feared my rage. But what does it benefit one to rail at the gods? For certainly, Amenhotep and his workers would have done their utmost to make a success of the task. Their failure must mean that the gods did not favour it. More than that: It must mean that the gods were angry. If that were true, it would be my fault, not his.

"Do you know why?" I asked calmly.

He drew a deep, wavering breath and coughed. "We had already excavated it on three sides," he told me, clearly much relieved at my response. "It is red granite. It would have been remarkable. We worked extremely hard, Majesty."

"I can see that you took a hand in it yourself," I said.

"Yes, Majesty, I did. We had extra hands on the team and we worked also at night by torchlight. All other work was stopped. We tried . . ." His voice broke and he coughed again. Stone dust, I thought.

"Well, then what happened?"

"The upper end is cracked," he said sadly. "I believe it was a latent fault in the material. There is nothing to be done. Nothing at all."

I nodded. A fault in the material. Not human error. Indeed, the gods were angry. But why? Could it be that danger was threatening Egypt and Pharaoh was not responding with sufficient vigour? Was it time to come forth as the destroyer? What was it that the gods desired of me?

"Majesty, I fear it is too late to try again," said Amenhotep. "Also . . ." he paused.

"Yes?"

"Also, the flood is not happening. It would be impossible, Majesty, to transport a giant obelisk on the river as low as it is. Even if we could complete one, which we cannot."

I nodded again. It is true. The water is extremely low. Lower than I have ever seen it in my life at this time of year, and there have been one or two years when the inundation was not entirely satisfactory

– once during my late father's reign and once during my husband's reign, may they both live. But never was it like this.

"Amenhotep, thank you for coming to tell me of this yourself," I said. "I am sure that you, all of you, did your best. It seems that the undertaking did not have the favour of the gods. You should go home now. I should think your wife will be glad to have you back. Rest for a day and then turn your attention to the arrangements for the Opet festival."

"Majesty will still hold it?" He was surprised.

"Oh, yes. It seems to me to be more necessary than ever. We must propitiate the gods." Never had the Opet festival seemed so important to me.

I have not had a chance to continue my writing for some time. So much has happened. Despite the setback with the obelisk, the arrangements and preparations for the Opet festival went forward, and on the due date all was ready. Normally this is the greatest Theban festival of the year and the people welcome it. They are free to take part, since it is the time of flooding: The harvest is long past and it is not yet time to plough and sow. It is usually boisterous and joyous and there is much feasting and dancing in the streets.

But this year the mood was sombre. The waters remain undeniably low. People are beginning to fear that there will be famine in a few months' time, and when the festival began they did not feel festive. I had however set my hopes on the Opet festival to turn peoples' minds to the positive message of rebirth and renewal, and I trusted that the familiar rituals and ceremonies would work their customary magic, restoring the connections of the Pharaoh with the gods and with the people of the Black Land.

The crowd that gathered on the first day to watch the priests enter the temple at Karnak to prepare the God for the procession was smaller than usual and subdued. The bright flags that festooned the route hung slack in the oppressive heat; there was not a breath of wind. Only a few garlands of flowers, already browned and curling from the merciless sun, hung from poles beside the way. I waited outside the entrance for the priests to carry out their prescribed tasks; I had to be there to greet the God and to escort him to the temple at Luxor. Slaves held up parasols over me and over my ladies and others wafted ostrich feather fans, but it was a long, hot wait nonetheless.

Inside, I knew, the priests would be bathing the image of the God and then dressing him in spotless linen robes. He would be adorned with precious jewellery from the temple treasury and placed upon a barque.

They seemed to be taking an age. We were becoming breathless in the heat. At last the priests emerged from the temple bearing the stately barque upon their shoulders, led by the tall figure of Hapuseneb, resplendent in his leopard-skin drape and enormous ceremonial wig. I greeted the God, making a deep obeisance, then turned to escort the barque, walking directly behind it.

Now the images of Mut and Khonsu, Amen's consort and their son, carried in their own barques, joined the procession. The Opet festival is the honeymoon of Amen and Mut, making possible the conception of their divine son. Nine months later the statue of Mut will be taken to the birthing house to give symbolic birth to Khonsu. I hoped that the renewal of the divine Theban Triad would bring about the inundation.

As we moved into the street, the crowd gave a collective gasp and a cheer went up. I began to feel more confident. On either side walked priests carrying incense and shaking sistrums. Behind us waiting dignitaries fell into step, followed by chantresses, musicians on trumpets and drums, acrobats, dancers and a motley group of commoners. The entire procession would make the journey to the temple at Luxor on foot. The road was lined with peddlers hawking their wares and kiosks selling items for offerings.

The musicians stepped up the tempo of the march they were playing and women clicking menat took up the rhythm. Bystanders began to clap and sing. This was better, I thought. I could smell freshly baked bread and saw people eating.

"Hola!" shouted a brawny farmer. "May we ask the God some questions?"

"You may ask," a priest told him, "and perhaps the God will answer. But only yes or no."

"Will my wife bear me a son?" asked the farmer. The barque hesitated for a moment, then dipped forwards, signifying yes. The man beamed and his mates clapped him on the back.

A thin, anxious-looking woman ran up. "Will my child get well?" she called. The barque did not move beyond continuing on its way. "Please!" she shouted as it went past. "Will my child get better? He is so ill!" The barque hovered, then retreated, signifying no. She burst out in desperate wails. My heart went out to her.

"Enough now! We must move on," said the priest. "But some people will be allowed into the temple, where the oracle may be consulted. If you have questions, you should try to get in."

At length we reached the Opet temple at Luxor. Now the three barques were borne into the dark recesses of the temple. Only the priests and I were allowed to accompany them. In a special shrine there was another image of the God embodied as Amen-Min, who, according to the ancient creation beliefs, inseminates the earth and brings forth fruitful harvests. For me to commune with Amen-Min is a particularly important part of the Opet ceremonies in any year, but most particularly this year when the inundation is in doubt.

I entered the dark shrine with a torch in my hand, dizzy with the heat of the day and the clouds of incense that swirled around me. I placed the torch in its socket and abased myself before the God. First

I needed to grow calm so that I could concentrate. I breathed deeply, smelling beneath the incense the dank, mouldy smell of the rocky floor. The perspiration cooled upon my skin. In the silence I could hear only my own uneven breathing, with the faint rattle of sistrums and sweet, high notes of the chantresses in the background.

Softly I began the ritual incantations:

"O my Father, my Lord!
All people sing thy blessings and praise thy name.
O hear our pleas!
The earth awaits thy precious seed!
Come thou and inseminate it!
Be thou generous, be thou merciful!
Praise thy glorious name!"

These words I repeated three times, breathing deeply and rhythmically all the while. Now I was calm. It seemed to me that the God spoke directly to my heart. This what he said:

"Greetings to thee, Son of Horus, King of Upper and Lower Egypt, Lord of the Two Lands. I have placed thee upon the throne to rule over Egypt. Thou shalt overcome the rebellious; thou shalt maintain the peace; thou shalt reject evil."

"Yes, Lord," I whispered.

"Thou shalt honour my name through the excellent deeds of thy Ka."

"Yes, Lord."

"Thou shalt maintain Ma'at."

"I hear thee, O my Father, my Lord."

I waited, but the God spoke no more. Somewhat stiffly I rose to my feet, took up the torch and left the shrine, moving backwards and sweeping away my footprints in the dust with the palm fronds the priests had provided for that purpose.

Now I entered the chapel where the coronation rites and ritual robing took place. As at my first coronation, and again at my Sed festival and annually at Opet, I was cleansed and anointed, dressed in the appropriate regalia, and at last invested with the crowns of Upper and Lower Egypt, the flail and sceptre placed in my hands. I wore the false Pharaonic beard tied on with loops around my ears. Hapuseneb, who officiated, spoke these words:

"Nothing is lost to thee, nothing has ended for thee. Behold, thou art renewed and powerful."

Renewed and powerful. Oh, yes, that was indeed how I felt. Now I would be escorted to an audience chamber where a privileged crowd would be present to be the first to welcome me. It was customary for the people to greet me with jubilation, to praise my accomplishments and forgive any wrongs I might have done. Once again I embodied divine power and generosity; once again I was the source of bounty and well-being for the Black Land. Surely now, I thought, the gods would once again be pleased with me.

As I entered the audience chamber, a cheer went up, but it seemed to me to be more muted than it used to be in previous years. The one who spoke on behalf of the people praised me as the custom was. Yet I thought that he too sounded less filled with enthusiasm than before. Or perhaps, I assured myself, I was imagining this. I took my place upon the throne at the far end of the room.

Some questions to the oracle would now be allowed. In a niche high up against the wall to my right there was a statue of the God. I knew that it was a hollow statue with an opening in its back into which a priest could speak, while standing in a passage behind the wall. The body of the statue magnified and distorted his voice so that it did not sound human at all, but resonated and echoed all around the room. The statue, which was covered in gold and had jewels for eyes, was softly lit, and when the voice boomed out it truly seemed to come magically alive. Unlike the barque oracle that accepted only questions that could be answered yes or no, this oracle gave longer answers. The right to ask questions of it was greatly desired by the Egyptian people.

An expectant murmur ran around the room as the Chief Prophet of Amen, Hapuseneb, took up a position near the statue. "Are there questions to put to the God?" he asked.

At once a man near the front stepped forwards. He had the burly build and large hands of a farmer. "I have a question," he said.

"You may speak."

"I want to know," he said, staring at the glowing statue, "why the inundation does not come."

Several voices agreed. It was a deep concern for all present, of course; only to be expected that it would be asked.

"*The tears of Isis do not swell the river,*" the statue intoned in its booming voice. Despite myself, I found that my arms had broken out in goose bumps. It was a very convincing presentation, one had to hand that to the priests.

"We know that," the man persisted. "But why not? Where lies the blame?"

"*Isis has turned her back on Khemet,*" proclaimed the God.

There were exclamations of horror. This was dreadful.

"*The mother and protector of us all withdraws from us,*" said the strangely inhuman voice, echoing from the walls. "*She no longer broods over us with her enchanted wings.*"

A woman shouted: "But why? What have we done?"

At first it seemed that the oracle would not answer. Then the voice came again: "*Isis wanders in the world. She is desolate. She seeks her son. She cries out in the wilderness: Where is Horus? He must sit upon the throne of Osiris. It is his rightful place.*"

I stiffened upon the throne. Fury threatened to overcome me. I almost rose and shouted at the God: "You lie!" But of course that was impossible. Consternation had broken out among those present. What did the God's pronouncement mean? I rose to my feet and raised my hand. The people grew quieter.

"We are all familiar with this tale," I said. "The oracle tells us that these events are once more being played out in the supernatural world," I went on, improvising as I went. "Isis is so taken up with the age-old battle between Seth and Horus that she cannot pay attention to Khemet. She cannot weep for Osiris. She must first intercede for her beloved son."

This seemed to be going down fairly well, although some still looked doubtful.

"It must all be played out again," I said. "Then, when Isis has vanquished Seth with the support of Osiris, all will again be well. Our mother and protector will remember us and she will grant us her tears in memory of her lost spouse. We must only be patient."

Even the first questioner now appeared to be satisfied. Before Hapuseneb could allow more questions, I announced: "The oracle will speak no more. The gods are weary and they desire to commence the journey to their homes."

Nobody dared to contradict me and the ceremony came to an end.

I was shaking with suppressed rage. Who had dared to speak such treason? For treason it was. If interpreted as a comment upon the current situation in Egypt, it was easy to conclude that Isis was displeased because the person on the throne was not the Living Horus, and that the mother god wanted another, a true Horus, on the throne – Thutmose. The people were not stupid. I might have confused the issue to some extent with my interpretation, but there would be enough people who would read the obvious explanation into the God's words.

I will demand the head of the priest who had supplied the voice, I thought. He will be fed to the crocodiles. How had he dared! It was insupportable. Yet Hapuseneb himself must have known this was going to happen – if indeed he had not instigated it. He did not look surprised. Well, I cannot not punish the Chief Prophet of

Amen, I thought. But I can punish a simple priest. I will have him found. And he will pay.

Here endeth the twenty-fifth scroll.

HER MAJESTY HAS tried hard to undo the damage done by the oracle, but I fear that her attempts have not been effective. The second and third days of the Opet festival were poorly attended, and all in all it was a dismal affair. The common people are convinced that Isis has turned her back on Khemet, for it is already obvious that the inundation will come late, if at all, and this is frightening. They are blaming this on the Pharaoh. Clearly something radical is wrong; so fearful a catastrophe could not happen if Pharaoh's magic was as potent as it ought to be.

So the criticism one hears in the taverns is growing ever more vociferous. Only yesterday Ahmose and I were drinking in the Wishing Well, and we heard some farmers talking morosely at a table near to ours. I watched in admiration as Saria, the Syrian slave girl of the ample charms, brought a large order of beer without spilling a drop, even while evading the beefy hands that were reaching out to squeeze her delectably round behind.

"Just as stingy as Hapi, this girl," complained one wall-eyed fellow, taking a huge gulp of beer and letting out a belch.

"Aye," grumbled his burly companion. "There's to be no flood this year, that's plain for all to see. No flood, no rich black earth, no seeding, and no harvest when the time comes. No food on the table soon. Nor beer."

"It's the fault of the Pharaoh, is what I say," the wall-eyed one whispered hoarsely. He knew he spoke sedition, but he was already fairly drunk and grown careless. "The Pharaoh must hold Khemet safe, and what I say is, no woman has the strength. Not over time. Not when the going gets rough." He drank some more.

"'Tis unnatural, a female Pharaoh is," opined the burly one. "We need a man on the Double Throne, and double quick too."

"A stronger hand, a stronger hand," agreed a small fellow with a bulbous nose.

"A warrior Pharaoh, like Thutmose the First, may he live."

"May he live," they chorused, and swallowed more beer.

"We should march," stated Wall-eye aggressively. He did not look as though he had ever marched anywhere in his life, having a pot-belly and skinny legs, but he had the attitude. "We should march north to Megiddo. I hear they have plenty, plenty stores of wheat. We'll be needing it."

His companions nodded sagely.

Ahmose was frowning horribly at me, probably expecting me to leap to the Pharaoh's defence, but it was clear that the two of us would come off second best in a fight with these persons, and I did no more than stare miserably into my jug. It is becoming undeniable that the gods are angry. But what the reason is for this, who is to say?

I shall not report these mutterings to Her Majesty. She will come to hear them soon enough.

THE TWENTY-SIXTH SCROLL

The Opet festival did not have the effects that I desired. The people have not been won over, nor have the gods been mollified. The inundation never came. It was not a matter of a more limited flood than usual; there has truly been no flood at all. Last month should have been the month in which the inundation peaks. The end of summer. Then the water should have receded, leaving the rich black earth ready for the planting. Farmers should have sown their seed and chased the sheep into the lands to tread the seeds into the fecund earth. But the Nile did not rise; it did not turn green, then red, then brown. The fields have not been blessed. Hapi has for once deserted me.

Also, the pronouncement of the oracle has done considerable damage despite my best efforts to contain it. Rumours run everywhere like water, and like water seeping into cracked foundations they may yet cause the edifice of the throne to collapse. All my offerings to my heavenly father, Amen-Ra, appear to be bootless and ineffectual. He too has turned his face from me, alas!

For months, now, I have felt helpless and bereft. It seems that, on the one hand, the gods have abandoned me; on the other hand I can no longer depend on the many men, formerly loyal, who have served me. Even after his passing, it became clear that Senenmut – but let me not write of that. *I will write no more of that.*

In my desperation I have not known where to turn. Wakeful night follows wakeful night, and though I yearn for the sweet ease of sleep, it eludes me. Or if it comes, it brings bad dreams. Then this morning when I arose, I stepped in a sticky patch of blood. Sekhmet had deposited a headless rat beside my bed. I felt quite ill.

Being sorely in need of a distraction, I decided yesterday to pay a visit to my beloved Djeser-Djeseru. It would be an unofficial visit; I was determined to go as I had gone before, once more in my life, without the usual entourage of ladies-in-waiting, royal guards, servants and slaves. Instead I called upon Mahu, who accompanied me to that place some years ago and protected me with his life. I told him what I wanted to do, and as I expected, he was aghast and tried to dissuade me.

"Majesty!" he cried. "It would be dangerous, extremely dangerous. Although the Pharaoh is beloved, of course, there are always . . . there are those who . . . It cannot be contemplated, to go without the guards!"

"I know there are those who seek my death," I told him. "But they will not expect me to do this. We shall go during the time of afternoon rest, when I am known to withdraw to the portico of the residential palace. Also there are not so many people moving about then."

"But, Majesty! How . . . how . . ."

"I shall be disguised," I said. "Perhaps I could pretend to be your sister. I shall wear a plain shift and a woven shawl covering my head and most of my face. You must order an ordinary sedan chair and accompany me to the quay, where there should be a simple boat that does not require a large crew."

"It will not work," he moaned, "the disguise will not work."

"Why should it not?" I was growing irritated with his opposition.

He rolled his eyes desperately. "People will see . . . it will be obvious . . ."

"I shall muffle my face," I said, "and remove all jewellery."

Still he shook his head.

"Why do you shake your head?" I demanded angrily.

"Even in a plain shift," he said, "Majesty will still have the manner of a Pharaoh."

"Oh," I said, thoughtfully. Perhaps he had a point. "Well, then, maybe I should wear an elegant, fringed linen robe with a faience necklace and a fine shawl, and I shall be a lady-in-waiting. Some of them are more imperious than the Pharaoh. Yes, I think that would do very well. You are so clever, Mahu."

He still looked miserable, but I knew he did not have the temerity to deny me, nor would he betray me in any way. "As Pharaoh commands," he reluctantly agreed.

So we went together. I told my guards to stand outside my bedroom as I would sleep for a while, exchanged clothing with a young lady-in-waiting and gave them the slip. As we left the gates of the palace, I looked around. "No sedan chairs?" I asked, surprised.

"Majesty, it is not far," said Mahu apologetically. "There is a short way down to the river. Ordinary people," he cleared his throat, "would walk."

"Oh, I see. Very well, then." It was strange to be on foot in the streets of Thebes instead of being carried along in a chair or seated upon an elevated throne above the crowds. Directly outside the palace, the broad avenue stretched ahead of us, leading to the temple of the God at Karnak. According to my orders, an impressive route has been established for the God and the Pharaoh to travel through Thebes during festivals. It links the palace with the shrine of the god Amen and also with that of his consort Mut. This paved processional way is a superb design that has added much to the dignity of Thebes.

Turning off from the broad avenue towards the river, we found ourselves suddenly in a very different environment. Here the streets were crooked and narrow, winding between tall but badly built tenements, pressed up against each other and blocking out the light. A pungent odour of fish, animals and sewage made me wrinkle my nose. A bearded goat peered at me through an open window, bleating mournfully. By the tears of Isis, I thought, these people share their living space with animals! I had much ado to avoid stepping in excrement.

It was not so very short a distance, either. Soon I was perspiring profusely from the sun and unaccustomed exercise. I wished that I was still as slim and fit as I was for my Sed festival, six years ago, but in truth, I am not. I glared at Mahu, who strolled along by my side whistling innocently. He did this on purpose, I thought, intending to discomfit me. I lifted my chin. But I would not give him the satisfaction of hearing me complain. I picked up the hem of my fringed and finely pleated robe and stepped delicately around the turds.

On reaching the river bank, Mahu found a pleasure boat for hire. It had an awning over a cushioned dais and was manned by a few stalwart sailors. One of them handed me on board with a firm grip, and I caught his grunted aside to Mahu: "Huh! An expensive one!"

We pushed off and the current took us along smartly. Mahu sat some distance from me in his scribe's position, looking nervous, but as the boat sailed on and nobody gave me a second glance he began to relax. Before long we were approaching the bay where the glorious temple stands.

"I had seen but eleven risings of the Nile the first time I sailed towards this bay," I said dreamily.

"Yes, Ma . . . Maya," he responded. I had told him to call me Maya, for he kept wanting to say "Majesty".

Once we had alighted, I instructed Mahu to sit down and wait for me. "I shall go into the temple alone," I said, brooking no opposition.

Steadily I mounted the broad, sweeping staircase leading up to the first terrace. Despite the poor inundation, I noticed that the trees my ships had brought from Punt still flourish. It seemed to me that Senenmut was very near. I know that I have written I would refer to him no more. I have tried to shut him out of my memory. But I cannot. His name is engraved on my heart just as it is upon the walls of the temple where I stood, looking around me. This, I thought, is the superb creation that the two of us together dreamed, designed, brought into being and finished in a manner that is surely pleasing to the gods. Without lingering, I walked past the relief carvings on the walls of the colonnades and chapels that provide a detailed record of my life and the main events of my reign.

In various places within the temple there are small representations of Senenmut, carved where the wooden doors of shrines and statue niches must cover them from public gaze when the doors are open for worship. Yet there they are, showing him kneeling or standing with arms outstretched, worshipping both the god Amen and myself, the Pharaoh, King Ma'atkare Hatshepsut. It was done with my knowledge and consent, and this is stated in a text carved on the reveals of the doorway leading into the north-west offering hall. It is written: *". . . in accordance with the King's generosity which extended to this servant in allowing his name to be established on every wall of the King's great temple in Djeser-Djeseru . . ."*

I stared at this text and I felt his presence. There was nobody else about. "Did you tell her, Senenmut?" I asked him. "Did you tell her, damn you?"

I have been so angry with him since discovering that he had a wife. Even more so because of the message that he sent through her. That was our secret that none other should ever have shared. Yet now I have had time to think about it and my ire has subsided. I do not believe that he told her the entire tale. The message in itself is quite neutral; it tells one nothing if one does not know what it implies. No, her demeanour would surely have been different had she known the whole. I think he kept faith with me after all.

I stood behind a door and I traced the outline of one of the secret carvings of him with my finger. Cold stone. No blood, no breath, no life force. Yet while he lived the life force was powerful in him. He was a man of great energy and appetites. And while he lived, I and none other had his heart. I know that now. Even when he was angry with me, he loved me still.

What matter that he took another woman to his bed; she was no more than a minor wife. It still hurts me that he spent his seed in her, and that she brought forth two boys. Yet I understand the urge to leave something behind of one's own blood and bone. Had it not been for the existence of my grandson Amenhotep, I would account my own legacy poor indeed, despite all the building done during my reign.

I have seen the boys. I told the guards to fetch them to my small audience chamber soon after they had been installed in the residential palace. They are as like each other as my own visage is to its reflection in a mirror of highly polished brass. They entered into my presence bravely, holding each other's hands, and knelt and kissed the ground as they had been taught. How comforting, I thought, to have another so like oneself always at one's side, almost like an embodied Ka. Surely then one can never be lonely. They looked at me with their mother's unusually light-coloured amber eyes. They had her small neat nose also, and the spindly legs of young children, the knees scabbed with play. I saw nothing at all of Senenmut in them. I was not sure whether I was relieved or sorry. I gave them each a tiger nut sweet and sent them away.

Standing alone in the temple he built for me, I traced the figure on the wall again. Its arms were outstretched in an attitude of worship. To this day I am not certain whether it was truly I myself whom Senenmut adored. Had I not been Pharaoh, would he have remained in thrall to me as indeed he did, despite the little wife who could hardly ever have had him by her side? Would he then have desired me just as a woman, would he have married me and remained by my side all his life? Or was his devotion to the Pharaoh only? It is possible, I know that.

Yet I remember how, here in this very place, he held my hand and put his fingers on my wrist and told me he could sense the voice of my heart and that it spoke to him. I remember those words and I remember how we were together, and I remember all those years of devoted service, and I think, now, that he loved me truly, loved none else but me; that he was faithful to me, in his fashion.

By the tears of Isis, I thought, what have I done? In my fit of destructive rage, I had your tombs stripped and your grave goods dispersed and your statues and images destroyed; most terrible act of all, I had your mummy taken from its resting place and given to the crocodiles. In my fury I tried to wipe out your name and bar your way to eternity. Have I condemned your Ka to wander forever homeless, forever seeking sustenance and finding none? Have I banished you to barren darkness? Or worse, to a never-ending battle through the dread Duat? Senenmut, what have I done to you?

Yet here you are still; your images are here, your name is engraved on these walls. Statues of you still exist intact. While there are such representations of your bodily form, you are not lost, you cannot be lost. You cannot be destroyed.

My heart prays for you: May Horus open your mouth. May all the shining beings see you, may they hear your name. Oh, you judges of the Afterlife, take the man Senenmut unto yourselves; let him eat what you eat, let him drink what you drink; let him live upon that which you live upon; let your boat be his boat, let him net birds in the Fields of the Blessed, let him have running streams.

I am heartsore, my love. Sad to my very bones. Sad that we could not have broken the jar and grown old together, with a pair of fine boys to look after us in our old age. Sad that we had only that one night when we could be together simply, a man and a woman, and know each other and be happy.

There will be no more destruction. No further attacks. I shall see to it that regular offerings are made to the false-door stela in your mortuary chapel, so that your Ka may feed. May you reach the Field of Reeds, the Fields of the Blessed. May you live for ever.

I turned and left the temple. I felt that I had in some way indeed communed with the one who built it for me. As I walked down the wide stairs towards the river, I was more at ease than I have been since that woman came to me.

A thought came to me while we were sailing back. I wondered whether I might yet contract a second marriage. A treacherous thought, for I have always been assured of my own strength, my own clear insights, good judgement and ability to rule. Yes, I have reigned alone and I alone have sustained Khemet. But in these times I feel beset on all sides; I have no single friend in whom I have absolute trust. I have nobody with whom to share my thoughts. Nobody in whose presence I can be simply a woman and not the Pharaoh and a god.

In Egypt itself there is no suitable mate for me. Quite simply because such a one would need to have royal blood. I have always believed that any marriage to a lesser person would weaken my position, not strengthen it, and that still holds true. Certainly I do not want a man who seeks to govern me as well as the Black Land. Besides, Thutmose would never stand for it. We would have civil war. No, no, that would not do.

Could I turn to the Mitanni, perhaps? Propose an alliance? Or is it too late for such a move? Are they in truth already preparing to go to war against Khemet? Lately my memories of that young prince of the Mitanni have revived. I remember our conversation when he visited our kingdom that night when I was but nine, when I heard the songs of the blind bard. Perhaps I should send an envoy bearing the golden bracelet that the prince gave me then to remind him of that meeting long ago. An alliance with him would make me more powerful, not less; together we would be doubly royal, and the two kingdoms would be united by ties of blood, perhaps more binding than the golden bribes we have been using. There would be an entire empire's army to call upon to help defend our throne should the need arise. That alone might be sufficient to keep the ambitions of the runt in check.

Of course I know that prince is probably dead by now. And even if he lives, the young prince is surely no longer young nor handsome. It may be that he has a pot belly, foul breath and no teeth. I do not look forward to a union with someone gross. I wondered how much older he was than me. About ten years, I should estimate. That would make him fifty-one, if he still breathes. No. Much too old. Since women generally age better than men – I do not think that I look particularly aged, even if I have been slimmer, and I feel no embarrassment in wearing a diaphanous linen robe – it would be better to seek a partner younger than myself. Yes, I thought, perhaps the prince in question has a younger brother; the King of the Mitanni has doubtless sired many princes. They could supply a young and virile man to stand at my right hand; also to share my bed. Perhaps such an invitation might serve to avoid a violent confrontation.

The idea grew more and more attractive as the boat sailed on towards Thebes. Even yet, my monthly flux is strong; I could still bear a son to inherit the Double Throne. A son to lead men and to govern wisely. Or a daughter who would be like Neferure was, may she live. Suddenly, as I sat alone upon the dais beneath the striped awning, my body ached with longing for a human touch. Oh, how I longed for a warm embrace, for a lover's arms, a child's hug, a baby's milky breath against my cheek! It seemed to me that my very skin was hungry. Hungry for other skin to give it sustenance. Perhaps that is how the Ka yearns for food in the Afterlife.

The scribe Mahu was sitting at a slight distance from me, looking somewhat less strained now that we were returning to Thebes. He has attractive hands, I thought: a scribe's hands, slightly stained with ink but not worn and calloused as a labourer's would be.

"Mahu," I said. "Come nearer."

"Ma . . . Maya?"

"I said, come nearer to me. I want you to sit beside me, on this cushion."

Stiffly and respectfully, he moved over, swaying with the movement of the boat, which was now sailing briskly before the wind. His eyes swerved from side to side, but nobody was paying any attention to us. He took place beside me, bolt upright.

"Hold my hand," I said.

"Ma . . . Maya?" He looked petrified.

"You heard me. Hold my hand. We are together on a pleasure boat which you hired for the afternoon. I am a lady-in-waiting whom you know well. Hold my hand."

Hesitantly, he put out a hand and I placed mine in it. I could sense a faint tremor in him, but after a few heartbeats he grew calmer and his grip intensified. I closed my eyes and held on tightly. His hand was warm and dry and strong. I could have this, I thought. A companion. A lover. Once more, I might know a close embrace, the pulsing of hot blood, the rush of delight coursing through my loins. With the breeze on my face, it seemed to me that Senenmut sat there beside me. I could smell him, a little musky. I could hear him speak, hear his deep tones, his rumbling laugh. He would make me feel young again. Together we would . . .

The boat gave a slight lurch as it changed direction to approach the quay. I opened my eyes. Of course it was not Senenmut by my side, merely the little scribe, his eyes huge, wondering now if we would reach the palace safely. I released his hand.

We reached the palace without any problems. I told Mahu to wait. I went to the chest where I keep my jewellery and delved deeply. Indeed, there it was, the golden bracelet from the prince of the Mitanni. Chased with an elegant design. A solid weight. I held it in my hand, thinking. Then I went out to the portico where Mahu waited patiently. I gave him the cedarwood box with the bracelet in it.

"This is for you, Mahu," I said. "To thank you for your services. I realise that you take serious risks for my sake. Your loyalty is appreciated."

"Majesty!" He kissed the ground. "It is not necessary . . . I serve the Pharaoh gladly."

"I know you do. Yet take it. It is for you, one day perhaps for your wife. You don't have a wife yet, do you?"

"No, Majesty. Yes, Majesty. I mean, I have no wife, but I will t-treasure the gift. Thank you, Majesty. Thank you." He took it with both hands, then scuttled off with a look of relief on his face when I dismissed him.

I think he will remember this day.

Here endeth the twenty-sixth scroll.

INDEED I WILL, indeed I will. I took the box home and only once I was inside, with the door closed, did I open it and take out the golden bracelet that it held. The bracelet is a thing of beauty, of fine workmanship. I looked and looked at it. According to what she has written, it might have been instrumental in bringing about a crucial change in the Black Land. It might now have rested in the pouch of an envoy as he rode to the north, on his way to invite a foreigner to come and take the hand of our Pharaoh, giving him great power and great riches.

Instead, I hold it in my hand. Majesty did not write whether she has dismissed the plan completely, but would she have given the bracelet away if she had not decided against it? It is a dangerous plan. I trust that she has realised that for herself. Very dangerous indeed. I do not know how long such a man would live. The Party of Legitimacy would reject him. In fact, I think someone would kill him; I do not believe that the Great Commander, General Thutmose, would countenance a foreign man upon the Double Throne. No indeed, it would not do.

I wrapped the bracelet in some old papyrus and hid it in a hole in the wall beside the fireplace, stopping up the opening with a mud brick. I am sure it will be safe. Nobody would expect me to possess such a thing, for at present I do not yet live in the best part of town and my house is simple. I am earning more as an assistant scribe in the palace than I did previously, and I hope soon to improve my circumstances; they will be modest gains – but honestly come by. But perhaps, while I serve the Pharaoh in this secret matter, it would be better for me to remain unobtrusive and maintain a modest style of living. In any case, the bracelet will never leave my hands.

Yet, precious and beautiful though it is, it is not the main reason why I could never forget this day. It was an extraordinary experience, to sail out to Djeser-Djeseru with the Pharaoh, just we two as if we were ordinary people. Well, of course I am ordinary enough, but she is not. Today, though, I did see her as she might have been had she not been the Pharaoh and divine. A lovely woman who conversed with ease about the many building operations she has undertaken during her reign. Her Majesty has healed and restored the scarred wounds perpetrated upon the Black Land by the Hyksos. She set out to do that and she has achieved it. For that alone she deserves our gratitude.

I noted that she looked tired and sad, but after she had spent time in the temple alone her step was lighter and she smiled on me. Most extraordinary of all was the fact that she called me to her side and made me hold her hand. It was the hand of a Pharaoh and a god, but it was warm and gripped mine firmly. I noted that she had her eyes shut much of the time and she did not speak much on the return journey. Can a god be lonely? It seems unlikely, and yet I would have sworn to it that she was lonely. Had she not been the Pharaoh, I would have taken her in my arms and held her tight. That is what an ordinary woman would have wanted. But only I myself am an ordinary person, and so I just sat still and held her hand.

Reading what she has written, I now know that my instincts were correct. Alas, I could have comforted her, but even had I known – even had I understood – I would not have dared.

I am not sleeping well. And I have a constant thirst. It is as if my body knows that Hapi has deserted me, as if the drought has entered into my very bones, causing the urge to drink a river. It is growing harder and harder to keep my attention on important matters. This morning I struggled through an audience with the governors of the nomes, all pleading for more rations from the royal stores. I tried to convince them that there is no need to panic, that nobody is going hungry just yet, but they kept on badgering me with greater and greater demands. More than once I lost the thread of the discussions completely. Finally I pleaded a headache – not, indeed, a lie – and ended the session early.

However, then Hapuseneb insisted on an interview, saying that it was important. He brought a young priest with him, a nervous-looking fellow with a cast in one eye.

"Majesty," said the Grand Vizier, "at last I have news about the oracle."

"The oracle?" I did not grasp what he was referring to.

"The oracle at the Opet festival. Your Majesty wished me to . . ."

"Oh, yes," I said, remembering my anger at the treasonous words that had been intoned by the false god. I had instructed Hapuseneb to punish the priest who had spoken them, but he had maintained that he could not find the one responsible. He knew who it had been, he said, but the man had disappeared. Of course Hapuseneb himself denied any part in the wording of the speech, claiming that he had been as aghast as I had been to hear what was said. Should I have believed him? I did not know.

"Speak to the Pharaoh," he told the priest, who was obsequiously kissing the ground. The man seemed to have been struck dumb in my presence.

"The priest who spoke for the oracle has been found," Hapuseneb informed me.

I looked at him sharply, my fury at the incident returning with the memory. "I trust you will have him suitably punished," I said. "He should hang from the walls of Thebes."

"Majesty, he is beyond our punishment," said Hapuseneb, "although doubtless his Ka is suffering greatly in the Duat. He was found drowned and the fish have fed on him. Some fishermen discovered his body in the reeds. They took his remains to the House of Death, where he was identified as a priest by the amulet around his neck. This man could tell who it was only by a ring that he recognised."

"You knew him?" I asked the fellow.

"Yes, Majesty. We entered the p-priesthood together." He seemed full of fear.

"Tell the Pharaoh what you told me," ordered Hapuseneb.

"Majesty, he was bribed to speak the words of the oracle," the young priest said. "A man came to the t-temple, and offered much gold to anyone who would speak what he told them to. I was tempted, but I was too much afraid," he added. At least he was honest enough to admit that.

"What manner of man?" I asked, my heart cold within me.

"A N-Nubian," he told me. "A tall Nubian with big shoulders. He had the bearing of a soldier. And a bag of gold."

I closed my eyes. It could have been Khani, I thought. He had returned from the North by the time of the festival. He could have made plans to lead a great campaign himself. Soldiers who return from foreign fields bringing ample wheat will earn the adulation of the populace, there can be no doubt about that. He who led them would be able to do exactly what he wished. The situation required deep and careful thought.

"The drowned man is to be fed to the crocodiles," I told Hapuseneb. "This sorry priest shall hang head downwards from the walls of Thebes . . ."

The man gave a fearful shriek.

". . . since he knew of a plot that affected the security of the kingdom and he did not speak. You are dismissed."

I ordered a sedan chair to take me to the palace, where I lay down on my day-bed on the portico. I allowed my ladies-in-waiting to minister to my headache and then sent them away, for I was in great need of privacy. The report of the Nubian who had bribed the priest disturbed me greatly and I mulled over it. The one who told this tale could be a liar. He could have been himself bribed or intimidated by Hapuseneb. Or the tale could be true, but the guilty person need not have been Khani. I was sorely troubled by the possibility. It seemed to me that I could see his face as he stood before me, bringing me information as he so often had. Was that the face of treachery? Were those eyes that have always held my gaze so steadily the eyes of one who wished me dead?

Suddenly I was overcome with grief. Tears poured from my eyes as if welling up from some deep fountain of sadness. I wept for my good friend who, I feared, had turned on me. The evidence against him was mounting up.

A miserable night I had of it. At first sleep would not come, and it seemed to me that I could not breathe in the stifling darkness. Shortly after I retired, a strange sound assailed my ears. It was a fierce, sustained growling, and it made the hair on my neck stand on end. For one wild moment I imagined monsters. Then I saw, in the faint light of the small oil lamp that always burns beside my bed, that it was Sekhmet. She was prowling my bed-chamber with a bird clamped in her jaws. Catching a bird brings out the lion in her. She took her booty under my bed and proceeded to devour it.

Faint peeps suggested that at first it yet lived; but soon only the crack and crunch of bones could be heard. I found it hateful yet oddly fascinating to listen to. It was impossible to sleep while that went on. I hate it when she catches birds. It is within the natural order of things for her to catch mice and rats, and even the occasional lizard. But it always seems to me that cats ought not to prey on birds.

Finally she was done. She emerged from under the bed, jumped onto my bed and washed herself delicately, licking her paws and fastidiously grooming her muzzle and then her ears.

"What has become of Bastet?" I asked her. My other pet disappeared some days ago and has not been seen since. I would not be surprised if Sekhmet chased her away.

Sated, Sekhmet curled up at my feet and went to sleep. But sleep eluded me until the small hours. Then at last my eyes closed in utter weariness, but it was not restful, for I had a dream – indeed, a vision – that chilled my heart. In my dream I stood in the Grand Audience Chamber of my main palace at Thebes, but not on the raised dais where I am wont to sit. Instead I stood amid the press of common people who were awaiting an audience with the Pharaoh. I could see the throne up on the dais, but it was empty. On it lay a bunch of flowers, indicating that the previous Pharaoh had died and the Double Throne awaited a new incumbent.

Then a figure appeared on the dais and a thundering cheer went up. This figure was a tall male person, and although his face was indistinct I could tell that it was a Nubian. He removed the flowers from the throne and threw them away as if in disgust. Then he majestically took his place upon the throne. I saw that he held the crook and flail, and the Double Crown was upon his head.

Still I could not clearly see his face. I moved forwards, the press of people parting to let me through. I must see who this person is, I thought, this imposter, this usurper, who has the temerity to sit in my place. I shall order him to be thrown out and the worst possible punishment shall be his fate. He shall be executed and fed to the crocodiles. He shall not live. His Ka shall suffer for all eternity in the Netherworld and Ammit shall devour his heart. I called for the Royal Guards, but I found that I could not utter a word.

Who was it? I feared that I knew, but I strove to see clearly to exclude all doubt. I approached the dais, and I was all but certain that it was Khani. As I mounted the steps leading up to it the figure on the throne seemed to shimmer, dissolve and coalesce into a new shape. Where a man had sat there was now a snake, its scaly black body curled upon the seat, gleaming as if coated with oil, its narrow head rearing up and back, forked tongue flickering, poised and ready to strike. Fear turned my bowels to water but I stood my ground.

Apophis, I thought. Companion of Seth, the destroyer. The enemy of men and gods. He who lies in wait for the solar barque of the sun god as it travels through the nether regions. Yet once he had spared me for my destiny. So, Apophis, I thought, have you come for me at last? But I refuse to bow to you. I faced a live cobra at my coronation. I shall face you down also. I am the Pharaoh of the Black Land and none but I shall sit upon the Double Throne. The voice I had heard so often in my dreams spoke to me again: *Kill him for Khemet! Kill him for Khemet!* And now at last I knew whose voice it was. It was my own. It was my heart speaking to me.

When I awoke, it was as if the dream had made matters clear to me. All my life I have trusted in dreams and visions. I have had a warning and I must heed it. Above all, no person from the wretched Kush shall govern Khemet. There shall be no black Pharaoh upon the Double Throne.

The sky is a bleached blue and a searing wind has begun to blow. It is now obvious that evil walks abroad in the Black Land. The wind that burns all growing things and strips the soil from the hard-baked ground is the foul breath of Seth. Aye, Seth and his devils are casting a blight on Khemet and they must be fought with all the might of

Osiris, Isis and the great god Amen-Ra. The Living Horus must rise up and smite the enemies of Egypt who gather and plot and breed in the darkness. Now must the Son of Light be resolute.

My heart aches for the brave young prince whose cause I once espoused when his life was forfeit. One who became my friend, one who has served me well. One who has loved me – truly, I believe it – and whom I have loved as a brother. Is it possible that pressure has been put on him? He still has ties of blood and no doubt loyalty to a foreign land, a vassal state. They may well be stronger bonds than those of gratitude, friendship or fealty. Certainly there are rebellious men of power among the Nubians who hate Egypt and who desire to destroy us. Perhaps they have had a directing hand in this.

Or perhaps not. Men go to the crocodiles of their own accord. The Double Crown is a glittering prize, for which all things might be sacrificed. Driven by ambition, what would Khani not do? Where would he stop? Not at regicide, it seems. Deeply as it grieves me, I must conclude that in the final analysis, he too is nothing but a foul barbarian.

And as for me, when it comes down to a choice weighted by the throne of Khemet on the one side there can be no doubt of where my interest lies. More than my interest – my sacred duty. I have been invested with the Double Crown. The God my heavenly father blessed me when I was anointed and became myself a god. I am his heir to whom he gave birth. The Divine Light placed me upon the earth of living mortals to reign wisely over this land.

It is clear to me what I must do. I have sent for Ibana.

Here endeth the twenty-seventh scroll.

THIS IS TERRIBLE. Ahmose had a tale to tell when we met as usual yesterday that convinced me of dire treachery – but the guilty parties are other than he whom Her Majesty suspects. I must beg immediate audience to inform the Pharaoh before something dreadful is done. I tried to see Her Majesty early this morning, but I was told that she had gone to the temple and would not be in the audience chamber at all today. I shall try to gain entry to the palace where she rests in the afternoon. I must see her, I must.

There are conflicting claims and accusations involved, but I am sure that Her Majesty will understand at once that Ahmose has no reason to lie, while those who have told her another tale have strong motivation to create their own version of actions and events.

This is what happened after I left Her Majesty's office with her most recently written scroll. Ahmose awaited me at the tavern where we meet. When I sat down opposite him at the small table, his crooked face was grave. Before he began to talk to me, he peered around very carefully, to be sure that none listened. But it was a quiet time of day and there were not many other customers; those who there were sat far enough away. Yet he leaned forward and spoke very low. Ahmose is often called in by Hapuseneb to act as scribe when matters pertaining to the records of food stores are at issue. So he has every opportunity to glean items of interest to pass on to me.

"The Grand Vizier sent for me yesterday," he told me. "Several scribes have been called in to help plan the distribution of food to the people. You know that already hunger stalks the land."

"I know," I said. "It is frightening."

"Well, yesterday, when the rest of the scribes left, I lingered for a few moments because I was to take a missive to the leader of the Party of Legitimacy. Hapuseneb wrote it as I waited. Then, just as I was leaving, a closed sedan chair arrived with a visitor. I saw them set him down before the gate and he entered without seeing me, for I drew back behind a pillar." He paused. He likes to be dramatic.

"Well? Who was it?"

"It was the Great Commander," he told me.

"Thutmose?"

"Shhhh. Do not speak the name. Yes, it was he. Aha, I thought, this is an interesting development. What could those two have to speak of? And why did he come unattended? Usually he has quite an entourage."

I nodded. The Great Commander has a considerable sense of his own importance and normally travels with several guards and slaves.

"So, I thought it might be advisable to linger a little longer. I was outside on the portico, so I slipped around to the side where a window to Hapuseneb's office stood open. There were palms in pots, and I could crouch down and approach close enough to hear without being seen. I crept nearer on all fours." He chewed another date.

"I have no doubt that you heard something of note," I said, "and that you will tell me in your own good time."

His crooked grin was a grimace. "You cannot imagine what I heard," he said, his voice so low that I had to lean forwards and listen carefully.

"They are plotting to do her harm," he said.

"What! To do harm . . . you mean, to the Pha . . ."

"Shhhh! Do not speak it."

"Are we speaking of murder?" I whispered, aghast.

"Maybe . . . not quite that. But evil spells are being cast. Dark magic. They want her to fall ill. Perhaps they are hoping that if she feels weak enough, she will abdicate."

"She has been very tired of late," I said. "She does not complain to me, of course, but it is clear to an observer who sees her often that she is not well. But what . . ."

"They were using wax figurines. You know how it is done."

"Yes, I do know. How did you find out?"

"I crept right up to the window," he said, "and I peeped in, and I saw the little figurines on the table. With sharp needles stuck into them. I heard Hapuseneb chanting incantations. He would not do such things in the temple, of course."

"No, he wouldn't." I was cold with dread. These actions boded nothing but ill for the Black Land, and for Her Majesty. Then I added: "But you said figurines, not just a figurine? There were more than one?"

"Two," he said. "The one was much taller than the other, and black."

I stared at him. "Khani," I whispered.

"Shhhh. Yes. And you know, it is said that the wound he suffered on his recent campaign festered badly and he is not yet properly recovered from it."

"He supports Her Majesty," I said. "He is probably her most loyal supporter. If he fails her . . . Oh dear, oh dear, what are we to do?"

"You must warn her. She must take counter-measures. And watch her back."

"Yes," I agreed wretchedly, "I know I must, and it is more urgent than you realise. You are . . . you are quite sure of what you saw and heard? There was no . . ."

"No mistake," he said, with finality. "I saw what I saw. Even with one eye. I heard what I heard. And then Hapuseneb put the wax models away in a chest."

I nodded. How fiendishly clever of him, I thought. To have previously told the Pharaoh a distorted version of a terrible truth. Her Majesty must know what is actually happening, who the real conspirators are. But oh, why does this responsibility have to rest on me? All I ever wanted was a quiet life. Work to do and enough to eat. How did I get into this situation? It is not good. Not good at all.

THE TWENTY-EIGHTH SCROLL

Truly, today I am surprised to find that I still live and breathe. Early this morning when I set out to the temple to conduct the dawn rituals, I did not expect to meet with violence. Of course Hapuseneb usually acts for me at the temple of Amen-Ra at Karnak. But lately, because of the many matters weighing heavily upon my heart, I have visited the shrine myself and I have tried my utmost to hear what the God speaks.

Already when I left the palace, before dawn, accompanied as always by two ladies-in-waiting and the Royal Guard, I noted unusual activity in the streets. There were undoubtedly more men abroad than on other days at that hour. Nor were they all Thebans, I thought. They had the look of rural folk and persons from the lower classes: peasant farmers, watermen and stonemasons – muscular, stocky figures in rough-spun loincloths. They seemed to be walking with some definite goal in mind.

I was puzzled. But once we reached the temple and I turned my attention to communing with the God, I forgot these men. Even so early the day was already sultry and the cool darkness of the shrine felt like a refuge. I fixed my eyes on the blue, jewelled gaze of the God. *Please, Lord*, I besought the holy one in my heart, *please, Lord, speak to me. I am thy seed, I am the fruit of thy loins, thou put me on the throne. I have need of direction and counsel. I have need of guidance. Lord, what would thou have me do?*

But the God was mute. I went through all the steps of the ritual, dizzy with hunger and the scent of incense; I bathed and anointed and clothed the God, I decked him with jewels, I offered food and wine, I abased myself. The chantresses sang sweetly outside the shrine and the priest intoned the magic formulae faultlessly. Yet still the God was mute.

For one mad moment I was filled with frustration and rage and I came close to dragging the golden statue from its niche and dashing it to the floor. I wanted to tear the gaudy costume from the lifeless doll, smash its immobile face against the temple wall, claw the unseeing eyes from their sockets and cast the broken statue into the depths of the Nile. I stood trembling as anger coursed through me.

In that moment I felt as if I were standing on the edge of an abyss. What if indeed this were merely a figurine, truly no god at all? What if the God – even all the gods – were merely inventions of the priests? What if the sun were but a ball of fire, Hapi but a course of water swelled from time to time by rain, what if there were no Amen-Ra, no Isis, no Osiris, no Horus, no Apophis, no Seth?

In that moment I had a frightful vision of a universe where there was no Afterlife, where the Fields of the Blessed did not exist; where all our steles and inscriptions, our magic charms and amulets, our grave goods, our tombs and our funerary monuments were meaningless and doomed to crumble into dust. Where there was no spirit world peopled by the transfigured dead.

Could it be that the high calling of the Pharaoh was but a waking dream? That I had given my life, had spent my strength, had renounced my one true love, for nothing? *Could it be that there is no Ma'at?*

It was a terrible vision, bleak and desolate. But it could not be true. I summoned all the life force within me to reject it. I could not live in such a world. For in that world, what was the meaning of my life? I had dedicated myself to the service of Khemet and its people; I had vowed to satisfy the gods; I had sworn to maintain Ma'at. That dedication was the reason for my existence. For that purpose Khnum had created my Ka upon his potter's wheel, had caused me to breathe. Ma'at is all.

Cold with fear, I bit my lip until it bled. I closed my eyes. *"For-*

give me, heavenly father," I whispered aloud. *"It was Seth who almost mastered my heart. It was the destroyer who tempted me. I am thy dutiful son, the Living Horus, and I honour Osiris and I honour thee."*

There was no response. On shaking legs I backed out of the shrine, sweeping the floor hastily. I left the temple as fast as I could, striding along the passage through the outer halls into the light.

"Make haste," I told the bearers of my sedan chair. "Pharaoh does not feel well."

They set off at a swift pace, but soon they slowed as a hubbub of voices sounded in my ears. I put aside the curtain and peered out, but I could not see what was causing the delay. The press of people was so close that my bearers were being jostled. I waited for the captain of the Royal Guards, a burly officer, to shout and clear a passage for us to pass, but I did not hear his commanding voice. Then he stood beside me and spoke urgently in a low tone.

"Forgive me, Majesty," he said, "but the danger is great. Pharaoh must allow me . . . Please, Majesty, come at once!" Unbelievably, he had gripped me by the arm and was hustling me out of the chair. One of my ladies had scrambled into my place. She was pale and her eyes were wide with fright.

"Majesty will please enter the rear chair," urged the captain, propelling me towards it. Always when we went to the temple one lady's chair went ahead and one behind mine, while guards marched in front and behind with one on either side of the central one. Now, with the customary order changed, we suddenly altered course. Each chair reversed smartly and we set off back to the temple, bumping as the bearers broke into a trot. The curtains were closed and I could see nothing, but there was shouting all around and I had to cling to the grips to avoid being thrown out.

Then the bearers swerved, moving swiftly along what had to be a side street, since we could not yet have regained the entrance to the temple. The chair was set down and the curtains ripped aside.

"Into this house, Majesty," the captain instructed me. "We must take cover until order is restored."

I saw two of my guards backing the terrified owner of the house into a lower room as our party clambered up onto the flat roof. Somewhere in the background a baby squalled. More guards were posted at the top of the narrow stair. I knew that they would protect me with their lives. One of my ladies threw her shawl over my head to hide the golden cap crown that proclaimed me Pharaoh. I drew the end across my mouth and nose. Cowering from my beloved people! I could not believe that it had come to this.

As we gained the flat roof I could see where we were: close to the wall around the temple complex, diagonally across from a side gate leading to a storage area. The street was crowded and as I watched the crowd surged towards the gate.

"Grain!" The single word was yelled repeatedly. "Grain! We want grain!"

So that was it. They were expecting handouts, sacks of grain from the temple stores. But to my knowledge no such order has gone out. It is not yet time for such an intervention, the situation is not yet as critical as that. People still have vegetables from the second harvest, limited though it was. Yet everyone fears the hungry months that loom ahead and a rumour of grain allocation would have drawn the anxious heads of households from many royal cubits around Thebes.

Now I noted that there were armed soldiers in considerable numbers amongst the peasants. It occurred to me to wonder how they had known so soon that they might be needed. Suddenly the seething mass of men seemed to boil up like a desert storm in a dry wadi. Everywhere fighting was going on, peasants armed with short staves or walking sticks grimly battling the soldiers with their short swords. The riot eddied around the house, shouted orders echoing over hoarse shouts punctuated by screams of pain.

"Guards! Stand fast!" commanded the captain, pushing past them to run down the stairs and check the outside entrance. There was no knowing what the enraged mob might do. Yet surely the soldiers must soon gain the upper hand.

I watched in horror as the struggle below grew uglier. A woman coming from the market with a small child on her arm and a basket of onions and turnips became caught up in the mêlée. The vegetables scattered as she dropped the basket and clutched the screaming child to her breast. A blow from a wildly wielded stave gashed the mother's forehead open and blood streamed over her face and drenched the child. Blinded, she staggered and fell. As she rolled in the dust she was kicked and trampled by the frenzied men.

"Majesty!" shrieked one of my ladies.

I turned, to see a man dressed in the loincloth of a peasant leap onto the roof behind me. He crouched, holding my terrified gaze intently. The sunlight glinted on a sharp blade in his hand. My ladies screamed in fear and skittered away from me.

Suddenly the noise of the fighting below seemed to fade away. There were only two people left in all the world. Only myself, undefended and alone, on this common rooftop in the bright morning light, facing a man with dusty bare feet, smelling his rank sweat, hearing his fast uneven breathing, knowing that he was Death finally come for me. So this was the destiny the gods had always meant for me: to be killed by a man of the people – my people, whom I had loved and governed and protected all the years of my reign. Once before it had almost happened, in a boat upon the water, but my little scribe had foiled it. Now it was time. I hoped he would strike true.

Then a second person's head appeared above the low ledge behind the crouching attacker. I had time to think that there had to be a ladder, before the lithe figure vaulted onto the roof and the attacker swung around.

"Khani!" I cried.

"Majesty, stand back!" he called to me, as he leapt forwards to engage the man in combat. It was immediately clear to me that despite appearances the stranger was no peasant. Sinewy and lithe, he fought with the strength, agility and cunning of a trained soldier. Feinting and lunging, he cut and parried with speed and skill. Khani overtopped him by a head and had a much greater reach in his powerful arms, but he was still thinner than he used to be and soon his breath came in gasps. To and fro they battled, ducking and weaving.

The attacker hovered like a hooded cobra gathering itself to strike. Then he rushed forward and somehow slipped under Khani's guard; a red gash opened on the taller man's upper arm. I gasped in horror and my women shrieked, but Khani kept his footing and his nerve and backed away, circling, drawing the danger away from me. Now the stranger had changed his grip on the knife and bent into a crouch; it was clear that next he would aim upward at the belly rather than slashing at the heart. Round and round they shuffled, bare feet scraping on the roof tiles, each one watchful, tense and deadly.

I was terrified for my champion. It was obvious that he had not entirely recovered from his recent illness, for he was visibly tiring. His colour was bad and perspiration gleamed on his drawn face. By the breath of Horus, I thought, let him not lose this struggle! How I have wronged him! Please, please let him not die for me!

Then, as his opponent's weapon flashed forwards again, Khani caught his wrist, threw him to the ground in a wrestling grip, and plunged his short dagger into the man's chest up to the hilt. Blood spurted in pulsing gouts. In a moment, the eyes that had held mine with such venomous intensity but moments ago had turned to pebbles of dull glass and the intended instrument of my death clattered from a lifeless hand. Khani let him fall and stood over him breathing heavily.

"I thank you," I said, shakily. "You came just in time."

"I followed him," said Khani, wiping the perspiration from his forehead with the back of his hand. "I suspected . . ."

Behind Khani's back, I saw the captain of the guard appear at the top of the stairs, dagger in hand. With two leaps, he had reached us.

"No!" I screamed, "No, no, no, no, nooooo!"

Yet I could not prevent his arm from rising, could not stop his downward lunge, could not hold back the fatal blade from skewering Khani from behind. Could not drag Khani back from the shore of the Netherworld to which he had been banished with one cruel blow. Could not restore his breath, could not cage his Ka.

He sank to his knees before me, a splendid warrior fallen like a broken obelisk. I clutched at him despairingly.

"Majesty," he whispered. "Majesty. King . . . Ma'atkare Hatshepsut. I salute thee." He bent his head forwards, apparently intending to kiss my hand. Blood welled from his lips and dribbled warmly across my skin. The morning smelled of it. He expelled a last breath and fell at my feet.

The captain had an expression of triumph as he wiped his blade on his tunic. "It is done, Majesty," he said. Clearly he expected praise.

"You have carried out your duty," I managed to say tonelessly. He had killed my faithful friend, my protector, whom I had loved since we were both merely children, who had spied for me and given me sage advice, who had steadfastly watched my back and had saved me from the blade of the traitorous attacker, and he expected praise! In truth I wanted to slap his smirking face. I wanted to weep and wail and tear my hair. I wanted to fall to my knees and beseech the gods to look upon my dear lost friend with mercy when he stood before them at their dread tribunal. To make him welcome in the Fields of the Blessed.

But I did none of these things. I walked, deliberately, to the edge of the roof and looked down. In the street below the fighting was ending as the soldiers chased after those peasants who were able to take to their heels; many lay wounded or sat groaning by the wayside holding bloodied heads. I could not see the woman or the child and I hoped they had escaped.

"We should be able to leave soon," I said. I showed no weakness, for I am still Egypt.

When we had arrived safely at the palace and I was at last alone, I noticed that my footprints on the painted tiles were smudged with blood. Then I shivered and shook as if I had an ague.

All day the acrid smell of smoke has hung in the air. There was rioting across the city, and the peaceful citizens of Thebes became a howling mob. It was as if Seth and his cohort of devils ran amok in the streets and set fire to anything that would burn, destroying all in their path, while the soldiers sent by the Great Commander to restore order did so as viciously as possible. By nightfall many bodies hung head downwards from the walls and the crows picked at their eyes.

Alas! What has become of my beautiful city, hundred-gated Thebes? What is to become of Khemet, deserted by the gods, bereft of its rich black earth?

When I went to my bedchamber, heartsore and exhausted, I fell upon my knees and prayed to Hapi, who had cradled me when I was a child, upon whose bounty all depends.

"*Oh Hapi, why do you not come forth and assuage the thirst of the earth? You, who have always been limitless! Since you are no longer generous, everything, everyone exists in anguish. The creatures suffer, the faces of men grow hollow. Upper Egypt and Lower Egypt suffer together: Work cannot progress, men have no food, the children no longer play. Since you have grown cruel to us, silence is everywhere. Denuded of all that is good, the country is close to collapse.*

"*Oh Hapi, our generous mother, why have you turned against us? Why do you refuse your children life? The priests pray tirelessly with magic spells and incantations. Offerings and sacrifices are made to you, birds and antelopes bleed on your altar. The harpist seduces you with pleading songs. The people of Khemet utter desperate supplications! Why have you not responded with the inundation?"*

But Hapi would not speak to me.

Last night I had the dream again. This time it was again different in some ways. As always, I was once more on that battlefield, on foot and alone. Armed with my dagger. As ever, I felt the burning sun beat down upon my head. But this time I was surrounded by absolute silence. There were no sounds of strife, no cries, no groans, no pleas for help. No horses whinnied, no chariots rolled by. Around me on the sand lay the corpses of our slain enemies. I could smell the sweetish stench of rotting flesh. The furtive dark shapes of jackals slunk among the dead. Looking up, I could see vultures circling overhead in the clear blue sky. I waited for the soldier to come towards me as he always did. But this time he did not come.

I have already killed him, I thought. Approaching a prone form, I rolled it over with my foot. My own face looked back at me. I myself lay among the dead.

All day I have been weak and shaky, as one who is ill. I need time to collect myself, time to grieve. But Pharaoh is Pharaoh and matters of state must be attended to. This afternoon my troubled rest was interrupted by the arrival of a courier from the North, bearing news of an attack upon the forts that protect the Horus road. At once I called my advisers to an emergency session. The counsellors, who had hastily gathered, looked grave. Nehsi, I noted, suddenly seemed to have lost his usual energy and appeared for the first time to be an old man, stooped with shaking hands. He was very fond of Khani, I know, ever since he took the young Nubian prince under his wing and introduced him to the Kap. He is clearly distraught at the sudden death of his protégé. I would that we could comfort each other for this loss that hurts our hearts, but there is no time for that.

"Majesty," he said when he saw me, "should you be here? Should you not rest . . . the shock . . ."

"I am Pharaoh," I said, "my place is here."

The courier entered the audience chamber looking travel-stained and utterly weary. He knelt and kissed the floor.

"Well?" I demanded. "What have you to report?"

"Majesty, it was a concerted action," said the courier. "Well planned and executed. They must have waited until our divisions returned to Khemet and then they swooped down and fell upon the forts in huge numbers. Our guards were decimated and the forts are burning."

Thutmose gave an exclamation of disgust. "We should have sent an entire army straight away, not merely a few divisions," he exclaimed angrily. "I said so at the time!"

"Who leads the rebels?" I enquired.

"The Prince of Kadesh, Majesty," replied the courier.

"He must be taught a lesson he will never forget," growled Thutmose, "one that his children will inscribe upon the tablets of their hearts. We must go to war."

"How will we feed an army?" I demanded. "Here our people can subsist on vegetables grown near the river, but that cannot sustain thousands of marching men."

"Precisely why we should take to the Horus road without delay," he insisted. "I have information that there are plentiful stores of wheat in Megiddo. We can mete out punishment and save our people, if we act quickly and decisively."

The counsellors present were nodding in agreement. "The Great Commander speaks the truth, Majesty," said Nehsi.

"I concur," added Seni. "The arrogant Prince of Kadesh must be taught a lesson. And we need wheat."

"And if the army fails to secure the wheat held by our enemies, those that are not killed or taken prisoner will starve," I argued.

"We will not fail," stated Thutmose. "We have the finest corps of fighting men the world has ever seen. We will prevail. By the breath of Horus, Majesty, I swear we will prevail! We must go to war!" Such was his anger that it seemed as if his protuberant eyes were starting from his head.

"The decision is still mine to take," I told him coldly. I would not let it seem that he had given the command. "I will consider it."

He looked as if he would like to spit. But he bowed, as did they all.

War is inevitable now. I know it. How we shall feed an army I do not know. Yet march we must. Egypt cannot allow its vassals to make a mockery of us. We must assert our absolute supremacy. And at the same time, we must wrest from them the wherewithal to save our hungry people here at home. Oh, yes, I know it – Thutmose is right. I can delay no longer, I shall order the soldiers to march forth. But my heart aches for Khemet. Already Thebes has a pall of smoke and blood. It seems that the time has come when, as it is written: *"Merriment has ceased and is made no more, and groaning is throughout the land . . . the land is left to its weakness like a cutting of flax."* Alack the evil day!

Here endeth the twenty-eighth scroll.

THE TWENTY-NINTH SCROLL

I am exceedingly weary. I cannot sleep, and I have pondered many things. I have looked back over my life and suddenly it does not appear so very significant. It seems to me now that many of the things that one believed important at the time were trivial. Men grow like the grain, and like the grain they are mowed down. One must provide a harvest as best one can, before going into the ground whence Khnum took the clay to mould one's body and one's Ka.

I tried to sleep, but I could not. So I arose again, and I have taken up my pen and begun a new scroll. Since I have nobody to share my thoughts with, I will talk to my journal.

I ask myself: Who have I been? What have I been? What can I say to the dread tribunal I must face in the Afterlife?

I think back to the time when I was a child and had great dreams. I recall the songs of the blind bard that made me dream of greatness. It seems to me that I can smell the perfume of the wax cone scented with myrrh that Inet tied on top of my head that night, the night of my first banquet, so that it kept me cool as it melted gradually. I remember that the hall was hot and noisy and that there was too much food and that the Syrians grew drunk and boisterous. But mainly I recall the songs of the blind bard, whose eyes gleamed milky white like pearls, with his bald head shining in the lamplight like polished cedarwood. I see still his gnarled hands sweeping across the strings of his small harp, and I hear the music that sang like water running over stones and the plaintive notes of the double pipes and the young girls clicking the menat.

First he sang of love, telling us all to cherish our beloved: *"Weave chains of blooms to give to your beloved, Rejoice in the days of youth . . ."* because the time would come all too soon *"When to the land of silence, You and your love will both be gone"*. Yes, the truth that a life is but a single breath, but one brief exhalation of Khnum, is one that only the old ever know, and for them it is too late. As for myself, I renounced my beloved; I put love from me. And yet it was there, always present. Even if it ran hidden like an underground stream, it sustained my life. Others – now, alas, gone to the gods – gave me their love. Also I had the love of my people; I did have that.

It is strange, now that I think about it, that the bard sang of the land of silence. Did he truly mean that the Afterlife is a place of silence? I have always imagined the Netherworld to be a dread place filled with the howls of monsters and the unregenerate damned, while in contrast there should be singing, the calls of the birds and gentle breezes sighing through the trees in the Fields of the Blessed; and surely the progress of the God's solar barque across the heavens must be accompanied by celestial music of the most marvellous harmony. Silence? But perhaps he merely meant that none speak to us from there, that we cannot communicate with those who have gone to the gods.

I remember that the Syrians, who were drunk, misliked the song about mortality and demanded instead a song of great deeds. That was when the bard sang *The Song of the Godlike Ruler*, a song that all my life thereafter has echoed in my dreams. Especially I would hear the words:

> *"He was a shining one clothed in power.*
> *And all the people praised him."*

A shining one clothed in power, whom the people loved: That was my dream, and it became my life. As Pharaoh, how do I compare with the godlike ruler whose praises the blind bard sang?

He told first of the Pharaoh who came forth as the Avenger and Destroyer, who smote the enemies of Egypt and bathed in their gore.

Only once, at the beginning of my reign, did I take the field of battle. We did triumph, but what I experienced then made me believe that war is the enemy of Ma'at, and ever since I have avoided it if at all possible. Nevertheless, when military expeditions were essential, I sent the army to do its duty. I did not shrink from it.

Now I must send the army forth once more, but this time it must be a major campaign of conquest. Nothing less will do. In the dark of the night, I took that decision. I will convey it in the morning. I will give the Great Commander what he wants, and send him forth upon the Horus road, be it to death or glory. Yes, I will do it. Perhaps, having decided this, I can sleep now.

Still, however, sleep eludes me. I keep returning to the song of the blind bard. I recall that he praised the Pharaoh's actions in repairing what he had found ruined. Well, most of what was destroyed by the Hyksos, who ruined our temples and desecrated our gods, has been restored under my rule. There has been much rebuilding and building anew in my time. In particular there is Djeser-Djeseru. It is like nothing that has ever existed; there is no other such in all the world. I believe the God may be pleased with it. Yes, all over the Black Land the temples are whole again, and the rituals are faithfully carried out. As Pharaoh I have given the Kingdom of the Two Lands a period of stability and healing. That much is true.

Of course the core of the bard's eulogy was that the Pharaoh had held the Black Land safe in his hands, that he had triumphed over evil. That he had restored Ma'at.

The night air is chill, and the oil lamp that lights my scroll begins to dim. I shall have to write faster. I have served Khemet; I have done my duty, I must write a full accounting. Even if my enemies strike my records from the living stone, my deeds must yet be known.

Throughout my reign festivals and feasts were held on their due dates. I have done what is prescribed, honouring the gods and renewing my kingship; the necessary daily rituals have been carried out, nothing being omitted. I have always been mindful of my duty to link the earthly and the spirit worlds, to guard against malevolent influences and to keep chaos at bay . . .

Finally, in the early hours of this morning, the oil lamp guttered and went out and I had to lay down my pen.

Yet still I could not sleep. I paced my portico, up and down, up and down. I saw the night grow pale and I watched as the barque of Amen-Ra cast its brightness over the sleeping land. My city was still covered in a haze from the fires of yesterday and it glowed like a cloak of gold. One might have thought it a sign of the God's benediction had one not known it was in truth the very opposite. For a brief while the scene was beauteous, scented with the sweetness of lotus flowers on the cool dawn air. Then the sun rose higher and the detritus of destruction was mercilessly revealed. The wind brought the bitter scent of ash.

This morning I sent a message to the Vizier that I do not feel well. I am unutterably weary and I cannot face any audiences today. All I feel able to do is to write once more in my journal. I must complete the record. I must leave nothing out.

The question that tortures me is this: Why is it that the inundation has not come? Why has the bountiful river god turned away from Khemet? Why in this time of sowing do the river banks lie dry and barren under the brilliant sun? Why have the priests' prayers, incantations and sacrifices failed to move the gods to pity? Why does Thebes groan under a pall of smoke and blood? I know not why the gods are angry and do not speak to me.

Or is it possible that I, the Pharaoh, have earned their anger and their enmity? Can it be my fault that the Two Lands suffer? Could I have been wrong in believing myself to be the chosen of the gods?

So much of my strength of will has been expended on keeping the young Thutmose from wielding power. I have held back from war, not only because I have had a horror of it – and indeed, indeed I have – but also, let me admit it here, to block him from great achievements that would have earned him the adulation of the people. My people. I wanted to be always first and foremost in their hearts. He has warned of grave danger, of losing our vassal states, of being attacked by a foe grown bold because we do not act. Now that I have decided to give the order I should – admittedly – have given long before, it may be too late. I may have failed to keep my people safe.

In the light of morning this thought has come to me: Perhaps, when the sacred barque bowed to the child Thutmose in the great temple of Amen-Ra, it was in truth the God speaking to Khemet. Perhaps, through my struggles to maintain my supremacy upon the Double Throne, I have spent my life in wrestling with the gods. Obstructing the will of my heavenly father, Amen-Ra. Perhaps the young Thutmose should have reigned.

It may be that the inundation failed because I, Pharaoh, failed. Nor will it return while I still reign. No, there will be no blessings from Hapi, and the lack will be due to my own actions. Humbly, I confess it. I have tried to reign wisely over this land that the God gave into my care; but I – I, Pharaoh – have contravened Ma'at.

This will hold back the flood: I gave the order to have Khani killed. Khani, my faithful informer, my loyal supporter, my dear friend. I allowed the devils of Seth to crawl into my heart and sow mistrust of a person who always loved me and who has always had my love. I believed that he was a turncoat and a danger to the state, and I gave orders to have him eliminated. I should have been patient and prudent; I should have waited and watched, and I should have had him followed to discover whether he was in truth a traitor or not. But I was afraid and I acted hastily, and I was completely and unforgivably wrong. But I could not reverse my orders before he had proved me wrong and it was too late.

I recall the words of my royal father, when we made the journey to Abydos: *"You should remember that it is easy enough to be ruled. To be a ruler, that is far more difficult. To rule oneself is the hardest thing of all."* My greatest failure has been that I did not rule myself.

So I grieve for my dear friend and I grieve for the Pharaoh Ma'-atkare Hatshepsut, whom the gods have rejected, and for good reason. Hathor no longer supports me with her everlasting arms. Horus does not stretch his protective wings over my head. Wadjet will not spit venom into the eyes of my enemies. Nor will Hapi be bountiful. In vain do I implore the mercy of the gods. Egypt lies barren and it is my fault. I, whom the Divine Light placed upon the earth of living mortals to judge human beings and satisfy the will of the gods, I who am sworn to displace disorder, lies and injustice with the harmony of Ma'at – I have not been worthy.

Yes, I grieve and I am much afraid. For I fear that my heart will weigh heavy on the scales of justice when I move on to the Afterlife. I see Anubis, the jackal-headed one, awaiting me with angry eyes, and I imagine that the hound of hell, Ammit, will have a heart to feed on when I reach the portals to the Netherworld. I greatly doubt that the best entreaties of the priests will effect a safe passage for me. All their amulets, scarabs, spells and incantations will not suffice. No, despite all that the priests can do, my heart will rise up to testify against me.

I shall not see my father Thutmose, may he live for ever, nor my mother Ahmose nor my beautiful Neferure nor my little son, he who was not named and should now be a man. I am sure that I would know him, and he should be beautiful. Nor shall I see my devoted Senenmut again. I shall not ride with my heavenly father in his solar barque. Nor shall I join the never-dying circumpolar stars.

Perhaps the bard was right. Perhaps we go to silence. Nothing else. If that be so, it will be more than I deserve. Whatever the truth of this, at least I will finally be free of the burden that my heart has borne ever since I lost my Neferure and my little son who had no name and never breathed. My mother told me that one carries the sorrow of a lost child like a large and heavy stone for all one's days; I did not believe her then. I have learned the truth of it. I shall be glad to lay that stone down at last.

One good thing has come from me and will, if the gods are kind, remain to be a blessing to this land that I have loved. That is the small Amenhotep, who should be Pharaoh if he lives to grow to man's estate. He has the pure blood royal, having passed from my loins through the pinched and narrow vessel that is his mother into the light. He has begun to take lessons in the palace school and his tutor speaks well of his abilities. He will, I do believe, be a good and a great Pharaoh.

He is coming to visit me today with his mother. I have fetched out the little war chariot that he loves and I have ordered his favourite grape juice and tiger nut sweets. I think I hear their footsteps approaching and his delightful laugh. He is a child of the sun. Heavenly father, please let him breathe. Let him become Pharaoh and give him the strength and courage to maintain Ma'at.

May his life be sustained by love, as mine has been. May he too understand this: To love and to be loved is the best way to face the certain knowledge that one must go into the tomb; that one must travel to that land of silence of which the blind bard sang.

Here endeth the twenty-ninth scroll.

AS I WRITE this, the tears are dropping onto the papyrus and I must pause to mop my eyes for fear of blotting the ink. Her Majesty called me to receive the scroll, as usual. Then she invited me to stay and share some cooled wine, and to meet her grandchild, whom she clearly adored. I did stay to meet the child, and I saw that his fond grandmother did not dote foolishly. He is indeed a happy child and a loving one.

But wait. I am when all is said and done a scribe and I must note what I observed as accurately as I am able. No tears, I shall shed no more tears.

I noted, first, that Her Majesty was looking ill and weary. She had grown very large of girth and had lost the energy with which she always spoke and moved. But when she saw the child, her eyes sparkled again and she called him into her arms. He is a sturdy boy, I think about eight or nine years old now, with a child's side lock over one eye, and he wore only a light kilt, for the day was warm.

I noted that he had no sense of the sanctity of Pharaoh's body, but ran to her as a child will and threw his arms around her joyously. She bent down and embraced him. His mother, I saw, felt the heat, even though they had been brought in a sedan chair and had not walked the streets. She had a linen kerchief in her hand and mopped her face with it.

She brought a gift of sweetmeats that her cook had prepared; it was arranged in a little basket on some leaves. They were pink and shiny. "Figs, stewed in sweet wine and flavoured with honey," said Meryetre. The child wanted one, but his mother would not allow it. "Have a tiger nut, darling, those are a gift for your grandmother," she said. "You should not eat them."

She herself did not eat anything but drank cooled wine which the slaves brought.

Pharaoh sat down with the child leaning against her knee and she took a sweetmeat. I had kept in the background, sitting cross-legged on the ground as I always do, but at that moment I could not keep silent. She had sent away her slaves, including the one who must taste all she eats and drinks. "Majesty," I said, in a low voice.

She looked at me with her lion's eyes, and they were tawny and as brave as ever. She looked at me and shook her head, very slightly.

Her daughter Meryetre did not notice this pass between us; she was circling restlessly around the room, picking things up and setting them down and chattering. She is not normally one to chatter much, but on this day she was chattering. Her speech ran on over our heads like a light and inconsequential breeze.

Her Majesty took a sweetmeat and ate it and then she took another and a third. She praised them, asking if her cook might have the recipe. Meryetre agreed, distractedly, as if she were thinking of something else. And then, as soon as the cooled wine was drunk, she made the child say goodbye and took her leave.

Now I come to what my pen does not wish to write. This happened yesterday afternoon; this morning when the God sailed into the sky, Her Majesty King Ma'atkare Khnemet-Amen Hatshepsut was no more. They gave it out that she had suddenly passed on late the previous afternoon. The palace officials said that she had been suffering from a serious flux for some weeks and it had sorely taxed her strength. She had simply stopped breathing and her slaves had found her lying on the ground.

Thutmose, the one who shall now be the King, has ordered that the seventy days of mourning must be properly observed, and Her Majesty's body has been removed to the House of Death for ritual purification. There will be a great state funeral and the poor will rejoice, for they will be given bread and beer; the royal stores are not yet totally depleted. She will be buried in the tomb that Hapuseneb has prepared for his Pharaoh. There will be sacrifices in the magnificent funerary temple at Djeser-Djeseru that the late great Senenmut built for the King.

The land is quiet and subdued. But I, I cannot sleep and I cannot eat. I am tormented by some questions that will never be answered, and they disturb me greatly.

Why, truly, was I there? Did Her Majesty really wish me to see the child? She could have given me the scroll she had just completed at once and sent me on my way. Or was I there to witness and to write what I had seen? Did she expect something of import to take place that day?

Did she know, when she took the sweetmeat, that her daughter had brought her death? She heard me warn her and she shook her head. To that I can attest. She heard me and she looked into my eyes and she put forth her hand very deliberately. But perhaps she only meant: How can you warn me of danger when it is a gift from my own child? No, no, Mahu, you forget yourself. Perhaps that was all she meant.

Did Meryetre know what she had brought? Had she a part in planning it? Or was she merely the messenger? Or had she no idea at all? She did perspire, that is true, but the day was hot. My face was damp as well. She would not let the child eat of the sweetmeats, but then they did look very rich and he is only little. She did not eat herself, but perhaps she does not care overmuch for sweet things. She was restless, but she often is. I was there and I cannot tell you truly what transpired. I do not know.

For that matter, who knows for sure that there was poison involved? Her Majesty had been tired and unwell for quite some time, and she was no longer young. It might all have been quite innocent. I would rather think that, for the other possibility is too dreadful for me to consider. I do not wish to believe it.

And yet I cannot sleep. The questions go around and around in my heart and I argue in circles. But about one matter there can be no doubt, and that is what saddens me most of all and will not let me rest. It is this: At the end, when death came for her, she was alone. There was nobody to hold her hand, to comfort her, to ease her passing. Nobody to speak words of love, no hand to mop her brow.

I should have stayed with her. Oh, I should have stayed. But I was craven and in her hour of need I scuttled away like a cockroach in the light. I expected her to die. I did. I could have been the last to see her breathe. I could have been with her. But she had entrusted the scroll to me and I knew I had to get it away and safely hidden before . . .

No, I write a lie. It was not the scroll, that was not it. In truth I was terribly afraid, and I still tremble. If indeed there was poison involved, I was a witness to something that it were better none had seen; those who could murder a Pharaoh would hardly hesitate to wipe out a minor scribe. I think I must find a berth on a ship and depart from Thebes as soon as possible. I might be crushed underfoot like a cockroach indeed. So that is why I deserted Her Majesty yesterday. A craven thing is what I am. I who have always loved her did not have the courage to stay with her when she had need of me.

I will hide the scrolls. That one service I can yet do for her.

But oh, by the Ka of Thoth, I should have stayed.

POSTSCRIPT

More than ten summers have passed since I hid the final scroll and fled. It was easy enough for me to disappear. Being an orphan, I was brought up by an uncle who also saw to my schooling. He had several other children, though, and was relieved when I was off his hands. At the time when the Pharaoh Hatshepsut passed into the Afterlife I lived alone with only one female slave to see to my wants. It did not take me long to bundle up a few items of clothing and the tools of my trade and pack the purse with some debens of gold and silver that I had saved. And the golden bracelet Her Majesty gave to me.

I booked a berth on a ship bound for the North and it sailed with the evening tide. When it reached Heliopolis I disembarked and soon found a post as scribe with the Aten priests. There I kept my head down and worked diligently and life treated me well. I missed the well-rounded and flirtatious Syrian slave, but perhaps she would not have suited me in the long run. After a while I took a wife, a small and quiet woman who speaks softly, treats me kindly and keeps my sleeping mat warm at night. We have two sons who will follow me as scribes.

The Pharaoh Thutmose is much admired for his military achievements. Directly after King Hatshepsut passed into the Afterlife the new Pharaoh began a series of highly successful military campaigns. He ruthlessly suppressed the rebellion mounted by the vassal states to the north-east under the banner of the Prince of Kadesh. He personally executed seven rebel leaders, returning home with their bloody, mutilated corpses hanging head downwards from the prow of his treasure-laden ship. Six of these he proceeded to hang from the city walls of Thebes, while the seventh was taken further south to Napata in the Sudan. Its horrific stench was an unforgettable testimony to the victorious might of His new Majesty.

Also the new Pharaoh confiscated the grain harvest from the stores in Megiddo and brought it home to feed his people. In the following flood season Hapi was bountiful again; the inundation came and brought the rich black soil just as it always had. Seeds could be planted, the harvest was a good one and everyone rejoiced. More military campaigns followed, all meeting with great success. He seems bound to conquer all the lands as far as the Euphrates.

Despite much time spent in the field of war he has managed to collect women like trophies. Besides two principal wives, he has acquired numerous minor wives, including three from Syria, and a considerable selection of concubines. Yet the one who takes precedence, who is the Great Royal Wife and will probably one day be the Mother of the King when young Amenhotep takes the throne, is Meryetre-Hatshepsut. However there has never been a God's Wife of Amen, for Thutmose has refused to appoint anyone to fulfil that role. Perhaps he remembers how much power it conferred on the late great King, his aunt, when he was young.

Meryetre has not grown more beautiful as time goes by, nor yet, I suspect, has her nature become sweeter, but the Pharaoh honours her and I have heard she sits by his side in the Window of Appearances, heavily bewigged and painted and beringed, when he rewards his generals.

Soon Hapuseneb died and I judged it best to keep the scrolls hidden. They are quite safe, tightly sealed in jars inside the cleft at the back of the cave on my cousin's mountain farm. I do not think they will easily be found. Now I write this postscript and I will add it to the rest and close the place up and then leave the scrolls where they are. Later generations may discover them and then the truth about my Pharaoh will at last be known. In my lifetime, it is now clear, this will not come to pass.

I have returned to Thebes with this latest rising of the Nile, before the full inundation comes. It is the first time I have been back since the death of the Pharaoh Ma'atkare Hatshepsut, may she live for ever. My aged uncle died and left me some gold in his will and I had to come to settle the estate. Also I wanted to check on the scrolls, which have been a great worry to me. I never handed them to the Grand Vizier Hapuseneb for I did not trust him – and with good reason, as matters turned out, for Pharaoh Thutmose gave him many rewards and there was no doubt that they were acting together.

When I arrived in Thebes, I went to look for Ahmose, my friend the scribe with the one eye for whom I had found work. He had prospered in my absence and now has a comfortable house in a good part of town. He invited me to dinner one evening and we dined well on fish steamed with ginger, quails roasted in garlic and honey and fresh fruit. Afterwards we sat on the ground in his inner courtyard, cross-legged as we were accustomed to sit while working, drank some more wine and talked. The evening breeze was cool and a fountain splashed in a fish pond studded with lotuses. A couple of earthenware lamps cast a golden glow and the faint scent of incense hung in the night air.

We talked generally at first, but then his tone became serious. "There have been developments," he told me, "of which you may not know, that I think would interest you." He looked at me assessingly with his only good eye. He had grown plump over the years and had acquired a painted glass eye in the empty socket that put me in mind of the Eye of Horus which the fishermen paint on their boats to ward off evil.

"And what are they?" I was feeling mellow after the good dinner.

He looked around him, as if to make sure that nobody heard, then leaned forwards confidentially. "You know there is a new Chief Prophet of Amen," he murmured. "In the place of old Hapuseneb, who died."

I knew, for the priest had visited Heliopolis. I liked him not; he was fat and unctuous and his naked face and bald head shone with sacred oil.

"He has decreed that the late Queen who claimed to be the King . . ."

"King Ma'atkare Hatshepsut," I said, not caring for the way he spoke of Her late Majesty, may she live for ever.

He put a finger to his nose and shushed me. "Do not speak the name," he whispered. "The Prophet of Amen has declared her to have been a heretic."

"A what!" I was astounded.

"A heretic," he repeated. "A female claiming to be King is against the laws of Ma'at, he says. It contravenes the natural order of things that the gods have ordained."

"I don't believe it. And the Pharaoh Thutmose? What says he of this?"

"He has given orders," whispered Ahmose, "that her name should be expunged. That her records on the living stone must be removed. That her images should be destroyed. That her building works should be torn down, her obelisks dismantled or hidden. He has omitted her name from the list of Kings he had drawn up. He desires that it should seem as if she had never been."

I was aghast. "I had heard that he has taken over her temple at Djeser-Djeseru and had his own images and records placed there, but I did not realise that he was actually destroying what was there of hers."

"Obliterating her," said Ahmose. He reached out and threw some crumbs into the pool. Fish rose to snap them up. "Gangs of workmen have been put to work hacking out her cartouches and her images wherever they appear. I tell you, brother, her obelisks at Karnak have been hidden behind a wall. At Djeser-Djeseru, the sphinxes bearing her head and her statues have been shattered and flung into a pit."

"That is dreadful," I said, and shuddered. Such actions meant that not only was Thutmose removing the late great King from the history of Egypt, but he was attempting to deny her eternal life. Vindictive in the extreme.

"It does not stop there," Ahmose went on. "The names, records and images of those who worked for and supported her are also being destroyed. Of Senenmut not much is left. Statues – and there were many, although some were destroyed while the late Pharaoh lived . . ."

"I know," I said.

"Shattered," said Ahmose. "And thrown into a disused quarry. Even the names of Nehsi and Thitui have been erased from the walls at Djeser-Djeseru."

That would be in the records of the famous voyage to Punt, I knew. The leader of Her Majesty's great expedition and her treasurer were being consigned to forgetfulness together with the late great King.

"But Thutmose accorded her a suitable ceremony," I said. "The time of mourning was observed. Her body was mummified and the rituals carried out, is that not so?"

"True," conceded Ahmose. "And everyone believed that he had her buried with her father, Thutmose the First, may he live for ever, in the tomb that was prepared by Hapuseneb. But Pharaoh Thutmose later reburied the mummy of Thutmose the First, in a new and most magnificent tomb elsewhere. And . . ." he glanced around again, clearly very afraid of listening ears. "The tomb where King Hatshepsut should rest has been robbed and desecrated, and the grand sarcophagus bearing her name and inscriptions stands empty," he whispered. "The grave goods have been destroyed or burned or have disappeared, and the mummy also. This is not generally known, but I have contacts. And I have been to the tomb. I went on a donkey and it was unconscionably hot. But I made the trip and it is true." He whispered even more softly, leaning towards my ear. "The lid of the sarcophagus lies to one side, intact, face up, as if it never was in place. The canopic chest of Hatshepsut is empty. The tomb is desolate and only snakes are living there." He turned his Horus eye on me. "I tell you the truth, brother," he said.

"I believe you," I said, cold to my heart's core.

Therefore it is of the utmost importance that the scrolls should be kept safe. Now is not the time to hand them over to anybody I can think of. Now is the time to bury them deep and wall them up. I shall add these last few words and hide them and I shall never again return to their hiding place.

One day, when her bones and mine are dust, they will be found. Let them bear witness to future generations. It is written: "*The strongest buildings crumble and disappear, yet the works of the scribes endure through the ages.*" Perhaps the faithful care of a humble scribe may be all that ensures everlasting life for Her Majesty, King Ma'atkare Hatshepsut.

For she did live. Insofar as she was divine, she honoured and she served the gods. She ruled her country wisely and well and Egypt bowed to her and worked for her. Insofar as she was a woman, she passed on the blood royal through the travail of her loins; she loved greatly and she was loved in return. I can attest to that. Oh, yes, she walked this earth and those who knew her observed her beauty of form and spirit. And though her corporeal body may be lost, yet I am sure that she has joined the never-dying circumpolar stars.

Mahu the scribe

AUTHOR'S NOTE

Although this is a novel and as such a work of fiction, most of the characters who appear in the story were real people. Even though they lived and died about 3 500 years ago, we know a fair amount about them. The written evidence we possess about the ancient Egyptian civilisation derives in the main from two primary sources: from formal inscriptions on monuments, tombs and temples (the "living stone"), and from more informal writings on materials such as papyrus and ostraca (broken pieces of pottery or bits of limestone). The stone records comprise what one might term official propaganda, providing impressive but not necessarily accurate accounts of the lives and achievements of nobles and particularly of pharaohs. The ostraca record items such as songs, stories and administrative lists. Deductions about lifestyle and customs are also made from artefacts discovered in archaeological digs and from items stored in museums.

Some complete papyrus scrolls from ancient times have emerged from storage places in a legible condition, due to the extremely dry climate. One such is *The Egyptian Book of the Dead*, a vast body of religious writings, a version of which was translated and edited by E.A. Wallis Budge in 1895 and is known as *The Papyrus of Ani*. I have gleaned much from this work.

However, the primary sources of information all have to be translated and interpreted, and there is often considerable controversy about the correct interpretation of known facts. We should not find this surprising. It is difficult enough to know the character and motivation of people who have recently died – for that matter, of people who are still alive. How much more difficult it must surely be to discover exactly what people were like over a gap of 3 500 years?

Hatshepsut is a prime example of a historical person whose life and character have been interpreted in varying and contradictory ways over time. We know that she did reign over Egypt for approximately twenty years and that her stepson Thutmose followed her to become one of Egypt's greatest pharaohs. It is less clear whether he was her co-regent or whether she effectively kept him from the throne all her life.

Two views of her are cited by Joyce Tyldesley in her informative biography entitled *Hatchepsut: The Female Pharaoh*. Egyptologists in the Victorian era saw her as "a valid monarch, an experienced and well-meaning woman who ruled amicably alongside her young stepson, steering her country through twenty peaceful, prosperous years". In contrast, by the 1960s, she had been "transformed into the archetypal wicked stepmother familiar from popular films . . . she was now an unnatural and scheming woman . . . who would deliberately abuse a position of trust to steal the throne from a defenceless child . . . her foreign policy was quite simply a disaster . . ." Current scholars tend to avoid either of these extremes.

In 2007, Egyptian authorities announced that the mummy of Hatshepsut had been identified. In 1903 Harold Carter, of Tutankhamen fame, discovered two mummies in an insignificant tomb designated as KV60. The smaller mummy, which was in a sarcophagus identifying it as that of Sitre, known as Inet, royal nurse, was brought to the Cairo museum. The larger one was uncoffined, and remained in situ until 2007. It was thought that the larger one might have been royal, because the position of its arm suggests the typical royal burial position. But since the two mummies came from such an undistinguished burial place, the larger one lay nameless for decades, until at last modern technology (DNA tests and CT scan) assisted in a definite identification. It has been declared to be the female pharaoh Hatshepsut.

This person was obese and had red-gold hair. She had damaged teeth and may have suffered from diabetes and cancer. Many questions about her reign still remain unanswered, though. Did she die a natural death? This is not yet clear. If not, who killed her? Why and by whom were her monuments and statues desecrated? The same questions apply to Senenmut, plus others that have never been answered: Was he her lover? Did he ever marry? Was he the mastermind behind her accession? The novelist has more freedom than the scholar to imagine plausible answers to these and other questions about these people who lived so long ago.

The following characters are recorded in history: Hatshepsut; the pharaohs Thutmose I, II and III; Queen Ahmose; the princes Wadjmose and Amenmose (although they may have been born to a different consort); Neferubity (also called Akhbetneferu); Neferure; Meryetre-Hatshepsut (although she may not have been Hatshepsut's daughter); Hatshepsut's stillborn son (some scholars doubt that this event occurred); Satioh, Thutmose III's first principal wife (who may however not have been a Mitannian princess); little Amenhotep (who became the Pharaoh Amenhotep II, one of the great pharaohs of Egypt); Sitre, royal nurse (known as Inet); Senenmut; Hapuseneb; Hapuseneb's wife and children; the steward Amenhotep; the architect Ineni; the treasurer Thitui; General Nehsi; Mutnofert, mother of Thutmose II; Isis, mother of Thutmose III; the tutor Itruri; the King of Punt and his obese wife; the people of Punt who came to Egypt with the returning expedition; the Hyksos invaders; the Prince of Kadesh.

The following characters are my inventions: Khani (although instances are recorded of Nubian youths captured in battle being trained in the Kap and later holding prominent positions in the army); Mahu the scribe; Ahmose the scribe; Hapu, royal physician; Minhotep, physician; Bek and Yunit; Dhutmose (although there were two viziers during the New Empire period); Ibana the enforcer; Captain Aqhat; Seni, senior counsellor; Ahmeni, head of the Party of Legitimacy (such a party did exist); the five daughters of Satioh; Nefthys, wife to Senenmut; their twin boys.

Hatshepsut's statues, monuments and inscriptions were indeed desecrated, as were those of Senenmut. Her name was omitted from King lists from the time of Thutmose III, so she was completely forgotten until Egyptologists deciphered hieroglyphs in 1820. Archaeologists from the Metropolitan Museum in New York were instrumental in retrieving and restoring many items from Hatshepsut's legacy. The temple at Djeser-Djeseru still stands (complete with images of Senenmut, of Hathor suckling Hatshepsut and of the voyage to Punt); having been carefully renovated, the site is now known as Deir el-Bahri. The caricatures exist, except that I have moved them from an unfinished tomb in a cliff above the temple to the temple wall itself.

MARIÉ HEESE
Stilbaai 2008

THANKS

I would like to express my heartfelt gratitude to the following people: my son Fritz for giving me the book by Fletcher that made me complete what was one-third of a manuscript; Melanie and Fanie Celliers for their support and suggestions; Willie Burger for a thoughtful report on an early version that prompted a major rewrite; my outstanding literary agent, Daniel Lazar, for his coaching (via email from New York) that helped me to write a substantially better novel than the one he first set eyes on; Mignon van Coller for coming to the rescue when technology baffled me; Mart and Koos Meij for bringing the manuscript to the attention of the publishers; Marietjie Coetzee and Charles Malan for their recommendations; Alida Potgieter, my publisher at Human & Rousseau, for further helpful suggestions; Louise Steyn for meticulous editing; Michiel Botha for the cover design; Chérie Collins for the page design, and above all, Chris, my husband, for insightful criticism, for taking me to Egypt to see Hatshepsut's temple and to New York for the Hatshepsut exhibition at the Metropolitan Museum of Art, and for putting up with my obsessions.

SELECTED SOURCES

Of the sources listed below, I am most heavily indebted to Budge, Tyldesley, Fletcher, Harris and Johnson. The genesis of the novel came from Wells. Johnson made me aware of the importance of the concept of individual conscience to the ancient Egyptians and I thank him for that.

PRINT MEDIA

Assmann, Jan. 1995. *Egyptian Solar Religion in the New Kingdom*. London: Kegan Paul

Breasted, JH. 1924. *The History of Ancient Egypt*. London: Hodder & Stoughton

Budge, EA Wallis (trans & ed). 1967 (1895). *The Egyptian Book of the Dead (The Papyrus of Ani)*. New York: Dover

Caldecott, Moyra. 2003. *Tutankhamun and the Daughter of Ra*. Bath, UK: Mushroom eBooks

Chalaby, Abbas. 1989. *Egypt*. Firenze: Bonechi

Cotterell, Arthur and Storm, Rachel. 1999. *The Ultimate Encyclopedia of Mythology*. China: Anness Publishing

Fletcher, Joann. 2004. *The Search for Nefertiti*. London: Hodder & Stoughton

Freeman, Charles. 1999. *Egypt, Greece and Rome*. Oxford: Oxford University Press

Gedge, Pauline. 1977. *Child of the Morning*. New York: Soho

Goetz et al (eds). 1988. *Encyclopaedia Britannica Micropaedia* Vol 5. Chicago: Chicago University Press

Harris, Nathaniel. 1997. *History of Ancient Egypt*. London: Chancellor

Harvey, G and Reid, S. 2002. *Encyclopedia of Ancient Egypt*. London: Usborne

Jacq, Christian. 1997. *The Son of the Light*. London: Simon & Schuster

Jacq, Christian. 1998. *The Temple of a Million Years*. London: Simon & Schuster

Jacq, Christian. 1998. *The Battle of Kadesh*. London: Simon & Schuster

Jacq, Christian. 1998. *The Lady of Abu Simbel*. London: Simon & Schuster

Jacq, Christian. 1998. *Under the Western Acacia*. London: Simon & Schuster

Jacq, Christian. 1999. *The Black Pharaoh*. London: Simon & Schuster

Johnson, Paul. 1974. *Elizabeth I: A Study in Power and Intellect*. London: Weidenfeld & Nicolson

Johnson, Paul. 1999. *The Civilization of Ancient Egypt*. London: Weidenfeld & Nicolson

Machiavelli, Niccolo. *The Prince and the Discourses*.

Mertz, Barbara. 1967. *Red Land, Black Land*. London: Hodder & Stoughton

Montet, Pierre. 1964. *Eternal Egypt*. New York: Mentor Books

Newby, PH. 1980. *Warrior Pharaohs: The Rise and Fall of the Egyptian Empire*. London: Faber & Faber

Patrick, Richard. 1972. *All Colour Book of Egyptian Mythology*. London: Octopus

Roehrig, Catherine H. (ed). 2006. *Hatshepsut: From Queen to Pharaoh*. New York: Metropolitan Museum of Art.

Schulz, Regine and Matthias Seidel (eds). 1998. Egypt: *The World of the Pharaohs*. Cologne: Konemann

Smith, Wilbur. 1994. *River God*. London: Pan

Steele, Philip. 2000. *My Best Book of Mummies*. London: Kingfisher

Tyldesley, Joyce. 1998. *Hatchepsut: The Female Pharaoh*. London: Penguin

Waltari, Mika. 2002 (1949). *The Egyptian*. Chicago: GP Putnam's Sons

Wells, Evelyn. 1965. *Nefertiti*. London: Robert Hale

INTERNET WEBSITES (ALPHABETICALLY ORDERED BY TITLE)

www.fordham.edu/halsall/ancient/hymn-nile.html 05/10/23
Ancient History Sourcebook: Hymn to the Nile

www.livius.org/ap-ark/apis/apis.html 05/08/22
Apis

www.mc.maricopa.edu/dept/d10/asb/anthro2003/glues/blackland/black_land.html 5/10/23
Fagan, Brian. *The Black Land*

www.maatkare.com/books.html 16/07/02
Book List & Fiction Guide

www.touregypt.net/featurestories/diet.htm 05/08/27
The Diet of the Ancient Egyptians

www.touregypt.net/featurestories/bull.htm 05/08/22
Divine Cults of the Sacred Bulls

http//nefertiti.iwebland.com/crowns/ 05/08/17
Divine and Royal Headdresses and Crowns

www.tyndale.cam.ac.uk/Egypt/ptolemies/chron/egyptian/chron_eg_cal.htm 05/07/19
Egyptian Dates

www.touregypt.net/featurestories/festival.htm 05/02/15
Springer, Ilene and Dunn, Jimmy. *Grand Festivals in Ancient Egypt*

www.maat-ka-re.de/english/personen/hapuseneb/hapuseneb.htm 05/01/29
Hapuseneb: Historical Data

http//xoomer.virgilio.it/francescoraf/cracow-2002/Krol.htm 05/07/17

Krol, Alexei. *The Heb-Sed and the Emergence of the Egyptian State*
www.touregypt.net/support/kadesh.htm
Kadesh
www.osirisnet.net/tombes/nobles/nakt341/e_nakt341.htm
Nahktamun No 341
www.mystae.com/restricted/streams/scripts/duat.html 05/02/05
The Nightmarish Underworld
www.touregypt.net/magazine/mag05012001/magf4a.htm 05/08/27
Parsons, Marie. *The Nile River*
http//ancienthistory. About.com/library/bl/bl_opet.htm 05/02/15
Gross, Kim Johnson. *Opet Festival*
www.philae.nu/akhet/Opet.html 05/02/15
The Opet Festival
www.maatkare.com/qhat.html 16/07/01
Pharaoh Maatkare Hatshepsut
www.crystalinks.com/egypt2.html 02/05/05
Pharaohs – Gods – Goddesses
www.maatkare.com 05/07/17
Prayer of Pharaoh Maatkare Hatshepsut on her Jubilee
http//nefertiti.iwebland.com/ceremonies/ 05/08/17
Public Religious Ceremonies in Ancient Egypt
http://findagoddess.com/display.php?HERNAME=Wadjit 05/02/05
She of Ten Thousand Names: Wadjit Egyptian Mother Goddess
http://members.tripod.com/-ib205/tuthmosis_3_1.html 05/09/13
Tuthmosis III 18th Dynasty
www.touregypt.net/magazine/mag03012001/magf6.htm 05/02/09
Arab, Sameh. *The Queens of Egypt – Part II*
file//A:\Hugh Nibley's, What is the Book of Breathings.htm 05/02/05
Shirts, Kerry A (ed). *What is the Book of Breathings?*
www.maatkare.com/women.html 16/07/01
Women in Ancient Egypt

ARCHEOLOGICAL EXHIBITION

Hatshepsut: From Queen to Pharaoh. New York: Metropolitan Museum of Art 2006.